Dancing the Loom

A Novel by Carol Craig

Dancing the Loom

by C. L. Craig

© 2022 by Carol Craig
Published by Ingram Spark
1 Ingram Blvd.
La Vergne, TN, 37086

Printed in the United States of America.

Library of Congress Cataloging-in-Publication Data

Craig, Carol, 2022
         Dancing The Loom / Carol Craig.
  p. Cm. -- YA Fantasy
         ISBN 978-1-73622227-4-4

Interior Design by Sara Rolat.
Cover design by Darrin Brenner: D. Brenner Art & Design.

Printed in the United States of America
09 10 11 12 13 RRD 7 6 5 4 3

Why fuss with the meadowlark
When the world is left unfinished?

–Brigid Anne Dunsmore

Prologue

Alaric the Third peered through the mirror, his beady brown eyes staring back at him, his black hair receding into a reverse widow's peak. But as he stared harder, he could feel rather than see something happening that caused his soulless heart to quicken.

"Where is the loom?" he hissed, turning away, unwilling to view what he knew to be there. He balled his fists as he surveyed his kingdom from a-high. For years he had fought his way to the top from a hardscrabble life as an orphan, his parents killed in the Great War while he had been left to the mercies of the orphanage and their machine. Now *he* was in charge of the orphanages, the manors, the entire kingdom save for a portion that hung like a ripe plum, ready to be picked, eaten.

He stood from his gem-encrusted throne, of which he had many, and felt the ring that acted as a weight upon his finger, each jewel bearing a meaning that only he knew. The holy trinity: an emerald, a ruby, and a blue diamond. He'd stolen them off the very leader of the free world who used it merely as a museum piece from the Dark Ages. But he knew the gems' powers. He caressed them as he often did when thinking. The emerald symbolized love, wisdom, and protection, but most of all, all things green and alive; the ruby wealth and prosperity. To his distaste, the blue diamond stood for peace.

"There will only be peace when I own everything," he growled, tugging at his oiled black goatee. Once again, he turned to the scrolled mirror with its onyx and sapphire inlay. It was here that The Citadel of the Jackals unfolded before him in all its glory. With a turn of his head, he could survey the different parts. His stomach soured when he saw those portions that were free of his domain. Beautiful rolling valleys, gardens strung out in opulent rows of green, lush woodlands surrounding tall manors with people who thought they could compete with him. Thought they were equal to him. But they would soon learn. He narrowed his eyes as he stroked his goatee. Nothing was sacred. Nothing. And he would see to it that everything that lay before him was his. For that was the irony of his name, Alaric. It meant "Ruler of All," and yet he wasn't ruler of all . . . not yet. For that to happen, he needed the loom. Because whoever owned the loom wielded the power. He laughed because although his auricles had been unable to reveal the exact location of the loom, they assured him that the owner would be a young woman. And eventually they would find her. But one thing he knew for certain. Whoever owned the loom, she was no match for him. No match at all.

Once, when I was seven, my mother brought home a treadle loom. It had a large shuttle and the threads had already been started. For months, my three sisters and I would take turns dancing the loom, our tiny feet pressing hard to lift the warp, our small hands pushing the shuttle in and out, stopping only to tie a new color onto the warp. I thrilled at the clack-clack-clack as my feet danced against the pedals, the weave showing itself as if by magic.

Where the loom came from, I never knew. Was it a family heirloom passed down through the generations, and how had we come upon it at that exact moment in time? I didn't know. Why had I not been more curious . . . *asked*? But that's the way of it with small children. We just accept.

Then as mysteriously as the loom had appeared, it vanished. Why didn't I ask where it went? Why had I never fretted or worried over the mysterious disappearance? But through my childish eyes, it was simply the way of the world. Things came. Things went.

So it came as a shock to see this loom, all these years later, locked behind the window of McGregor's Five and Dime in Upstate New York. I knew it was ours, or had been . . . once. See, it had six pedals, and a beater measuring 36 inches. And although I was too young to recall the reason for it coming and going, I recalled these most unusual of things because I had counted the pedals and sung a ditty to the clack of the weft.

> Six pedals pumping, Mama's gone a'hunting.
> Thirty-six inch beater
> Caught a chicken dinner
> Made that chicken simmer
> In a porridge pot
> Hey, diddle dumpling, Mama's gone a'hunting.

But that wasn't the half of it. No, I had carved my initials in wood with one of the skeleton keys that Mama kept on a hobnail in the kitchen. I loved the keys, and when Mama was away, I would climb onto an opened drawer, push my way up onto the counter, and kneeling, grab a ring of those keys, shimmy down on my belly, push the drawer shut with my feet, then plop down onto the worn linoleum that Mama kept shined like a newly minted half-dime. Then I would press the keys into the locks, and listen to the tumblers turn, wait for the satisfying click, feel the reassurance of the lock. I would do that to each and every door and when I had that done, would go through the house and unlock them all, then repeat the process of climbing onto the counter to deposit the keys on the hobnail. Once again, I would shimmy down with a plop, my self-appointed job done for the day.

Yet today, as I stared at the loom through the window of the five and dime, I felt it calling to me. Unwittingly, it had drawn me in through the door, the bell overhead dinging my arrival. The store clerk looked up, then unceremoniously went back to his work of counting out change for a customer. Whereas I felt the pull of the loom as if I were the thread, and it was the shuttle, weaving me into the fabric of the loom. As I stood in front of it, I saw passersby stopping to stare, as though I were a store mannequin, merely a prop for the loom, my dark hair fanning the shoulders of my dress, my navy blue skirt cinched tight at the waist, my white shirt billowing at the sleeves, the cloth-covered buttons, running the length of my v-neck blouse. People often peered at my eyes and then drew back, as though in alarm, for they were the clearest of blue, so at odds with the color of my hair. They were like none other. No, they fairly sparkled. Mama called them The Blue Mists, as though a place rather than a color and had named me after a Celtic saint, Saint Brigid of Kildare, a follower of Saint Patrick. Brigid's father was a pagan, her mother a slave. My namesake believed in helping the poor and downtrodden, as did I, even though one might think *me* poor and downtrodden. But it hadn't always been so.

Now, as I witnessed my reflection in the window, I saw that the loom framed my face, made my eyes appear that much bluer, my hair that much darker. In this moment, I could see why children often stopped to stare, their mothers pulling them along quite unwillingly. It was as if they had set the brakes on their feet and had determined to gawk as long as humanly possible. But their disconcerted mothers would grab hold, and through sheer force of will, drag the children to themselves. Yet I had caught the women's backward glances, the moment of fear and wonder that eyes could be so blue, so flecked with bits of gold, as though a fire were burning within, or perhaps ice. Mama explained it to me once, that the reason arctic ice is so blue is because the air bubbles are squeezed out as the ice compresses, allowing the ice crystals to enlarge. And perhaps my eyes had been compressed in some way, the air squeezed out. I know not. I only know that I am a misfit. One of a kind. Odd. And yet I am no different from the average girl. Am I? No, I am simply a normal girl with odd eyes.

And now, as I stood gazing at the loom, dust settling over it from lack of use, I was determined to own it once more, but how *could* I on my scullery's salary?

Think! Think!

I snapped my fingers. The loom had obviously been here for some time, as evidenced by the amount of dust covering it, so I sought out the manager, a thin, dour man with a hook nose and wolfish features.

"May I purchase the loom?" I asked. "On payment," I rushed to add lest he think I meant to purchase the whole thing outright.

For a moment, he scowled, raked in my appearance--the average dress, plain shoes. He could tell my means were paltry at best. He peered at the loom, at the dust revealing its disuse.

Finally, he frowned, thick bushy eyebrows descending over a ledge of misgiving, then gave one quick nod of his head. "Five dollars a week," he growled.

I gave a low whistle. One-fifth of my monthly salary. I barely made ends meet as it was. But I could not let the loom get away from me again. We shook on it. Then he sent me to the clerk, who wrote up a chit with the down payment of my first five dollars securely in his hand. As I turned to leave, I made my way over to the contraption for one last look. I blew at the dust, assuring the loom that I would be back someday to bring it home with me. The cost? Ninety-two dollars and sixty-seven cents. In just a little over five months, the loom would be mine.

That night, as I lay in bed in my tiny upstairs flat, tossing and turning in my sleep, I heard the clack-clack-clack of the pedals grind into motion, saw the weft pulling loose and the colorful silk thread sewn by an unseen hand. Back and forth, back and forth. I would like to say that I could see the tapestry, but I could not. I only knew that it was beautiful and sewn just for me, though how I knew it, I couldn't say.

At the end of the week, I made my way back to McGregor's Five and Dime. But before I could even enter, I noted something strange. Odd, really. For there, in the window, sat my loom, but on it were the beginnings of a tapestry that had only the barest of threads, gold, a border I believed. I wondered who had operated the loom. The manager's wife perhaps? Surely not the disinterested clerk who could scarcely be bothered with me when I entered to the sound of the bell.

I was determined to ask. So up I marched to the front counter, demanding to speak with the manager. Moments later, the manager appeared from behind an opaque muslin curtain, his eyebrows raised in question and his hands behind his back, as though he had something to hide.

"My loom," I said, nodding to where it sat by the window,

not nearly as dusty as before. "Who is creating the tapestry?"

"Tapestry?" he said with a frown. He wiped his hands on his white apron that he used when dusting shelves. Then he followed my gaze and paused. Seeing I was right, that indeed someone had been using the loom, he hurried over, his head moving back and forth as though he were trying to decipher this oddity.

"So, it wasn't you or your wife?"

He gave a mirthless laugh. "My wife would do well to keep up with the house and children. As for myself, I have never set hand to a shuttle in my life."

He spoke with such utter disdain that I had no doubt he was speaking the truth. Who then? The clerk with one drooping eyelid and a mop of unbrushed mousey brown hair? "Could your worker be the one?"

"Impossible." The manager shook his head with vehemence. "I can barely get him to wait on customers. He is the laziest man I know."

"Anyone else, then?" I squeaked.

But the manager would have none of it. "Perhaps it was there all along, and we hadn't noticed," he said, as though that put an end to any further questioning.

"Perhaps," I murmured, but I planned to keep an eye on the loom from here on out. I knew what I had seen, and there was no gold thread on that loom the last time I'd been here.

For the next several weeks, I found more and more reason to pass in front of the window, and each time a thread had been added, the shuttle poised, as if by an unseen hand to add yet another strand come nightfall.

When nearly a month had passed, word got around and

people began to gather, just a few at first, then more, until at last I had to push my way through the throng to see the miraculous loom with its unseen weaver.

"Look," one mother exclaimed, a bairn on one hip. "Some green has been added. Grass, perhaps."

"And is that the start of a shoe?" another man queried, pointing to what might be the toe.

Something odd was happening, something that gave me shivers, for no one had come forward to claim the miraculous work, and it was clear by the weave that none other than a master craftsman had taken up the loom. I quickly entered the store, which had been barricaded to all except those agreeing to a purchase beforehand. And apparently many were willing to buy in order to more closely inspect the loom, which was now being dubbed a miracle. As such, it became a long, arduous ordeal to make my five dollar payment, although the manager did seem quite happy that my loom had put his store on the map, so to speak. For the fixtures had grown more luxurious as the customers entered in droves, and even the manager's clothing was new, imported from New York City proper so that he looked almost dapper despite his vulture-like appearance. I knew that come the five months, he would be sorry to see me go—and more importantly--the loom.

"What do you think it means, Brigid?" my friend Emma asked one day when she accompanied me to the store.

Three months in, the tapestry was just over halfway finished. Around the glen, for indeed it was grass that had appeared in the beginning, sat small stone cottages, and in the center, a tall strapping young man with golden-red hair that fell in waves down his upper torso. He wore a tunic, in finest linen, white with a gold thread design, and deep green leggings with soft suede boots.

"I don't know," I whispered to my red-haired, freckled friend. Irish, like my namesake. But what I *had* noticed is that in the beginning, it seemed to me that my loom and I had gained celebrity, but as the loom continued on, that celebrity had turned to suspicion.

And five months later, as I came time to make my last payment, I once again tossed and turned in my bed the night before the final remittance. In my dreams, the clack of the loom worked at full speed, so much so that I felt exhausted by the time I awoke the next morning, as though I too had been working throughout the night.

Slowly, I dressed in my Sunday best, but before I left to make my last payment on my loom, I reached underneath my blouse and pulled out a locket. It was round with a metal button that, when pushed, opened to a hologram of my family in better days. I had only to wish for the place and time, and there, as though made of painted clouds, was the family I had lost, at different stages of our life. Today, I chose Christmas, because it indeed felt like Christmas now that I would be getting my loom. I watched with tears in my eyes as my family and I opened our gifts. I couldn't have been more than five, all told. My gift that day was a toy horse and buggy on a rail. My five-year-old self set one of my smaller stuffed toys into the buggy and I watched it go round and round on the track. Sadly, I closed the round locket, my memories tucked as securely as the stuffed animal inside my locket.

I dried my tears, then quickly made my way down to see what the loom had drawn. What was left could only be sky, so I was unprepared for the shock of what lay before me, and the wide berth people gave me when they saw me arrive. It was as if I had been bewitched, though truth to tell there is not one thing bewitching about me, for I am nothing if not normal. Plain. A scullery maid, nothing more.

The same could not be said for the loom. There, in full view of half the townsfolk, was a story, richly told, in the finest of silk and by the best of weavers. For I had been drawn into the weave, though how that could be, since only sky was left, I have no idea. But I was not the only one. There too, in plain daylight, were many of the people from our very village, women mostly, looking as though they had appeared as if by magic from the stone huts, each dressed in the standard of the village. Warriors mostly, quiver and arrow at their back. I, too, wore the standard, the quiver and arrow, as did the man standing beside me, though how that had occurred overnight is anyone's guess. A chill settled over me that could not be shaken, no matter the warmth of my cloak.

"How?" I whispered.

All around me, eyes filled with both suspicion and wonder, in equal measure, as though I had had a hand somehow in these strangest of events. As I stood there, rubbing my icy blue hands together in terror, I wondered if the weave in the loom, that I had found so fascinating, would foretell my future. Not only mine, but the futures of those around me.

2

Alaric paced the length of the room on the third floor in the fortress high atop the hill. He'd had the fortress built by the best craftsmen around, praising their work, demanding more before final payment, squeezing every last ounce of work he could muster out of them no matter the cost to their health. This was how one became rich. Little pay and long hours. Only fools worked for free, or nearly free. He peered through the opened window to the courtyard below, the horses of the men he'd been waiting for long since stabled.

"Where *are* they?" he groused, his boots clicking on cobblestone he'd had shipped from a grotto far away. The auricles had finally revealed the owner of the loom. As such, he had immediately dispatched two of his henchmen to find the loom and bring it to him. Just as he opened the door to deliver a heated command to his guards, the two henchmen appeared, looking quite startled.

Alaric stroked his goatee, then bade them enter. "Did you find the loom, buy it out from under her . . . that Brigid whats-her-name?"

Forgoing the usual pleasantries, not even allowing the pair to sit before turning on them, Alaric launched at the two men.

The two appeared ashen as they licked nervous lips. "We tried, sire," one said.

"We did," agreed the other.

"But something strange happened," the first insisted, turning weasley eyes to the other.

"Yes, the other agreed." Both men appeared hawkish--hawkish brown eyes, hawkish noses or rather beaks--by Alaric's standards. Even the way they lowered their shoulders reminded Alaric of a hawk, or perhaps more aptly a buzzard. Yes, that was it precisely. Two buzzards.

Alaric rubbed his hands together, the friction helping to warm his frigid fingers. "What do you mean, something *happened*?" he demanded in a booming voice that was certain to intimidate.

"It's just that--" the first man began.

"--we tried," the other man added, both of them bobbing their heads like two magpies.

"But every time we attempted to enter the store--" said the first.

"--we were stopped by a phalanx of people," the other finished.

"People, what people? And why didn't you just barge your way in?" Alaric demanded, turning on his heel and pacing once-more, the sound of his boots ringing out one after the other. He paused only to pick up his riding crop, which he smacked against the cobblestones now.

"We did, sir," said the first of the men, his compatriot leaning into him as if to protect himself by showing a united front.

Alaric stopped to scowl at his henchmen. Where had his underlings found such weaklings?

"But they stopped us," said the other, his voice quavering and unctuous.

Alaric halted his pacing. "Stopped you, how?"

"We don't know," the two men said in unison, as though of a single mind.

"It was as though--" The first man halted mid-sentence.

It's then that Alaric could smell the metallic odor of their fear, that and something else. He sniffed, unable to hide a *moue* of disgust, as clearly they hadn't bathed recently. He pulled a chatelaine from his coat pocket and placed a dab of perfume from his vinaigrette onto a handkerchief, then held it to his nose as he spoke.

"--there was a wall. It was--"

"--immovable," the second man finished. Then they both dipped their heads in agreement.

"A wall." Alaric normally liked walls. It kept people out. But he didn't like this one, for this one kept his people from getting what he had demanded of them.

"Those little . . ." he growled, pretending to crush the invisible people who had thwarted him in his quest. "Well, not to worry. We will find that loom, and I shall have it. By the end of the week, if at all possible." And with that, he turned on his heel, and cast open the door, yelling down the hall for the maid to escort the two men out and a certain Josiah Herman in. He rubbed his hands together in glee. Five hundred dollars. A fortune for anyone, least of all a scullery maid. That should secure the loom. Surely, someone of her means couldn't afford to look askance at such an offering. No, the deal was all but done, he decided with a laugh that sounded more like a growl. Then he yelled once more to the maid.

"Where *is* that blasted woman?"

I'd had a devil of a time finding someone to transport my loom from the five and dime up the three flights of stairs to my small loft in the attic. By the time the chapman had it placed in a location nearest the window, the poor man was out of breath and sweating. Feeling sorry for the trouble I had caused him, I gave him a small gratuity, all that I could afford on my meager salary, thanked him, and was glad to see him off, for now I had the loom all to myself. The first thing I planned to do was to lift the tapestry, ever so carefully, off the loom, edge it in a silk border, and add in a pocket for a rod so that I could hang it on the wall above my bed. I had yet to afford the actual thread for my loom. That would take weeks if not months to secure, but at least I had the loom, and for now that was enough.

But before I could get started, I heard a knock at the door. It was Betsy, our head housekeeper in charge of all lower staff. I knew then that something was afoot, for she rarely if ever made the trek up the stairs to the loft, which was drafty in the winter, stifling in the summer months. I could only imagine what had brought her here. And sure enough, upon opening the door, she peered past my shoulder to the loom, clearly as eager to run her eyes over the magical mechanism as those in the village.

Finally, when I made no offer to bid her enter, she asked, "May I come in . . . er . . . to speak with you about a certain matter?"

My heart sank to my boots, but I dared not deny her entry, so I stepped back to allow her room to do as she pleased. She immediately rushed over to the loom and bent down to give it a thorough once-over. When she stood, she peered at my eyes just long enough to cause me discomfort. But I forced myself not to squirm, not to stare back in a manner unbefitting a scullery maid. No, I stood there, head slightly bowed and waited for her to say what she would.

"It's best you know, Brigid," the housekeeper said, her shoulders thrown back and her bun appearing more severe, if at all possible.

"Oh?" I replied, not to be outdone.

"Mum is watching you. People are talking . . . about the loom. The weave. It is causing a stir both downstairs and outside of our home."

As if to make clear her meaning, she ushered me over to the window and peered down. I followed her gaze and felt a check in my spirit, for there, outside the wide lawn and the iron gates, lingered a variety of people. When they caught sight of me, some of the more brazen ones, men mostly, yelled up to me in a smattering of name calling, whereas others begged to see the miraculous loom. And still others asked if I would sell it, no doubt believing it would issue a tidy sum to the right buyer.

One cheeky boy even had the nerve to ask me to marry him in order to obtain said object. But I was wont to give it up so soon after acquiring it, for it represented not only memories of my childhood, but a piece of my heritage as well, despite the fact that we had owned it for no more than a year, if even that. And I had yet to learn which of my ancestors, if any, had owned it before us.

I peered up at Betsy, uncertain of her meaning. Had the commotion caused a stir within the household? Was she placing me on probation for a sin I had yet to commit? How could I be responsible for the townsfolk's reaction to something I'd had no hand in? It made no sense.

"In case you misunderstand me, Brigid," the woman said with a newfound authority, her hands clasped at her breast, "we can not have these people standing watch at all hours of the day and night. If the lingerers do not go away, and go away soon, then you shall either have to give up your loom or your residence. The choice is yours."

But even as she spoke, I knew which way I would choose, for this was the only piece of my past that I owned to say that I had once been born a Dunsmore--Brigid Anne Dunsmore of the illustrious house of Dunsmore. See, I had not been born poor as some might suspect. No, I had been born to a wealthy household that had seen it all lost to a bad wager, the economy being the worst wager of all. We, like many people in our circle, had wrongly invested a huge portion of our wealth in gold. But after the Civil War, gold was snapped up for a pittance to right the government's coffers. Suddenly, with our wealth gone, we could no longer borrow to keep the cotton mills going, and cotton had fallen to ruin in any case. And therein lay the rub, for it had broken our family, and flung us to the four winds like clocks, the dandelion-headed seeds that we'd made a wish on as children before setting them to the air currents to reseed. And so we had reseeded, my mother alone in her single-room apartment, my father in a factory in a city far away, and me, a scullery maid, earning what I could to help out the family, what was left of it. Even my three sisters and two brothers had been farmed out to places unknown.

When the housekeeper left, I walked over once more to the window and peered out. Some of those who had been there before had wandered away to stave off the chill from an afternoon of clouds and wind, while the still curious took their place, trampling Ma'am's flowers, some climbing the ironwork to get a glimpse of the girl with her loom. As one spied me, I stood back, heart pounding as though they might see me from my hidey-hole of an attic that even now left me patting my hands together for warmth.

I barely had time to gauge what to do next when I heard another knock at the door, this one more timid than the last. Fortunately for me, it was Emma, who was just as low on the totem pole as I. She, however, had not come from wealth, but had been only too happy to take lessons in elocution so that she might sound more proper in hopes of snagging a groomsman or a butler some day.

"Come in," I said, nearly dragging her in and shutting the door as quietly as possible so as not to create a stir among the downstairs help. "Have you seen?" I demanded pointing toward the window. "It's a fair circus down there."

"That it is," she agreed, her eyes wide, her skin even paler than usual with its tinge of pink to match her red hair and freckles.

"What have you heard?" I asked, wanting to learn everything she knew before telling her my news--the ultimatum the housekeeper had given me on behalf of Ma'am.

Her eyes peered back and forth as though someone might pop out of the very woodwork to cuff her for what she was about to say, but nevertheless, she withdrew a crumpled note, hastily written by its appearance.

"I will give you $500 for your loom, J. H.," the note said, whoever J.H. was among the many people below.

Despite my earlier determination to keep the loom, I whistled. Five hundred dollars would go a long way toward home ownership, something I had dreamed of since the very first day I'd been thrust into the cold dusty attic. Each day, as I peeled potatoes or sliced up cucumbers, the oven providing the only warmth I'd had that day, either that or on summer days simply adding to the relentless heat, I imagined what it would be like to live in my own home. To dust my own furniture, to have a small garden in which to grow vegetables and the occasional flower. Still, even with the sale of the loom it would be thousands of dollars out of my reach, whereas with any luck, the loom might provide me a living, albeit small. A side business to supplement my job here as a scullery maid. I closed my eyes, hoping the answer would come to me.

"Are you going to sell the loom, Brigid?" Emma's eyes wandered to the loom and then suddenly grew wide.

"What is it, Emma?" My eyes followed hers. It took a moment to register what had affected her so, but there it was in large, gold letters that made my spine tingle. For on the top of the tapestry, it said, "Save Our Kingdom."

But what kingdom? And save it from whom?

For the rest of the afternoon, I worked in the kitchen, below stairs, toiling over a pot of boiled mutton with roasted red baby potatoes coated in oil and chopped rosemary. With the hem of my apron, I wiped my brow, the heat and humidity stifling.

"Brigid!" Cook admonished. "Manners!"

I scowled but continued stirring. The cook was a severe woman, as short as she was round, with a bun at the top of her crown and tendrils of gray lying limp, having escaped the bun but not the humidity.

My thoughts strayed once more to Emma and the tapestry, to the words I had seen written into it. Why had I not noticed those words when I'd made the final payment? And what did they mean? Furthermore, the woman sewn into the tapestry alongside the tall, handsome warrior was clearly me. No woman had such bright blue eyes. The silk that had been chosen for my eyes seemed to fairly shimmer, to give off sparks of light that caught one's attention no matter where one moved within the confines of the small attic. For the entire workday, I'd been impatient to get back to the loom. One more hour, and I would be able to rush up to my room to see if anything would be different this time, or if it was finally finished with its weave.

But no sooner had I completed that thought when I heard a commotion in the upstairs dining room, a series of screams and shouts followed by crashing dishes. Moments later, Emma came bounding into the room, panting and out of breath. I dropped my stirring spoon with a clatter and felt the cuff of Cook's hand as a result of my clumsiness. I quickly picked the stirring spoon from the floor and ran it under hot water, soaping it down to make certain that I had cleaned it to Cook's satisfaction.

Emma curtsied, then rushed over to where I was standing. But instead of speaking to me, she turned to Cook and said, "Someone was caught trying to steal the loom."

No one needed to tell Cook what loom Emma spoke of, for the entire household was abuzz with the news and the stir it had caused outside the iron gates.

Cook gasped and muttered, "I knew that loom would be nothing but trouble. Miss Betsy told me she spoke with you today about ridding the household of the loom." As if in admonition, she peered at me over her glasses, head lowered.

The room seemed to shrink, and me with it, for I had never said I would sell my precious loom, only that I would think about it. But now, the potential thief had forced my hand.

"What will you do?" Emma murmured.

She worried her hands together in a nervous habit she

had developed upon working at Ma'am's household, where the slightest infraction could cause one to be cuffed or forced to work long hours at the worst jobs as a reminder never to make a mistake of any kind. But being human, the staff seemed to make daily mistakes, sometimes hourly. As such, the lower one fell on the totem pole, the more nervous tics one developed, the more fearful one became of making mistakes. And of course, the more mistakes one made. It became a self-defeating loop that I too had suffered, Emma and I being the lowest on the totem pole in the grand household.

"I don't know," I said, on a sigh, my head spinning from the sheer weight of my dilemma.

"There's nothing you can do about that now," Cook said, coming over and planting herself between me and Emma to let us both know that she was in charge and that there would be no shirking duties in *her* kitchen.

Surprisingly, I felt better about this because it gave me a task to focus on and time to come to a decision.

"Back to work," Cook ordered. "Both of you," she added pointedly to Emma, who curtsied briefly, offered me a brief look of apology, then ran upstairs to her duties.

Cook watched me with squinted eyes, but I merely turned to the task at hand, my back to her so that, hopefully, she would return to her work, her focus no longer on me. Fortunately, that did the trick and I was left to my musings. Should I take the five hundred dollars and be done with it, before I lost both my job and my place of residence? And if not, where could I go? The room felt as though it had warmed a good twenty degrees in the past few minutes and once again I wiped my brow with my hem.

To my relief, Cook hadn't seen me so let me be.

What to do? What to do? I loved the loom. It held such precious memories of me and my sisters, as well as my brothers, before tragedy had struck and we children had gone to different households. I hadn't seen my sisters or brothers for well over a year now. I wasn't even sure how they fared, though I'd asked all who entered if they had heard of them. None had.

The hour that followed stretched painfully long, but at last I was able to leave to the privacy of my own room. Gratefully, I removed my apron and rushed up the stairs, but just as I was about to take the back stairs to the servants quarters, Housekeeper grabbed my shoulder, and said, "This way, Miss."

Her grip was made of iron as she steered me toward the dining room, a place I was never allowed. Fear gripped me as firmly as her hand, for there, seated on a straight-back chair was none other than Ma'am herself. She quickly excused herself from the table, thanked Housekeeper Betsy, then said, "Come with me."

My legs quivered, for if I had angered or offended Ma'am, I knew that my stay here would be short indeed. With a quiet regalness gained through prestige, Ma'am led me to the drawing room, a room where the men retired to at night to smoke cigars and drink their nightly port, or the women met during the day to discuss events over tea and fresh scones.

Once there, she bade me sit. I did, but only on the edge of the Edwardian chair with its talon feet and blue tapestry cushion showcasing a young woman and her dog. For I wished to flee as soon as possible from what could only be bad news, for seldom did Ma'am deal with the help herself.

I stared at her high lace collar, at her poofy sleeves that tapered down to her narrow wrists, at the fullness of her green skirt with its crinoline petticoat, anywhere save her green eyes, which I imagined bore an expression of deep disdain.

"Look at me," Ma'am commanded.

I gulped at the order but did as told. "Yes, Ma'am?"

"By now, I am sure you have heard that a stranger was able to get past the gates."

Once again, I gulped, for indeed I, and probably every servant in the household, had heard of the break-in by now. I fanned myself with a hand, to which Ma'am drew out a genuine fan from her skirt and handed it to me, one from Paris by the look of the plumage and the scene—The Eiffel Tower being the biggest giveaway in that regard.

"Now, tell me about this loom," she began. "I hear it has . . . . powers."

I glanced anxiously toward the open door, wishing myself on the other side of it, away from the prying eyes of Ma'am who held my fate in her hands. In moments, I and my loom might very well be outside those gates, the loom smashed, me on my keister. I didn't know what to do to save either myself or my loom. And I had nowhere to go, not to my mother's apartment, as she had so little room as it was. And the added burden of rent and food for another mouth would only burden her further. No, I could not go there. Nor would my father want me, for he had trouble enough of his own. As to my sisters and brothers, I wasn't quite sure where they had landed. I only knew that I had little saved and few prospects. One bad word from Lady Engstrom and I would never work in this town again.

My skin fairly burned as I awaited her judgment, but to my surprise, she simply said, "May I see it?"

"Ma'am?" I said, believing I had heard wrong.

"The loom," she said, as though I might be dense. "May I view it?"

"Uh . . . yes, of course." I sat there as though dumb.

She stood and urged me to do likewise. Then she pointed a hand for me to lead the way. Shocked by this turn of events, I forced in air and tried to stand tall as I proceeded through the doorway and down the hallway, Ma'am trailing me with an urgency that surprised me.

"But what about your dinner, Ma'am?" I asked as we twisted through the servants quarters and up the backstairs.

Ma'am seemed almost giddy, as though doing something unbecoming a lady by entering such lowly quarters. For the first time since beginning work here, I wondered if Ma'am had ever taken this path, or had she left it up to her staff to peruse these quarters, having never actually stepped foot in them herself? *So many questions.*

Slowly, we made the ascent. Even she seemed out of breath and heated from the exertion by the time we arrived at the attic beneath the eaves of the topmost portion of the manor. Now that she was here, outside the humble door of my abode, she paused, as if suddenly fearful of entering such a hovel as mine. Steeling herself, she gave a nod and I clicked open the door with the skeleton key at my waist. Then I stood back, as was proper, to allow her first entry.

She gasped, her eyes quickly scanning the sparse furnishings—alast alighting on the loom itself, the item she had come to see. I felt a check in my spirit, eyes welling in surprise, for indeed my loom had been adding to the weave. For there, in the arms of myself, or rather the sewn version of myself, was Emma, bleeding from a wound to her chest, and I . . . well I had a look of shock and anger. But more than that, determination. Because someone, somewhere, had hurt Emma and I would not stand for it.

4

"What do you mean Brigid wouldn't take the money?" Alaric scowled as he sat on a bench at the edge of the garden, stroking his greyhound, one of many he kept on the grounds. The sun overhead was tepid at best, and yet for mid June, one had to take what one could get. He pulled his waistcoat tighter around him as he sucked on a butterscotch candy, with just a touch of rum to give it flavor, savoring its sweetness. "Of course she will take the money."

"No, sire," Josiah Herman said, his face as narrow as his eyes and lips, a most decidedly reptilian look about him. "She turned down your offer."

Alaric stuttered, unused to women, or anyone else, for that matter, turning down a "request" of his. Everyone knew that his requests were orders, and yet his lackey hadn't told her who was making the offer, leading her to believe instead that Josiah himself had made the offer through an intermediary who lived near the manor. Yet, if Brigid were a discerning woman, she would see by the intermediary's clothing– threadbare at the seams and buttons sewn and resewn–that Josiah's lackey was not a man of means, and especially someone able to come up with such a handsome sum as that.

"When you sent the carrier falcon to the intermediary, why did you not add that the man should steal the loom if she refused the sum?" Alaric demanded, swiping at a butterfly who dodged his wrath with a smooth upward motion as it continued on its way.

"He tried," Josiah said, speaking more softly as a lithesome young woman moved their way, one of Alaric's many relatives, twice and thrice removed. "But he failed in his attempt."

Before Alaric could throttle Josiah for his failure, the man leaned in and in a voice filled with *gravitas* added, "The place is a virtual fortress since Brigid brought the loom to the manor. Lady Engstrom has hired guards."

"For goodness sakes, why would she hire guards?" he demanded, the early scent of winter honeysuckle saturating the air.

"Well," Josiah said, his brows gathering to indicate his confusion, "surely you've heard that Brigid has become a celebrity. The loom is known far and wide for its . . . *powers*." Josiah dipped his head knowingly.

"That is a dilemma, is it not, Josiah?" said Alaric, twisting his goatee as he thought about what the younger man had said. "Where is she now?" Alaric rubbed at the greyhound's ears, the dog looking steadily forward, never at Alaric.

"In her attic loft, I would imagine."

"Well, we must find another way to reach her. From within, perhaps?" He raised a brow in glee.

"Sire?" Josiah said, cocking his head.

Surely the man was dense. "We shall send someone as a trainee, free perhaps? The Lord and Lady of the manor aren't likely to look a gift scullery maid in the mouth, no?"

Josiah's face fell in on itself as the meaning became clear. "Oh . . . oh!" he added, a slow smile forming on his face. "I suppose they wouldn't." Then together the two men laughed as they planned their path forward.

Despite my obvious discomfort at the sight of the tapestry, newly changed to reveal Emma in distress, Ma'am seemed not to notice, but how could she? The woman had never set eyes on the tapestry before today. She didn't know that it had changed. As if this new fly in the ointment had affected the very air itself, the room suddenly felt hot and humid, so I moved to the window and opened it to allow in air. But no sooner had I done that, then I realized my mistake, for below me, the lingerers, or should I say *ma*-lingerers, were waiting, ready to pounce the moment they caught sight of me, and caught sight of me they did. One stalwart man yelled to the others, "There she is!" and soon the area outside the gate was awash with people climbing the gates to get a better view of the "woman of the loom" as I was now being called. I quickly shut the window, but not before Ma'am had seen my distress and appraised me with wonder. My heart beat double-time. I didn't know what to think, what to feel at the sight of her judging me so.

But to my surprise, she cocked her head ever so slightly and blinked at a rapid pace. Then she asked me the most peculiar question. "Are you happy here? In this attic."

How to respond to such a question? Sequestered alone in a cold attic, hot in the summertime, forced to do her bidding at the drop of a hat, even though I had seldom set eyes on the woman, having been holed up in the kitchen all day. *Was* I happy here? I decided to be truthful.

"I've always dreamed of a home, a husband, a garden with fresh vegetables." And not content to leave it there, I continued, "I have always wanted to write . . . books," I added in case she misunderstood my intent. "Novels of women who have succeeded against all odds."

At this, she raised her eyebrows as though I had said something either amusing or perplexing perhaps. More to my surprise, I thought I saw respect, as though she, too, had dreams that had gone unfulfilled.

"You can write, then?" she asked, as though the thought had never occurred to her that someone of my station could write.

"I can, Ma'am," I said, eyes down at my feet.

"And how, pray tell, did you come to learn to write?" she asked, lifting my chin so that I was forced to look her in the eye.

"By my nanny," I said, before I realized how that might sound.

"*Nanny*?" she said, drawing back as though I had just said that I was a three-foot green-eyed cyclops. "You had a nanny?" She began patting herself, unaccustomed to the apparent cold.

I shrugged, reluctant to explain to this woman, who might not understand at any rate, that fortunes can come and go, so that even a woman in her station might not always be well-heeled, should she fall on hard times.

But she seemed to feel otherwise, as she grabbed me by the elbow and said, "Follow me." Then she led me once more downstairs, only this time to her private chambers where she asked her personal maid that lunch be served and that we be left in peace, afterward.

Once the door was closed, she bade me sit, but not before I had the opportunity to take in her palatial quarters, so different from mine. For every creature comfort a woman could want lined the chambers, from a mahogany bed with pineapple finials to a large tapestry hanging on the wall beside her bed displaying a garden filled with delights including a fluffy white dog chasing chickens who hastened to escape the furry little animal. On one wall stood a bureau with a menagerie of glass bottles, some filled with perfumes, others with lotions, a boar hairbrush next to a mirror. No expense had been spared in seeing to her comfort, and I, for one, thought it odd that she would entertain a waif like me in a room such as this.

"So, now that you are here, tell me how it is that you came to have a nanny and learned to write? More so, how one with a nanny could become a servant in a house such as mine?"

She sat down gracefully on a high-back chair with lilies carved into the slats above the blue tapestry seat that cushioned her. As she did, she gathered her skirts, green, as it were, and patted them gently so as not to crease the fine crinoline.

Dare I tell her the whole sordid story? In the end, I decided to tell her a partial truth, that my family had lost its money in high finance. "Isn't that the way of the world?" I added with a shrug.

"No it is not!" she countered firmly, as if to acknowledge the truth of it, she would be acknowledging that it could happen to her, a most unseemly proposition in second light. Realizing that she had spoken too harshly, perhaps, she softened her approach. "So, you want to write . . . books."

I detected a sliver of distaste in her words and wondered whether she read for pleasure or learning. Surely, a woman of her stature must read *something*. But before I could ask, she turned the topic on me with such a hairpin twist that I had little time to prepare.

"What do you plan to do with the loom?" she asked, falling back in her chair as though the matter she had really wanted to speak about had finally been broached.

"Do with the loom?" I asked, remembering Housekeeper's warning that I must be rid of the loom or risk being tossed out of Ma'am's house. A shiver of warning ran down my spine at the realization that she was to have the discussion with me herself.

"Do you plan to keep it or sell it?" she demanded, her straight and narrow nose huffing with indignation.

"I . . . well, I had planned to keep it," I said, feeling boxed in suddenly. I had hoped to stave off this conversation for at least a few days.

"I see," she said, her eyes now icy. For several seconds, she tsked, her eyes blinking rapidly as though thinking.

Just then a knock sounded at the door and Ma'am bade the maid enter. With tray in hand, a cheery looking girl who I knew only as Jesse, rushed in as best one can when carrying a heavy tray, and laid it on a table that sat between my chair and Ma'am's. My mouth watered at the delicacies there, sliced meats of every kind, cheeses too. Grapes graced a silver tray while another dish bore three kinds of bread. Moments later, another maid entered, this time with drink, glasses, and desserts. It was a veritable cornucopia of delightfully delicate foods. And to think, I would partake in this, rather than sneak a piece of bread when the cook wasn't looking to add to my meager stores that barely kept me fed most days.

Ma'am thanked the servants, then bade them leave. She nodded for me to fill my plate and fill it I did, though I must say my face warmed to think how gluttonous I must appear to her. I couldn't recall the last time I had eaten so, and I daresay it would have been as a child, not as an adult, for I was too busy working to have time for such things. Nor were such things on offer. No, mine was a simple fare at best. So, as I filled up on the variety of foods before me, I barely heard her words until she repeated them.

"It's not safe for you here with that loom."

I stopped what I was doing. "What do you mean?" I asked. Did she mean that I was causing trouble for her household by having it here? I frowned and sat my plate down, chewing slowly on her words and the food, both in equal measure.

"I've heard—" Here, she looked around as though the walls had ears. "—that there are those who mean to have the loom."

"I don't understand?" I said, still uncertain of her meaning.

She set down her plate. "Must I spell it out for you? The loom has a reputation. *You* have a reputation."

"Reputation for what?" I asked, my naivety on not-so-proud display.

"They say the loom is bewitched," she whispered.

"Bewitched?" My brain felt fuzzy, as though its signals were muffled. "But how could a loom be bewitched? It's simply . . . odd."

"And that's another thing," Ma'am said, fingering her necklace, a beautiful one carat amethyst in a bronze setting. "How is it that it only began weaving when you purchased it, never before?"

I fanned my face from the heat emanating from inside me. What on earth was the woman getting at? As if I had something to do with the loom acting as it did? Surely, she could see that I was a young woman, nothing more. A serving girl, on the lowest rung of the ladder in the Engstrom house. No one wanted to be me, and why should they? I answered to everyone, but no one answered to me. It was as simple as that.

"You really don't get it, do you, Brigid," she said, nodding her head as though she were talking to a simpleton. And maybe she was, because I bore no pretense, and in a house such as this, that was most unusual indeed.

"What don't I get?" I said on a sigh, wishing this conversation over and me back in my quarters, a serving girl once more.

"Whether you like it or not, Miss Brigid–" Here, she gazed pointedly at me, causing heat to rise to my cheeks once more. "This loom has made you a celebrity. And as a celebrity, you draw attention to this house."

My shoulders slumped. So, I was being kicked out of the house, to be sent packing with nowhere to go. I worried my hands together until I thought I might draw blood, so frightened was I by the prospect. She paused as though thinking, only adding to my inner torture.

At last, to my intense confusion, she said, "I want you and Emma to go to my friends' summer house. Take your loom. I will send for a carriage after dark. No one will know you are gone until it is too late. You will leave out the back gate."

I sat in stunned silence. I was being sent away, but not away from the people of this house, just somewhere . . . safe.

Before I could ponder her words further, she added, "I will be there in one month's time. Until then, you are to speak to no one outside the house, do you understand?" When I didn't react quickly enough, she said more firmly, ""*Do you?*"

I nodded my head, and yet it was spinning with all the twists and turns that had taken place since the purchase of the loom. I was going away. But where? Where was this summer house? Maybe Emma would know.

5

Henry paced the ramparts of the high manor, its palace-like walls thick and covered in ivy. Where was Brigid? Surely, she should have been here by now. He peered across the landscape, at the rolling hills, a long, thin winding road stretching out for miles. If she were on her way, he would know it.

"You've been waiting for weeks now," his brother Thomas said.

Thomas was spindly and tall, taller than Henry himself who was of decent bearing, six foot, if a day, whereas Thomas had a good one and a half inches on Henry. As if to improve his station, Henry stood taller and placed a spyglass to one golden brown eye to scan the horizon yet again. For one brief moment, he thought he saw something, but realized it was only a large stump, put there by the Jackals, a seamy sort bent on destroying Henry's kingdom. And the Kingdom of the Jackals was headed by none other than

Alaric himself. A shiver ran through him at the thought of them. Though related to both dog and wolf, they might just as well have been a different beast entirely, for they held no allegiance to anyone or anything but themselves. And expected total allegiance from all others.

"I put a call out through the loom," Henry said, lowering the spyglass to inspect his brother who was waving at some comely lady below. *Beatrice.* That lanky girl with curly black hair and green eyes who had bewitched his brother. She was a peril of a different sort. Always batting her eyelashes at poor Thomas who seemed besotted of her. Thomas, for his part, waved, his curly sandy brown hair—so different from Henry's straighter red hair, which was tied with a leather strap and blowing in the breeze. Worse yet, Thomas was wearing a dumb smile as if he had not a brain in his head.

"Maybe this Brigid girl didn't get the message," Thomas suggested, shrugging, his eyes never leaving Beatrice's.

"Can you think of nothing but Beatrice?" Henry said, shaking his brother. "Snap out of it. Imagine what is at stake."

Thomas frowned, then nodded, his expression suddenly more serious. "Right. Of course." Still, he stood on his toes to peer around Henry to get one last glimpse of Beatrice before she disappeared around the corner of the building.

Henry tried to ignore his brother's antics. Instead, he turned his ire on himself, thinking about the kingdom. If only he hadn't been so impetuous, hadn't . . . His eyes moistened with tears for it had been he who had cursed the gods for taking Soren too soon. Soren had been his best friend growing up, a little sprite compared to the larger Henry. He had been his sidekick all throughout childhood, and then "the troubles" came. It started as a cough that wouldn't cease and soon turned into pneumonia. Despite the ministrations of the best doctors in the land, Soren had died, his sweet, angelic face upon his death bed belying all the pranks they had pulled, the mischief they had managed, two bright minds coming up with what one alone could not. And now . . . now the kingdom was in dire straits . . . because of Henry. Because of the curse he had yelled upon Soren's death, damning the gods for not looking after one such as him while allowing the worst of the worst to survive, unchallenged. And everyone knew that there was none lower than Alaric the Third. Henry pictured the man with his reverse widow's peak, his dark oily hair with matching goatee that he often plaited. And his teeth. Henry shuddered at the memory of them. For Alaric had shown up on Henry's parents' doorstep that fateful day that Soren had died, a smile upon his face, his teeth glistening gold and silver, every other one a competing metal. Henry shivered, feeling even now the unctuousness of the man. *The evil.*

No, only the loom could save them now . . . and Brigid. The prophecy had foretold it. He turned his head and swiped at his tears before his brother had time to see, then shoved down all feeling. Once he had his emotions under control, he turned back to Thomas and forced a smile.

"What if she hasn't even seen the loom?" Thomas continued. "Or perhaps she didn't understand it?" Thomas said, more serious now.

The very air around Henry seemed to still in that one brief moment. What if Thomas was right? What if Henry had been sending Brigid messages all along and she hadn't received them?

Or worse. What if she was *illiterate* to the way of the loom? Panic seized him. For some time he stood there, the birds silenced as though understanding this watershed moment. But then all the air he'd been holding whooshed out of him as he came upon a plan. He would speak to the maze mage. Ask for assistance. And then . . . *then* he would wait.

One might think that darkness would be frightening, but for me it was freedom, for I had escaped the confines of the attic in this foray to the countryside. Hope stirred in my chest as I listened to the clack-clack of the lorry's wheels on the pavement. The chill caused me to pull my shawl tighter around my shoulders, the stars winking in the night sky as though letting me in on a secret. The secret being that freedom had been within my reach all along. And yet, after my imprisonment in the attic, I would see the countryside only in the dark. Still, I could almost imagine it. The sound of geese in the yard. The pump that would pour clean water into the buckets that I would carry to my garden to feed the vegetables and flowers, and all manner of rich organisms. Even now, I knew in my very heart of hearts that the fertile earth was waiting for me out there, needing me to tend it, to care for it as though it were mine. Mine.

Nothing is mine.

I shrugged in tighter to Emma whose teeth chattered like the beak of a magpie, those noisiest of birds. It would be hours before we would arrive at the village, according to Ma'am, and even more hours until daybreak, and yet nothing–not the cold, not the jolting ride, not even my fear of the unknown—could hold back my joy at this simplest of freedoms. To be one with the night and it with me. Because only here, beneath the canopy of stars, did I truly feel known, heard, understood. Always before, I was someone's chattel. "Throw the bucket here, Brigid. Tuck the bed like so. Have I not told you before, the beans are to be snapped in thirds, not halves." It was all I could do not to wither under the constant glare of one person or another. I could scarcely remember those rare moments when my mother had held me to her and whispered words of kindness. How I missed those times. For it seemed as though the world was made to test one's very desire to be in it. As though those living were not happy unless everyone else was miserable. How many times, in the wee hours of the morning, when I couldn't sleep and would listen to the rustle of the downstairs patrons, had I wondered why it was so. Why would so many people demand the misery of others when all their lives could be better should they just treat each other, well . . . *better*? But I suppose there are unwritten rules that determine the exact misery required of every human being. That some quota exists that demands it. As if to punctuate the point, the lorry hit a pothole and I bumped my head on the wood siding.

"Ouch!" I rubbed at the bump, which I felt certain had formed a red knot.

"Can't you ever sit still?" Emma groaned.

All I could see of her in the waning moonlight was her red hair, plaited for travel, and glowering eyes that appeared black against the night. She'd worn pointed shoes and her only travel garment, the one she wore when accompanying Housekeeper to town for supplies, a plaid frock woven in simple cotton.

"Aren't you excited?" I breathed, wishing I could stand up in the lorry and spin circles of delight to anyone daring to be out this late at night. "We're going to the country."

"Yeah, yeah," she said in a rather grumpy manner, should I say so myself.

Why could she not be as excited as I? But I suppose she was rather miffed. After all, she had planned to work her way up to marrying the doorman, or perhaps the livery driver. In the country, all prospects of marriage might be lost. So why wasn't I more upset at the idea of living life out on a farm in the country with nary a soul to turn to should I so need? I can't say. I just knew I didn't want to be a servant for life. Perhaps it was my upbringing. Mother had been such an artistic soul, always painting, setting tea out for friends and neighbors. And she had loved her piano though she pounded away at it like it were the gears of a locomotive heading out of the station. *Pound. Pound. Pound.* In response, my head had done the same. Needless to say, I had avoided her sessions at the piano as often as possible.

"What are your plans once we get to the countryside?" I gushed.

Emma simply turned over and grunted, her head resting on a hay bale.

"I, for one, plan to start a garden. I wonder if they will have a pond . . . and fish."

It's then I heard her snoring. I sighed, disappointed that she couldn't share in the joy I was feeling at being set free into the countryside. I suppose I was being insensitive to her wants and needs. Yet how anyone would want to spend the rest of one's life in a dusty attic at night, a basement kitchen during the day, I had no idea. No, for me the outdoors was as close to heaven as I could get. With a sigh, I laid back against my own hay bale and stared up at the stars. I had heard they had names. Ursa, the bear, Orion, the hunter, the Big and Little Dippers. I recalled my studies, lo those many years ago, the Greek literature I had been forced to recite.

I peered over to where Emma lay sleeping, relieved that I hadn't awakened her with my recitation and amazed that I had recalled such learning, though what did I have to while away my hours of toil but to remember all that I had gleaned.

As the minutes ticked by, I too was lulled by the lorrie's movements and felt my mind drift and my eyelids grow heavy. They had scarcely closed when I heard an odd humming sound and saw a golden glow beneath my eyelids. With a shake of my head, I forced my eyes open, too tired to know what I was seeing. But there it was, a chimera for sure, as it could not be real. For placed in front of me, my loom, which took up the entire rear of the wagon, all but shimmered, as though it had snatched up the halo that surrounded the moon in a haze of color and had made it its own. And furthermore, this haze of color seemed to be dancing a virtual jig across the loom as it moved to and fro beneath the skylight of stars, giving the entire evening an unearthly glow that had my hair standing on end. Afraid that it might stop, should I show my hand, I lay low against the wagon floor and watched it work its magic. The blood in my chest thumped a rhythm as I regarded the light that danced the loom, click-clack, click-clack, the steady rhythm never once alerting either the driver or Emma, who lay cradled amongst the hay, her breathing shallow.

For hours, it seemed, I watched the weave grow, but all I

could see were faint glimmers where the light fell, never seeing the heft of the weave or what it might portend. I would have to wait until morning for that. And indeed the nighttime hours moved nearly as quickly as the shooting stars that angled the sky from above, dashing as though frantic to be somewhere before daybreak. In the cradle of the wagon bed, the constant rhythm of both the wagon and the loom lulled me further, until I finally fell into a deep slumber, wherein I saw my family, once again in the bosom of home. We were young still, we children, none of us yet jaded, adulthood soon changing all that.

I awoke with a yawn, my mind cloudy but quickly clearing as I struggled to sit up. But when I did, I saw that Emma had beaten me to the punch and was even now rubbing at her eyes and staring in awe in the direction of the loom. She turned to me with wide eyes.

"It's changed, Brigid," she said in a Yorkney accent, having been born in England and set sail as a small child. And although she'd garnered a proper American accent, when astounded by something or afraid, or, as in this case, in the presence of someone she trusted, she reverted to her childhood accent. "The weave. It's gone bonkers, it has."

And I had to admit, the loom had indeed gone "bonkers." For in the weave, it showed me and Emma riding a wagon such as this, and in the far distance an estate surrounded by lovely gardens. But what grasped my attention most was the person on the west turret waving as if to get the attention of the pair in the cart. Emma, normally a chatterpie, had gone as silent as a churchmouse. Before I could say anything to allay her fears, I felt a prickling sensation along my back and turned ever so slowly.

For there, in the far distance, was a manor house, with gardens in front and two turrets, just as the loom had foretold. Furthermore, when my eyes drifted to the west turret, I indeed saw someone waving. A man. And not just any man. It was the young man who had inserted himself in the earlier weave of the loom. This, the kingdom I had come to save.

6

Alaric the Third sat atop his large black Friesian horse, brought to the northwest by early Dutch settlers. From a distance, he spotted his messenger riding toward him as though an army of bats was giving chase. A fissure of worry gnawed at Alaric as he and his brigand rode out to meet the man. The messenger's horse was at full lather, by the time he made the clearing. The messenger's eyes fairly shone with a fire that made speaking difficult.

"The loom," he said, dipping his head and gulping air. "It's gone. Brigid is gone along with one of the other servant girls, an Emma somebody or other."

"What do you mean?" Alaric boomed through gritted teeth. How hard was it to contain one young girl? "Gone where, and when?"

"She stole out in the middle of the night," the man said, panting and out of breath.

"Why didn't Josiah tell me this himself?" Alaric fumed, his fists balled around the reins of his horse.

"I could deliver the news faster."

Alaric read the lie in the other man's eyes. More like Josiah didn't want to face Alaric's wrath. All in good time. He pulled at his riding crop and held it up, causing the messenger to shrink in his saddle.

"Again, where . . . is . . . she?" Alaric said in a voice so low and filled with menace that the man froze, only responding when Alaric shouted, "Tell me!"

Fear flickered across the messenger's face, then in a small voice, he said, "Josiah doesn't know."

"Doesn't know." Alaric sat perfectly still, causing the other man further disquiet. "Well, well. You tell Josiah that he had better find her and the loom, and he'd better find her soon. Do you hear me?"

The messenger gulped, but nodded. "Yes, sire. I will tell him."

"Good," Alaric said. And then when he found Brigid, he would call on the Harridan of Nature to help him in his quest, to restore the loom to its rightful place . . . with Alaric the Third, son of Faineant the Foul. To win the kingdom for Alaric and his followers, The Jackals. But most importantly, to show all who knew him that *he* was in charge, *he* held the power. No longer would he be ridiculed as Alaric the Orphan. Yes, everyone would soon know his name and speak it with awe and respect. Or he would see to it that they would rue the day they had met him.

It was him, I felt certain. Shivers ran down my spine and tears formed in the corner of my eyes even as I struggled to make sense of what I saw. No longer was the man from the loom dressed like someone from a continent away. No, now he was dressed in a midnight blue waistcoat and vest, long white trousers replacing the earlier breeches. His auburn-red hair blew wisps in the wind, even as he clung to the turret with one hand, waved with the other. Had he known I was coming? But how?

"Emma, do you see what I see?"

Emma nodded, her normally hearty pink complexion now sallow and her expression piqued. She gulped before speaking, her voice coming out a quiver. "It's him, ain't it, Mum?"

Emma had never called me Mum, only Brigid, so I didn't know what to make of it. "Aye, I do believe you're right," I concurred. "But what do you think?" I asked, hoping that one of us would be the more stolid of the pair, but apparently that would have to be me because she simply shrugged, hands trembling ever so slightly. When next she spoke, her words came out as a squeak.

"Do you suppose he's a ghost, Brigid?" she whispered, as though he might hear, even from this distance.

He hardly appeared to be a ghost. No, this was a real flesh and blood man, albeit with a strange history, where the loom was concerned. I nearly jumped out of the lorry to rush to meet him, to ask him questions, though I would have to go about it carefully. Thankfully, I decided to wait until the lorry came to a halt.

As if reading my thoughts, the man in question yelled down to me even as we pulled up within the safety of the manor. "I'll be right down! Don't move." He started to run off, then came back for only a second to add, "Not a muscle."

"Not a muscle!" I shouted in return, and once again he disappeared. I could hear him open a door and clamor down stairs at an ungainly pace, all the while thinking what an unusual start to a meeting under odd circumstances indeed.

The birds chittered in the trees, starlings, I believe, while the driver climbed down out of his cab. He pulled a folding stair down from underneath the wagon for us to step down carefully, so as not to trip on our dresses. He held out a proprietary hand and helped us from the wagon, me first, then Emma. We had barely stepped onto dry land, as it were, when the gentleman we had seen atop the tower came stumbling out of a side door, doubled over and out of breath from having run the entire way.

The lad who had waved to us from above placed a hand on his knee to steady himself, and once he could speak, he said between breaths, "So glad you could come. I've been waiting all week for you."

I turned to Emma, wondering if she found this as odd as I did. Apparently, she concurred, because she held her valise tight to her chest to lend distance between her and him. The driver, however, seemed to notice nothing odd because he lifted out our steamer trunk that carried our meager belongings then turned to the young man and said, "Where do you want this?'

"Upstairs. My brother Thomas will show you where to take it, or one of the maids." The young man nodded toward the door that ended at the top of a wide portico with several steps leading up to it. The driver appeared nonplussed as he muscled the heavy steamer trunk up the steps on his shoulder.

"So, you've finally decided to answer the call," the young

man continued, grasping my hand as though he'd known me his whole life rather than just moments.

Again I eyed Emma, agog at this turn of events, but she merely shrugged and shook her head, as confused as I.

"Who *are* you?" I asked, realizing too late how rude this might sound.

"Henry, of course," he said, as though it should be common knowledge. "And you are Brigid and this is Emma," he added, pointing his chin in her direction. "Now come. We have work to do."

He was about to sweep me away when I remembered the loom and set my brakes. "We can't go until my loom is secured," I insisted. Already, it had been nearly nabbed once. I didn't want to risk a second try.

To that, Henry frowned. Then his eyes brightened and he let loose a loud, shrill whistle that made me flinch at the sound.

"Don't worry," Henry said brightly. "Red will take care of it. He's my horse," he said by way of explanation. "Best guard dog there is, only he's a horse. Can put out an eye, that one can. Loves children though. Odd," he said, then shrugged as though it made no difference to him that the horse loved children but hated people in general. Perhaps the horse'd had a bad experience with humans. I know *I* had.

Seconds later, a roan-colored horse came galloping around the corner of the manor, tail up, eyes wild, as though headed to a fire. His pale blond mane set off the lovely almost ginger color of his coat. Henry spoke unfathomable words, but the horse seemed to understand as he nodded his head and then backed up to the rear of the wagon and stamped his hoof several times before releasing a loud whinny, head up, ending on a snort. I couldn't help but laugh at his antics. What a strange pair, these two. Emma seemed just as impressed by the display because her mouth had opened so wide that a fly could have mistaken it for carriage doors.

But this was not to be the only oddity of the day, for as soon as the horse was firmly in place, Henry grasped my hand tighter and yelled, "Hurry!" as he rushed me off toward the back of the manor. Emma, who held her valise tight to her chest, determined at the last minute to drop it and follow us at an awkward walk-run.

"Where are we going?" I asked, breaths coming in short bursts as I rushed to keep up.

"Where do you think?" He pointed toward a tall European hornbeam maze. *Carpinus betulus,* I knew from my studies.

I barely had time to acknowledge the height and breadth of the maze before he had found a secret entrance and had pulled me into it. Emma's emerald green eyes widened in panic at the fear of being left behind, or worse, getting lost all alone in the maze. At least I had a guide who knew the way in and out, I assumed, but she had only me. As if she understood this, she lifted her skirts and ditched her slippers, preferring to run to keep up.

For the next several minutes we made rapid hairpin turns, first right, then left, sometimes turning in on ourselves so that we seemed to be going in the direction we'd just come. The maze appeared to have no end, and finally, I once again set my brakes, refusing to go further until Henry explained what exactly he had in mind. For the maze went on forever and I suspected that if I kept going, I would find some poor soul who had never made it out, only bones and clothing to ever show that someone had entered this hall of mirrors.

When Henry tugged once more, I stomped my foot, not caring that I looked like a petulant child. "Henry," I said, as if we had indeed known each other forever, "I demand that you tell me where we are going."

He rolled his eyes, clearly unused to having to deal with stubborn young women, but I was not to be put off. He would answer me or by god . . . by god, what? I peered around me, realizing that I was lost, totally and completely lost. I had no choice but to trust him and hope that I made it out of this living venus flytrap alive. Tears formed at the edges of my eyes, maddening, for they showed me a fern in a world filled with snapdragons.

"We are going to see the head gardener. Don't you know that the plants are at war?" He shook his floppy red mane. "You arrived just in time."

At that moment, I heard a tremulous mewl from Emma who had lost us on that last turn.

"Don't move," Henry called to her. "You either," he said to me, lifting one eyebrow to let me know I should broach no opposition.

Yet the moment he disappeared down the artery of the hedge that veered sharply to the right, my heart began to flutter in my chest and my breathing grew so shallow that I thought I might pass out right then and there. For how would I ever find my way should he never return? Panic set in, but I forced myself to focus on what he'd said, for surely he was mad. The plants—at war? I had never heard of such a thing. Even as I drank in the earthy smell of the hornbeams with its serrated edges and lovely gray bark, my thoughts returned to the tapestry, to the words written on them: *Save My Kingdom*. Was this the kingdom the tapestry was referencing? A kingdom of . . . *plants*? And how did Henry fit into all of this? My head was spinning like a top.

Suddenly, the realization that I was alone . . . completely and utterly alone in a world of mazes, in a land so foreign that I might as well be one of those spinning tops searching for purchase, I spun in circles, wondering which way to go. I called out to both Emma and Henry, my voice coming out a quiver, but received no response. *Where are they?*

Admonition or no, I could sit here no longer, waiting for fate to play its hand, and from the look of things not in my favor! With an abandon bordering on terror, I began to run when a hand reached out from behind me and snatched me into an embrace so tight that I fought with both fists, only to sink into those arms with immeasurable relief when I saw that it was Henry, his smell at once both primal and woodsy. His normally chipper outlook had suddenly been exchanged for deep concern. Beside him stood Emma, appearing as fraught with panic as I, though at least her panic seemed to be subsiding now that we were all together.

"I told you not to move, Brigid," Henry whispered into my ear, his breath brushing against me like hummingbird wings.

"I tried, Henry, honestly I did, but . . . ."

"I know," he said, placing me at arm's length so he could take stock of me. "I had the same reaction the first time I entered the maze." He ran his fingers across my right cheekbone, brushing away a tear that had fallen in my haste . . . my fright. "You're mine now. I will take care of you, yes?"

I could only nod, my throat tight with emotion. For the first time since I'd arrived here, my heart stilled, his confidence giving me pause. Solace. So much of my life had felt out of control since I'd been separated from my family. It seemed my fates had been thrown to the winds with few ties to anchor me. No, I was as untethered as the seeds of a dandelion, scattering this way and that to the four directions: east, west, north, and south.

"Good," he said, once again taking my hand and, with a lift of his chin, encouraging Emma to follow. "Then we shall go meet the person leading the charge."

"Oh?" I said with a frown, not sure what he had planned.

"Come with me," he said with a sly wink. "You'll see what I mean." Then he squeezed my hand and bade me follow him.

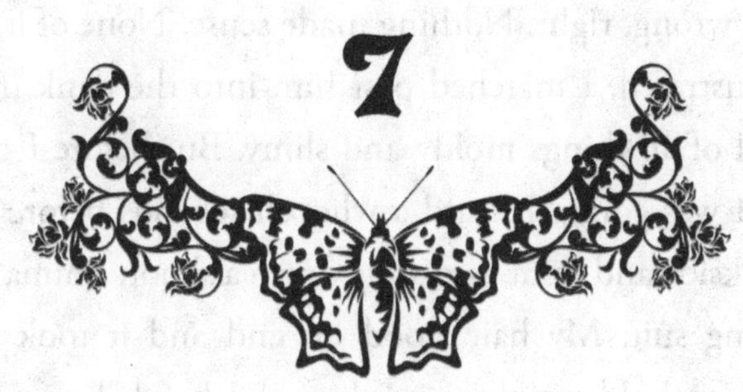

I was hopelessly lost and out of breath by the time we reached the cavern, which came as a surprise both exciting and terrifying. We had been running for what felt like an hour now. For some reason, I had expected to reach the center of the maze, not the edge of it, but indeed we had come to the only terminus possible.

"Stop!" I pleaded, holding up a hand to show I meant business. For several moments I bent over, hands on knees, struggling for air. Once my nostrils had stopped burning along with my chest, I peered over at Emma, whose feet were bleeding, having long since shed her shoes.

"Who's in there, Henry?" I nodded toward the cavern, which dripped with ferns and strange, unfamiliar flowers, both fragrant and towering in size. Faint voices echoed from deep within the moist chamber.

Henry looked around, as though the hornbeam had ears and

said, "It is not for me to say. It is for you to find out."

"Oh, for the love of . . . ." I balled my fists. So many riddles . . . mazes. I was tired, frustrated, but most of all angry that everything I had known of the past was gone, wiped out as cleanly as the slate blackboard that my school marm had taught on. The world seemed to have tilted, everything now upside down. Right, wrong, wrong, right. Nothing made sense. None of it.

Frustrated, I marched past him into the dank interior that smelled of all things moldy and slimy. But before I could think where I was going, I heard a whoosh seconds before I slid onto my backside and went careening down a shoot, Emma and Henry following suit. My hair stood on end and it took all I could manage to hold my dress in place as I hurtled ever downward, shrieking the entire way until at last my lungs gave out, and nearly my heart.

By the time I reached the bottom with a loud thump, I was both in awe of the jewel-colored stalactites and stalagmites that looked as though we'd been eaten by an alligator with rainbow colored teeth, and in a lather, ready to do fisticuffs, if it came to it. And indeed, I must have looked a fright, for both Emma and Henry rose to their feet when they landed, then stood back in order to give me a wide berth.

"How dare you, Henry . . . what's the rest of your name?" I sputtered, feeling fierce now and betrayed.

"It's Henry Jay Bookbinder at your service," he said with a bow and what could only be termed a goofy smile.

"Well, darn you, Henry."

Emma gasped, unaccustomed to hearing me behave so badly. No doubt I would be doing penance for days to come in her zealous mind, but I didn't like being mucked about. I believed in fairness, and so far, I had seen little of it at best. Was this how things worked? Did war make people infinitely uncivil? I had the horrid feeling that I was about to find out, and I was afraid that my suspicions would soon be manifest. As such, I closed my eyes, forcing my breathing to slow, my mind to settle. *What does one do when the world comes apart?* I wondered in as calm a manner as I could muster. How I longed for normalcy, for sanity, but it was clear there was none to be found here.

For a moment, I took in my surroundings, the golden pathway made up of shimmering pebbles that led where, precisely? Deeper into the cave, that was for certain. And I could see tiny crustaceans, a crab that moved sideways and turned jewel colors so that it could fade into any color of background. And there was a translucent spider in one corner who spun a rainbow web. Unnerved, I stepped in closer to the others.

"Okay, Henry," I said at last. "It appears that I have been hijacked." Here, I narrowed my eyes to let him know I was not pleased. "Take me to your . . . gardener." Then we would see what's what, but even as I thought it, I trembled, for nothing about this place was right, and as if to mirror my fears, I heard a wailing from deep within, a sound so frightening as to be evil by its very nature.

Despite the number of times Henry had entered the cavern, the eerie screams never failed to unnerve him. As he explained to Brigid, the sound came from those that could not be saved, a reminder to all of them to try harder, to be better. But she seemed nonplussed by what he'd said, as though blaming him in some way for the horrid wails. And as if to exacerbate her already fragile state, the cavern began belching a sulphuric odor that had all three gasping. Henry, having thought ahead, pulled three masks from within his waistcoat and handed the two women each a moretta mask that looked as though it belonged in a Venetian Carnival rather than a cave, only the nosepiece covered in cloth to lessen the odor. Once their faces were covered, he placed a more masculine looking mask over his own face.

"What is that . . . *odor*?" Brigid asked, her face askew as she rushed to put on her mask.

"It's the headmaster of the garden. He uses the stench to keep people away."

"Even us?" she asked, the surprise written in the arch of her brow.

"Even us," he reiterated. "One can never be too careful during times like these."

With a sadness bordering on melancholy, he recalled all he had witnessed over the past few weeks—the suffering. The loss. Until now, he had been so focused on finding Brigid and Emma and bringing them here that he hadn't allowed himself to feel. Yet now, as they edged closer to the inner chamber, it all came rushing back at him and he stopped, rubbing tears from his eyes.

Brigid, who until now had seemed angry with him, cautiously grasped his hands and squeezed. "It will be alright," she said, her eyes scanning his—empathy written in the unusual blue irises with the little gold flecks. For some reason, this simple gesture soothed him and the trepidation he'd felt slowly faded into the ether. He peered back at Emma and saw that she too seemed more vested in the venture than she had at the start.

"The head gardener is a good man. He, and many others, are trying to save the kingdom."

"The plant kingdom." Brigid seemed confused, either that or she didn't understand the urgency.

He felt as though he were talking to a child, but he had to try to make her understand, as his worst fears had materialized, for Brigid was most assuredly illiterate to the ways of the loom. And he had just a short time to bring her up to speed.

"It's like this," he explained. "The plants feed us, they provide oxygen, they clean the air, they nourish insects, animals, and humans alike. If we lose that, we lose *everything*."

She shook her head, clearly confused. "If that's the case, then surely we all have a stake in preventing that. Who would oppose such a simple concept?"

So naive. He tsked, all the while summoning the courage to make her understand things that had taken him years to learn, if not a lifetime. Had her parents taught her nothing?

"Surely you must have heard about this," he said, gesturing around him and to the entrance above that was merely a speck of blue light in the distance, "been taught about the loom and all that it represents." But he could see by her puzzled expression that she had no idea what he was talking about. "Saints preserve," he murmured, a weight settling on his chest. So much to do to save the kingdom, and now this. He closed his eyes, then opened them and saw both women peering at each other, eyebrows coming together in a frown.

"It's clear I know nothing," Brigid said, rubbing at her brows as though fighting a headache. "So, enlighten us."

"Enlighten you," Henry repeated.

"Are you a parrot? You keep repeating my words," Brigid said, once again sullen and unforthcoming, arms crossed as if to ward off any further assault to her sensibilities.

He breathed a sigh born of frustration. "See, it's like this," he said. "The plants, animals, and insects have all taken sides."

"Sides?"

"Now who's the parrot?" he said with chagrin, the dark and dank cavern suddenly feeling claustrophobic. "The rats and the cockroaches have teamed up with the poisonous snakes and mosquitoes. And some bats are becoming rabid-ized. They are becoming a scourge to our kingdom."

"But why? What's in it for them?"

Henry peered at the ceiling of the cave, at the multicolored stalactites dripping water rich with minerals from above. "Do you know nothing?" he said, once again turning his attention to Brigid. "These insects and animals proliferate. They need more space. Some evil men have teamed up with them to take over the kingdom. We good humans and animals and insects are in the way. With us gone, the evil ones would have the kingdom to themselves."

"Oh!" Brigid and Emma said in unison.

"But wouldn't that upset the balance?" Brigid said, while at the same time reaching for a beautiful lime green crystal that shimmered in the light pooling of water at the edge of the cave.

"Don't touch that!" Henry said, rushing to her side and nearly slipping on a mossy stone. He dragged her away before she could snag the crystal.

"Why?" she asked, perplexed.

"It could be booby-trapped. That's how the opposition tricks us. They offer beautiful, shiny objects that attract us to them. They use it to capture us, to manipulate us. They'll stop at nothing, so beware!"

His point must have hit its target, for Brigid shivered, gooseflesh playing up her arms. Emma huddled in tighter, glancing around the cave with dread, as though every corner held some secret trap to ensnare them. Yet, better that than to be caught in the sticky web of deceit, as that could be deadly. Sadness gripped Henry as he thought of his best friend, Soren. They had been close as children, had done everything together. They had even studied the art of warfare together, until . . . . Henry's throat tightened and he fought back tears. No, he would not go there.

For a moment, both women said nothing, sharing fearful glances as they once again perused their surroundings for any potential dangers. Then, Brigid seemed to regain her equilibrium, standing now with arms akimbo and sporting an expression so fierce that Henry took a step back.

"If what you say is true, why had my family never spoken of any of this?" she challenged, her blue eyes piercing and just as captivating as the crystal.

But before Henry could respond, a booming voice echoed through the cavern, a voice so deep that it rocked the very ground beneath them—so much so that Brigid, Emma, and Henry were forced to clasp hands to form a human chain, should anyone lose their balance.

"They tried," boomed the voice, eyes like burning coals firing the darkness with twin points of red light. "But they were separated too soon to provide the needed training."

"Who is that?" whispered Brigid, hand trembling as she gripped Henry more tightly.

"That is the head gardener," Henry explained, trembling nearly as much as Brigid herself, despite the many times he had spoken to the sacred entity. "He is responsible for the gardens, for nature. For our survival."

Brigid gripped him tighter still, and Henry had to say, he didn't mind. Not at all. In fact, it sent chills racing through him, a pleasant feeling at that.

The red lights blinked, sending rays into the darkened cavern. Then, in a more ominous tone, the head gardener said, "She does not know the language because she speaks the language of the heart. It is different from ours. Because of this, she is hard to reach. Hard to teach. But just as she cannot speak our language, we cannot speak hers, and as such, it causes much confusion and misunderstanding. You, Henry, are tasked to teach her."

"Me?" Henry squeaked, pointing at his chest wondering if he had heard correctly. If neither her parents nor her teachers had been able to reach her, how did the head gardener expect *him* to get through to her?

"Yes, you, Henry. But I must warn you--"

Henry's heart pounded as he waited for the final edict, his thoughts racing. What if he couldn't teach her? What if she was illiterate to this language . . . could only ever speak her own? What then? He held his breath as he waited for the head gardener to finish his sentence.

"She doesn't learn as we do—through pain. It . . . *stunts* her growth."

"Stunts her growth?" Henry had never heard of such a thing, but as he peered over at Brigid, he could see that the very word "pain" had caused her to recoil and draw in on herself, as though she were shrinking right before his very eyes. How very . . . odd.

"Should you fail–"

But suddenly the light was fading, as was the voice.

"Should I fail . . . what? What will happen?" Henry realized that he sounded frantic now, but he feared the unknown consequences even more than the task itself.

Too late, the light was gone. They had learned all they would for today. With trepidation that left his knees weak, he turned toward the ladder that he knew was built into the cave. It would be a long, exhausting climb out of the cavern, but he had no choice. Now he would need to do the seemingly impossible. Teach Brigid the language of war.

8

"We have found Brigid, M'lord," Josiah said, having come to the castle himself this time.

Alaric noted the weasel-faced man ruefully, as he sucked the very marrow from one of his latest victims, a moose bagged from the Adirondacks and shipped to him via overland carriage. The knowledge that Brigid had been found made the meat taste sweeter still as he peered 'round the room at the generals and their retinue.

"And? The loom?" Alaric raised a single brow which he'd recently had pierced, the stud a silver and gold pirate ship.

"The loom has been found also."

"Good!" Alaric leaned back from the wide oak table and patted his belly, then swiped at his oily mouth with a brown linen napkin. "Where is it?"

Up until now, Josiah had beamed with beneficence, but now

he appeared more hesitant, unsure of himself.

"Well, sire, it is being well cared for. It is at the manor--"

"The manor?" Alaric growled so loudly that everyone at the table immediately stopped talking and peered up, only to peer down again when he turned his malevolent gaze their way. "What do you mean, the manor?"

"The Bookbinder's manor. It's like this," Josiah stated, his lips held together in a tight line. "I have placed someone on staff to watch over the loom, to report back to me."

Alaric pondered that for a moment. He supposed it was wise to use tact rather than might to go after the loom. For the moment, it would have to do, but the thought didn't sit well with his stomach and he burped, a sour taste in his mouth.

"Give me a week," Josiah said. "I promise you, you shall have your loom."

Suddenly the sour taste in Alaric's mouth had left a sour feeling in his stomach as well. Angry, he stood, tossing the napkin onto his plate.

"You will get me that loom, or else. Is that understood?" he commanded, once again lifting a brow.

"Yes, sire," Josiah said, but it was clear by the bitterness of his expression that the threat had not gone over well with Alaric's lackey.

Alaric turned on his heels, his boots clicking as he yelled over his shoulder, "Dinner is finished. You may all leave!"

Alaric had spent the better part of the afternoon deciding what to do. He didn't like relying on others to do his dirty work. Therefore, he hurried to the aviary where the falcons were kept in traditional mews, partitioned areas with individual perches for each of the falcons. The falconer, an older gentleman with a craggy face who had raised falcons even in Faineart the Foul's time, had always seemed larger than life. A big man, it was said that he was of Kazakh blood, and it was true that he had dark skin, but he had the bluest of eyes, so pale as to be almost translucent. How he had arrived here from so far away was anyone's guess, but Alaric felt certain he'd been obtained in one of his father's numerous adventures where he collected people as readily as he collected revenue . . . *before* Alaric had been sent to the orphanage as a child to be raised by nuns. Only to return home as a teen once his father had passed, to live with his uncle, who by that time needed a successor.

Even as a young child, Alaric had been slightly frightened of the Kazakh, a mystic if ever there was one, for he lived and dined and spoke with falcons from birth on, as though *they* were his family rather than the more typical human family. He had found it disconcerting that the falconer spoke their language, and they seemed to understand him, too, responding to his slightest beckon. To add to the sense of mysticism, the Kazakh wore a fox fur jacket and a large red hat and boar skin gloves. Mostly, he trained eagles for all manner of hunting, but this Kazakh had branched off, including falcons in his arsenal, but the falcons were used as messengers and fighters, unlike eagles which were strictly hunters.

"I need you to send this message to the Bookbinder Manor. It's of utmost importance. Send your finest eagle to protect the falcon. Do you understand?"

Like his birds of prey, the man merely blinked, his large eyes having taken on an almost avian quality as though he'd indeed been birthed into the family of predatory birds. He gave one brief nod. Alaric didn't dare challenge him as he might others for he'd heard whisper of the last person who had done so. Found pecked to death in a valley not far from here. No, better to remain on friendly terms, as much as one could with a man who lived and trained with the greatest hunters on earth.

The moment our trio reached land above the cavern, I fell to my knees, unable to take another step. I would have kissed the very earth I had walked on earlier that same day, had I not worried what the others might think—believing that perhaps I had gone mad from the caverns below. But it was not madness that afflicted me. It was pure and unadulterated relief that I had survived such an ordeal as this, today being the strangest of days. For how often did one meet a head gardener in a cavern filled with brightly colored stalactites meant to enslave a person, should one be so foolish as to reach for them? Thankful that I had been properly warned, I said a silent prayer of gratitude and took the hand that Henry offered. When I rose, my legs felt weak, as though they might collapse again at any moment.

"So, let the lessons begin, Brigid," Henry said. "For you, too, Emma, though you are of less use than Brigid."

"What? After all we've been through?" I demanded, furious that he had spoken so rudely to Emma and me.

Emma, who was nothing if not mild-mannered, bristled, her normally placid green eyes sparking with a fury I had not seen before.

"What do you mean, I am of little use, Henry Bookbinder?" Emma demanded.

Heretofore, she'd been leaning against the hornbeam maze, catching her breath and peering up at the bright sky, layered with just the wispiest of white clouds. Now, however, she stood upright and had taken to placing her hands on her hips in challenge, her bright red hair only accentuating her pale skin further.

"Well . . . it's just that . . ." Henry stammered and stuttered, then threw up his hands. "The oracle has said that *Brigid* is to save the kingdom."

"Me?!" I spat, feeling at this point as if the earth might swallow me whole. "How can *I* save the kingdom?" Cold prickles of fear ran up my arms, followed by a resounding wave of heat, as though I had suddenly come down with ague and was feverish.

Henry puffed up, then immediately deflated, all the air he'd stored in his lungs releasing in a sigh. "*That*, I don't know. I just know you'll never save the kingdom if you don't know the language, so the lessons begin the moment we return."

"Return to what?" I asked, taking in the scent of the lawn and hornbeam, and some mysterious sweet smell I couldn't name.

Henry regarded me curiously. "You smell it, don't you?" he said, with a hint of accusation in his voice.

"Smell what? That sweet smell?" I answered innocently enough.

He grabbed my hand and began pulling me through the maze, Emma clutching the back of my dress so as not to be left behind this time.

"We must hurry. You are to stay away from the sweet smells," he said, the aroma immediately generating a torrent of sneezing in both Emma and Henry.

For some reason, the smell didn't overly affect me, but I didn't want to chance getting whatever Emma and Henry had, so I hurried along, one in front, one in tow.

We returned through the maze faster than we'd come, and even before we found the exit, I heard a man calling Henry's name at a distance, becoming more frantic each time he repeated it.

We were running through the twists and the turns of the maze so fast that when we exited, Henry ran into the person with a thump, all of us falling like dominoes, one after the other, splayed out in the grass like so much windblown flotsam.

"Get--off--of--me--Henry!" the other man managed to say through shallow breaths.

One by one, we rolled over to gaze at the sky, the sun no longer overhead but far on the horizon. Dusk would soon be here, and as though the thought had registered to my stomach that it had missed the afternoon meal, it began rumbling painfully from within so that all three sets of eyes were staring at me.

"What?" I demanded with a shrug.

Emma just shook her head, a look of disgust imbuing her narrow features. But to my intense delight, her stomach too began growling until moments later, a near symphony had begun to play as we struggled to gather air into our overused lungs.

"I see you still don't know how to treat guests," the young man said, rolling on his side and leaning on one arm. "First, let me introduce myself. I am Thomas A. Bookbinder, Henry's brother."

He stuck out a hand toward me and did an imaginary shake

in the air, while I did likewise. "I'm Brigid," I said, "and this is Emma who is like a sister to me."

All of Emma's earlier pique seemed to fade away at the compliment given her and she, too, gave an imaginary shake.

For his part, Henry stuck out a hand toward his brother as if to give him a shake as well, when Thomas rose to his knees and said, "Oh for the love of . . . ." He waved a hand as if to ward off any further antics from his brother. "Follow me." He offered first me, then Emma, a hand.

I nearly laughed when I saw the pout that had settled over Henry's face, as if he had found us first and had determined that we were now his, "finders keepers". But I also saw that Emma seemed instantly smitten with Thomas, for when she clasped her hand in his, she didn't let go. Not immediately. Not at all. It was as if they'd come to an unspoken agreement and that was that. I had never seen Emma like this, for she fairly glowed. I peered over at Henry, who peered back at me and then we both shrugged. With trepidation, Henry held out his hand toward me, his lightly freckled cheeks paling, as though I might reach out and slap them instead. But just to show there were no hard feelings for taking me into the cave, I took his hand and gave it a squeeze. For a moment, he didn't move. Then an angelic smile lit up his face, and I do believe he stood a bit taller as if to prove to me that he was knight material, or some such nonsense.

Before long, we were back at the manor house, seated at a narrow table with a huge repast unlike any I had seen before, even at Ma'am and Sir's manor house. For here, in resplendent glory, dotting the table were yeasty breads with butter and jam. A roast, unlike any I had seen, with potatoes and carrots, onions and garlic. To set it off was a gravy boat filled with the most delicious smelling gravy I'd ever hoped to taste. In the middle of it all was a swan-shaped gelatin mold that seemed to swim in a moat of pansies in every color, shape, and size. Blue, purple, orange, but my favorites were the yellows, each of them looking like a miniature person with a lovely bonnet, as though dressed for Sunday dinner. And at the head of the place setting, fluted glasses filled with what I could only presume was mead, as I had heard that this was the drink of the gods and smelled quite sweet.

To my left, I was introduced to all manner of people, including an aunt and uncle, Lady Penelope and Sir Roger, who were said to be from the old country, though what old country I had no idea. Across from me and Emma sat Henry and Thomas, as well as two giggling daughters belonging to Lady Penelope and Sir Roger, their hair done up in curls, and each dress meant to outdo the others with a large yellow bow on one, a green bow on the other. But for all their insincere charm, they were quite pretty and I could see Emma steaming in silence beside me, for she had claimed Thomas as surely as one claims one's shawl after a dance. But her most ardent competition seemed to be Beatrice, a comely young girl who Thomas had set his eyes upon with a smile akin to a lovesick cow.

For my part, I simply eyed Henry to see what he thought of these two simpering young ladies and the lovely Beatrice. Clearly, he adored the flattery, used to being a star among men. Yet when he glanced over at me, his cheeks flushed, as though recognizing this weakness in himself--the need to be the center of attention. I offered him no absolution. It was a weakness he would need to cure, if he ever hoped to find either love or to save the kingdom, because although I had only just heard of the kingdom's need, I knew enough to know that such a weakness could be one's downfall. I had enough on my plate already to realize I didn't need *that* to take me down. No, in my lively imagination, I had enough dragons to slay without adding that to my repertoire.

"So, Lady Brigid, where did you say you were from?" the girl in green asked, her name Joclyn, I believe. The other's name was Gertrude, according to Henry.

"Uh . . . where I'm from?" My eyes widened and I searched my memory, trying to decide which life to tell her about. The one before we'd lost everything, or the one after, where I would have to explain that I not only was no lady, but worked as kitchen staff and lived in the hot and stuffy attic of a manor house.

Henry seemed to understand my dilemma, for at that moment, he reached for the tureen of gravy. "Would you care for some--?" But before the words were finished, he unceremoniously spilled most of the gravy in Joclyn's lap, all over her satin green dress with swirls that reminded me of aging wood.

She jumped to her feet and yelled, "Stupid--"

"Joclyn! Really!" Lady Penelope admonished, apologizing to those around her, especially to Henry and Thomas's parents, who were seated at each end of the table, a stolid pair, if ever there was one.

"But he spilled--"

"Not another word!" Sir Roger growled, raising a brow in challenge.

She stamped her foot once, then stared down at the floor. "Yes, Papa," she said, but not before she glared first at Henry, then at me, as though I had caused her distress by my mere presence.

Then she unceremoniously took her leave from the table.

I discreetly smiled my thanks to Henry for coming to my aid. So, he must know about my fall from polite society into the bowels of Sir and Ma'am's manse, or in my case, the sweltering attic. In my previous station, I would have no more been allowed in this room, than I would have been allowed to speak to people such as these at a table such as this. Come to think of it, why *had* Henry and his family allowed me a place at their table? Was it because of the prophecy that I would save the kingdom? Is that why they had foregone protocol, or were they different, less zealous about one's place in the pecking order?

"Now, Brigid," Lady Bookbinder said. "You were saying that your parents were from upstate New York, no?"

For a moment, I froze, but she gave me a knowing look. She was offering me an olive branch, a way out of an uncomfortable situation. How had she known about my family?

Lady Bookbinder turned back to Sir Roger and Lady Penelope. "Brigid's father was in finance, isn't that right dear?" she said, smiling sweetly at me. For the first time since I arrived, I took stock of the woman. She had a splay of sandy brown hair that curled atop her head, and she sat very erect, a rather large emerald ring gracing her hand and matching her gown. Though no longer svelte, it was easy to see that she commanded attention, even now. Perhaps this was the reason Henry expected the same.

"Right," I managed to squeak, betweened lips narrowed from nerves. I just wanted the meal to end so that I could go back to the room the maid had taken me to when I arrived, the manse being so large that Emma had her own room, as did I.

"Oh, how lovely," Lady Penelope said.

While we are waiting for Joclyn to return, Lord Bookbinder said, "We should discuss some important issues. Perhaps Gertrude would like to wait in the drawing room until we are finished?"

Though asked as a question, I knew it to be an order, one in which Gertrude could hardly refuse, as the guest of Lord and Lady Bookbinder. Sulking nearly as badly as her sister before her, Gertrude rose, tossing her linen napkin aside in a huff, her golden ringlets dancing in the candlelight. All we saw was a cloud of yellow chiffon as she made a dramatic exit. Catching the glint of humor in Henry's eyes, I looked down quickly so as not to betray my mirth at the petulance of both women, who were obviously used to getting their way. It was easy to see they had never had to soil their hands, to have them become chapped from days in water peeling potatoes and yams, slicing onions and all manner of vegetables. They had never toiled so that sweat dripped off their brows and down their noses. No, those two had been pampered. In that moment, I wondered. Did Henry like pampered women, women who were used to having their way, like Beatrice, who now seemed to be flirting at Henry to make Thomas jealous? Or did he like . . . ? No, I would not go there. I was nothing to him but a means to an end. And yet . . .

"Beatrice, you may want to keep Gertrude company," Lord Bookbinder added purposefully.

Thinking she'd escaped having to stay behind, she too huffed out of the room, chin up, flashing one last glare at Emma who wore the grin of a North American lynx on her pretty pink lips. According to my studies as a child, the word lynx was derived from the Greek word *leukos*, meaning bright, which described Emma's smile perfectly, for it nearly lit up the room now that she had Thomas all to herself. I presumed the only reason *we'd* been allowed to stay was because of our proximity to the loom. And because of the prophecy.

"So, now that the young ladies are gone, we must speak hurriedly," Lord Bookbinder said, standing and pacing. "Alaric the Third is our nemesis. He has sent an avian messenger warning of a pestilence headed our way if we don't give him the loom. But if we do, it will be our undoing. Whoever owns the loom rules the kingdom." He looked pointedly at me. "Until recently, we had no idea where the loom was located. But now that it belongs to Brigid . . . to *us* . . . we must stop Alaric, and stop him quickly, but how?"

All eyes turned to me. Heat rushed to my face. How could I possibly know what to do? I had never even heard of Alaric the Third before today. I thought and thought, but my mind was known to go blank whenever confronted with a dilemma such as this.

Then, with a snap of my fingers, it came to me. The loom. I would ask the loom. It would know what to do, but not until nightfall. The weaver never showed him or her self, merely worked his or her magic in the night.

"One evening, Lord, Ladies. Give me one evening to speak to the loom. Then I shall have your answer."

For one moment, no one spoke, the tension rising inside me like an unpopped silk balloon. Then, it was as if a pin had pricked it, spilling relief among the gathering. Now, I just had to pray that I was right. That the loom would advise me on this most precarious of topics.

I was wrong, for despite my tossing and turning later that night, or perhaps because of it, the loom had nothing to offer by morning. As I dressed to descend the stairs for my morning repast, I felt numb from lack of sleep, and number still at the bad news I would soon impart. Slowly, I trudged down the stairs and met Emma at the landing.

"Has the loom revealed anything yet?" she whispered, wrapping her crimson shawl tightly around her to stay warm.

"Not a thing," I said, hearing the early stirrings of the manor in the adjoining room.

Emma's pale green eyes widened in alarm. "What will you tell Lord and Lady Bookbinder?"

"I don't know." I shrugged. After all, what could I tell them?

Soon, over soggy oatmeal, I revealed the awful truth to all present at the table. "I wish I had better news," I added, peering down at my oatmeal, no longer hungry. "I only know that I can't give up my loom. I *won't* give up my loom."

Lord and Lady Bookbinder glanced nervously around the table, seeking the reactions of Lady Penelope and Sir Roger.

"So, it's decided," Lord Bookbinder said with resignation. He dropped his napkin next to his oatmeal and pushed away from the table, then stood. "I will prepare Alaric's falcon for the return trip with a note of our own stating that we will not give up the loom. Agreed?"

All those present nodded reluctantly, all except Gertrude, Beatrice, and Joclyn, who just appeared confused, having been sent away while we tossed around the obstacles we faced.

From that point on, we waited well into the day for word. Surely the falcon had arrived at Alaric the Third's fortress by now and we would soon have our answer. All of us were on pins and needles, jumping at the slightest sound or a hand on the shoulder.

Finally, it was Henry who turned the tide with his usual cheerfulness. "We can't just sit here waiting, and we can't change the outcome at any rate, so why not spend the day playing batball, then we'll learn what we'll learn when it's time.

Everyone agreed with his analysis, and soon we were outside playing to our heart's content, until tired and spent. We came in for supper, none of us overly verbose after such a strenuous day. Instead, we tucked into our dinner in silence. I, more than most, believed that perhaps Alaric had heard Lord Bookbinder's reasons for keeping the loom and had come to accept it, such was the reason for his delay in answering. The delusion I was under satisfied me to no end and I smiled for the first time all day.

But before I could settle into a cozy retreat after dinner, a rush of noise came barreling through the front doors of the manor and down the hallway, shouts from the serving staff coming in wafts. "You can't go in there. Lord and Lady have guests. Really! Stop!"

At that moment, the doors to the dining hall burst open and a short man of muscular stature strode through dressed in military uniform. I looked to Henry for an explanation, but he only shrugged, as curious as I to learn the reason for the man's outburst. We didn't have long to wait.

"Lord Bookbinder, Sir Roger." He nodded to each man in acknowledgment. "You and the young ladies and gentlemen need to follow me. Quickly!"

We all peered at each other to see if anyone knew the meaning of the intrusion, yet it was clear that none was the wiser. As one, we stood, each man and woman falling in line according to their perceived rank, poor Emma coming in last.

Henry waited for me. "Who is he?" I whispered once I came within earshot.

"Private Tucker, at your service. He's a courier. He's tasked to deliver messages from the front."

As I rushed to keep up, I wondered what news was so important that he'd interrupted Lord Bookbinder's meal with Sir Roger. But I soon saw the disaster that lay before us, as each of us gasped, Lady Bookbinder screeching her fright for all to hear. For there was a fearsome swarm of insects in a swath so wide that it blocked the sun, millions of shiny black beetles, perhaps, whose shell, when lit by the sun, gave off a watery display of color like that of a rainbow. I grabbed Emma's hand, my heart racing as millions upon millions of the wee beasties fanned toward us, no more than a faint hum as they approached. I watched in horror as the sky darkened and people from the village screamed, engulfed by the hoard of insects that had turned daytime to nighttime in a matter of seconds. All eyes of those around me grew wild with fear as did my own.

"Quick! Inside!" Lord Bookbinder commanded.

He didn't have to ask twice, for we skittered indoors like the very insects we'd seen, the door slamming shut just as the black cloud burst around the mansion, bugs spattering the windows, the hum louder now as we weathered the eye of the storm.

Lady Bookbinder, who had only recently met me, placed a reassuring arm around my shoulders, while Joclyn, whose dress was not nearly as spectacular as the one she'd worn last night, and Gertrude, who had paled markedly, huddled beneath the wings of Sir Roger and Lady Penelope. Thomas and Henry stood stoically side by side, Emma huddled between them. The only one without comfort was the poor courier who stood close to the window, watching the mayhem as it passed.

At last the hum that seemed to shake the very windows and reverberate off the stone walls faded into the distance and was gone. A low murmur replaced the hum as each of us spoke in turn, our relief evident in the sighs that shadowed our murmurs. But that relief didn't last long, for when the courier marched to the door and opened it, each of us straining to see beyond those double doors, shock replaced relief and the murmurs turned to dread.

"What is it?" I asked, standing on tiptoes to get a glimpse of the land beyond the manse.

Henry brought me a stool that he'd found in the drawing room. I stood on it and nearly fell off when I realized what I was seeing. Those wee little beasts, that alone seemed harmless, had formed a phalanx so large as to cut a swath through the countryside, eating everything in their path except for those plants deemed unpalatable. As a result, stands of trees or bushes that apparently lacked taste to the tiny beetles, were left standing, while other areas had been stripped clean, mere stalks remaining of what once had been a thriving ecosystem. I shivered at the complete and utter loss of vegetation. Our world, which only moments before had been lush and filled with all manner of leaves and grass now appeared gray and lifeless. Even the birds remained silent as they shuttled back and forth in search of the world they had known before this plague of beetles had descended upon it. I wondered what this would mean to the kingdom. The lettuce was completely gone, while only thin strips of fiber were left of the kale. And the pea stems . . . well, only the nubs remained. I thought of the large spread of food that lay on the table in the other room and cringed when I realized that the manor house vegetable gardens were in utter disarray.

As if the thought had occurred to Lady Bookbinder as well, she ordered the maid to remove the grand meal she'd prepared and to bring us sandwiches instead, then discreetly whispered to the maid, "Put any remaining food in the larder," she hissed. "We begin rationing now."

9

Henry felt the squish beneath his feet and grimaced as he and Thomas began the cleanup process, along with every other hand the household could spare. In a hodge-podge line, the motley crew headed to the cistern with buckets. To Henry's unending surprise, Brigid and Emma insisted upon coming along. They hauled water with the best of them, the wooden harnesses no doubt heavy upon their shoulders. But neither woman complained. Instead, Brigid began humming, clearly used to such heavy labor. Though he couldn't say she was gifted in the art of music, the sound she made wasn't totally unpleasant.

"Do you suppose Alaric was behind the attack?" Brigid asked as they walked back and forth to the well, dipping their buckets into the water and then rinsing away the black beetles that remained, the ground thick with them.

Henry promptly stepped on her foot.

"Ow! What did you do that for?" Brigid demanded, nearly dropping her buckets, water sloshing everywhere.

"It's time you learned. We don't talk openly about such things. Only behind closed doors and only with family."

"What?" She halted, but he urged her to keep walking. "But you were talking openly in the cave," she said, skipping to keep up, water running down her arms and onto her dress.

Though he read the anger in her voice, he was determined to ignore it. Despite what the head gardener had said about her uniquely odd manner of learning, Henry felt it best that she learn as all citizens did.

"That was then; this is now," he said cryptically, nodding his head slowly in the hope that she would get his drift.

She did not. Instead, she turned on him with unparalleled ferocity, nearly dropping her buckets once more. "Why, you ungrateful . . . I'm helping you and your kingdom," she said through gritted teeth.

"Shh! Relax!" he whispered, hoping to calm her the way one would a savage beast, for that's what she was, it appeared from everything he had just witnessed. And dimwitted besides.

Just then, the sound of wings appeared in the distance. Henry bent an ear, listening.

"What's that?" Brigid cried in alarm.

"I hear it, too," Emma concurred.

Before Henry could explain, a cloud of black birds filled the sky, turning daylight into night time in a matter of seconds. The sound was so ferocious that Henry's voice couldn't be heard over the beating of wings. Then, to make matters worse, he felt a moist wet plop on his forehead. Soon, they all dove for cover as the sky opened up with offal from above. Henry ran for the nearest Red Oak, Brigid and Emma trailing behind.

"What are they?" Brigid yelled, leaning in close so Henry could hear her better.

"They're black birds. They must have been sent by the Master Birder."

"Master Birder? What is that?" Brigid asked, squinching her eyes.

"Who do you think trains the birds? She sent them to eat the black beetles."

"A woman raises this many birds?" Brigid peered up, as though counting them as they passed, only to shake her head in amazement at the vast number.

"Aye, she has acres and acres of all kinds of birds, depending on the need. I'll take you to her aviary sometime."

True to his word, the birds began not only flocking after the beetles that had just passed over the manor, but a whole host had come to make the cleanup easier by feasting on the many insects that hadn't made it past the manor in their riotous feeding frenzy. Henry danced with delight because although plenty remained to be rinsed and cleaned, the bulk of the work had been done by the birds, saving them hours of hard work and sweat.

As if his joy were a contagion, both Brigid and Emma began to dance with excitement as well. And as if that weren't enough, clouds began scudding in along with the birds, and soon a downpour served to wash away any remaining detritus so that their work was all but complete.

"They did it! They did it!" Henry cried, cavorting in the rain, no longer seeking shelter, for now they could begin the task at hand. Rebuilding the fields before summer.

Together they danced, Brigid's earlier snit gone. And yet an ominous thunder roared in the distance, as though a prequel for what was to come. Henry felt it in his chest and knew that this first volley might be just that, a mere volley. Next time they must be more prepared. He just hoped there would be no next time.

As I lay my head on my pillow later that night, no matter which way I turned, or how many times I plumped the pillow or fussed with the quilts, I could not get settled. At last, when sleep had eluded me completely, I climbed out of bed and lit a candle, then carried it downstairs, the shadows playing off the walls and paintings only heightening my sense of unease. Because although the manor seemed perfectly benevolent by day, by night it seemed . . . well, downright frightening. I tried to tiptoe quietly, so as not to wake any of the others, but as I made my way to the kitchen for a midnight nosh of some sort, I saw that nearly everyone had made it there ahead of me. Lord and Lady Bookbinder, Lady Penelope and Sir Roger, and Thomas. Even Henry was there, chewing on a leg of lamb and wiping his mouth unceremoniously with a linen napkin.

"Oh, Brigid, there you are," said Lord Bookbinder, wearing a cream-colored dressing gown and a matching nightcap.

Earlier this morning, he had taken charge with such vigor as to seem almost young. Today, he appeared much older and more staid, his mustache flowing over his upper lip in two perfect waves and his cheeks rosy from the coolness of the hour.

"What say you about all that has transpired, wee one? Has that loom of yours provided an answer to our current dilemma?"

Everyone leaned forward, expressions intense. The only one missing from our little excursion were the maids and Emma, for neither had stirred.

"Yes, tell us," Lady Penelope encouraged. "I've heard that this loom of yours reads the future. Have you seen what it has in store for us?"

How could I gently let them down, for the only way my loom could work was for us to be asleep. I explained it as best I could and watched as, one by one, their faces grew crestfallen. I sighed, but then felt a tongue lick my fingers in sympathy.

"What?" I peered down and there was a dog, an English mastiff, if I was not mistaken, running its warm, moist, sandpaper tongue across my hand. Unlike some of the other dogs I had seen around the manor, this one was red with a dark face and sagging jowls. I petted it, to which the great beast leaned into me and peered up, its sad eyes the picture of content.

"Sit," Henry ordered, handing the dog a small piece of beef. The dog did as commanded. "Good girl," he said, patting the dog, who stared up at him appreciatively, no doubt hoping for another command. Then he turned to me. "Care for a plate of roast and potatoes left over from the noon meal? We've decided not to count them as rations just this once."

I gratefully accepted his offer, taking the proffered plate along with a glass of mead that Lady Bookbinder handed me.

"That should help you sleep, dear."

"Indeed it should," I concurred, reveling in the ordinary after a day like today. After all, what would tomorrow bring? Plants run amok? Dancing squirrels? After today, I could believe anything, for normal had flown out the window along with the birds.

When I and the others had our fill, Lady Bookbinder hurried us to bed warning of a possible early morning. "After all, we need to be ready, come what may," she said in her best schoolmarm voice.

And perhaps she was right. I hoped not, but what did I know? If someone had told me a week ago that I would have fled in the night with a magic loom, to a place filled with mazes and caverns and all sorts of incredulous magic, I would have undoubtedly told said person that he was off his rocker. But today, it was I who had skipped a rail.

The next morning, we all dragged through the manor as though lead had been poured into our shoes. But gradually, as each of us began to awaken fully, the day commenced. It began with Henry yelling, "C'mon troops!" and holding up a knobby pine that he used as a walking stick.

Both Joclyn and Gertrude, Lord Roger and Lady Penelope's daughters, gladly lined up behind Henry while Thomas followed. For her part, Beatrice had resoundly refused to join the excursion as long as Emma tagged along. But I knew Emma well enough to know she would never leave Thomas' side, not with those other piranhas lurking about. And true to my prediction, she hovered so closely that I heard an "ouch" every now and again when she would accidentally bump into him or step on his foot. Poor Emma, I thought with a smile. She was clearly besotted. Whereas Henry, for his part, was on a mission.

"Tally ho!" he cried to which both girls giggled.

"We're not in England," I bristled churlishly. But no one listened, least of all Henry.

So, in the end, I trailed this odd grouping, always keeping an eye out for some insect or bird, or whatever peculiar thing this area had to offer. But to my pleasant surprise, the world around me was infused with all sorts of entertainment, from the dragonflies that hovered momentarily overhead, flitting about, then doing loop-de-loops around me as if in play, to the furry caterpillars that came in all glorious shapes and sizes. I picked one up and placed it on my hand.

"What is this one called?" I asked Henry, who was up ahead showing the two young ladies a purple butterfly that had landed on his hand.

Henry, who had been preoccupied up until now, turned. Upon seeing the caterpillar, he quickly released the butterfly to the sky above and came rushing to me crying, "Put it down. Put it down, now! Have you no sense?"

I tried to brush it off my hand, but that only sent him into a further frenzy.

"No! No!" he cried. "Carefully. You don't want it to bite!"

"Bite?" I gasped, more determined than ever to get it off my hand, but the wee little beastie seemed just as determined to cling to me. No matter how hard I shook my hand, the caterpillar only gripped it more tightly.

"Are you crazy? You don't want to endure its wrath," Henry all but wailed. "Stop shaking your hand. Talk nicely to it. They're our friends."

"Friends that bite?" I asked, not at all certain I wanted friends that nipped now and again.

"They help us, so long as you don't upset them." His eyebrows came together in consternation at my obvious lunacy.

"I don't understand your world at all!" I said, stamping my foot. To my surprise and delight, at just that moment the caterpillar's shell began to harden and to become a translucent green.

"Now look what you've done. It has formed a chrysalis."

I looked around at the others to determine if this was bad, and if so why, but the girls only shrugged, while Thomas merely leaned into my ear and whispered, "I'll tell you later." Then he winked. At least *someone* was on my side. I yawned, feeling exhausted from a poor night of sleep and from the beating my ego was taking at knowing virtually nothing of this new world I had popped into.

I placed the chrysalis gently in among a stand of woody leatherleaf that bordered a boggy waterway complete with hobblebush and ferns. There, it would be well hidden from the many predators that might find it tasty. It's then that I spotted a very green and lush pool of water, a waterfall nearby. I leaned down to grab a handful of the inviting liquid, when Henry, livid now, his eyes shining and his face beet red, came rushing toward me and grabbed me by the back of my dress, pulling me onto my rear. Now, not only was my ego bruised, but my backside as well.

"What'd you go and do that for?" I yelled, allowing the anger to wash over me.

"I already told you not to touch anything without permission back at the cave!" Henry admonished, begrudgingly handing me a leather pouch filled with water. "Here. Drink, if you must."

I jerked the leather pouch toward me, not at all polite as I might normally have been. "What have I done wrong *now*?" I demanded.

"Everything. Just everything," Henry sounded like a petulant child.

"What Henry's *trying* to say," inserted Thomas, coming to my aid, "is that the water might be non-potable."

"What does that mean?" I asked.

"It means you can't drink it," the two men said in unison.

"Or it could make you sick," Jocylyn added.

I got the undeniable feeling, from the smug expression on her face, that she wouldn't find that such a bad thing. Trying to tamp my frustration and anger down, I drank from the leather flask, the smoothness of the liquid soothing my wounded ego.

"Well, why didn't anyone remind me ahead of time that I wasn't supposed to touch anything?" I demanded once I'd had my fill of the water, not willing to let my snit go just yet.

"Be . . . *cause*," Henry said, drawing the word out to show how much he was annoyed by the question, "you have to learn for yourself."

"What sense does that make? If all of you know that the water is bad or that the caterpillar can bite, why wait until I make a mistake? Why not tell me in advance?"

Thomas and Henry shared an uncomfortable silence, then finally Thomas spoke up. "You see, these are the rules. Each of us must learn for ourselves. It teaches us to think."

"Besides, no pain, no gain," Henry said, his normal cheeriness returning.

"That's just a saying."

"Maybe in your world," he said with a laugh, then he was

off again, a knapsack at his back, his knobby pine walking stick in the lead.

The two girls followed suit, Gertrude twirling around merrily, an insincere smile widening as she watched me struggle to rise. Seeing my dilemma, Emma and Thomas helped me up, each offering me a hand. I wiped the back of my dress, which was now covered in mud. I would have cried in frustration at all the indignities I'd suffered that day, but I wouldn't let Henry or the two women see me shed a tear.

We marched for what felt like hours, away from the wide swath of destruction the beetles—from the order *Coleoptera*, if memory served—had wrought into the more lush surroundings. Finally, we came to the location Henry had intended, for he set us all around a wide clearing with rocks that ran in a semi-circle, each one flat so that it made a rather fine seat. In the middle of the clearing was a long-used firepit, by the looks of it. Thomas, who seemed used to the drill, immediately set in collecting firewood, Emma doing likewise.

Once we were all situated and Henry had a fire going, he said, "Each of you must provide an offering."

"An offering to what?" I asked, looking around for something to use as a tithe.

"Why, to the gods and goddesses, of course," Joclyn said, her very aquiline nose lifted ever so slightly, her features perfect, her eyes round. Apparently, her family had made quite the offering to the gods and goddesses because both of the sisters had not a flaw among them, save perhaps their personalities, which seemed tolerable at best.

With that, Joclyn stood and marched over to the largest rock made of granite with intricate design, the one that faced the fire. From her sleeve, she drew the most beautiful plume I had ever laid eyes on, its colors changing with the light so that it drew images from the mosaic that resembled unwittingly the very countryside and manor from which they'd come. She set it onto the rock, then curtsied slightly.

Next came Getrude, who made a production of plucking a barrette with the finest pearls and abalone from her hair and laying it beside Joclyn's feather. Afterward, she eyed me, one brow raised, as if to say, "Top that!"

"Emma?" Henry turned to her and invited her up.

My breathing stilled as Emma marched forward. What on earth had she to offer to the gods and goddesses, she, who like me, had known nothing of the offering beforehand? But to my amazement, she laid a writing nib onto the granite, and not just any writing nib. One crafted of the finest silver, a mighty oak drawn into the very handle.

Thomas scarcely waited for her to finish before hurrying over to land his token to the gods. And what a token it was. A coin with latin words written into it: honesty, integrity, fraternity.

All eyes paused to stare at me as I scrambled to come up with something. Surely Thomas had been the one to clue Emma in to the ceremony, to supply her with the needed gift. I, on the other hand, had no one to guide me. My heart stuttered in my chest as I fought to come up with something, anything, that might change my fate, which hung in the balance on this one treasure.

What? What? What? I wracked my brain to think of a way out of this predicament. I already had two strikes against me. This surely would be my undoing.

But my mind went blank, the blood rushing to my head as I walked the death march to the granite stone that would decide my destiny. If the gods and goddesses had disliked me before, they would no doubt hate me now for I had nothing to give.

I was within steps of the altar when in front of Emma and Thomas something came skidding my way. I nearly tripped on it, but halted just in time. With a frown, I bent down to look at it. It was a book, but not just any book. A book made of the finest parchment, the edge of its pages gilded in the most beautiful gold with a painting on it of a clipper ship. As I peered up, I saw that both Emma and Thomas had prepared for my dilemma and had seen fit to aid me in my hour of need. I said a silent blessing, thanking them both. And in their eyes, I witnessed their welcome. Reaching over, I picked it up and ceremoniously walked it to the altar, placing it next to the other offerings. I didn't breathe a sigh of relief until I made the short walk back to my rock and took a seat. When I glanced over, both girls were staring at me with disgust, certain that they would have bested me in this most important test. But I hadn't failed. For once, I hadn't failed. Once again I eyed Emma and Thomas, and this time when no one was looking I mouthed my thanks.

Henry was the last to deliver. To my surprise, his gift was neither astounding nor expensive. Instead, he laid a nest with the most lovely blue eggs atop the stone. Robin's eggs.

"For the cause," he said.

It was then I knew that, like his gift, Henry was a good egg.

10

Inside the barracks, Alaric stood in front of the large wall map wielding his varnished witch hazel staff like a baton. He surveyed his troops, each man or woman gifted in a single aspect of the art of war. Of course there was the Kazakh with his many species of eagles, from the booted eagle to the crested serpent eagle, from the griffon vulture to the bearded vulture, each having its place in the food chain.

Then there was the Council. Among them was the entomologist, who, oddly enough, went by the name Cricket, not surprisingly a tiny woman with odd brown eyes, no irises whatsoever, and her clothing shimmered with jewel beetles that flashed green, blue, and purple when lit by the sun, while her golden hair wafted up like so much cotton candy with little ringlets cascading down both sides of her face. She kept all manner of insects, from the miniscule parasitic wasp to the enormous elephant beetle and everything in between, including the assassin beetle which most people abhorred.

Next came Tempestous, the harridan of both weather and nature in its entirety. Like her name, which sounded remarkably similar to tempestuous, she had a fiery nature which showed in the way she dressed, from her flaming moire robe to red hair that shot out in all directions framing a narrow face and full red lips. She controlled all of nature, the meaner portions of it that is, and she took her position in the web of life seriously.

A pair of teens worked with the reptiles. The girl's name, Liz Herd, reminded Alaric of the lizards that she cared for, and Chame Leon worked specifically with chameleons and other more snake-like reptiles. And like many of the reptiles, both had smooth skin, not a blemish nor a flaw among the pair, their eyes wide set and almond shaped with golden irises and the most beautiful iridescence that flamed outward at the far corners of their eyes.

Sitting next to the pair in a long line of chairs made available was Fishmonger, whose skin was scaly like the very fish that he raised, each scale flashing colors of the rainbow. The man preferred predator fish like the shark and the piranha. Alaric couldn't pass by him without feeling a shiver of unease.

Lastly came the Queen of all Mammals. Alaric stopped, frowning as he came to her. She was decidedly ordinary, a humanoid, and average at best. For years, he had wondered what she was doing among the rather ferocious team he'd assembled. For one, she was mild-mannered and truly loved her animals. She did not abuse them as the others had their charges, with the possible exception of the reptile handlers who were known to keep clean cages and fresh water for their serpents and the like. He wished he could pick her brain as he had the others, but she seemed oblivious to his machinations. He shrugged. No time to worry about that now.

He strode back to his wall map and pointed to the errant kingdom who had refused him the loom. "Our plans begin today." A murmur arose among the members of the group, but he quickly silenced them. "We shall take the loom by force, if necessary. And you shall all play a part." Then he began outlining his plan.

For the next two days, things seemed to improve. The head gardener had his workers reseed the barren land, while the junior gardener of the manor, a young man named Poppy, redoubled his efforts at producing a vegetable garden for the manor and all those living in it. Fortunately, each and every start from the greenhouse had gone untouched and because summer hadn't yet begun in earnest, he was able to replant, being sure to feed the plants with the richest compost in the land. It was into this welcome sight that I toured the gardens, helping out where I could.

For the next couple of days I dug, planted, and tilled a portion of the garden, the others doing likewise. It seemed that everyone put their backs into restoring the vegetable gardens to their former glory. Fortunately, the ravenous beetles hadn't touched the hornbeam, sparing the maze for future generations.

"Maybe the worst has passed," I ventured when Henry neared with a shovel in hand.

"How can you say that?" he hissed, peering over his shoulder as though someone was watching them, even now.

I shaded my eyes to peer up at him, but the sun haloed him and all I could see was his silhouette. "What do you mean?" I asked.

"You're tempting Fate."

"Fate?" I asked, unable to stifle a giggle. Surely he didn't believe in such hocus pocus. But I soon discovered by the utter fear that lined his face, that indeed, he did.

"Fate rules our kingdom," he whispered. "With an iron hand," he added for good measure. "You never want to tempt Fate by speaking of possibilities."

"What *can* I speak of?" I groused, feeling boxed in by all the words I could and couldn't say.

Henry indulged me with a sigh. "Each of us learns what one can or cannot say from infancy on."

I pondered that. "But what if someone hadn't been taught that? What then?"

"Then that person must *learn*," he said, his brows raised to include me. "Quickly."

"So what words can't I say?" I asked as I dug a hole and plopped in a beetroot, which I resoundingly detested, preferring celery, green onions, potatoes, almost anything except the detestable beet.

"I can't tell you. You must learn for yourself."

I wiped my brow with the back of my hand only to have Henry laugh because I had left a wide smudge on my forehead. "How does one learn if no one will tell you what's right and what's wrong?"

"Oh, you'll know," he said cryptically, and not two minutes later, when I asked a question about the cave, a raven swooped down and pecked me on the head. "Ouch!" I said, wondering why the raven had targeted me. I felt my head and saw that I was bleeding. I would need to put something on it so that it wouldn't become infected. "What was that for?" I demanded.

But Henry only raised his honey-colored eyebrows as if to say, "See, I told you so."

"I'm not allowed to speak of the cave?"

Suddenly mute, Henry merely shrugged.

So caves were out, apparently, and I had the cut to show for it. How many other cuts and bruises would I have before I learned the language, and what if I could *never* learn the language? The thought chilled me. I had never been good at languages. Instead, I had picked up small snippets of languages, but rarely could I string an entire sentence together except in my own tongue. Worried, I shivered.

As I set back to work, I fumed. What sort of people used pain to teach life lessons when rewards worked so much better?

Over the course of the coming week, I quickly learned what sort of people, for I was covered head to toe in all sorts of strange wounds, from boils to prickly rash--from a smashed toe to a swollen eye. I had made mistakes too numerous to count, and the truly horrendous part was, I didn't know what had caused most of them, so I didn't know how to make them stop.

I sat in front of the mirror above my dressing table back at the manor, tending my latest wound, a swollen lip. Fortunately, I knew how to treat it by cutting off a piece of aloe and squeezing the gooey juices of the cactus onto my finger, then rubbing it onto my newest injury. Although my lip stung, it didn't take long to settle down.

"How will I ever survive this?" I whispered to my reflection. I wasn't a stupid person, but I also had a keen sense of justice, and this felt extremely unjust. I recalled the few times I had seen an animal mistreated and the sense of outrage I'd felt at the time. Now I was to be the mistreated animal and like those most wretched of beasts, I would have no say in the matter. Whenever I brought it up to Henry, he merely shrugged and called it tradition, as though that explained everything in a nutshell.

"But surely, traditions can be changed," I argued one day as we set out into the woods to learn to shoot with a bow and arrow.

"No they can't," Henry said, very matter-of-factly, focusing instead on the target, in this case a bale of hay with a series of circles painted onto a linen sheet. "A tradition is a tradition." He walked twelve paces then turned. Lifting his bow and setting an arrow into a notch, he pulled back and the arrow flew through the air in a shallow arc, hissing as it moved ever closer to its target. Then "thwack," the arrow landed . . . directly into the middle of the circle, as though some unseen thread had guided its landing.

"Bravo!" Thomas said, Emma clapping her enthusiasm.

For some odd reason, Emma had not a scratch on her, whereas I was covered in every manner of pestilence. I had a sneaking suspicion that Thomas, to his credit, had guided her in private about the dos and don'ts of the kingdom. Why my dear friend would not help me too, I had no idea. But as soon as I could get Emma alone, I aimed to find out.

I was up next. Henry tried to explain how to hold the bow

and arrow, even going so far as to guide my hand and peer down the sights. But, for all of his training, I was as inept at the bow and arrow as I was at learning the language--the customs.

It wasn't long before I had my chance to get Emma alone and to ask her what had been bothering me so. After an hour, everyone was tired, and the men had gathered in a corner laughing about some shared history. I saw my opportunity, and I was determined not to waste it.

"So, Emma," I said, offering her a piece of venison jerky that the cook had sent packing with me. "You're faring well here?"

"Very well," she said, chewing the jerky with gusto and washing it down with some cool water from her leather flask.

"How fortunate," I said cooly, guiding her to a spot beneath a dogwood for added shade. "Aren't you going to ask how *I'm* doing?"

Emma gulped, her expression one of distaste, as though she had just sucked on a sour lemon and was not at all pleased with the bitterness left on her tongue. But to her credit, she had the decency to blush and peer down at the grass beneath her feet, plucking one particularly succulent blade and sucking on it before answering.

"Quite frankly," she said, "I was afraid to ask. And I felt a bit . . . guilty that I am doing so much better than you."

I sighed with relief that finally the unspoken was out in the open. "And why *is* it that you are doing so much better than me?" I splayed my hands in search of an answer.

She sighed too, but with frustration. "Truthfully, Brigid, it's because I follow the rules."

Defeated, I rolled my hands into fists, for I had tried. Truly I had. "But that's just it, Emma, how do you know the rules and I don't? Is Thomas teaching you?"

Emma looked around as though the woods had eyes and the person behind those eyes might have reason to smite her right then and there. Through gritted teeth, in a whisper she hissed, "No one, but no one is allowed to help a person learn. You must learn on your own."

Once again, she surveyed her surroundings as though the woods had not only eyes, but ears as well.

"How is it then, that you are picking this up so easily whereas I--" I held my hands out so that she could see the many scrapes and bruises that graced my body. "--I look like this!"

But she would not budge. At least now, I understood why. But how did she and Thomas communicate if they couldn't speak such things out loud? I had *so* many questions and not an answer to be found anywhere or from anyone.

"Can't you at least *try* to help me?" I pleaded, but the very fact that I had asked had put her at risk as evidenced by the tears forming in her eyes.

So, I couldn't even speak to my best friend about such things. It left me feeling isolated and vulnerable. Anyone with a chip on his or her shoulder could use me as target practice, I realized, and I also knew I was a lousy shot, from my earlier try at the bow and arrow. No, all I had was my wit and what good had that done me? I could have lain on the cool soft grass and slept my life away had it not been for the announcement from Henry that we were headed to our next destination, which was once again, like everything else in this kingdom, secret.

For the next hour, we trudged through brook and dale,

through valley and high peak, until I nearly collapsed with fatigue. "Are we there yet, Henry?" I asked.

Henry, who had seen me floundering, had taken my sleeve and hauled me along with him, grabbing my hand on those especially difficult climbs--waiting behind as I struggled for breath.

"We're almost to the Kregs," Henry said, hauling me up the final leg of a mountain peak.

As we finally came within sight of a clearing at the top, he allowed me a few moments bent over, hands on knees, to catch my breath. When I finally lifted my head, I saw what he had intended, because a gap stood between us and a flat rock that extended over a deep canyon, a ribbon of water winding through it and disappearing off in the distance.

"Oh, no," I said, shaking my head for emphasis. "You don't expect me to jump!"

"Just to the other rock," he explained patiently. "See?"

He urged me to look down, but the sight below was dizzying, and I felt a sense of vertigo. Seeing that I had paled, Henry placed an arm around my shoulder and encouraged me to take deep breaths, but no matter how much he tried to calm me, I could not be calmed, for I had a definite fear of heights.

"It's easy. A simple leap. See?" he said, jumping back and forth, back and forth.

Logically, I understood that the jump was not hard, but somewhere in my reptilian brain, my legs had decided not to cooperate and until now the expression "knees knocking" with fear had only been an expression. But I could see now that the expression had some merit, for my kneecaps *were* literally knocking.

"Try it. In fact, I'll stand on the rock and Thomas will stand on this side to catch you should you fall."

His blithe smile won me over in the end, for how could his blind faith in me be wrong? For several seconds, I closed my eyes, finally opening them. I tried not to look down. Yet as I attempted the leap of faith I made the error of peering down for one small moment. That's all it took to breach my confidence, and suddenly I was flailing as I flew through the air, my body sinking like a stone. Just as my foot found purchase, it slipped over the edge, rocks falling to the chasm below. But before I could fall with it, Henry reached out to me and clasped my hand tight, his eyes on mine willing me to help him help me onto the flat stone that straddled the canyon. The moments seemed to crawl, each moment drawn out--the sun reflecting off of the pitch from the firs, the smell of the moist earth and pine, the strong pull of Henry's hand in mine, his strength giving me renewed energy. With a will I hadn't known I possessed, I let out a guttural cry and clung to what ground I could manage while Henry yanked me inch by inch onto dry land. When I finally reached the other side, I turned over on my back, panting, as everyone around let out a joyous cry of relief. Although I knew I would have to manage the leap back, for now, I savored the moment, refusing to give in to fear.

Soon, the others made the leap onto the Kreg, only Emma nearly falling as had I. Fortunately for her, she had both men reaching out to her and was pulled to safety in no time. We cheered the moment, Henry having brought mead, giving us only a single drink so that we would have clear heads for the return jump.

Once we were all relaxed and refreshed, Henry urged us to sit in a ceremonial circle where we all clasped hands, Henry at the center.

"Close your eyes," he said, "as I invite the Wind Spirit to protect us in the upcoming battles."

A shiver of apprehension raced through me, but I closed my eyes along with the others, but opened them as she neared. And true to Henry's word, the Wind Spirit began to howl, to dance around us like a lithesome spirit, her pale wings brushing up against me in a cool caress, her sheer shimmery blue dress fairly floating on the breeze. For what seemed like forever, but could have been five minutes, no more, she danced. When she was done, Henry thanked the goddess who howled one final goodbye, then disappeared down the canyon. Slowly, one by one, the others opened their eyes.

"The Wind Spirit has left each of you a gift. She has assured us that we will know instinctively when we see it. This will be your totem. It will guide you, so guard it carefully. You will find it in nature before the end of this journey, so be on the lookout for your gift."

He thanked the goddess one last time, then peered at the sun which was in its zenith. We would have to leave now if we were to make it back to the manor before nightfall. But that also meant that I would have to jump the wide chasm, and though I knew in my head that I could jump it quite easily, whenever I looked down, my stomach would flip and my head would spin. I said a silent prayer, forcing my mind to concentrate on something tangible, something that gave me joy. Instantly, the loom popped into my head as though it were calling me from a great distance and with one deep breath, I stood as far back as possible and took a running leap. This time no one was there to catch me. As if outside my body, I saw myself flying through the air in a slow arc, the sun burnishing my skin, the wind at my back, encouraging me onward. And then my feet touched earth and I rolled, only coming to a stop when a mountain laurel cushioned me, preventing me from rolling further.

One by one, the others made the leap off the Kreg, all of them finding purchase in the end. And one by one, we rose to our feet and continued on. Thomas was the first to find his totem, yelling, "I found it! I found it!"

He held up a root shaped like a spear, the handle of the spear twisted into three segments like a French braid, the end sharp and shaped like an arrow. Next, Emma came to a halt when she reached up to find an abandoned bird's nest with the most delicate splotched brown and cream colored eggs. Nuthatches, according to Thomas.

Henry discovered his totem shortly after Emma had found hers. His was unusual to say the least. We all stood around him to peer in awe at what he had found, for it was not a thing, but an animal. A horse to be precise, but how this horse had come to be in the woods was anyone's guess. We called around us, hoping to find its owner, but no one answered and so we fashioned a bridal out of both my and Emma's leather belts, which we tied together to use as a halter.

Now all that was left was for me to find my totem. We walked at length, my legs once again growing weary. I had all but given up any hope of finding my totem when from a distance I saw the finest feather I had ever seen. It was from a rare Blue Falcon, according to Henry, its feather the softest white with stippled blue.

"What does this mean?" I asked Henry, my eyes filled with wonder and hope that my totem might portend something wonderful.

Henry never dropped his stride as we marched down the narrow mountain path between the firs with an under canopy of smooth white beardtongue, common milkweed, and the tiny star-shaped pale bluets. In similar fashion, he went down the list in the same order we found the totems.

"Your totem is perhaps the easiest to fathom," Henry said, pointing to Thomas' spear. "You will be a great warrior."

Thomas let out a whoop and shook his spear in the air.

"But don't get cocky," Henry warned. "A spear is two-edged, so you must hold it in high regard and use it only when necessary."

Thomas appeared chagrined, but only for a moment. Next, Henry turned to Emma, who held out her nest and eggs, eager to hear his take on this new find.

"The nest and eggs suggest a new beginning, spiritual growth. It also represents motherhood."

Emma beamed up at Thomas, her green eyes flashing her joy at this announcement. Thomas cupped her in his shoulder and held her tight as if to reaffirm their shared joy that she would provide a brood of little chicks of her own.

I soured slightly at the thought, for what could a blue falcon possibly represent in light of the other gifts? As if to chasten me for the thought, the wind howled a warning.

"Okay, okay," I whispered churlishly.

"What does the horse represent?" Thomas asked, pointing to the cream-colored steed with a dark brown mane. A buckskin, by his reckoning.

Henry appeared sheepish while at the same time lifted his head with pride. "The horse represents many things, but most of all courage and freedom. It displays power and heroism while requiring independence. It is the noblest of animals."

"Courage and freedom?" I echoed. "Independence?" And yet this kingdom allowed no freedom or independence whatsoever, save for possibly heroism, as I could not fault Henry on his courage.

He must have realized what I was getting at because he halted mid-stride, the rest of us nearly running into him in the process. "I know you think we have impeded on your freedoms, Brigid, your independence--"

"Well, haven't you?" I asserted, refusing to back down though I knew there would be consequences, for there were always consequences. For every minor offense, no matter how small.

"You have to understand," he hissed, his eyes scanning the forest for any manner of spy, "it is for the greater good."

"Greater good for whom?" I challenged.

"For everyone." He dipped his head in frustration. "People's *lives* are at stake."

"And you think the only way to save people is to take away their freedoms?"

"You're putting words in my mouth, Brigid," he said, and the horse stamped and nodded its head as if in agreement. "An open mouth draws flies."

I recognized the saying from a former military leader from a battle I had long forgotten. "I understand that," I said, standing my ground. "But why use punishment when honey is so much sweeter? Why not a simple reminder, one that possibly even *I* can understand. Surely, there must be a way of conveying a necessary warning without constant punishment. No one should have to go around looking like a pin cushion for their entire life!" I said, fighting back tears.

"Fortunately, most people are not like you," he said, then blinked rapidly when he heard both Emma and Thomas gasp at what he'd said.

For my part, I grew silent, inwardly fuming because he had all but called me stupid in front of my peers. And perhaps I was to the ways of deviousness. Perhaps I looked at the world through a different lens, a kinder one. Undoubtedly, I was more naive, but at least I wasn't cruel. Yet in this world I wasn't certain if those who were not cruel could survive. Or would even want to, when push came to shove, and yet I had a kernel of strength in me that even now was taking seed. Once again, I wondered at the meaning of my totem and what it would portend.

Gritting my teeth, I said, "What does my totem mean? We know that Thomas is to be a great warrior, and Emma nurturing. And of course you will be a hero that prides himself at independence," I hissed, spearing his conscience with my words. But I refused to protect him from the irony of it all. "So what, pray tell, does a blue falcon represent?"

The heat of Henry's ire had been dampened by my outburst and he soon deflated like a leather parfleche, emptied of its water.

"A falcon represents vision, freedom, and victory," he said so softly that I leaned in to hear him. Yet it was clear by his defeated expression that something had been left unsaid.

"And?" I pressed.

He looked first at Thomas, then at Emma, as though pleading for reinforcements, but like me, they longed to hear what he had to say.

"It also suggests salvation from bondage whether it be physical, moral, or spiritual."

I clapped my hands with glee, startling the horse who reared up on its hind legs and whinnied. "Sorry," I said, "but that reaffirms everything I have been saying. One can't have freedom and independence when kept in bondage. Don't you see the irony, Henry? I know we're all in this together. We have to be to save your kingdom. I understand that. But save it for what, Henry? Is this the world we want to leave our sons and daughters, where we are divided up, thrown to the winds? Where we use and abuse the very people we call our heroes? Is this the kingdom you seek to save?"

It was clear I had nicked at his conscience for he bowed his head, angry tears welling in his eyes. "You think I want this?" he countered. "Your body is not the only one to bear witness to the beatings that bring us to the point that we no longer have a voice."

At that, he rolled up his sleeve and revealed a series of scars that ran the length of his arms in angry welts that ran circular fashion around his arm. "There," he said. "That is what happens when one receives the lash for insubordination. I have the scars," he growled, "just like you. All of us have them."

"Tradition," I said, but the word held no judgment now, only pity and sorrow for the wounded man who had borne such pain.

"Tradition," he concurred, and I saw him swipe at a tear, hoping I hadn't seen.

For a moment, we all stood in silence, each with our own thoughts, the wind sighing through the boughs of the trees, a mournful sound that left us all feeling melancholy.

After much thought, I said in a low voice so that only they could hear, "Then why don't we change it? Why don't we make it better for future generations?"

For several seconds, Thomas and Henry looked at each other, then in unison said, "How?"

But before I could answer, I heard the loom clacking in my head. Clackity-clack, clackity-clack, each additional clack sounding more urgent. Something was wrong with the loom.

I turned to Thomas. "Can you and Emma find your way back?"

Both Emma and Thomas frowned, but Thomas nodded his head.

"I can't explain, but I need to get back to the manor now." I turned to Henry, beyond panic. "Can you ride this horse?"

"Of course," he said, shaking his head in confusion.

"Then give me a push," I cried, lifting my leg for him to help me onto the back of the buckskin.

He paused for only a second before my meaning became clear to him. Quickly, he folded his hands together, fingers entwined and I placed my foot in his care as he lifted me onto the back of the mare, holding tight to the horse's mane with my fingers.

"Now you," I said, offering him my hand.

Once again he paused for only a moment before taking it as I helped to lift him onto the bareback horse. I prayed that he was as good a horseman as he had alluded to before. Then I said a hurried goodbye, as Henry lashed the horse and we raced away. I could only hope that I would return in time to save my precious loom.

11

The horse, who Henry had nicknamed Windtamer—both because the Wind Spirit had given him the horse, and because of the animal's ability to cut through wind like the surest of knives—was in a lather by the time we reached the manor. Yet even at this distance, we could hear the drums and the ground beneath us rumbled.

"What on earth?"

Windtamer rose up on her hind legs only to fall fast to earth, pawing at the soil that seemed to move beneath our very feet.

"What is it, Henry?" I demanded, holding tight to the buckskin's mane, Henry leaning over me in an attempt to keep us seated on the horse.

It didn't take long to find out. "Ants," Henry yelled. "Millions of the cursed pests!"

And true to his word, a phalanx of army ants marched in a

wide procession, drummer ants at the forefront, the ones in the middle bearing miniature banners proclaiming their affiliation with Alaric's kingdom. According to Henry, Cricket had seen to it that they were more human-like in their manners through years of breeding and crossbreeding.

"Call the birds," I yelled, but Henry only shook his head.

"The birds can't help on this one, I'm afraid."

"Why?" I asked, fearing for poor Windtamer whose nostrils were flaring and whose eyes were wild, the whites showing in unguarded measure.

"Formic acid. The smell is horrible. They give off a noxious odor and their taste is even worse. We're doomed."

Henry held me tight as if clinging to his last bastion of hope. And maybe that's what spurred me on, for I thought of what I had learned as a child--about the honeydew ants who lived in the bowels of the ant colony and clung upside down while filled by the other ants with honeydew they had collected from the aphids. I released a high squeal of delight.

"Honeypot ants!" I yelled to be heard over the marching.

"What?" Henry said, bending toward me with a frown.

"The ants. They have what's called a honeypot ant. Its tummy is loaded with sweet honeydew nectar from the aphids. The honeydew is allowed to ferment until it turns to wine. The ants use it in celebration. But I read once that other ant colonies would sometimes use that time to attack a colony, when the others have been drinking."

"So . . . ?"

"So, Henry, you have a wine god, isn't that so?"

"Bacchus?"

The sound of the marching grew steadily louder. They could be no more than a mile or two from the manor by now, and I could see that they were starting to swallow up the village below as they entered upon the southern outskirts of the town.

"We've got to hurry. Send them wine. Lots of it . . . before they take over the village."

Henry took action. He let loose a shrill whistle and within moments, a carrier pigeon came at the ready and immediately sent word to the wine god. The wait seemed eternal as the ants moved ever closer, my skin nearly crawling with fear that we would be beset upon at any moment. And indeed, I heard cry upon cry as one by one, the houses were seized. I held tight to Henry's back, silently bidding him farewell, as I knew we would be done for, should they reach us.

I had just about given up on any hope of salvation, when I spotted something in the distance, something that made my breathing grow shallow. Before the village could be completely swallowed whole, out of the sky came a bombardment of wrens, each carrying miniature sinew pouches filled with wine that they poured onto the unsuspecting ants below. I let out a gasp, while Henry shouted his joy to anyone who would listen. Within moments, the ants realized the manna sent from the heavens, as it were, and their orderly phalanx soon turned to disarray as they scrambled to partake of the wine offered them. Both Henry and I let loose a cry of joy, the horse bobbing her head up and down as though she too understood the significance of the occasion.

Soon after, the drunken ants broke rank and were stumbling in every direction, many of them turning toward home, some lying supine on their backs, legs up, while others scrambled to escape the torrent of wine headed their way.

Henry and I whooped and hollered, and heard both Henry's parents and staff do so as well, as they realized what was happening and came rushing outside. "We did it!" Henry yelled.

I cleared my voice.

"I mean Brigid did it. She thought of the wine."

Soon, we were all celebrating, dancing around the clearing, relieved to have the ants and their formic acid gone. We would have to clean up the sticky mess of wine, but for now, we were all safe.

Lady Bookbinder came over to me in the clearing. We had so much to talk about . . . at least I hoped that we *could* talk about any of it. But for now, everyone was safe and we had forestalled yet another catastrophe.

"How is my loom?" I asked, when everything was settled and the horse placed in a stall and given fresh oats.

"Come. I will show you," Lady Bookbinder said mysteriously, taking my hand.

I peered over to Henry wondering if he knew what she had up her sleeve, but he merely shrugged.

She took me inside and marched me upstairs to where my loom stood off in one corner of my room. And the strangest thing happened, for the tapestry showed my poor loom engulfed in ants ready to be carted off to Alaric the Third's lair. For the first time since I'd purchased the loom, it began to change with someone present. Right there, before our very eyes, the ants began to wobble drunkenly and to fall away from the loom and to slowly recede until none remained. In its place was the kingdom and the loom. On the top of the tapestry, one word and one word only was written in golden thread. And that word was *efcharisto*, Greek for "Thanks."

I was relieved to learn that Thomas and Emma had made it back to the manor safely the night before. Already, the place was beginning to feel like home as I prepared myself for the day ahead inside my new room, a real room so unlike my former place in the attic. As I rinsed myself with a washrag from the blue willow ewer and basin, I relished the cool clean water. I had to say, I was starting to like Lord and Lady Bookbinder very much. And even Gertrude, Joclyn, and Beatrice were beginning to have a begrudging respect for me. More than all that, I loved the freedom to be outdoors, no longer trapped at every waking hour in a stuffy attic or a below ground scullery kitchen, rarely if ever seeing daylight.

Once I had washed and dried, I threw on a linen shift. I would need more clothes in the coming days. Perhaps I could speak with Lady Bookbinder about my dilemma. She would know what to do. As I sat lacing my shoes for the day ahead, I felt at peace for the first time in many days. At last I was contributing to the safety of the kingdom, and so had made new friends. But at the same time, I knew my trials weren't over. If only we were a team working toward the same end, instead of endlessly punishing each other over the slightest offense. I shook my head, wanting desperately to fit in, but not at the expense of my body, which I inspected now, in the mirror over my nearly empty chifforobe. I shuddered at the sight, for I looked a right mess. Bruises here, cuts there, rashes taking up residence on the few remaining empty spaces. No . . . justice was at the heart of everything I did, and this did not feel like justice. I dabbed on creams and lotions, trying to hide the many places that stung, burned, or itched.

I lifted my speckled blue falcon feather, closed my eyes and made a wish. *Please, please help me change this world for the better.* And as if in answer, when I opened my eyes the wind gushed open the closed transom and danced about the room with a loud roar before departing, only to be replaced by a blue falcon. He came in on such silent wings that, for a moment, I thought I had dreamt him. I blinked at the sight of the beautiful and sleek blue raptor, while he sat on my finial as though he were the finial rather than the pineapple that had been carved for that purpose.

At first I was taken aback by the bird's arrival, for I knew nothing about predatory birds, much less falcons. For several moments, I hesitated. But surely the Wind Spirit wouldn't give me a dangerous totem, so I squared my shoulders and stood taller. I knew he needed a name, but what? I looked once again at the finial and it came to me. Phinney! "Phinney it is," I said. Yet I quickly realized that if I were to keep him, I would need a leather glove, a hood when transporting the falcon, a perch, and anklets. Perhaps Henry could help me with those. Now I had two quests for the day--to speak to Lady Bookbinder about the clothing, and to speak to Henry about falconry supplies.

"Come," I said. To my surprise, the blue falcon followed, flying through the doorway and down the stairs, landing on the newel post, which had been fashioned to look like Big Ben, a clock tower in London. Phinney blinked placidly as he waited for me to descend the stairs.

Henry, who just then rounded the corner, stopped when he saw the blue falcon. For a moment, they stood enrapt, blinking at one another.

"What do you think? I now have a blue falcon!" I cried with delight. "But I need some falconry supplies," I added as I descended the stairs.

"Of course you do," Henry said, as though it was a normal, everyday request. "Come, let's go to the bird sanctuary to get you supplied, then we'll come back for breakfast. Mother is waiting."

From that, I gathered we must hurry, so the bird, Henry, and I dashed out of the side door of the manor and set off at a crisp pace to a hidden oasis within a copse of eastern white pine just south of the main house. The route into it was hidden by a hedge of Canadian yew and some lower lying Canadian anemone. The path led us into a massive clearing fit with equally massive aviaries from which the birds were kept, and towering all around us in a wide circle were the pines, that gave off an odor at once both sweet and pungent.

At the far end of the aviary was an outbuilding and it's there Henry led us, calling all the while, "Conestra! Conestra! Where are you?"

I had expected a human, of some sort, envisioning the rugged birders I had seen in picture books. But this was no ordinary birder, for she fairly glowed, and her plumage, for that's the only way I could describe it, was iridescent from the many feathers she had collected. How she had managed to sew them onto a gown, finding only those most vivid of colors and patchworked them in so that they created a design of birds in flight, I could not say. I only knew that she fairly took one's breath away, for it was clear by Henry's reaction that he found her stunning. And indeed, her nearly blonde hair flowed in waves mixed in with flowers, and if she had feet or sandals, I could not see them.

"Ah! There you are," Henry said with relief. Then he pointed to Phinney, who had taken up residence above us in an especially large pine tree and was blinking down at us with his golden round eyes. "We need equipment for--" Here he turned to me. "What do you call him?"

"Phinney."

"Oh, I see, Phineus."

"No, just Phinney," I said.

"Right then." He turned back to Conestra. "Phinney here needs--"

But before he could finish, Conestra had turned on her heels and ushered us to the outbuilding where inside, the building was dark and lacked much light, which seemed odd for a woman who dressed so brightly. Once my eyes had adjusted, I saw that she kept bird supplies of all kinds from cages to large pottery urns of seed kept in rows with the bird type painted onto the front in a dull blue.

She led us to a dark corner on the back wall where all manner of supplies were hung in an order that made sense only to her. She ran her finger through the air, stopping when she came to a large leather glove.

"A little big," she said, "but it should do. Now, for a perch." She bent down to peer at a shelf near the bottom of a variety of supplies and pulled out a padded perch, handing it to Henry as it appeared rather heavy. She finished by providing me with anklets for the bird and swivel, snaps, and perch rings. Conestra gave me and Henry a detailed explanation of how they should be used. She started to turn away when a thought came to her, and blinking rapidly she said, "I almost forgot. Here's a lanyard and a whistle so you can call Phinney. Its pitch is so high that no one but the bird will hear it. That could be important if you're being stalked."

"*Stalked?*" Henry and I said in unison.

"Why stalked?" I added.

"These days you can never be too careful. This will help you . . . in case."

On that ominous note, for the next half hour, she trained us to call Phinney to the glove. I hoped the training would be enough for me to work with Phinney when needed.

It wasn't until we'd offered our thanks and were working our way out of the clearing that I turned to Henry. "What do you think Conestra meant when she said we might be stalked?" I asked.

Henry shrugged. "Dunno."

But I could see that Henry was just as disconcerted as I was at her words. I whistled to Phinney, who followed at a polite distance, and felt relieved when we finally arrived once again into the bright sunshine.

Alaric paced the interior of his chamber, his eyes alighting on the empty space where the loom should be, beside his Arthurian five poster bed. Next to the window, he kept a spyglass so that he could peer out on his kingdom and note anything untoward. But today, he wasn't interested in that. No, instead he seethed at the losses first of the black beetles, formerly the scourge of Egypt back when the pyramids were being built, then of the ants. *Wine!* Who could have thought of such a thing? Then with a shuddering anger, he recalled that Brigid hadn't been raised a commoner, according to his intelligence. She'd been tutored by nannies, taught about all manner of plants and animals. But a girl. Surely he couldn't have been bested by one of the weaker sex. He ground his teeth together, thinking. Strategizing.

What? What could he do that would affect her personally? What indeed? Then, with a flash of inspiration that had him rushing toward the door and down the stairwell, it came to him. Girls loved to be girls, hence their interest in their appearance. Well, he would fix that, soon enough. He ground his teeth together and laughed a deep guttural laugh as he raced out into the brilliant sunshine.

Henry had tired of lugging the blue falcon on his arm as

Brigid and his mother marched around town, entering one shop after another in search of clothing.

How can women enjoy such drivel? he wondered as he offered the blue falcon a spot on a bench next to him while welcoming the shade from the mitten-shaped leaves of the sassafras tree. The only time he entered the town to shop for clothes was on pain of death, or rather when given the alternative of digging out latrines, which was as close to death as one could come here on earth. All one had to do was offer him a shovel, and he was more than ready to clothes shop. Even so, he'd never enjoyed it.

While he waited, he watched the villagers stroll by--women in long gowns, men in breechcloths and stockings with tailcoats, their station in the community only visible by the wear of the clothing or the fineness of the material or lack thereof. Here, along the northeastern coast, the area was known for its contrast of large brownstones and cobbled streets versus those that were mere shacks, the unimproved roads turning to a quagmire of mud in the wintertime; that and horse manure created a stench so awful as to make the city nearly inhabitable in summertime. Fortunately, they were on one of the finer streets and the manure was picked up by the ignominiously named "dirt carter".

Henry had lapsed into such a fugue from the long wait that he'd fallen asleep and his head was lolling when the sound of giggling woke him. He turned in time to see his mother and Brigid laughing and carrying on about the dressmaker and her rather awkward son who had tripped over one of the mannequins and had nearly landed on top of Brigid. For some odd reason that brought in him an instant reaction of chivalry and jealousy all rolled into one to think that someone other than himself might lay hands on her. However he had no time to explore these rather overblown feelings for Brigid that had taken him unawares because the two women were already off at a trot headed toward a shop, oddly named Goose and Gander.

Once more he searched for a seat from which to wait out the pair, Phinney perched behind them on the wooden slats. Here, on the far edge of the central plaza, the more pedestrian shops began, whereas the well-heeled businesses lay nearer the center of the village. In the center, you had your clerks, your lawyers, even your clocksmiths and bakers, whereas the further one went the more industrious the business, from butchers to blacksmiths, bricklayer to fisherman, in the more coastal locales.

At noon time, the city fairly hummed with activity. Henry was lured toward a bakery shop drawing him in with fragrant aromas of breads and pastries of every kind. He told Phinney to cool his heels outside, or talons as it were, as Henry entered the small shop and waited his turn, wherein he put his nose up to the glass as he gazed over the vast array of delicacies. Before him in a tantalizing display were Boston Creme pies and a hummingbird cake, monkey bread and biscuits. He finally chose a rye bread and an apple set in pastry and coated in egg wash. Then thinking better of that, he ordered three of the apple pastries, one for each of them. That settled, he strode back to his seat next to the shop both Brigid and his mother had last entered, Phinney fluttering in his wake.

But even before he could take a seat he heard a hum on the horizon as though a vast amount of wings were beating as one, some louder, some having a softer whoosh. Phinney emitted small screeches. Moments later, Henry heard people murmuring, then yelling. Soon there were screams, and before he knew what was happening, Brigid and his mother were exiting the store just an eclipse of moths descended upon them all, eating away at their clothing and those of the remaining few who hadn't been fast enough to enter a building and lock the door behind them. For his part, Phinney was devouring the winged creatures as quickly as possible, but even he was overcome by their beating wings.

"Quick!" Henry shouted, running toward Brigid who let out a high-pitched squeal, arms flailing. He snatched her up in his arms and yelled to his mother, "Run!"

He had hoped to reach the side street where their carriage was kept, but too late he realized they could not outrun the ravenous webbing clothes moths which were even now gnawing at their clothing and chewing it to shreds. And as if that weren't bad enough, they were followed by the common grackle, a type of blackbird with an iridescent blue head and a nearly bronze body, which tended to congregate in numbers. The grackles swooped in and around the heads of his mother, Brigid, and Henry himself, plucking at their hair and pulling it out in large strands so that Henry feared they would be bald before they could escape the meddlesome creatures. Even Phinney was no match for the horde.

In the nick of time, Henry saw a side door to the bakery and opened it, shoving the two women, who were still screeching and covering their heads with their hands, in ahead of him. When he had both the pair and the blue falcon inside and the door shut, a few remaining moths fluttering around them, the owner came running and shouting. Henry explained what had happened. The man, who introduced himself as Constantine, set his bakers to work trapping the moths and disposing of them. Before long, other stranded victims of the onslaught came pouring in through the front door where they all waited out the beating wings.

A murmur of cries from the townsfolk went up, all ending with the name "Alaric." And Henry had to concur. This could be the work of only one man and his minions. But why? Why did he want the kingdom all for himself and what did he plan to do with it once he had it?

As if she'd read his thoughts, Brigid said, "He wants to enslave us. To have everything, while we have nothing."

Apparently, that was the central line of reasoning among manyl, for most huddled together, each of them nodding their agreement. But then one couple stood with narrowed eyes, their teeth pointed and their lips snarling. "This is your fault!" the wife hissed, turning on Brigid, her features thin and angular. "If you had just given Alaric the loom, none of this would be happening to us."

I quailed. How did they know about the loom? And so soon? Someone had leaked the fact that I possessed a magic loom, but who? I trusted everyone at the manor.

"And you protect her," the husband added, turning on Henry and his mother.

By their shocked expressions, this was the first that Henry and his mother had heard from any of the townsfolk about either the loom, or their involvement in taking it and me in. How had word traveled so fast? But then, having spent time in Ma'am's manor, I knew that gossip ran rampant in a world where gossip was the coin of the realm.

"Alaric cares about us," the husband continued. "He has promised to take us back to the way things used to be before you started allowing in outsiders like her!" He pointed a gnarly finger at Brigid, coming within inches of her face. "Always trying to protect nature. Well, what about us? We used to be able to hunt anything we wanted, to cut down the forests and to use the water for our needs, but you have stolen that from us."

Henry stretched out his arms, trying to get them to see reason while Phinney squawked his displeasure at Henry's quick movements. "We saved those forests. Men like you were cutting them down at such an alarming rate that none would remain if we left it to you. And as for the waters, you were pouring your waste into them. People drink from those waters. They're being sickened. Surely, you can see that it is in all our best interests to protect the entire community, not just one group."

"Alaric will let us do anything we want," another more sanguine fellow said, surely taught this by his parents. "He doesn't make us pay taxes."

A cry went up among the others as well as a nod of heads.

Brigid strode forward, facing them each in turn. "But how will you build roads? And we need people to watch over us. Surely, the night watch can't stand guard forever without *some* form of payment. This is why so many are caught drunken or asleep and unable to protect us. Nor can schools operate without income. And the government can't run itself without money."

For a moment, her words seemed to have affected those assembled, but then the shrew-faced woman bit back saying, "That's what all you elitists say. Want the money for yourself, you do, is more like it."

Until now, Henry had stood silently by, fuming, but hearing this, he stepped forward, shielding Brigid from what was quickly becoming a mob. "Elitists? *Elitists?*" he said more loudly. "Then why is it that Alaric lives in a golden palace, eh? Why is it that he pays workers like you a pittance, huh? Have you ever thought of that?" Like a general, he marched down the line of them, taking to task each in turn. "Why is it that he pays no taxes and yet uses *our* roads for *his* own purposes. Does he care if your children are educated?" he said, stabbing the air for emphasis. "He is making slaves of us all."

"Here, here," Brigid agreed, yet all the while the silence was deafening.

"Is it elitist to want our children educated, a roof over our heads, food in our stomachs? Alaric would control the very fields that we use to feed our families. Just look what he has done to poor Brigid." Henry pointed dramatically to her missing hair, her clothes that were now full of holes and nearly useless, hanging on by mere threads. "Is this how you would have us all look in the end, like paupers?"

A smattering of murmurs rose like flies, Phinney chattering along with the best of them. Some nodded their heads in agreement, some argued beneath their breaths, certain that the very rich and spoiled Alaric would indeed have their best interests at heart.

Until now, I had been mostly listening to the others in silence, still smarting from the loss of my hair at the nibs of the birds. I peered down at my clothes which had holes everywhere so that I looked like a rag lady. Ever since the Poor Law had been enacted overseas that forced one into workhouses and families to be split up, men going one way, women another, and children yet another, people had poured onto American shores seeking refuge. And yet if America continued down this path, it might soon look like the more unfortunate nations of the world which had sat their eyes upon this nation as a beacon of hope.

Just then, I peered over at the metal oven and saw my blurred reflection in the silver sheen. I froze, hardly daring to believe it was me, what with my hair torn asunder and my clothes so disheveled. Phinney peered back at me from his perch on Henry's shoulder.

"Why do the birds tug at our hair anyway?" I demanded, outraged when I saw the mess that had once been my beautiful auburn hair.

"In this case, it was simply Alaric being Alaric," one young woman said with a curtsy. "But normally, one loses hair because of–"

"Stress," they all said in unison.

"Stress?" I queried, eyeing them carefully. "What sort of stress?"

"Well, it can be anything," one of the women said, a particularly short and stout woman at that. "Have you cried recently? Been upset about anything?"

I put a finger to my chin, thinking. "Well, yes. I've lost my family, my home, and now Alaric is trying to take my loom. Plus, I am trying to learn the customs of your people and suffering greatly. So, you could say I'm stressed."

More murmurs arose and they all nodded knowingly.

"What?" I peered from one to the other.

"You're never to cry, least of all at the loss of a family member," one man said, tsking. As if to ward off the very idea, he pulled a pouch of tobacco from the pocket of his pants and a Meerschaum pipe and matches from a coat pocket, and began lighting up the pipe. He sucked on it, causing the bowl to turn a fiery red, the smell of the cherry tobacco surprisingly cheery on such a fateful day as this.

"But why?" I shook my head at the very idea. "Why can't one cry at the loss of family? We cry because we care."

To that, almost as one, a hue rang up and those assembled stepped back just enough so that if anyone were watching, that person would know they weren't with me, Brigid. Only Phinney and Henry remained at my side.

When no one answered, I repeated myself.

"Because," one rather intrepid older man said, "it's simply not done. You are to laugh, act as if it's of no matter that your family is gone." For emphasis, he began to laugh deep within his belly and urged me to do likewise.

This time it was I who took a step back. What kind of people laughed at the deaths of loved ones? I turned to Henry for answers. "I don't understand."

But Henry only shrugged, and as one, the whole lot of them cried, "Tradition."

"Well, tradition be damned," I said, to which I heard a unanimous intake of breath at the very idea that I would speak such blasphemy out loud.

And as if that had broken the dam that kept them all inside, they began filing outdoors in a rush, willing, apparently, to risk birds and moths rather than to face me and my foolish ideas one more second.

For several moments, I stood in the empty room, the only ones left the breadmakers themselves. And, of course, Lady Bookbinder, Henry, and Phinney.

Lady Bookbinder grabbed me by the elbow and said, "We'd best get you home before you cause any further damage."

"Damage?" I peered over Lady Bookbinder's shoulder to Henry, who stood with an awkward expression upon his face, one that conveyed both his apologies and an "I told you so," all in one measure.

And just like that, I once again had been censured in this strange land of contrasts, one that supported tradition, while failing in kindness and common sense. And yet, even as Henry and Lady Bookbinder escorted me hurriedly away through the now empty streets, I couldn't help but sense that there were people who longed to be kind, who wanted to show real human emotion. Who wished for greater freedom and autonomy even as they cared deeply for the community they'd been born into. And yet how could an outsider like me ever hope to improve the very foundation of a world that had been set in stone for centuries?

As I moved toward the stables and into the carriage, Henry and Phinney at my side, Lady Bookbinder seated across from us, I felt the weight of the world settle on my shoulders and slumped in accordance. Worse yet, I felt more alone than I had ever felt in my life, even during those years holed up in the hot stuffy attic, like an old rag doll, lost and forgotten. Tears started to well as the carriage bucked and rolled down first cobblestone, then dirt roads, but I forced them back. Whether I liked it or not, I now belonged to a world where I neither belonged nor understood the many intricacies of communication. I just knew that nine times out of ten, I seemed to have stepped my foot on every tradition known to this part of the world and that I would probably do so in the future. For now, I could only promise to do my best. But would it ever be enough? Would *I* ever be enough? I sagged backward onto the seat, no longer caring that I looked like something dragged out of the sewer. But even as I held fast to the seat that seemed to want to launch me out the window at the slightest bump, I wondered if I could thrive in a world without emotion, a world so rigid as to be frozen in amber. And like an insect, I felt trapped. Trapped and lifeless. The only thing holding me to it was Henry and Phinney, as well as Lady Bookbinder, who, despite my unorthodox ways, seemed to have taken me under their wings, and for that, I owed them everything.

For the coming week, I nursed my wounds, my poor hair looking like it had been hung from a clothesline. Even Phinney had found me too depressing and had gone to be with Henry. As for my clothes . . . well, I'd simply thrown them away, for they were useless to me now. Fortunately, the new clothes that had been bound in brown wrapping paper and tied with twine had fared much better. Despite their strong beaks, the grackles and moths hadn't discovered the hidden treasure within and had left the clothing intact. Looking back on it, as I sat in front of the dressing table, brushing what remained of my hair, which wasn't much, I puzzled over all the things that had happened in the short time since I'd purchased the loom.

As for the loom, it had quit clacking after the grackle incident as though it, too, was depressed at the many awful things that had transpired over such a short period of time. I turned to give it my full attention. Once again, it was developing a fine coat of dust. I pushed my chair back and stood, then walked over to it and knelt down, fingering the fine weave lovingly. Hoping to encourage it to take up the weft, I pushed the pedals with my hands, but the loom gave no response, instead I felt resistance, as though it had simply decided to stop working. Understanding the deep sadness that it must feel, I ran my hands up the wood, offering it comfort.

"It's okay," I whispered. "We will save your kingdom."

But still it remained silent, whether ignoring me or simply too depressed to go on, I couldn't say. We sat like that for a while when suddenly I heard a knock on the door.

"Brigid? Are you in there?"

Emma. My one connection to the past. For some reason it made me think of my father, mother, and all my siblings. It had been so long since I'd seen them that I wondered if they were still alive. Anything could have happened in the past five years. I forced back tears, knowing they would only cause me further grief to shed them.

"Coming!" I called as I heard her turn to leave. I hoisted myself up off the floor and ran to the door, throwing it back in case she hadn't heard me and had already left. Instead, I nearly ran into her.

Emma took one look at me, at my hair and the peck marks still dotting my head and face, and threw her arms around me in consolation. "Poor thing! It will get better soon. You'll see."

But her eyes told a different story and I realized that she was saying it for my benefit only, that she didn't believe her words any more than I. Still, I was grateful that she'd said them.

"You've been holed up in this room so long that Lady

Bookbinder worries that you may be ill."

Today, Emma's red hair was offset by two small braids at her temples, tiny white baby's breath adorning them, and she wore a long green gown with a cream-colored lace inset that ran the length of her bodice all the way to the floor. When I compared the two of us, I was the ugly stepsister with the unruly hair.

"I suppose I should make an appearance," I said, on a sigh. I glanced back longingly at my poor lifeless loom one last time before exiting my room. Then I accompanied Emma down the stairwell.

"I think you should know," she said, pausing on the stairwell and causing me to collide into her. "Ma'am is here. From the manor house. She's come to look in on you and the loom. Her husband couldn't come. Matters to attend to back at home."

Funny how quickly I had forgotten about Ma'am, about her promise to visit the country house soon. She had seemed a world away, a lifetime away, from where I was now. Did she know about all the odd "goings-on" in the house, in the village, in the kingdom? She had seemed so . . . so *staid*. Nothing could have clued me in that she led such a life as this. For some reason the thought of meeting Ma'am now, in such different circumstances, made my heart flutter.

I didn't have long to wait because I had no sooner stepped foot on the landing than I heard Lady Bookbinder call, "Oh, there she is."

She stepped aside to allow Ma'am to view me. Shock and awe played across Ma'am's lips at the sight of me. First and foremost was my hair, but then her eyes ran the length of me down to my clothing, much finer than my scullery maid's clothing, which I'd had the good fortune to toss. But what had her brows knitted in curiosity, I imagined, was the change in my demeanor. For here, in Lord and Lady Bookbinder's house, I had regained my status as a human being and so I held myself erect, no longer staring at my feet when replying to a question. Here, I was an equal. That seemed to have thrown Ma'am for she stood, mouth agape, inspecting me. Finally, she found her voice.

"Ah, I see you have made yourself at home, Brigid. May I ask how you're doing?"

Ma'am, who normally wore her hair up with tiny ringlets falling from the sides, appeared rather worn from her travels, fine wrinkles forming at the corner of her eyes. And her clothing was even more wrinkled from having been confined to such a cramped space as the carriage. Still, she kept her regal bearing, her back straight, her green eyes never wavering from mine.

"I'm doing well, Ma'am," I said, but even as I spoke, I could see her eyes going to my hair, to my face and hands, which like my upper body was pocked with bird pecks, some more angry and swollen than others.

"Ah!" she said, tilting her head slightly. "I can see that. Well, this does seem to be a rather trying year, does it not?"

How to begin? In the end, all I could do was nod. Never knowing the right or wrong thing to say, I determined it best to say nothing.

"Well, let's retire to the drawing room so we can all speak, then I will let you get to the noonday meal. You are eating, are you not?" She looked at me with genuine concern, referring no doubt to the recent weight loss.

I had been so busy and so harried, and perhaps more than

a tiny bit depressed at having lost so much of my freedom, only to have gained other freedoms, like the freedom to be outdoors, for all the good it had done me. I patted the hair that remained on my head and bit my lip to stave off any emotion that might betray me and only make things worse.

When I didn't answer about the weight loss, she simply nodded and said, "Follow me."

We entered the drawing room, a large room with mahogany paneling. Here, she commanded a seat at the one lone chair, ushering me and Emma to a spot on the daveno, while Lady Bookbinder stood to the left of Ma'am's chair, as was her due, waiting, as were we, for Ma'am to begin. And begin, she did.

"So, I suppose you know now that Castle Kreg is under threat."

She had only to look at my head and hair to know that I was well aware, though this was the first time I had heard the kingdom called by its rightful name. The name must have come from the many crags that dotted the region, or perhaps the location where each person received their totem. Or maybe simply that the manor had been built from the stony kregs.

To her statement, I nodded, hands held neatly in my lap, the room around me bathed in a soft golden glow of lamplight, its gentle flame flickering and creating images on the silver and black wallpaper that adorned the southern-facing wall. A Persian carpet lay between us, an exquisite marble-topped mahogany table laid out with a teapot and cups, along with delicate pastries that Lady Bookbinder had managed to scrounge up from the kitchen. Lady Bookbinder did the honors, pouring us some of the finest Ceylon tea I would have the pleasure to taste. I thanked her, then sipped slowly, savoring the sweet taste that had once been customary, but now was simply heavenly, for I hadn't enjoyed it in a very long time. Thick damask drapes flanked the beveled windows looking out at a garden filled with hedgerows of pink roses set in squares, each square filled with a menagerie of flowers from pink malvas to blue delphiniums, white daisies to lavender hydrangeas and everything in between. Despite Ma'am's pronouncement that the kingdom was under threat, I felt a peace at that moment, knowing that this might be the calm before yet another storm. Still, I could hope.

"We can no longer sit idly by," Ma'am said, "waiting for the next salvo. We must act."

Inwardly, I moaned. Although this was not what I had hoped to hear, it was clear she was right. The kingdom had endured much over the past week. As much as I had prayed late into the night beneath my eider quilt over the past several nights, and regarded my loom with vigilance, I knew that I was acting the rube, hiding my head in the sand when I should have been making plans, coming up with ideas to help the kingdom, meager as that might be.

"I doubt that any of you have heard," Ma'am continued, "but we have spies in the Citadel of the Jackals, Alaric's kingdom. We have recently learned that he is planning yet another assault. We must be prepared."

I was the first to gasp because I hadn't known that Ma'am had such connections. Had she had them all along but I had missed them? Me in my attic or scuttled below stairs while living at Ma'am's manor? My thoughts rapidly turned to Alaric, to the suggestion that he was planning more assaults, but what could he do that he hadn't already done?

"Some very brave souls are even now behind enemy lines, gathering information that should help us, but we cannot be lax," Ma'am warned, her lips drawn into a bow, her eyes stern. "We must take the helm before we lose it entirely."

Of course she was right. And as if by magic, I could hear the loom begin to clack, slow at first, then gathering speed. Inside me, it was as if a steam engine had fired up and even now the wheels were turning, chug-a-chug, chug-a-chug, the high-pitched whistle blowing as the train left its station, full speed ahead. And then, the oddest thing happened. It was as if I had become the conductor and knew--truly *knew* where we were going.

"Ma'am," I said, rising to my feet and pacing. "You're right. We've sat back for too long."

Ma'am turned to Lady Bookbinder with a questioning look to which the lady of the manor simply shrugged, just as surprised as Ma'am herself that a young upstart such as myself should deem to offer an opinion.

"Don't you see, we are sitting ducks the way it stands," I said, turning on my heel as I wore a path across the red Persian carpet that had seen more feet than mine. "We must act, and we must act now. I have an idea."

"Oh?" Ma'am said, the one arched brow suggesting she would reserve judgment, but didn't hold out much hope for one such as me.

"Please listen carefully, before you come to a decision." Inwardly, I cringed at my poor choice of words and I could see by the way Emma had retreated into an almost fetal position on the daveno that she had as well. Still, I pressed on. "We seem to be weakening ourselves," I said, pointing to the many bruises I had sustained over the course of the past couple of weeks. "Attacking each other instead of concentrating on the external threat."

Ma'am straightened her spine ever so noticeably and wore an air of haughtiness at the very notion that anyone, and especially a young girl, might hazard a change in tactics and age-old traditions.

"It makes us stronger," she insisted, setting her teacup firmly on the plate, spilling some of the precious tea in the process.

"I promise you, it does not. It only makes us resentful."

"Poppycock!" she cried, waving her hand in the air as if to ward off any further foolishness.

"I am living proof of it," I continued, despite the baleful expressions flashed my way from both Emma and Lady Bookbinder, as though silently pleading for me to remain quiet as was befitting a woman.

At that exact moment, Henry entered the study with Phinney on his arm. He must have been listening to our heated discussion down the hall because he said, "Women can never be decision makers. They are too high maintenance."

Ironically, it was this that finally united the women because all sets of eyes turned to him in shock, his mother the first to rebut. "Silence, Henry. How dare you say that we are too high maintenance, as though you men are not high maintenance, always running off half-cocked, expecting women to drop everything at a moment's notice to be at their beck and call whenever it suits them. Never thinking about how their absences affect us."

I wondered if she'd longed to say more, but she merely trembled with anger, and I could see that it had struck a chord with Ma'am as well, for she sat in silent fury, plucking at her dress as though it were covered in lint.

Finally, she spoke. "Huh! High maintenance. Well, we shall see who is high maintenance, Henry." Then she turned to me and in a voice filled with righteous anger said, "So tell us your plan then, young lady. And you," she added, pointing an accusatory finger at him, "you shall help Brigid execute her plan. Yes?"

Henry stood looking from one to the other, clearly stunned, Phinney making soft cooing noises on his arm. But Henry knew he was outnumbered in this, and knew too that his father would back up the women when they came to him as one. For a single brief moment, he blinked rapidly, then he nodded and swallowed hard. For the next half hour, I laid out my plan that I *hoped* would bring about change—for all of us.

14

Two days later, I stood on the lawn that fronted the manor, a group of women assembled around me and wagons filled with supplies for the days ahead. Ahead of our meeting, I had sent word throughout the village and countryside that I was forming an army of women to counter the scourge that had invaded Henry's land, and I had asked for volunteers. Fearing Phinney might be a liability while on the road, he had been resigned to the Master Birder's quarters. Besides, if we needed him, we could always send for him later.

In the meantime, as I stared out at the vast number of women arriving, I noticed Beatrice's gaze drift toward Thomas, who had decided to come along in case Henry needed him as backup. The raven-haired beauty had taken to flirting with Thomas again, driving poor Emma out of her mind with worry. Next to Beatrice stood Joclyn and Gertrude, outfitted in men's pants and boots. I shook my head in consternation. Clearly, they hadn't received the message that we were to appear as feminine as possible. Behind them, hundreds of women from the village had volunteered to join us in our quest to stop Alaric from further incursions. I took a calming breath. It would take much bravery on all our parts in the days ahead.

Out of my element now, I climbed up onto the stump, left there by the Jackals, so that I could see the vast group of women gathered before me. The sight left me breathless, for scattered there before me was a virtual mass of people from every walk of life. Women who had toiled, suffered, worked for better lives. Women who had supported men and families. Their communities.

I said a silent prayer and felt a shift, the smallest of breezes that lifted my skirt, the scent of jasmine filling the air. It was now or never. With a calm I hadn't known I possessed, I called upon my internal reserves. "I want us to divide into three groups," I shouted so that those around me could hear. I marched down an imaginary line and urged one group to the left, the other to the right. Once again I made an imaginary line and divided them yet again. When that was finished, I pointed to Beatrice. "You will take the third group."

Emma immediately bristled until she realized that I had sent Beatrice with a group that would not include Thomas.

"Jocelyn," I said, and noticed her puff up slightly, "you and Gertrude will manage the second group."

Emma once again bristled until she realized that I planned to have her on my team. I then provided the two teams with a messenger in case they might need either Thomas or Henry to come to their aid. Although it would seem more logical to send the men with the others, I knew that bringing them placed them in great danger and therefore decided to keep them together for safekeeping.

"Before you go, I want to add that we are to work as a team. As such, there will be no punishments given."

The meadow was awash with murmurs of surprise and dismay that traditions would be set aside in this way, but Ma'am had given me the reins of this mission, and I planned to operate in a different way.

"All of us," I said in as commanding a voice as I could muster, "have families and lives that are at stake. If you choose not to cooperate, we're all doomed. But there will be no backbiting, no punishment and revenge. We either work together, or we die together. You decide."

Again a murmur arose like a cloud of bees buzzing ever more loudly until Henry finally whistled for the noise to stop. I didn't know whether I was being overly naive to trust these people who I barely knew, or had yet to meet. I just knew that brutality breeds discontent, and if we were to survive as a people, we needed to work together, not to tear each other down . . . to treat each other with respect rather than as the enemy.

"Some of us may not come back alive," I added, an immediate pall settling over the throng of women before me. "But not if I have my say. There can be no egos in this endeavor. We are going to march into enemy territory and we are going to rally in the main square."

Beatrice furrowed her brow, her raven hair glistening in the sun so that it gave off a blue-black sheen, ringlets cascading onto her shoulders. "But why?" she asked, giving voice to the question that others no doubt had wondered. "What do we hope to accomplish?"

It was a question that I had asked myself numerous times throughout the night, but the loom had assured me I was on the right path. The loom that Lord and Lady Bookbinder had promised to keep locked away for safekeeping in their room while we were gone. That same loom had maintained that Alaric's men would be unlikely to besiege a group of women for fear of the negative impact it would have should word get out that he had attacked women. Singularly, any one of us might suffer a gruesome fate at the hands of Alaric's thugs, but together, we stood a much greater chance of surviving while creating a stir. But I had yet to answer Beatrice, I realized with a sigh as the crowd of women nervously awaited my response.

"We hope to get the men to stand down."

"But for how long?" one very tough looking townsperson asked, her dress mere rags, stains and dirt covering her apron.

"True, one attempt will do nothing. We must put the pressure on. Repeatedly. We must show that we are not afraid, that we women will stand up for our beliefs."

One young woman, who looked to be in her twenties, stood forward and yelled, "They will say our men are cowards, that they send their women to do their dirty work."

"True, they will say that, but they will be wrong. And we will know they're wrong, and that's all that matters."

"I still don't know what we expect to accomplish by doing this," groused a mother with a young teen at her side, even as she wrapped her daughter in her arms as if to protect her from what lay ahead.

"We are going to show the women of the town what it is like to be free--to live without fear."

The crowd buzzed as sweat dripped down my face and beneath my clothing. Then one courageous young girl came forward, perhaps fifteen if a day. "But how *can* we, when we live . . ." Here, she paled, her cheeks flushed red as a *Belle de Boskoop* apple. Uneasy laughter followed.

I recognized her concern and finished for her. "When we are not free? When we do not live without fear?"

She nodded, while the crowd gave a collective gasp that she would be so frank in the face of the danger it posed. But all would remain the same if we were not allowed to speak openly about what we wanted. As if recognizing the danger, a woman stepped forward, no doubt her mother, and drew her into the crowd and away, out of the sight of probing eyes.

"Please, do not punish her. She speaks the truth," I said, but to no avail as her mother whisked her away. The last I saw of them were of their skirts as they darted down the path toward town, moving at a crisp pace.

A clamor arose such that I thought I had lost every one of them, but I shouted to be heard above them. At last, the clamor died down so once again I could speak.

"Are you happy with the constant punishments, the pain?" I asked.

Every one of them tittered softly and peered down, as though afraid to look one another in the eye.

"Nor am I," I said, to let them know they were not alone. "We need to change things, but we can only do so if we are willing to work together."

Here, Henry finally spoke up through gritted teeth. "But Brigid, we have *always* done it this way. You go against hundreds of years of tradition."

"So?" I said, just as vehemently. "Just because something has always been done one way doesn't mean it *should* always be done the same. If we followed that line of reasoning, we would never get anywhere. For heaven's sake," I said, imploring him with my hands, "if we had adhered to that notion, we would have never had the steam engine . . . batteries. We would have said it's always been done this way, so why complicate things by doing something other than walking or riding a horse? Don't you see, Henry? We have a chance to make things better for *everyone*."

A murmur of assent arose from the crowd and I could feel the tide turning, a sense of unity among the group gathered on the lawn and in the meadow beyond. As if nature itself was in agreement, butterflies floated in on a breeze, their many colors enchanting, for there were the Eastern-tail Blue butterflies, the Falcate Orange-tip, the Baltimore Checkerspot, and the Cloudless Sulfur butterflies, and many others, too numerous to name. They floated about as if in a dance where only they knew the steps. Soon, the women were giggling, and even Thomas and Henry had to laugh at the joy it brought the women.

The butterflies began to float in the direction we were to head. Soon, all three groups of women followed, many of them gamboling in frayed and tattered gowns, their cries of joy filled with renewed strength and drive. Inwardly, I thanked the queen of the butterflies for her help in reaching our destination united. Our quest would take us to Jefferson County, near Watertown, close to Lake Ontario which bordered Canada. It was alleged that

Alaric himself was holed up somewhere amongst the boulders. We would follow the Black River Trail that skirted both the Lowville Formation and the Chaumont, where it was said that water cascaded over a stair step bed of limestone in waves.

The air of frivolity continued, scented by the smell of Blue Cloud calamint springing up around us as if by magic, which the butterflies favored. They stopped frequently to feed on the blue-gray shrub, their wings so numerous that we could hear their rhythmic beat. I couldn't help but join in as Emma grasped my hand on one side, Thomas grasping hers on the other, Henry clasping hands with mine. Together, we ran to catch up with the group and gain ground, lest I lead from the rear.

As we moved ever westward, the homes changed from that of the bleak gray and white federal-style houses or big white two-story colonials to old stone farmhouses or even older saltbox homes with their brick chimneys that helped to warm the hearths of common folk in wintertime when lit. I smiled, inwardly. To think that I had gone from privilege to the lowest of the low, outside of actual homelessness, and had regained my status, all in the course of a handful of years. I still hadn't recovered from the whiplash left me.

Like a herd of bison, we funneled down the valley, and up the low-slung hillside, over rock and dale, stopping only when we were too tired to go on or too hungry. At last, we halted for the night, our feet sore and our bodies aching. I found a slab of granite to rest my weary bones where I rubbed my sore feet and stretched my tired back.

"Here, let me do that," Henry said, pressing his thumbs into the muscles tightened by overuse.

I closed my eyes and moaned. "Thank you, Henry," I murmured. "I didn't think I could walk another step."

For a second, he paused and I opened my eyes only to find him staring. "What?" I demanded.

Henry inspected me as though I were one of his specimens. "Has anyone told you that you have very unusual eyes?"

I flushed beneath his gaze. No one had to tell me. Someone was always gazing at them when they thought I wasn't looking. I'd heard all sorts of theories regarding the unusual color. "Touched by the gods," one had said. "Mark of the devil," said another. "A seer," yet another had insisted, but it was none of these. I had neither the gift of sight, any ounce of true devilishness in me, and if the gods had touched me, they had failed to inform me of said event. No. It was just the way I had been born is all. I sighed, wishing for once that someone would see beyond my eyes to the heart beneath it.

"I know. People stare at my eyes all the time."

"Hmm," Henry muttered.

"What?" I asked, certain that he had more on his mind than just my eyes.

"Brigid," Henry said, almost shyly. "Did you mean what you said about not wanting people hurt anymore?"

I glanced around at the tents going up, brought along by the wagons of supplies from the caravan. In that moment, I realized that we had formed a small city of our own filled with disparate groups of women, all with unique lives, most searching for a better one for both themselves and their families.

"Yes," I said at last, and then hung my head in remorse. For I *had* experienced true anger at the injustices done me. I *had* longed for revenge in the hardest part of my heart. But just as soon as the anger had subsided, I once again believed that love outweighed evil, that human kindness eclipsed meanness. "But Henry," I added, "I have experienced anger--unlike anything I have ever known. Despite the many slights or the sheer drudgery of working as a scullery maid, or even the attacks from Alaric, never have I experienced what I have experienced here, in your land. The traditions, I mean—the punishments for not knowing how to behave to the satisfaction of those running the Kingdom. They seem cruel at best. There must be a better way to teach people the necessary skills to contribute to the kingdom." I took his hands in mine and felt them tremble at my touch, or perhaps it was my own hands trembling. "But change starts with one person, Henry. And if we are to change things, we have to set the example. And yet I'm human, Henry. I am fallible. And forgiveness comes hard." My throat tightened at the admission.

Henry peered down at his feet, which were just as swollen as mine from the marathon hike. "Once," he said, laying his head on his knees, "I was beat senseless."

In his voice I could hear the tremor of a confession, one that still haunted him now. I bent down and drew his chin up so that I could look him in the eye, but it was as if he had gone to some dark place well beyond what I could reach through touch alone.

"Mother said it was for my good, that I was to take it. That it would make me a better person in the end."

"And did it?" I asked, scarcely daring to breathe.

He blinked rapidly, staving off any tears that might betray his emotion. "No," he whispered. "It only made me angry, made me hate my mother for not protecting me."

And almost the moment he had made the admission, I knew he regretted it, for his eyes grew large and he stuttered in an attempt to take it back, to explain away his feelings of grief, of loss . . . for the innocence he'd once felt in the belief that the ones he loved most would or could protect him from evil.

"It's okay," I murmured, my eyes filling with the tears he could not shed despite knowing that I might pay for them later, when we returned from this trek.

"Henry," I said, reaching for his hand and capturing it in mine, holding tight to prevent him from bolting before I was finished. "It isn't wrong to believe in fairness. To believe that the ones you love should be able to protect you. To believe that we should live in a world filled with caring and empathy. We *need* such a world. But don't you see, Henry? We are kept off balance, always looking askance at each other so that we won't look at what's being done to us."

Henry's green eyes darted in all directions and his breathing became rapid and shallow, utter fear written in the whites of his eyes and the rise and fall of his chest, for we were not allowed to speak of such things.

"How are we any better than Alaric if we're too frightened, too unwilling to take a stand?"

"You don't understand!" he hissed, tossing my hands aside and standing. He ran his hands through his hair. "We cannot take a stand. No one can take a stand."

"Why, Henry? Why?" I asked, truly at a loss.

"Don't you see?" he hissed once again, bending down so that he could speak more candidly in tighter quarters. "People are watching, always watching and listening. Listening to see if a wrong word is spoken. Watching and waiting for a single mistake. Listening in on even the most private of conversations between husband and wife, much less mother and son. They don't want us to communicate with each other, so they keep us apart. By race, by class, by rumor, whatever it takes. They mean to keep power."

"Who are *they*?" I asked, still not understanding.

"That's just it, no one knows," he said, throwing his hands in the air.

As he spoke, the daylight dimmed, nighttime approaching and with it a hint at something sinister. Firelight began to flicker around the encampment as meals were cooked over open fire pits that dotted the landscape. We would have to make up for lost time, but right now I needed to understand the odd and frightening nuances of the world I had entered.

"Why do you all comply?"

He simply shook his head, as if I were a dolt without a clue to the mores of such a place. And perhaps I *was* a dolt. But I would never understand if I didn't ask, at the very least.

"Because, if we don't, we will lose our friends, our family. Our lives."

I felt as though the wind had escaped me and even now was hovering just out of reach, for I could scarcely breathe because of what he had told me. "Surely, you jest," I said, once I had refilled my lungs with air.

Henry plopped down on a log. "It's true. We are all kept hostage to the powers that be."

"How do you know that they are not controlled by Alaric?" I asked, the smell of roast beef cooking over a spit causing my stomach to growl from hunger.

"That's just it," he said, picking at some small stones and tossing them into the space between us. "I don't know. None of us do."

"Start from the beginning," I commanded, the murmur of voices around us comforting, despite what I knew.

"See, we were once ruled by two factions, but we shared the power. For many years, it worked out well. But then Alaric, and his father before him, decided they wanted more power. They no longer wanted to share power. They began subjugating large numbers of people. It was subtle, at first. His father claimed it was necessary because of a protracted war to the south. He began secretly filling every segment of society with people who would do his bidding for the right incentive."

"Money," I said, stating the obvious.

"And power," he added. "Soon, every position within the government was infiltrated with his people. They rose to high ranks."

"And started rumors that would cause people to distrust each other, I imagine." It was my turn to stare at my feet, the realization suddenly dawning on me that this was a far bigger problem than I'd first understood.

"That, and then they encourage retribution so that everyone turns on each other."

"Which keeps the rest of us busy while he's got his hand in the pot." I finished for him.

"Exactly," he said, appearing weary now, his eyes hooded and his shoulders slumped.

"So where do we go from here?" I asked, but knew he had no answer. If he'd had one, he would have done something about it by now. With every segment of society filled with Alaric's people, there could be no peace, no joy in the simple acts of raising a family, earning a living, learning a skill. Instead, turmoil reigned.

As if he'd read my thoughts, Henry simply shrugged and said, "I don't know. But Brigid?" He peered directly into my eyes this time. "I want to apologize for what I said earlier . . . about women being high maintenance. I was wrong. And thanks for being here. I don't know what I would have done without you these past weeks. It's as if you've shined a light into all our fears and brought clarity to what has been ailing my people for the past many years."

I bit my lips, wishing I could provide some words of wisdom. But we both knew there were none. We were all drowning in a sea of discontent. We just needed a way forward. But how? How could we come together to bring light to a world battered by darkness. That was the question that nagged at me now. The question that would nag at me for weeks, possibly years, to come. The thought weighed heavily on me as we sought to join the others in preparation for the night ahead. Tomorrow, we would move ever westward, and closer to Alaric's lair.

15

For all of his life, Alaric had sensed his opponents, felt them as surely as he had felt the wind just now, brushing against his skin as he stood out on the ramparts of his palace. The palace, or more accurately a fortress, was set into the stony face of the rock cliff and hidden by a stand of pines. A perfect vantage point from which to view the valley below, whereas someone looking in would see only trees, despite the fact that Alaric stood just feet in front of the person's face. It had always given him a special thrill to be so close to his opponent with the other person none the wiser.

He tugged at the spyglass cinched to his belt and lifted it, studying the landscape below. Funny how much he'd aged over the past few years, he realized as he scanned the horizon for movement. He had always been handsome, which had been a great advantage among the ladies. And yet lately, he had begun to feel old—had wondered what it would be like to cede power. But then he would remember his father, a man so massive in both stature and vision that the thought evaporated almost the instant it had arisen. No man worth his salt would cede power willingly. If a man was lucky, he would live to a ripe old age and die at his post. If he was unlucky, power would be wrested from him but only through violence. That thought sobered him. Though he couldn't fathom cowardice in a man, the dreams he'd had lately of his demise left him unsettled. In a sour mood. Though he knew he had tested his adjunct's patience more than once in the past few days, he couldn't seem to quell the nagging feeling that someone was out there, getting closer by the minute.

"Siegfried."

"Sir?" the young man said, clamoring to his feet from his station by the door.

"What have you heard from the scouts?" Alaric growled as he lowered his spyglass and hitched it to the belt below his tunic.

"Scouts?"

Heat rushed up Alaric's face and neck. Was the man deaf or simply an idiot? "Scouts! Scouts!" he repeated. "What have they found? Surely you have heard from them by now."

The lithe man shivered, his gown whipping in the wind so that he looked as if it might pick him up and carry him away. Though he, along with Josiah, was possibly the most loyal of Alaric's servants, the man's acne scarred face grew crimson and the whites of his eyes flecked with fissures of red, as if he never slept well or at all. And yet Alaric often grew frustrated with the utter denseness of the man. Fortunately for the inane young man, at that moment a crow flew in, a small cage-like apparatus on a leather string around its neck. Alaric lifted it off of the bird, shooing him away. The crow simply let out an angry caw, then lifted its wings and flew northward, but not before it had deposited a load of white bird droppings on the rampart closest to Alaric.

"The insolent bird," Alaric cried. But he soon forgot about the bird and its insolence when he read the note.

An army of women is on its way west. Stop.

Reasons unknown. Stop.

They are unarmed. Stop.

Alaric whistled and shook his head. An army of unarmed women. For what purpose? And what could a lone group of women hope to accomplish? Were they merely a foil for a much larger army of men? Again, Alaric couldn't fathom it. But why then? Why was an army of mere women at this very moment marching northwestward toward his territory?

"Siegfried?" Alaric said.

"Sir?"

"Call the council to order. We will gather in the meeting hall in precisely one-half hour. And make sure that the Jackal Guards are present as well. The elite group of guards must be notified of what may transpire. Am I clear?"

"Clear as mud," Siegfried said with a laugh. Then seeing that Alaric hadn't laughed as well, he added, "Right. I will send word immediately."

Alaric narrowed his eyes at the man. He didn't like being ridiculed, and he couldn't help but think that the man had ridiculed him just then. Humor was not tolerated in his army. Neither had it been tolerated in his household growing up. Whenever he heard the words joy or happiness, the understanding of such things eluded him. The only joy he had ever experienced was in humiliating others as he had been humiliated as a child by his peers who thought him odd. Spoiled. But he soon learned that eliciting fear in the other children won him respect, so he sought to use it against them to avoid being humiliated as he did now.

"And Siegfried?"

"Yes, sir?"

"You ever ridicule me again, and it will be the last time it happens." He lowered his eyes to be sure the man understood his meaning.

Siegfried gulped, too afraid to move even a muscle.

Alaric couldn't help but smile, his meaning eliciting the desired response. "Off with you then," he said. Then he turned back to the landscape below, pulling his telescope once again to his face. Only this time he knew what he was searching for. An army of women. But why? That was the question he had yet to answer. Now he needed to make plans. To capture each and every one of them. With that, he lowered his spyglass once more and smiled. Maybe he understood happiness more than he had let on. He chuckled, then set out for the tower to prepare for the meeting ahead.

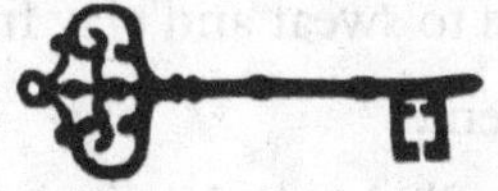

I shivered, having heard the strings of my precious loom as though it were stationed before me, clacking back and forth. But more than that, it was as if the loom and I were now connected, as if I understood its meaning, even this far away, in the encampment that bordered the Adirondacks, beside steep mountains with its dwarf ginseng, dwarf rattlesnake plantain, and common sorrel. The smell of sugar maple filled the air, reminding me of pancakes and the fact that I hadn't eaten. Once again I shivered, even as my stomach growled.

With more than a tingling of fear, I searched the horizon, the hillside dotted with American Beech and yellow birch, besides the aromatic maple. And in that moment, it was as if I were already inside Alaric's fortress, witnessing the exchange between Alaric and his generals. *He knew.* The loom was forewarning me our nemesis knew we were on our way to his lair so he would have time to plan, to counter. But what frightened me most, as I prepared for the long march ahead, was the realization of what he planned to do. To capture every last one of us. I struggled to breathe. Then what? We had to come up with a better plan than the one I had outlined, but first, the Adirondacks lay before us. We had hired a guide to take us through Avalanche Pass, and as if the guide had read my thoughts, I saw him head toward my tent. He was a burly man with a full beard and knit cap, a trapper by trade. He wore a tired set of boots held together by twine. He also wore denim pants held on his round paunch by a set of suspenders, while on top he sported long johns, a slight pink tinge to them due to sweat and clay from the rivers, where I assumed he washed them.

"You Brigid?" he called in a deep voice, manners apparently set aside while in the mountains. Or perhaps he'd never had them at all.

"That's me," I said, nodding toward one of the several logs that we'd drug to encircle the campfire last night.

He took a seat, but not before he gave my hand a hearty

shake. "So you headin' this motley bunch?" he asked, closing his one lazy eye so that he could peer up at me.

I sat on the log opposite him. "I am."

He whistled and shook his head, clearly not expecting that a woman would take the lead when two men were readily available. "Well, I never." He chuckled, no doubt thinking this a good story to tell the men at the local pub when he returned from his trek. "And you're planning to go in search of this Alaric fella?"

"I am."

"Well, then," he added, "what do you plan to do once you get there? This Alaric is no one to mess with, I can tell you that."

I flushed, knowing the guide was right. But I bided my time by offering him a cup of coffee brewing over the remaining campfire, which he readily accepted. I lifted the steel coffee urn and poured some into a tin cup.

He reached for it and immediately began blowing across it before taking his first sip. "Ahh!" he said, closing his brown eyes in dramatic fashion and smacking his lips. "Best cup o' coffee I've had in a long time, Miss," he added, opening his eyes and piercing me with the one good one. "None of that chicory for you, no siree!"

For a moment I wasn't sure if he was making fun of me, but in the end I decided this was just his way.

I was about to ask if he wanted food when he said, "You got any grub there, Miss?"

I sighed, not sure what to think of the trapper nor my predicament. For a moment, I stared up at the great wall of mountains, wishing I were already on the other side. Wishing I hadn't been naive enough to think that sentiment alone could save us from capture. It was a naivete I could no longer afford. With that, I turned to the trapper and began preparing him breakfast for the long trek ahead. We would need every bit of energy we could muster, if we were to make it to the top of the Adirondacks and back down the other side before the snows set in.

Henry arrived shortly, along with Thomas and Emma. For her part, Beatrice had taken to glaring in our direction, discreetly turning away when she thought I was looking. I took it as unrequited love, and yet more than once, I had seen her whisper among her team of women only to have them all glance our way with a good deal more than suspicion. What on earth did the woman have up her sleeve, I wondered? But I couldn't deal with that now. I needed to speak to Henry, Thomas, and Emma. We must come up with a plan more solid than the simple hope that Alaric would not attack us for fear of what that might look like to others in his kingdom or the backlash it might cause. If any one of us were hurt, he would no doubt receive condemnation at the least, a full-scale war at worst, but if he simply captured us . . . My head felt heavy and I rubbed it, having managed very little sleep the night before. I pointed to a spot not far off, an open meadow where we could be alone to talk. The others followed as the trapper focused on his "grub".

Once we were together in a small circle, I posed my concerns. Henry, bless him, said, "You should have thought of this ahead of time, before you brought nearly a thousand women on an impossible mission."

"I know, Henry," I said, dipping my head, realizing what a true novice I was in this whole thing. "Maybe we should stay put for a bit, begin training in earnest." I realized now that we couldn't go in empty-handed, that we had to put up resistance if we were to avoid capture. "Emma, I want you to tell everyone that we will stay here another day, maybe longer. Get the runner. We will need supplies. We begin training today."

"Training for what?" Emma asked, pulling on her skirt which had tangled with a gorse bush.

"For resistance, first and foremost, for combat, if necessary."

Thomas whistled and Henry snorted, until he realized I was serious. "But you're . . . *women*," he said, as though Emma and I didn't know that already.

"Henry," I said, "it's high time you learned that women are more than housekeepers and cooks, wives and mothers. We have untapped potential. But we need people who *care* about the common good. Who see beyond what we can do, to who we are and what we need to be happy. It's not just okay to survive, Henry. We should be able to thrive, but we're never going to do that if we women are not part of the equation, if we're only divided in terms of the labor pool instead of as full-fledged human beings. Don't you see, Henry?"

At that, Henry picked up a stick and began poking at the dying embers, a few remaining sparks flashing as they rose up into the sky and disappeared. The smoke from what remained of the fire felt somehow comforting, as though a testament to what we were about to go through.

"They can go after one of us," I continued, "but they can't go after *all* of us."

"How do you propose to get everyone on board?" Thomas demanded.

"We speak to the women about the proposed changes, and

we will do it now." I called for the messenger who hastened on winged feet to meet with each of the groups of women and call them to a meeting at the stump near the clearing. It would give me a height advantage from which to view their reactions.

One hour later, we assembled around the stump, Henry at the ready to help me up. My dress caught on a knot and tore slightly. I hoped it wasn't an omen of what was to come. When at last the women were all assembled I cleared my voice.

At each village, we had picked up more followers so that now we needed a bullhorn to speak, which thankfully I had acquired at the previous stop. "I've made a change of plans," I announced into the bullhorn. "We will stay here for a month and receive training in the meantime."

"Training in what?" Beatrice shouted.

"Resistance and combat." A murmur arose at my announcement.

"Combat?" one of the more matronly women said, hands on hips with a scowl on her round face. "I didn't sign up for no combat."

Once again a murmur arose, not unlike bees seeking meadowfoam. One matronly woman stepped forward, a glint of anger in her eyes.

"I thought you said we wouldn't be punished anymore–that we would forego tradition. That's the only reason I agreed to sign up." Her eyes sparked with fury, her face as bright as a red trillium.

Her words caught me off guard and I nearly slipped off the stump. If not for Henry's skills in agility, I would have suffered a disastrous fall onto my derriere. Once I had regained my composure, I said, "Who is harassing you?"

At that, the woman merely peered down at her feet, her tongue suddenly struck silent. One brave soul stepped forward and said, "It t'isn't her has been bothered, ma'am. Twas her." She pointed a pudgy finger toward a raven haired waif, who tried to hold her ground despite the women urging her forward.

Yet, even at this distance, I could see a bruised cheek and a red welt on her arm. And when she turned slightly, a patch of missing hair became visible. My insides grew molten with a fire that nearly sent me flying to right the wrong that had befallen her. Fortunately, Henry held me back while I pulled myself together and formulated a strategy to determine who had done this to her.

Taking several deep breaths, I pressed on. "Bring her here," I urged.

To that, several women prodded her along, though she protested all the way, until at last she stood before me where I could see her wounds more clearly. I stepped down from the stump.

"Who did this to you?" I asked, bending down so that her eyes met mine. Fear kept her pupils moving to avoid mine, tears hovering close to the rims, those too a reason for concern in days past because of the consequences of that simple action. "Please. I won't let anything happen to you."

But I could see by the way she squirmed that she believed me incapable of such power to protect her. And I could see why, for it had always been so. With a steely resolve, I determined to change that. "You," I said pointing to one woman. "You," I added, pointing to another woman. "Surely one of you saw it."

Most women merely averted their gaze, refusing to jump in the middle of something that could cause them the same punishment, if not worse. The silence among the women grew deafening as bees buzzed and cattle lowed in the distance.

Finally, one brave woman, someone of approximately the same age and no doubt a friend to the woman who had been beaten, stepped forward and said, "It was her!" She pointed at Beatrice, who stood defiantly with her shoulders held back, as though it were her inalienable right to abuse any subordinate she saw fit to attack.

I couldn't help but wonder if it wasn't the poor woman's beauty that had been the source of the retaliation, but no matter the reason, it simply could not stand, or no one would be safe.

"Beatrice, you are no longer commander of your women. Step down."

Beatrice, who I'd only ever seen flirting with Thomas, a coquettish smile upon her flawless pale skin, blue eyes bright with desire for the aforementioned, now showed her true self, her eyes alight with hatred and bitterness.

"I will not," she said, arms akimbo, her legs splayed outward in challenge. "These are *my* women and I will do as I see fit. You're not going to let her get away with this, are you Thomas?"

She lifted her chin in opposition, certain that Thomas would come to her aid. But to Thomas' credit, he said, "This is between you and Brigid, not me. Though I know this puts me in an awkward position, I agree with Brigid. I am tired of the constant bickering and fighting amongst ourselves. Tired of the unending punishments as though we are all living pincushions to be poked and prodded, enduring constant retribution. Sometimes I wonder who the real enemy is, us or them."

A collective gasp filled the impending silence, followed by

low murmurs that ended in a hushed sigh. Inwardly, I thanked him for his candor, for his bravery, especially in light of his earlier words about upholding the values of tradition. For even he could see how much happier the women had become over the course of the last couple of weeks. And yet few would take so kindly to his words, while they filled me with something I had been lacking for a very long time. Hope. Hope that we could change our circumstances. Hope that we could make life better for us all. Hope that we could become civilized, kind, caring.

The awkward stillness continued for some time until Beatrice broke the silence with a stamp of her foot. "I won't have it," she said, pointing a finger at the wounded young woman who looked as though she might keel over at any minute. "Tell them, Thomas. It's either me or her. Tell them."

For several seconds a hum filled the air as though bees had set up a colony nearby. Thomas' eyes sparked with indignation. Then in a voice so low as to be almost unheard, he said, "I choose her."

Beatrice drew back as though slapped, her cheeks red with fury and surprise. "B-but . . . " she stammered.

"Go!" he said. When she didn't respond he shouted, "Go!"

"You heard him, Beatrice," I said. "Pack your things and be gone. Emma will replace you."

Emma, who had been watching the exchange with guarded optimism, threw her hand to her chest, clearly unprepared for this turn of events and in such a short span of time.

"How dare you!" Beatrice turned to Gertrude and Jocelyn. "You're not going to let them do this to me are you?" As though convinced of their allegiance, Beatrice faced me once more. "If *I* leave, *they* leave."

Gertrude's eyes darted around her in apology to the other women, but at last she caved and followed the other woman's lead.

"Jocelyn?" Beatrice demanded, pushing the issue. "Are you with me or against me, and mind you, I don't easily forget disloyalty."

Beatrice's pale skin was apoplectic with rage, but to my surprise, Gertrude's sister didn't cave so easily. Instead, Jocelyn held her ground and said, "I'm with the women. And Thomas is right. You should leave. I, for one, am tired of all the bitterness and fighting. I want to work together as a team, to have my teammates' backs." And with that, she crossed her arms and turned away from Beatrice so that the woman couldn't cajole her further.

Furious, Beatrice turned to the waiting crowd. "Who is with me?" she shouted. "You!" She pointed to one poor girl who obviously didn't have the wherewithal to withstand a brute such as Beatrice. "I've known your family since we were children. Surely, you won't allow someone from the outside to tell you what you will and won't do."

The girl, who had paled almost to the point of passing out, now turned a deep shade of crimson, fear making her tremble. For a moment she stood as though frozen, then suddenly she bolted toward Beatrice. A few, realizing the tide had turned and that they would soon be next, fell out of line and moved begrudgingly toward Beatrice. Once Beatrice discovered that no more would follow, she turned on her heels and growled at me, "You just wait! You'll be sorry." Then she waved a hand in the air. "You will all be sorry!"

Everyone stood in stunned silence, as we watched her retreating back. Then to my surprise, Gertrude held back. Not only that, but she stood close to a peach tree. Suddenly, without warning, she grabbed a ripe peach off a branch and hauled it at the retreating form, hitting her squarely in the back. The pink flesh of the peach dripped, leaving a sweet smell despite the stain. For several moments, no one spoke. Then suddenly, they all began talking at once. Beatrice let loose one final blat, then stormed out, the few retreating women following her at a skip, their eyes peering around sheepishly. Nervous laughter followed.

I sighed, relieved to have her gone. And yet after all my exhortations about no fighting, I couldn't let it go. Yet I couldn't blame Gertrude either. In the end, I put her on dishwashing duty. But to take away some of the sting, I helped her with it so that we got the job done in half the time. As for the other women, Jocelyn included, they cleaned Gertrude's tent and washed her clothes so she wouldn't have that waiting for her when she was through with kitchen duty. Thomas nodded at me as he passed by. And I don't know if it was my imagination, but I registered a glimmer of newfound respect for me that left me aglow the rest of the morning. Now, I just needed to figure out how to best Lord Alaric, a man who had unleashed evil onto the land and would make us his slaves, if at all possible.

16

Fortunately for Alaric, the council was in his pocket. He peered out over the group of men and women that surrounded the huge oak table, determining who he could count on for support, who would require a little extra muscle to get them to do his bidding. In the end, only a few would oppose him and the only reason they had the audacity to try was their prior loyalty to Alaric's father. One would have hoped that this same loyalty might extend to him, Faineant the Foul's son, but it hadn't. The generals had thought him weak. Well, he would show them. He pounded his fist on the table to call their chittering to a close.

"Listen up!" he said, allowing his gaze to linger on Generals Cedric and Weathermore who chafed under his unblinking glare. "Right then," he added when all were silent, "we shall begin. I have just been informed that an army of . . ." He puckered up his lips, unable to speak such blasphemy. ". . . *women* is headed this *way!*" he spat, the word reeking of bile on his tongue.

As if one, the word passed around the table. *Women?* To Alaric's unerring delight, the elite Jackal Guard and even the women at his table seemed both shocked and surprised by this unsettling news. No doubt they were thinking as he did. *How could a group of women hope to fight an army the size of Alaric's?* He rubbed his hands together in glee. But no sooner had he expressed such delight than one of the women spoke in an irritatingly grating tone that never failed to make his jaw seize.

"But Lord Alaric, sir, you cannot go against an army of women without--" She paused, letting her words hang in the air like musical notes.

"Without what?" he growled, the sound so low that it fairly rumbled with rage.

The woman appeared to shrink in her seat, while the two generals coughed in their hands.

"Without creating a stir," she squeaked, peering around the table as if to gather support from her cohorts. Only a few nodded, ever so slightly, then shrank like her to make themselves appear smaller in an attempt to avoid Alaric's wrath.

Alaric turned to the two soldiers. "Do you agree with her assessment?"

Cedric peered toward Weathermore, his eyes glistening. Cedric stood, a cluster of medals on his breastplate.

"To attack women on the battlefield would be the height of arrogance and cause us to lose face, here and abroad. Furthermore, it would cause us to appear barbaric on the world stage. Would you really risk such an endeavor?"

Alaric growled in the back of his throat. Why did his generals always ruin his plans by wedging a stick into the gears of his operations? Why, indeed? He balled his fists.

"So, what do you have in mind?" he demanded, his words slick with honey.

Weathermore stood this time, as if to bolster support for Cedric. "We suggest that *you* attack first, halt them before they get here."

"How will that change anything?" Alaric asked, though feeling somewhat vindicated.

"We could wait until the women arrive in one of the villages, then attack the village. If anyone protests, we merely say we were attacking the town and knew nothing about the women."

Alaric snickered. No wonder his father had relied on such men. He peered around the room once more, palms up, his smile contagious, now that the worst had passed.

"So then, men . . . and women," he added reluctantly. "We have a plan, and we will implement it shortly." Then he turned to the two generals. "Wait here, until the others are gone. After all, we must nail down the specifics, eh?"

The generals regarded each other carefully, then nodded their assent.

"Good, good." Alaric shepherded the council out the door. Shutting it behind them, he turned to the two generals and said, "Now, where were we?"

The next few days passed in a blur. One by one, each of the four of us--Emma, Thomas, Henry, and I--began keeping our totems close, as though we all understood we were being called to do something extraordinary. As I moved from group to group, the blue falcon feather now on a leather cord that hung from my neck beside my hologram necklace, my bird whistle safely ensconced back at the manor, I watched the progress the women were making. Fortunately, Beatrice's performance the other day had settled the remainder of those who had stayed, any like-minded women having left with Beatrice. Yet despite that, the women's fighting skills were definitely lacking. But why? I felt certain the women were just as capable as the men.

I had been so lost in thought that I hadn't realized that Emma had come up behind me until I heard the words, "Women don't fight the same as men, do they?"

"Wh--?" I frowned, pondering her words. "Oh, true, they don't."

"I've been working with the women since I took over Beatrice's spot, but we're all flailing. I don't know what to do." Emma's green eyes appeared duller today, as if worn down by the struggle. And she'd switched from a dress to leather breeches with fringes and a fitted shirt. Leave it to Emma to manage to look feminine in clothes better suited to the trapper. Her totem, the nest and eggs, were kept on a wooden stool inside her tent, next to her bed. I had noticed her setting little gifts she had collected in nature around it, as though by making offerings, the totem would think more highly of her and help guide her in her quests.

For the next few minutes we watched as the women thrusted and jabbed at each other, missing nearly every time. They were better at firing rifles, which we'd procured through the trapper, and yet at least half of the shots missed their targets when the rifles bucked. As I took stock of the women, it soon became apparent that nothing was designed with a woman in mind. Nor were women's attributes that of men, and yet they were expected to fight like men, to *be* men. As Henry had explained to me earlier, women must learn to curb their emotion, but it was their very emotion that drove them. Why not use that emotion rather than squelch it?

I scratched my head, thinking. How could we harness the best attributes in women? I would never know until we had defined those attributes in the first place.

"Emma," I said, "have the women meet me in the meadow in exactly one hour. We need to begin making a list."

"What kind of list?" Emma asked as she called out instructions to the women who had begun their obstacle course training.

"A list of women's strengths and attributes—how we can use them to help in our quest."

Just then, I turned my eyes to the training ground and stifled a giggle to see the first girl doused in mud when she tried to traverse a fallen log above a mud pit. The next girl made it to the rope, swung on it so that her feet found purchase on the wooden wall that Harry and Thomas had erected with the help of some of the ladies. But try as she might, the new recruit slipped down each time she attempted to scale the wall. The final portion of the obstacle course involved swinging on bars to help with agility. One able-bodied woman had made it over both the log and the wall, only to be stymied in this final challenge where she dropped to her feet time and time again bent over, hands clutching her knees and panting at the exertion. No wonder the men found us incapable, and yet I felt certain if the women could use their greatest talents, they could outshine the men, or at the very least be on par with them. But how?

I left Emma to speak to the women, to let them know what I had proposed. Then I headed back to the tent to begin my own list. I started by inventorying women's greatest attributes. Most of the women I knew were smart, honest, empathetic, kind, caring, and capable. But none of those abilities directly translated to what we were proposing.

As I sat in the green army tent that had the slightest residue of mold, its odor now familiar, I heard a flap outside and ducked my head out to see what was happening. To my surprise, Ma'am had arrived by horse and she had brought me a gift.

"A miniature loom," Ma'am explained, handing it to me.

To my surprise, it was an exact replica of the one at the manor, as though the loom had given birth to its tiny doppelganger. I let out a cry of delight.

"Thank you!" I gushed, relieved to have it near me, even if only in miniature.

"The Bookbinders and I thought it might come in handy," Ma'am said with a wan smile. "In the days ahead. May we talk inside your tent where there are fewer ears?"

"Certainly," I replied, ushering toward my tent which was at the edge of the clearing.

I watched her as she entered, and then invited her to sit on one of the two folding chairs. For all the pomp and circumstance of her former life, Ma'am now appeared a different person altogether. She wore khaki pants and brown boots that came up just below her knee. Her shirt was also khaki. But what struck me most was the very sturdiness by which she carried herself, her shoulders erect, head back, as though of even higher stature than before.

"Things haven't gone well at the manor," Ma'am explained, launching in without so much as a hello. "Alaric has thrown every possible pestilence our way," she added on a sigh. "Lord and Lady Bookbinder are beside themselves."

"Pestilence?" I hazarded, fearing her answer.

"Weeds. They have popped up everywhere, Brigid. But fortunately, your blue falcon called upon all the other birds to eat the seed as quickly as possible so we were not overrun as we might have been. Bless her. And then there were the jackrabbits," Ma'am said, throwing up her hands in utter frustration. "Ate almost our entire garden. The only plus to that is that you and your women shall have meat for some time to come."

She pointed to a caravan of cargo that she had brought with her in a mule train of sorts, whereupon I thanked her profusely.

"Fortunately, Lord Roger and Lady Penelope are keen hunters and have spared us from further damage, but it is only time before the next volley ensues." Ma'am, who seemed capable of mounting any charge under any situation, now appeared haggard, her normally glossy brown hair lifeless, as though it had suffered as she had under the hands of the malevolent Alaric.

Just then, the miniature loom that Ma'am had brought began to clack, slowly at first then louder and faster as though a locomotive picking up steam. It must have had quite a headwind, as its spindle-like shuttle moved with an invisible hand, not even bothering to wait until nightfall when the rest were asleep as my original loom had. The realization sent chills through me that could only be cured with an explanation.

As if reading my mind, Ma'am said, "We don't know how it works."

"But where did it come from?" I asked, perplexed.

"We woke up one morning and there it was, as though the loom had given birth."

I noted the awe on Ma'am's face, her eyes alight with an inner glow, the loom's essence having somehow transferred itself into Ma'am herself. The thought made me shiver. And yet I, too, felt it. As though a soul had drifted through me and made its way out the other side on its journey toward heaven. And indeed, the ground on which we stood seemed to quiver along with the air, as though we were merely ripples at the bottom of a pond that had just been stirred by a strong breeze.

"Do you see it?" I asked Ma'am, my chest heaving.

"I do," she said, with just the slightest quiver in her voice.

The clacking continued on and on, the ethereal manifestation making my heart beat erratically. Suddenly, just as quickly as it had started, the loom halted its clacking and we both took a collective breath, the loom included.

For several seconds, neither of us spoke, but I felt certain if I had, I wouldn't have been able to hide my emotion. For there, on the loom, was a picture both beautiful and tragic in equal measure--so much so that I couldn't have spoken if I'd tried.

Ma'am was the first to give voice to what we'd witnessed just now. "Do you see what I see?" she said, no longer trying to hide the quiver in her voice.

I merely nodded, fearing my words would come out a whisper, or laden with tears. For there on a field in front of what I felt certain was Alaric's castle lay the very women I had hoped to train, splayed out in various death poses. In that instant, I knew what a fool's errand this had been, and yet no sooner had I thought of it than I heard a whisper in the wind that said, "It doesn't have to be this way. You could still win."

"But how?" It took a moment to realize I had spoken out loud.

I stood, as did Ma'am, the wind whipping all around me as though dancing a furious rhythm, blowing my hair upwards, swirling leaves and dust into my eyes until I cried out as bits of sand dug at my arms and legs like stinging nettles, scouring me with their sharp edges.

"How?" I yelled, while pleading silently for help. Just then, the wind gave one final glancing blow and flew off, a woman's voice calling me from the distance saying, "Make them believe . . ." And then the wind was gone, flying off to greet some other unsuspecting person, while I stood rooted to the spot, spent.

"What just happened?" I managed, once the flotsam left by the wind had finally settled back to earth. "Who was that?"

Ma'am set her jaw and I could see that she, too, found it difficult to speak. "It was Mother Wind. And she's right, you know. Until the women believe, all is lost."

"But how, Ma'am? How can I make women believe that they can have a say in their lives when all of their lives have been spent caring for others, their very personalities subverted for the greater good of men?"

My legs weak from what I had just witnessed, I plopped down heavily onto one of the folding chairs, urging Ma'am to do likewise. With a nod, she took a seat opposite me.

"A few of us have managed to live a more fulfilled life," she said, her eyes reaching across to me, urging me to believe so that others might as well. "But we are scattered here and there. We work separately. We are the lucky few who are ungoverned by men but work alongside them."

"How is that possible?" I asked, throwing up my hands.

"Only by the grace of our circumstances. Unfortunately, it is not the same elsewhere, and each of us knows it and therefore are grateful for it."

My mind reeled at the implications. Somewhere, out there, were women who could dream a life and make it happen, who could be who they were meant to be rather than in the cage designed for them, trapping them into a life of submissiveness, of kowtowing.

"But lest you think that men are any less imprisoned by life, be certain of this, Brigid," she said, once again capturing my eyes with hers, "they are just as caged by this design of their own making, which is the true irony of it all."

I ran my hands through my hair, trying to grasp all that she was saying. "But how, Ma'am, how can we change it? How can *I* change a system designed to ensnare and imprison an entire people?"

Ma'am stood and came to sit beside me. She took my hand in hers to emphasize how much I needed to truly understand before I could be of any help to anyone, least of all myself.

"You must realize," she said, "the system was designed to keep an unwieldy population in check. Without that, there could be no society, no security. But the system has run amok. Those running it have forgotten that *we* are not the enemy. That most of us love our country and our people. That we want only good for our country, for us. But we also want freedom and equality, to choose what we want to pursue in our lives, to love the people we love, to care for others without always caretaking them."

I shook my head, unsure of her meaning.

"Think of it this way, Brigid. Women are assured from birth that they will grow up, marry and have children. They will care for their household, and that is the sum total of who they are. Men are assured that they will become soldiers, whereupon when they return from their duty, they will go on to entertain a certain line of work supported by a system set up to help men attain those goals. In return, in time of need, they can be called upon again, at any time, to help protect society at large from those who would harm it. In the end, neither men nor women have a choice of what their lives will look like."

"Why does no one change that, if both are unhappy?"

"Because it supports a *system*, Brigid. We are merely the caretakers of that system."

My head felt thick from everything that had happened on this most unusual day. I rubbed my temples to ward off a headache. In the distance, I could hear the women marching, hear the occasional laughter which lightened my load. I wondered if men were allowed to laugh under similar circumstances, but I had my doubts. I pondered this system Ma'am spoke of and wondered why happiness hadn't been factored in . . . for anyone. Why freedoms hadn't been factored in as well--the freedom for women to pursue their dreams *while* they worked to keep the household running. The freedom to choose marriage or a career. For those women who wanted to be soldiers to stand alongside those men who did, while setting men free of the responsibility whose natures made killing other men repugnant. It was as though all of us had been placed, from birth on, inside a box of someone else's making.

Just then, a hummingbird flitted by with an almost superhuman speed, while across from it, a jay sat squawking on a branch, pounding on a nut of some kind. And it came to me then. One had only to look at nature to know that not every bird was the same, not built for the same task, so why were people forced into areas they were unqualified for or simply miserable? Once again, I rubbed my temples, the headache that I had been fighting returning for a second volley. I decided to lay it all on the line to Ma'am.

"I have a dilemma. Maybe you can help. I'm training my women to go against Alaric, but they're having trouble learning how to fight. And as you can see by the mini-loom, they are doomed at this rate. I've called a meeting to try to figure out women's strengths. So far all I've come up with is courage, kindness, empathy, nurturing, all the things that make us excellent wives and mothers, but not fighters.

"That's because women are the glue that holds a society together, whereas men rend it apart in order to gain land, power, status--"

"And to protect their families," I added, unwilling to believe that men sought solely their own gain.

"And their families," she conceded. "Unfortunately, many don't realize the importance of family until it's too late." Ma'am sighed, a deep sadness seeming to ooze from her very pores. It made me wonder if she had suffered such a blow in her own life.

I picked up a twig and began digging in the dirt, drawing

loops, little flourishes, wishing I could pull the answers from the very soil itself. "I'm struggling to find balance between goodness and standing up for what's right, Ma'am. I don't want women to lose those parts of their natures that are kind, compassionate. That's what makes them wonderful. But we can't live like this forever, and if we don't take a stand then nothing will ever change. I don't want us to *become* like Alaric in order to *fight* Alaric." Angry that I couldn't come up with the answers that seemed just outside my reach, I tossed a twig into the dying embers of the fire nearest my tent and watched as bits of it sizzled where it met with pockets of coal.

"Help me up," Ma'am said, reaching an arm to me as I stood.

I offered her a hand, which she took gratefully, still tired from her long journey inland.

"So where is this meeting going to be held?"

Her eyes lit with a kindness that made her crow's feet all the more pronounced. For the first time since I'd met her, I realized I liked her. Here, she exuded a calm, quiet confidence that seemed admirable. And she didn't look down her nose at me, though she had every reason to, given societal norms. No, she peered straight across at me, as though I were her equal, and truly I felt it, the sheer genuineness of her smile.

"Actually, we will be meeting just over there." I nodded toward a clearing where some of the women had already begun gathering, along with Henry and Thomas.

"So let's go brainstorm how to make this motley group of women successful!" Ma'am said, the cheer having returned to her voice as we marched over to the others.

For the next hour, we sat cross-legged around the glade.

Many of the women had brought woven mats or pieces of hide on which to sit, me and Ma'am included, as I gave her one of mine.

"I'll start," Ma'am offered, quickly introducing herself, "since I have years of experience being in charge of women. First, I have found most women to be team oriented, to work well with others, to search for answers rather than to go it alone or to grandstand. But there are also those who will backstab for their own gain. Those we should weed out as quickly as possible."

A chirping arose like a cluster of chickadees, disturbed by a brief bluster of wind. But just as quickly, the chirping stopped and everyone settled.

"I've noticed that some women make great hunters, but many do not," Ma'am added.

Nods followed all around with a hearty murmur of agreement.

This time, I was determined to speak. "Then why don't we separate the hunters from the rest and have the best person with weapons train these women."

Another woman raised her hand—Giselle, who was tall with long hazel-nut colored hair. "I could train the women how to shoot."

Another woman raised her hand as well and said, "Some women are good with dogs. That could help make up for natural hunting abilities if they had a dog to help them."

I saw nods all around.

"Some women are great with planning," said one rather quiet, studious-looking woman with oval glasses. She'd tucked her mousey brown hair behind her ears and sat ramrod straight. I had learned earlier that her name was Winnifred.

"Are you such a woman?" I asked.

Ma'am's eyebrows rose and she ventured a smile as though my stock had just risen in her mind.

"Do you think you could put together a team to help in planning?" I asked Winnifred rather pointedly.

The girl's eyes lit up and she said, "Sure thing."

In that moment, I realized that I hadn't demanded decorum as in a proper army, and yet even as the thought occurred to me, I was swift to decide against it. I wanted this to be an army of equals, giving all of us a stake in the outcome. Yes, there must be structure, but not the structure I had seen which demanded punishing respect. This respect must be earned. Not everything could be decided on a consensus, I knew, but anything that could be would.

"Okay, then, you will head that committee and I'll be on it as well. And Ma'am," I added, "if she'll stay."

"Possibly," she said noncommittally, but I could tell that she was thinking about it.

"Righto!" Winnifred said, a smile lighting up her entire face.

"Okay, so we're making progress."

"Brigid?" Emma called from her spot next to a babbling brook. "Won't we need a negotiator?"

I nearly laughed at the audaciousness of these women. Here I had thought my problems insurmountable, while the women knew all along what they needed. Of course we would need a negotiator, and who better than women to plan strategy, women who had spent their lives in negotiation with children, husbands, neighbors, and family.

One problem remained.

"What if we end up in hand-to-hand combat with Lord

Alaric's forces?" I said, the knot of pain at my temples that I'd experienced earlier returning.

That's when Ma'am spoke up with a glint of humor in her eyes. "Oh, Brigid. Dear, dear Brigid. I guess you do need me after all. We will outwit them," she said simply. "Surely you have heard of the Trojan horse."

"Or how about divide and conquer," one woman called out.

"How?" I countered.

"Send out false information on your opponent, or your brethren."

"We'll have to be careful with that one," I said quite warily. "What could be used against an opponent, could be used against oneself and breed distrust all around. You lose trust, and you lose the war."

A hum of disquiet filled the warm afternoon air which smelled of sweet apples and pears ripening in the sun.

"What else?" I asked.

"Attack where it hurts most," one enterprising woman said.

"And what would hurt Alaric most?" I countered, not to be outdone.

"A bruise to his ego!" Emma said and everyone laughed.

And it was true. Alaric was said to be a vain man in the extreme, always seeking adulation, standing for nothing more than an entire band of sycophants around him to kiss his royal feet and to agree with every word uttered from his mouth. But how? How could we attack his ego without looking small ourselves? Or worse, cruel, like the very man himself. I tapped the front of my teeth, thinking. It would do no good to wrestle in the same mud pit as him. But we could make the people around him question their loyalty to such an evil, manipulative man.

Winnifred, in her own quiet way, waved a goose feather quill in the air, hoping to get a chance to speak.

"Winnifred?" I asked.

All eyes turned to her and she flushed with embarrassment. "Well, it seems to me that Alaric will be expecting a bunch of weak women to enter his city to appeal to his better side."

"As if he's got one," one woman harrumphed.

The group erupted as one, but I held up my hands to silence them and to bid Winnifred speak.

"Go on, Winnifred," I urged.

Winnifred stared down at her feet as though fearful her idea might meet with derision. "Well," she said, slowly lifting her eyes, if not her chin, "what if we send a third of our women in and try to appeal to him, beg him to see reason."

This time the group erupted, but for a different reason, believing that she had surely gone mad. And I have to admit, that I too thought her idea naive at best. I was beginning to think that maybe I had chosen poorly when I'd chosen Winnifred, but then she held up her hands demanding silence.

"Let her speak," I encouraged. "Go on."

"Once we have Alaric's men believing we are helpless and naive, we bring them into the center of town. Then we attack on either flank. We could create a diversion so that their focus is elsewhere. That way they will not be expecting us." She straightened her shoulders.

"So," I said, my earlier worries gone. "We have a plan."

"That we do," Ma'am agreed.

17

Before I could leave for my respective duties, one young woman who couldn't have been more than sixteen years of age, all told, came up to me amid the clearing which was thinning out as people dispersed toward their given locations. She was small and timid, not what one would expect from a woman warrior, her features almost mouse-like. I nearly expected her nose to twitch, she shook so. She worried her hands together then cleared her throat while her voice came out a squeak.

"Ma'am--"

"Call me Brigid," I interrupted, intent on keeping to my promise of a level playing field.

"And I'm Yesimeh," she said bashfully.

"Yesimeh. What an unusual name." I rolled it around on my tongue.

"It's from my mother. It means Jasmine."

In what language? I wondered, but kept any further musings to myself.

"At any rate, I hesitate to say anything, but I think you missed something. Actually, quite a few things."

"Oh?" I said, cocking my head in surprise. "Like what?"

"Well, we will need nurses and doctors, if we are to fight. There are many capable women among us."

Her movements were quick and furtive, once again reminding me of a mouse. Yesimeh the Mouse.

"You're right. I will take care of that next."

She nodded, her green eyes focused on the departing women, her pained expression making it clear she wished she were departing with them.

"We will need scouts, as well. People who are either invisible or great actors."

I shook my head, marveling that so much thought came from such a small package as this. "And I assume you have identified those people as well?"

Her head bobbed up and down so quickly that I feared she might have jostled something loose.

"Thank you. I will look into that," I said, then turned to take my leave.

"Ma'am--I mean Brigid?"

"Yes?" I said, turning back to face her.

"You've forgotten one other thing." Her brown hair, though thin and lifeless, seemed to bounce on the very air currents, as though just as eager as the girl herself to divulge all her thoughts at once.

"Oh?" I asked, raising my brows.

"The gifts. Many women have them, you included . . . or so
I am told," she murmured, head down.

"I see. And what gift do I have, pray tell?"

"Well, the loom, of course." She puzzled her brows, as
though I were daft. "And that." She nodded toward my blue
falcon feather.

Without thinking, I fingered the feather on the leather thong
around my neck. The thong also held pictures of my family in an
orb-shaped globe. I had almost forgotten the blue falcon feather
I had placed next to it.

I peered at Yesimeh, whose brown eyes lit with an internal
fire. "You said some of the other women possess 'gifts'?"

"They do." She peered around her to make sure no one was
close, then leaned in. "Roseland has a carrier pigeon that can ferry
notes, should the need arise."

"She does?" How had I not known this before?

"She hides it in her tent, Ma'am--I mean Brigid."

"Hmm." I stroked my chin, thinking of all the uses we could
have for a carrier pigeon.

"And Peke has a snake."

"A snake?" I drew back in alarm. "Why on earth would she
bring a snake with her?"

"Be-ca-us-e," Yesimeh said as though speaking to a child, "it
can scare the enemy. The element of surprise and all." She tapped
her index finger against her temple.

"Good thinking . . . I suppose. Anyone else?"

"Oh there are many of us."

"*Us?*" I threw up my hands. "How many exactly?"

Here, she giggled like a schoolgirl speaking out of turn. "Oh ten, twenty. Who's to say? It's not like we all go out promoting ourselves, now is it?"

I was about to ask her what gift she possessed, when I saw in the distance a great storm brewing. It had taken shape so quickly that I hadn't had time to process what I was seeing. Yesimeh turned to see what had caused my mouth to form a wide "O." Before I understood what I was witnessing, she grabbed me by the arm and yelled, "Run!"

It took only a second to gather her meaning, for the clouds had gone from an amorphous mass to the shape of a giant man, Alaric I assumed, or one of his minions. It stomped toward us, thunder and lightning following in its wake. The ogre-shaped cloud had within it a funnel that picked up houses and people, tossing them from side to side with its great arms. Where its eyes should be, a red glow flashed fury upon the land and all its contents, people in particular. I searched frantically for Emma, Thomas and Henry, but to no avail.

"We must go, now!" Yesimeh cried. "There's no time to get the others."

Even as panic filled my chest, I could see that she was right. I cleared the cobwebs from my head with a violent shake, then ran like the wind in search of shelter.

"A cave. We must shelter in a cave," Yesimeh shouted to be heard over the storm.

"But where?" I yelled in return, as we raced toward the hills. For if indeed there were a cave, the mountains appeared the most likely place to find it. Together we climbed the cliffs of massive boulders, the wind already at our back and tearing at our clothing. Others must have had the same idea, for all around me women scrambled to beat the storm from sucking them up inside it, only to swirl around like a giant cauldron filled with this week's laundry. Then I saw it. "There!" I shouted, pointing so that the others could follow suit. Soon, we were all scrambling in the same direction.

I fell inside the cave first, then Yesimeh. We pulled others inside, and before long we had a chain of women working to retrieve the others, yet still there was no sign of Henry, Thomas and Emma, I realized with a sinking heart.

Just as the storm was upon us, one woman, Hannah I believe she was named, struggled as the wind sought purchase around her. She fought valiantly against it. I could see the cloud's fingers pawing at her smaller digits one by one so that she might lose her grip and be consumed by the ravenous beast of a storm.

"Grab my feet!" I yelled. "Make a chain. I'm going after her."

Yesimeh was the first to act, but she was too small and I feared the two of us being sucked in with Hannah. Fortunately, Yesimeh saw the error of her ways and stood back for a more sturdy girl to give aid. Soon an entire chain of women had formed, the stoutest at the end forming the anchor by which to hold us.

I crept along the ledge yelling, "Hang on! I'm coming."

I could see the fear in Hannah's muddy brown eyes as her thin coat whipped behind her, pulling her inch by inch from my grasp. "Fight, Hannah!" I growled. "Don't look back." For if she looked back and saw the monster that even now held her in his grip, I knew that she would panic and all would be lost.

I clamped my teeth together and growled anew as I fought my way over to her. My fingers touched hers, but I couldn't get my hand around her hand, her wrist. If only I could . . . I let out a yell as I pushed myself to the limit of my ability, straining every muscle in my body to reach her. Finally, my efforts paid off, and my hands made contact with her wrists. I paused for only a second to gather my reserves. Then I nodded, hoping the women could see me and would reel me in. Fortunately, Yesimeh, who was not strong, was a capable watchman. She lifted a hand in the air and dropped it hard so that every woman in the line would see the order she'd given. My ankles were yanked backwards so that I feared they might break, and yet I held tight to Hannah whose eyes were pooled with tears, the pleading in them filled with such yearning and need as to bring tears to my own eyes. Silently, I prayed. Prayed that we could save Hannah. Prayed that we both made it back to shelter and safety. Prayed that the storm . . . the ogre, would disappear. And as if my prayers had been answered, the ogre's arm came off at the elbow and he let out a shriek of pain that filled the air in a thunderous roar. All around me, rocks began to fall and I feared an earthquake, so impacted was the ground by the noise. Nevertheless, I held tight to Hannah, as the women did to me, and though bruised by the day's event, we were pulled ever closer to the entrance until at last, the two of us were pulled through the cave's mouth.

I sat panting as women gathered around each of us in turn, inspecting us for injury. Fortunately, though we would be sore and in pain in the coming days, we were alive, truly and totally alive. When I finally was able to calm my breathing, I began laughing, softly at first, then with gusto as the realization wore on that we had survived. Soon the others were laughing as well. Yet we sobered when we saw the cloud's arm wrapped round Hannah's leg give a violent jerk. Then a black cloud of steam escaped from it, creating a foul odor that had us all gasping. Like a souffle that had been brought out of the oven too soon, the arm seemed to puff up, then give one last gasp before collapsing in on itself. Moments later, the arm shriveled up and turned to dust. Ceremoniously, we swept up the dust with pine branches to feed the very soil around us. From a distance, we could hear the faint stomping as the ogre returned to its lair, minus one arm.

My relief was short-lived, however. For I knew that I could no longer be complacent. Too many lives depended on me. Now that the trauma had passed, I searched around the cave and, with trepidation, realized that only a handful of our women had made it into the cave. Where was everyone else? Further, where were Emma, Thomas, and Henry? Fear settled over me, every bit as malevolent as that cloud. Now I had another prayer to add to the rest. That they and the others were safe, and that we would once again be reunited.

18

The night proved cold, the entire group of women huddling together in the cave. Even as I ached with fatigue that touched every single portion of my body right down to my fingertips, I longed for sleep but it wouldn't come. Instead, I shivered in the dark dampness, drips of groundwater seeping through the ceiling of the cave and landing on each of us in turn. I was not the only one to suffer sleep deprivation as evidenced by the coughing, the chattering of teeth, and the constant movement among the others in the group. I hadn't realized that Yesimeh was so close at hand until I heard her whisper into the darkness.

"Brigid," she murmured, "that was a brave thing you did back there."

Numb with cold, my lips formed words yet I struggled to speak. "Y-you w-were b-brave too."

"No, Brigid. I was too small to help you."

I wondered how she could talk so easily, under the circumstances, but saw that she had a pair of woolen gloves on her hands which she used to cover her face when silent.

"N-no. You h-heard my c-cries and o-ordered t-the women t-to pull. T-thank y-you."

"Oh, Brigid. You're freezing. Here," she said, using her woolen mittens to warm my face.

I was about to protest, but felt instant relief as gradually my face began to thaw. She kept the mittens there for several minutes, then pulled them away to once again warm her own face.

"Earlier, when you said that many of us have gifts . . ." I began, my lips not functioning fully, but at least I could get the words out without my teeth chattering. "What did you mean? Do you have a gift?"

In the darkness, all I could see was the glistening of her eyes and a faint silhouette. But I could feel the movement when she nodded as the motion further chilled the already cold air. I shivered and patted my arms to stay warm, wishing that I had thought to dress warmer, but I hadn't planned an overnight stay in a cave when I'd set about meeting with the women earlier in the day. I peered out the entrance of the cave, at the night sky, wondering what time it was and how much longer I would have to endure the cold.

"We're nearing morning," Yesimeh said, as though reading my thoughts. "Daybreak will soon be here. Then we can leave the cave and find the others."

Her words sat between us, leaden with portent. What would happen if I and the other wayfarers couldn't find the remaining group? Or if the others were no longer alive? My throat thickened at the thought, my stomach in turmoil, and not just from lack of food or drink.

"We'll find them."

She spoke so softly that I wondered if I had heard her or just imagined the words, wishing them so.

"As for my gift--" she added tentatively. Here, she peered around at the others to see which ones slept, which ones stirred. "Just as you have your loom, I have this."

Carefully, she pulled something out of her pocket. All I could see in what moonlight prevailed was a rolled up sheet of something clear that reflected slightly when the moonlight touched it.

"W-what is it?" I asked, scrunching my nose, the cold returning to my lips.

"Isinglass."

"A windowpane?" I asked, not understanding.

"Like a windowpane, but a gelatine made from the air bladders of sturgeon."

I would have laughed had she not seemed so serious.

"I know you must think it silly, compared to your loom. But it works."

She broke off a piece and placed it in a rivulet of water that had dripped from above. Then she touched it to my skin and I yanked my hand back. It stuck to me. I hurriedly washed it off in a pocket set among the stones before it could dry.

"It turns into a glue-like cement. Handy if you can find enough of it to do any good."

"And can you?"

"I can prepare it, but we would need to go fishing."

"Fishing," I said, absentmindedly.

Such a leisurely pastime, and yet now fishing might very well save our lives in more ways than one, food being the greatest need for a group our size. Between food and air bladders, I would have two uses for fishing. I wondered how many of these fish bladders I could procure. We could dry the fish to take with us, though an invading army might smell us coming, I realized with a chuckle. It felt good to laugh after such a difficult night.

As we sat talking, the sky gradually lightened, until before I knew it, the sun had arisen. Those lucky few who had slept awoke with a yawn and stretched, whereas I would get little sleep today. No, I would have to wait for tonight and hope that it would come quickly. I thought about what we might discover once we arrived back at camp. Where would we find new tents and supplies, now that the ogre of a storm had passed through, destroying everything in its path? I rubbed my eyes and sighed, then stood, my lips once again going numb with cold.

"I-it's time we r-returned to camp, to i-inspect the d-d-damage done to our belongings." I could barely wrap my lips around the words, so frozen were they. "A-and to f-find the others," I added, on a somber note.

A mumbling of words greeted me as the women prepared for the long trip down the mountain. Fortunately, though our legs were weak and wobbly from last night's trek up the mountain, the cold was slowly seeping from our bones and we were able to make good progress. At times we nearly galloped down the hillside, amazed at the speed by which we moved, at other times we stopped to catch our breaths before pressing on.

When we finally made it to the valley from which we had

started, we all took a collective gasp, for not only were our tents and supplies scattered in every direction, there were no signs of life either. The few women who remained had all perished. Once again my throat tightened and the familiar ache returned to my stomach, any desire for nourishment gone, replaced by a weight of responsibility so heavy that I felt as though it might crush me.

"This is not your fault," Yesimeh said between gritted teeth. "It's Alaric's fault. He did this to our community."

"I know," I said, but in my heart, I bore the entire responsibility, for I had led them out here onto a battlefield, completely unprepared. I wouldn't make the same mistake again, I decided with a determination that had my fists in balls and my jaw clenched. No, I would not make a similar error in judgment.

Though I wished for it, we couldn't carry the dead to their homes. We needed every single person here to help in the fight. If this was to mean something to the women still living, we must make positive changes to each and every one of their lives, so that these deaths would not be in vain.

The tears that I had been trying to hold back fell freely down my cheeks. For one brief moment, I sought to quell them, to stick to the adage that one must not cry, that women were to appear stoic alongside their men. But that had been part of the problem, had it not? That festering wounds were never allowed to heal under the ministrations of the body's release of its toxins, its tears. Instead, people held them in, as society insisted upon. Buried the pain just as they had buried their dead, the sorrow and misery bottled and shaken until it presented in ways so much more violent and costly. Knowing that, I allowed myself tears. And when I looked around, I saw that most were crying as well.

When each of us saw what the others were doing, we one by one began to laugh, for the tears were a release long since forgotten, suppressed.

Once the grief had passed, we mounted a charge, each group performing a different task. Yesimeh offered to put together a team to dispatch the dead while Hannah sought to put together a group of women who would gather what remained of our camp. In the meantime, I rounded up a search party to go in search of the missing warriors.

"We'll meet back this afternoon in the clearing and go from there. Then we will say our farewell to our friends."

The mood had once again turned somber, as each group stirred to its task. I had only a small party of eight, none of whom I knew, save for Gertrude who had quit her snooty attitude with Beatrice gone, and now seemed only too eager to help.

I didn't know where to start, except to walk to the nearest town where perhaps someone might know something. So together we set off. The town was nearly an hour away by foot. How I wish I'd had Henry's horse, but like Henry, he was nowhere to be found.

An hour later, we limped into town, still tired from yesterday's doings and today's hike down the mountain and into the village. We had only an hour to find what we were looking for before we would need to head back to camp. Perhaps I could send two of the women to purchase new supplies. Since I knew only Gertrude, I sent her along with a pudgy woman named Ida. Although a plain woman with dark hair that hung to her shoulders, her full round face lit up with a smile, despite our circumstances, and she giggled, promising to do the ladies proud.

"Okay," I said to the others, "let's start at the market stalls." Surely someone had seen thousands of women with two men. Make that three, counting the trapper.

And it didn't take long before one of the women from my group, Jessie, an unusually tall and lanky woman, called me over to a stand that held a variety of fish. I would be sure to mention the fish to Yesimeh. Flies buzzed lazily above the fish, which smelled only somewhat fresh, the swarthy seller swatting the insects away with a rolled up newspaper. My stomach turned, despite my hunger. It's then I thought to buy us all a meal before we left. We would need food for thousands, if we could ever locate the others.

"This man here says tha' the lot of 'em swarmed in after the storm and are put up at a farm just west of here," Jessie said, pointing in a vague direction. "Says the storm blew in but passed over before touching down 'side our encampment. Says tha' group of ours scattered in all directions so that ogre of a storm only got some of 'em. Our group planned to return t'morrow to bury the dead."

All six women went silent at that. An uneasy hush followed as we processed what we had heard. We knew this was only Alaric's latest volley. There would be many to come, and the thought sobered me. Sobered us all.

"Well, let's purchase food for the encampment--"

"Miss," the fishmonger said, wiping fish guts onto his apron, "a man named Henry already ordered food for the lot. Enough food for a month, he did."

"Is that so?" Inwardly, I thanked Henry for having the foresight. Still, we all needed food and we needed it fast.

As if the wheels of my thoughts were visible, the fishmonger said, "There's a tavern down the way. They'll set you up with a hot meal until you can make it to the farm. It's the Langlois farm-- Frenchman and his wife, so I'm told."

I quickly calculated the logistics of getting everyone at the same place. "Do you suppose we could get some people with carts to pick up the remainder of our group, perhaps thirty people or so?"

"Course we can. You just say the word."

But before I could say a thing, he shouted over to a boy sitting in front of the livery down the way and told him to get Jake, presumably the stable master. Before he could shout further orders, I waved him closer.

"We need someone to tend to the dead, perhaps bring them to town where they can have a proper burial."

He held up his hands. "I understand." He began untying his apron. "You go have your meal. I'll take care of everything and meet you there."

"Oh, and the women located at our previous camp haven't eaten," I added. "They will need food to tide them over until they can get to town."

"We'll take care of things," he said. Then the fishmonger called to the butcher in the stall next to him and asked him to watch his stall, a long-standing arrangement that benefitted both, no doubt. That done, he flew off to the required tasks.

Relief seemed to take hold of each and every one of us for we all began talking at once, the smell of the nightly repast filtering into the cobbled streets as we neared the tavern. The smell of warm food was gratifying after weeks of roughing it. One by one, we barreled through the saloon doors and took a seat at a rather large round table. Before we'd even had a chance to order, the two other women entered.

"How did you find us?" I asked, surprised to see them so soon.

"Asked at the market," Gertrude said. "Gossip is as easily traded as wares, apparently." We all laughed. "Henry already took care of the supplies," she added. "Plus he left a message, should we come enquiring, to find him at the Langlois farm."

"We heard," I said, surprised at how quickly the gossip had made its rounds in this small community. "Well, then, I suppose we should eat."

We ordered from the rather limited menu of stew, biscuits, and a round of ale. Yet nothing had ever tasted so good, in my opinion, the biscuits light and fluffy, the stew bubbling with carrots, potatoes, and fresh peas from someone's garden. By the time we had all eaten, our stomachs round and ripe, the fishmonger arrived to take us to the farm by cart.

"We sent a message to Henry and Thomas that we found the lot of you," he said, insisting that the town would pick up the tab for our meal. "Heard about what you women are trying to do. It's quite brave of you to go up against the likes of Alaric and his goons. They're a hungry lot, always stealing from our stores, claiming theys taxes for protectin' us, but the only ones we got to worry about is them goons of his. They're a sorry lot, they are."

We followed him as he grumbled his way out of the tavern, still going on about Alaric and his men. He walked us to the livery, where a man named Jake had prepared a cart, determined to drive us himself.

"For the cause," he said, doffing his hat.

"For the cause," we said in unison.

I didn't know it at the time, but that was to be our catchphrase from then on, a word that was whispered as men and women passed each other, doffing their hats just slightly to hide their lips from prying eyes. It also warmed me to know that we had support among those in the town.

The ride, although much appreciated, was bumpy, the road littered with potholes often filled with water that would splash up, leaving us covered in wet mud. We squeezed in tighter so we were less apt to get splashed. When at last we were in sight of the farm, I leaned forward and called to the driver, who bent down so that I might have his ear.

"I thought you were paying taxes to Alaric. Why are the roads so filled with potholes?"

Jake snorted, pressing his two quarter horses on with a "Hah!" and a slapping of reins. "Naught of it goes for us, Ma'am. Only insofar as it helps his cronies, that one. And they pay nary a tax." He snorted again, then blew out a wad of phlegm that the horses side-stepped. "It'll be a cold day in hell afore the likes of him helps the likes of us. Too good for us, that one. Thinks he's above us. Looks down his nose as do the others."

I knew that it went both ways, as the poor and middle class looked down their noses at the wealthy as well. And yet when the rich were unwilling to pay their fair share of taxes, and yet received more than their fair share of benefits, one had only to guess at the reason for the ire of men such as Jake.

"The irony is that the rich need the poor and middle class, and the poor and middle class need the rich. Things just need to be more fairly divided."

"Got that right!" the man grumbled.

But before I could ponder further the plight of the masses or the livery driver's threadbare clothes, Jake pointed out the Langlois farm, a lovely farmhouse, white with green shutters. Off to the right of it sat a pinkish brick barn.

"They's in there," the man said, pointing to the barn. Even at this distance, I could hear the hum of people talking and moving about. Surely not *all* of them were in there.

And as if he'd detected my disbelief by the set of my brow, he nodded toward the backside of the barn. "Th' rest is camped out there. Townsfolk supplied them with tents and the like, seein' as most of theirs blew away in the storm."

I thanked him profusely, pumping his hand until I had to apologize for the inconvenience.

"Okay, ladies. We're here," I shouted, turning to face the barn.

They didn't wait for any further word as they took turns jumping down, some of them falling and laughing in mud-soiled dresses and petticoats, some in pants. When they had finished disembarking, they turned to give me a lift. I wanted to say I wasn't helpless, but seeing how dirty and worn they all appeared, I gratefully accepted their hands and help, knowing it had cost them.

Once I was safely on the ground, Jake tipped his hat one last time and said, "If you ladies need anything, anything a'tall, just send one of the Langlois children around and we will be happy to help ye' out."

"Thanks so much," I gushed, hoping that he understood how truly grateful we were for his help. Then I turned to the women and said, "Let's go!"

We made so much noise as we ran toward the barn that a gaggle of women came to see what all the fuss was about. When they saw us, they set up a cry of excitement, running to greet us.

Henry came to the door, and when he saw me, safe and alive, he came sprinting toward me, catching me into his arms and twirling a circle so that I thought I might collapse then and there.

"Oh, thank God," he said once he'd stopped twirling me about and had swept me into a tight embrace, his cinnamon smelling breath against my ear.

Without thinking, he kissed me fully on the mouth, then drew back, shocked by his own audacity. But I didn't care. I was so caught up in the moment, so happy to know that he was alive, that I jumped into his arms anew and we stayed like that until Thomas came over and tapped him on the shoulder.

"I believe it's impolite to monopolize the lady." Though I blushed, he smiled and hugged me tightly, once Henry released me, followed by Emma who did the same.

"I was so afraid I would never see you again," she said in a rush. "What happened to you?"

"I could say the same for you," I chided but with a hint of teasing in my voice.

As they welcomed us inside, we took turns telling them everything that had happened, ending with the most frightening and exciting part of the episode, the ogre having lost its grip--literally--when we tore Hannah away from his clutches.

"Thank goodness she's safe," Emma said, appearing almost matronly now in her new role as mother to the younger girls. "And you," she added.

Then I told them about the dead we'd encountered back at the camp. One young woman cried when I listed the women who had survived, the women who had not.

"That was my sister," she said to which Emma scooped her into an embrace and rocked her as the woman sobbed quietly.

I explained that the fishmonger had gathered a group of men to go after the others and bring them here, along with the dead. A heavy silence descended upon the gathering as even more women from the camp out back heard the commotion and word got 'round about the missing and dead. Only three women were unaccounted for, that we could gather. Where they were was anyone's guess. We would send a search party out in the coming days, but right now, it felt good to be in the embrace of the community of women.

"Where is the trapper?" I asked, suddenly remembering that he had been close by when all of this had begun.

But no one seemed to know, they merely shrugged their shoulders when they realized he'd been lost in the shuffle. Well, that too would have to await another day. Then it occurred to me. Ma'am. Where was Ma'am? Panic seized me as I darted my head searching for her.

"Ma'am. Where is she?" I cried, tears rushing to my eyes.

Henry snorted. "You want to tell her, Thomas?"

"I'll let you do the honors, Henry."

"Take a look."

He grabbed my hand and led me to the back where fresh tents had been set up as well as a makeshift camp. I took one look and laughed. For there was Ma'am, teaching the women how to shoot guns while another woman taught the women how to shoot arrows. And Ma'am's style was more than a little intimidating.

"Quite the little huntswoman, that," Henry said with a laugh.

"I suppose," I said, shaking my head. "Oh, Ma'am," I murmured. "What are we going to do with you?"

20

As the days progressed, the women improved at their newfound skills, so much so that my miniature loom had set to clacking again, only this time the scene showed fewer and fewer women dying on the battlefield. Indeed, many of the women had been set to right, their injuries gone. I invited Ma'am to my tent to see what she would make of it. She bent down to examine the miniature loom, then rose to her feet, exclaiming with delight at the changes.

"So," she said quite cryptically. "We can alter the future, with enough preparation."

"My thoughts exactly," I said, just as excited as she.

We regarded the loom for a while longer, and when nothing more was forthcoming, we ambled outside to take stock of our troops. The area around the barn was different from the last place we had encamped. Gone were the dale and fen. All around us were fields, some fenced to house cattle or sheep. We had been given a spot in the south forty, just this side of the rustic white farmhouse with clapboard siding and dual chimneys that smoked at all hours of the day and night, the closer we got to fall. Henry had gone out to purchase cold weather gear and should be back shortly.

We decided it best to speak to all the women at once. One of the women had brought with her a trumpet that she blew with gusto whenever needed. Soon, the women had gathered around while Ma'am and I told them what we had learned--that the future could be changed through hard work and determination. A murmur arose like a cloud of hornets. I had just lifted my hands to quiet everyone down, when Henry pulled up his horse cart filled with supplies. Everyone rushed to greet him, but before Henry could quiet the lot, more carts pulled up, not with supplies, but with fresh recruits from the nearest town and a few beyond.

"What is this, Henry?" I demanded, both excited and a bit frightened at the prospect of more women to train. Worse than that, men had dispersed among the women, insisting that they be allowed to help the cause as well.

Henry bent down from his spot on the bench of the cart, his riding crop still in hand. "How could I say no, considering what we're up against?"

"You should have asked me first," I hissed, not at all certain about this. The women around the village had all been people Henry's family had known for years. Here, I knew no one. How could we be certain that we weren't being infiltrated by some of Alaric's men?

"I know what you're thinking, Brigid," Henry said, "but

they seemed genuinely as interested as we are in stopping the onslaught."

One of the men, having caught what Henry was saying, spoke up. "You don't know what he's done to our people," he said with an undeniable vehemence. "He has stolen many of our women, for what purpose we have no idea. And he has raided our fields, taken our only means of survival. We have struggled to succeed, but we're becoming poorer and poorer with each raid. We can no longer stay the course."

With a wariness bred by recent events, I took stock of the middle-aged man. This man was no poor farmer as evidenced by his dialogue. Surely, he'd had schooling, and quite a bit at that. And his silk vest and linen breeches were not that of a field hand either. No, this man was of some station in life, and yet he too had been impacted by the vagaries of Alaric's whims.

I looked to Ma'am for guidance but saw that she was just as concerned as I. "We could put them in auxiliary positions for now," she said. "Make sure that we can trust them before giving them anything more pivotal."

Henry caught my eyes and refused to look away, imploring me to give them a chance.

With a sigh, I said, "Alright, Henry, Ma'am. We'll give them a go."

After that, much whooping and hollering gave way on their side. I just hoped I hadn't made a mistake. I pointed to a vacant spot closest to the cattle and bade them to set up their tents there. In the meantime, I would have Henry speak to the new recruits to see if any had skills we might use.

Two hours later, Henry arrived with a list of the new recruits' various skills, just as I was inspecting the horses Henry had purchased for what would become our cavalry.

"Some of the recruits are good at handling horses. We could put them on stable duty. And of course, Thomas is great with horses, as am I," Henry stated matter-of-factly, hands behind his back as we surveyed each new horse in turn. All were of good caliber, all save one who appeared scrawny and malnourished.

"Where did you get this one from?" I demanded, determined to rescue all that had been starved, as this one surely had.

"A miserly old coot, that one. Poor horses. I took the best of the lot."

"There are more?"

"Why, yes, but Brigid--"

"Get them," I all but growled, furious that such a person as that was allowed to tend horses.

"But Brigid--"

"I said get them," I ordered.

Clearly Henry wasn't used to seeing me so demanding, but when it came to abuse, I would not tolerate it. Henry turned a deep shade of crimson and stammered at my reply.

"But Brigid," he pleaded, hands held out in supplication, "we're not in the business of rescuing animals. Our focus must be on Alaric."

"You don't understand," I said through gritted teeth. He had not been there when the tax collectors came for our horses. To hear their snorts and cries. It lived with me to this day. I had found out where the animals were taken to auction, had watched them tied onto the back of the slaughterhouse wagon. Had listened to their almost human-like screams as they had been slaughtered, one by one, each knowing what lay ahead of him or her.

I hadn't realized that my fists were in balls and that tears were streaming down my face, and snot down my nose until I felt Henry's hands come round my fists, felt him pull me to him in a tight embrace.

"It's okay, Brigid," he whispered into my hair. "I'll rescue them. I promise."

It was as though the words released a torrent of pent-up anguish I hadn't known I was harboring until then. For the next several minutes, I allowed him to cradle me into his arms, to soothe me of the memories that even now filled me with both fury and sorrow, in equal measure, so much so that I shuddered at the images they produced. The sounds. The smells. All embedded in my psyche in a way that nothing had before or since, except for the loss of my family. That had been especially painful. Somewhere in my child's mind, I believed I should have done something, worked harder, fought harder for my family. Maybe then we would still be together. But then my logical mind would kick in and I knew the picture was much larger than what I could see. That the die had been cast by the almost fortress-like monolith of the rich and powerful out to claim every last penny anyone owned. Had all of us worked our fingers to the bone, we still wouldn't have been able to stay together. But maybe here I would have a new family, one that loved me just as well. I could only hope.

Henry reached down and cupped my chin, lifting my lips to his as he gently kissed me, his lips drying my tears. It was a balm to my battered soul. But what struck me most in that moment was the fact that he had allowed me to cry, hadn't punished me for releasing the tears of the festering wound I held inside me. Despite his training, his upbringing, he had allowed me in that moment to be fully human, and I cherished him for it. I shivered at the delicate touch, the taste of him, both manly and yet sweet at the same time, as though he had pear on his lips with just a touch of brandy.

Before I could dwell further on this precious moment, I heard a commotion at the back of the barn and feet on the path, someone calling out "Henry!" in a most frantic tone.

Henry pulled back, but not before he smoothed my hair and set me to rights. "Over here!" he called. "What is it?"

And indeed, it was one of the new male recruits whose name I had yet to catch. His blonde hair was disheveled, and he spoke with a funny accent, from his home country perhaps, as he clearly wasn't born here. Scandinavian, perhaps.

"A fight has broken out among several of the new recruits."

Henry and I shared a glance, then in an unspoken message we raced to stop the fighting before it spilled over to create havoc among the others. We had just fled the barn, sunlight blinding us as we came into the open. We shielded our eyes, the sight before us coming into focus. There, not fifteen yards away, I saw a ruffian, not someone we wanted as a recruit, surely, whose meaty fists were targeting a much smaller man. The smaller of the two had unwieldy hair that went every which way as though he'd been struck by lightning, and he was now sporting a bruise in the middle of his forehead.

"Stop!" I shouted, but the beefy man's eyes never wavered from his target. "Stop!" I shouted again, pulling on his arm just as he went in for another punch.

Though I hadn't halted him, he missed his target and the smaller man managed to land a blow before stepping out of the way of the meatier man's fist. The women were at odds to keep them in line, so it was up to me. Thankfully, before the larger man, who saw me as nothing more than an annoying gnat, was able to sink in another strike, Thomas rode up on his horse and proceeded to separate the man from the others. Using his horse, he nudged the man farther and farther back as though he were herding cattle, until finally, to everyone's great relief, the man fled. A cheer erupted and many gathered round the smaller man, roughing up his red hair and singing his praises for having the fortitude to stand up to the brutish man.

"What happened here?" I demanded, once the commotion had died down.

Emma stepped forward. "Jax, here, was protecting my honor. The lout tried to land a kiss." She grimaced at the mere thought of such a thing. "He with the putrid breath." She shuddered, her shoulders nearly reaching her ears as she imagined what might have ensued had Jax not saved her.

"Did you know the man?" I asked.

"Knew of him, is more like," Jax said.

The boy was clearly Irish, by the color of his hair, the pale skin and freckles, and the slightly offset nose. He had a quirkiness to him that was instantly likable, as though he was every woman's ornery younger brother. And it's true the women had taken to him, each of those nearby offering to care for his wounds or to fix him something to eat. It was easy to see he was relishing every moment of their attention. I had to laugh, in spite of myself.

He would be one to watch as his presence could create jealousy among the women. For now, he would be a welcome addition.

"That there was Heinrek. The boys back home called him Heiny for, well, you can guess, I'm sure." His face turned a deep crimson that flushed all the way up his ears and to his hairline.

Again, I laughed. "I take it you didn't like him very well."

"No one does," he said, his expression exaggerated to show his distaste. "Always bossin' the rest of us around. Actin' like he's somethin' special. Chasin' the skirts, if you get my drift."

"Oh, I do." I eyed Emma carefully to be sure she was alright. But despite the indignity of the man's actions, she seemed none the worse for wear. "Okay, well, back to work. Emma, you can take Jax around and show him the grounds. But first, get him ice for that bruise."

Many of the women let out groans, while Thomas watched from a distance, jealousy causing him to pull hard on the reins wherein his horse bucked his head back and forth and he pranced impatiently to have the reins loosened.

Yes, I would need to monitor the green-eyed monster carefully. We couldn't have disruption in the ranks, not if we were to work as a team. The sooner Jax found a proper mate, the better. And somehow, I had a feeling it wouldn't take all that long. Not with his boyish charm and good looks.

Heinrek drove his horse at a rapid clip, never caring that the beast was lathered in a coat of sweat that made his black hair glisten in the sunlight. He couldn't wait to tell Alaric what he had learned in the short time he'd been at the women's camp. Although he knew he should have been more circumspect, should have stayed longer to gather more information, he had enough to bring him a pretty penny for his troubles. He sniggered with glee at his foresight. It would be a three day ride at a sound clip. He had already sent his white raven ahead with a message attached to a small barrel secured around his neck. The bird was said to be divine. Ironically, he'd won it in a poker game. At first he'd balked at such a thing, but the more he had learned about its rarity and its association with the gods, the more he had thought it a good omen.

Now, as he whipped his horse ever onward and felt the ground give way beneath its hooves, he chuckled with glee to know that Alaric would soon learn of his importance. See what an asset he could be to the leader, and bring Heinrek untold wealth as a result. Like Alaric, he understood the machinations of power. Of greed. Now everything was within his reach, just as it had been when he'd won the white raven.

"Godforsaken horse!" he shouted, wishing himself in Alaric's camp already. He would need to stop at the next town. Trade his horse for another that could be worked into an equal lather. Whatever it took to get what he wanted, and he wanted as much as he could finagle. Everything he so desperately deserved. For the first time all day, he smiled just as the town came into view. He slowed his horse long enough to catch his breath and to taste the air filled with pines and white birch. While the stable hand was saddling his horse, he would stop for a pint and a meal. He could taste the mutton stew already. He licked his lips, then pressed his horse onward, eager to barrel toward his future.

20

"We must go now," the trapper said, licking his finger with his tongue and holding it to determine which way the wind was blowing as we sat around the warm campfire.

Fortunately for us, the trapper had returned after an all-night bender, or should I say two-night bender, at the tavern and had brought the three missing women with him who had holed up in a nearby inn until they could relocate us. Had they not run into each other in search of breakfast, we might not have found them so readily.

"The winds are coming from the west," the trapper continued, rubbing his hands together for warmth. "I fear an early winter. If we don't hurry, there will soon be snow and all will be lost."

"But it's only just September." Two weeks had passed since the ogre's visitation and the village had been eerily quiet. I had received no news from the manor either. That, in itself, felt wrong somehow. Prior to this, we had received almost daily word and instruction, which we roundly ignored if it went against our new precepts. Still, I had the innate feeling that something was indubitably wrong. Now, to make matters worse, we had the warning from the trapper. Worried, I summoned Ma'am. She would know what to do.

When she arrived ten minutes later, I told her what the trapper had said and also apprised her that we had yet to hear from the manor house.

"That's odd," she said, pinching her lower lip.

"And I can't get over that Heinrek fellow. I don't know why, but I have an awful feeling about the man. He was like none of our other recruits--so, so . . ."

" . . . vile!" Ma'am filled in the word for me.

"Precisely," I said. "Could he be one of Alaric's men?"

"Would it surprise you?" she asked, tendering a raised brow. "I wonder why Henry didn't catch that. He's usually so astute about character."

Henry, who had been nattering around his tent in search of something, popped his head out of the open flap. "Did someone call my name?"

I looked to Ma'am for courage. "It's just that . . . well, why did you recruit such an awful man as Heinrek?"

"*Recruit* him?" Henry bent his head slightly, as though puzzled. "I didn't recruit him. He was here when I returned from gathering supplies. I thought one of you ladies had recruited him."

Alarmed now, both Ma'am and I stood. "You speak to the women out back," Ma'am said. "I'll speak to those inside the barn. Someone must know something about him and his arrival."

For the next hour, we interrogated all of the women, but none admitted to knowing where the second-generation German had come from.

I snapped my fingers. "Jax! Where is he?" I demanded.

"He's up at the Langlois' house running an errand."

"The Langlois'?" I peered up at the farmhouse, quite large by most standards. I'd had yet to meet them, though Henry and Thomas held the pair in great esteem. It did seem high time I introduced myself.

I nodded my thanks and had Gertrude run to tell Ma'am of my intended trek to the main house and the reason. Then I tottered off, feeling out of my element

When I arrived on the doorstep, no sooner had I knocked than the door opened to a large strapping woman I could only presume to be Ms. Langlois. A head taller than me, she had snowflake-blonde braids that wrapped 'round her head. And she wore a dress and apron--a dirndl--that reminded me of something one might wear in the Swiss alps. And indeed, she was of Swedish descent, I soon learned, her husband of French stock. How they had met, I had no idea, but I felt certain the woman planned to tell me, as she never stopped talking from the time she bid me to enter.

"My name's Ingrid," she said, not a blemish on her face. "Sit, here, ya?"

She pointed to a wooden rocking chair next to the fire, the entire room done in knotty pine. The chair was so low to the ground that it must surely be a child's chair, but I avoided the subject, not wanting to offend her so soon into our visit, preferably not at all.

"So, I finally get to meet the woman warrior. Everyone is talking about you, no?"

"Me?" I squeaked, unaccustomed to being the center of attention. For years, I had lived in a household where children were to be seen and not heard, only to be demoted to scullery maid where again, our voices were to be kept to a mere whisper most days.

Ingrid frowned, appraising me from all sides. "I think you big woman, not . . ." Here, she giggled, her cheeks twin apples on her rosy cheeks. ". . . tiny." To avoid my probing gaze, she bowed her head.

I suppose I *was* tiny by her standards. But I had a hard time concentrating on what came next as the most savory, aromatic smells came bubbling up from the cauldron over the hearth. A caramelized mix of lamb and potatoes, carrots and fresh onions.

When Ingrid realized how absorbed I'd been with the stew, she laughed as though it was part of her very nature, and flounced over to the cupboards, if they could be called that. Rather thick plank shelves hung on each side of the window above the kitchen sink, the window a view to the pasture beyond—to the cows and the dairy. She pulled a heavy crock bowl from its place on the shelf and drew a ladle out of a drawer. Then she set about filling the bowl with stew. Afterward, she brought me some cheese made fresh from the farm, and I do believe it was the best cheese I'd ever had the privilege to taste. I was so wrapped up in this blessed introduction that I'd completely forgotten why I'd come.

When I finished eating, I wiped my mouth with the cloth napkin she'd brought and set the bowl and saucer onto a small wooden table made of an indeterminate wood, possibly maple, though that smell could be coming from anywhere in the room.

"I actually came here to find Jax. Have you seen him?"

"Ya! He's with my husband, Bernard. That young Jax fellow, he is good with the animals, no? He is helping milk the cows now since our young dairy man went missing during the storm."

"Oh!" I gasped, her answer having caught me unaware. So many had been impacted by Alaric and his men. I took her hand in mine and felt the callouses from a lifetime of hard work. "I see. I came to ask Jax about a man who was among us, a Heinrek."

Before I'd scarcely uttered the words, she tsked, her normal good cheer driven away like the wind before a storm. Even her eyes seemed more hooded, as though the very thought of the man had her guarded and ready to seek refuge from the danger that seemed to hover over the man like a swarm of hungry locusts.

She leaned forward and spoke in hushed tones. "That man is evil. Alaric is bad enough, but Heinrek draws human insects to him like the dead flesh of a badger." She shook her head as if to be free of the man and the image he produced.

"Heinrek showed up at our camp. No one knows how he got there."

Ingrid peered around as though the walls had ears, and I had to admit, I was beginning to think that perhaps Alaric had some special skill to magnify our voices, to sniff out anything that might smack of dissent to his tyrannical rule. And yet, he was not our ruler. That was the rub of it. But he wanted to be. To let that happen would be to nail our own coffins, for we surely couldn't survive a man such as he.

"Do not trust him," she hissed. "And whatever you do, place

a guard around the camp. For your sakes, *and* for ours." She raised a single brow and leaned away, her expression once again placid, her face registering nothing of what we had spoken about only seconds before.

A chill settled over me. I intended to heed her words. I thanked her for her hospitality and rose to leave. "One thing--" I said, taking one last look around at the small but sturdy room with its blue-and-white gingham curtains and a checkerboard throw rug. "The trapper has returned--" I started to say from days of debauchery, but held my tongue, instead saying, "--and tells us we must leave soon or the pass will close before we can return."

"Do you really want to go?" Ingrid pleaded. "Why not stay here, where it's safe."

How I wished it were possible, but I had seen the evidence of what could happen should we merely hope that Alaric went quietly away. "None of us is safe," I said, conveying my sorrow with my eyes. "As long as Alaric is out there, determined to control us and our kingdom, we will never be free to pursue our lives as we have before."

"But why you?" She ran her eyes across me as though determining if I were fit for the job, the sacrifice. "Surely there are others--stronger . . ."

"More qualified?" I added.

She closed her eyes, nodding reluctantly before opening them again.

I thought of all the reasons that I should step down. All the reasons I should sit back, let someone else reach for the brass ring. And yet if not me, who? If not these women, who surely had the most at stake--who had almost no representation for their hopes, their dreams, their livelihoods--if they could not do it, who could? I recounted the many battles I had been made to memorize as a child, and what struck me most, looking back, was not the might of the battle. No, what struck me most was how many Davids had smote their own particular Goliaths. Had succeeded against all odds. Had brought down the mighty, corrupt, power-hungry leaders. And few of those women. And those who hadn't? I shuddered at their personal histories.

Finally, I peered at Ingrid, who I was quickly coming to regard as a sister, and said, "Because I must."

In her pale blue eyes that so matched my own, I saw my family, uprooted and tossed to the four winds. Each cast about by a system braced in corruption and greed--a greed that had left my family without means. How many like me had lost everything as a small band grew richer, amassed more power? Soon, we would be like the countries we had escaped, we of the great melting pot--America. Divided by religion, race, sex, politics. No, I would not go back to the poorhouses of Ireland, to be like the *dalit*--the untouchables--of India, or forced into slavery that had begun with the very founding of our nation. Nor would I go back to being merely chattel to men, unable to teach once married, unable to seek loans, to own property. We *were* the property.

Ingrid seemed to understand the shift that had taken place inside me. She paused, then held up a single finger. "*Vait*. I have something for ya."

She toddled off into the other room with the clickety-clack of wooden clogs, her socks knitted in bold stripes of color: fire-engine red, canary yellow, cerulean blue. Moments later, she returned with a small leather pouch. From that pouch she plucked out six coins, all Morgan silver dollars. I gasped, for this no doubt accounted for a tenth of her and her husband's yearly income.

"This is my yearly tithe," she explained. When I tried to protest, she threw up her hands. "I think *Got* will understand. And Brigid . . ."

"Yes, Ingrid?"

Ingrid peered toward the door, her voice lowering to a whisper. "I have sent word."

"Word to whom?" I said, not catching her meaning.

"My people. The Martins. They live on the outskirts of Alaric's fortress. I have told them of your plight. They are preparing ahead for you. They will give you shelter and food through the winter . . . if you make it through the pass."

Her words lingered, an unspoken acknowledgement of the sheer lunacy of the plan. *My* plan. My breathing grew shallow, the fire roasting me now, as if in agreement. She nodded toward the six coins, which I attempted to return to her.

"What you're doing is for all of us, ya? Now go."

She shooed me toward the door, refusing to listen to any further protest. More grateful than I could ever say, I hugged her tightly, then I eased out the door, the coins jingling in my pocket.

The first hail of the season had fallen, peppering the ground in a hoary white coating. By the end of the month, the pass would be closed and any worry that the female army might breach Alaric's defenses, gone, for this year at least. Alaric removed his gloves and puffed warm air into his frozen hands. He had ridden out to the valley below to watch the men go through their maneuvers, their black leather breastplates intact. The ribbed contours of the breastplates reminded Alaric of the underbelly of the black racer snake that lived in wooded thickets and ate rodents and small amphibians.

"Sir," Siegfried said as he rode up beside Alaric on a small mount no bigger than a pony.

"Eh?" Alaric said, making a show of putting his gloves on, finger by finger. When he was done, he turned to the man, giving him his full attention. To his surprise, Siegfried had brought someone with him. He hoped his adjutant had scrutinized the man carefully or it would mean his hide.

"M-Mr. Heinrek would like to speak with you." The adjutant quavered, hands kneading the reins of his pony.

"Oh?" Alaric inspected this Heinrek fellow, his greasy brown locks, his grizzled appearance and yellowed teeth.

What could Alaric possibly have in common with such a man? As if to lend credence to his theory, the man hawked phlegm onto the ground below, causing Alaric's mount to lift its legs and take a step back. Alaric narrowed his eyes.

"You have exactly five seconds to speak or I will have my guard take you away in chains," he hissed through gritted teeth.

"I know where them women warriors are located."

Alaric's horse whinnied and threw his head back, forcing Alaric to dig in his heels to remain mounted. "How?" Alaric demanded. "How do you know?"

The man paused just long enough for Alaric to raise his riding crop just slightly. But it was enough to spur the man on.

"Because I was inside her camp." The self-satisfied smile

sent a wave of anger coursing through Alaric, a thrill of discovery riding on its wake.

"Inside her camp you say. A spy?" Before Heinrek could answer, he yelled to his second. "Keep an eye on the maneuvers."

"But--" his second started to protest.

"But nothing, just do as I say." Then Alaric kicked his horse and took off at a gallop. When no one followed, he yelled. "What are you waiting for? Come along!" Together the three rode off to the fortress to form new plans.

Henry had spent the day in town gathering cold weather gear for the trek ahead. Something about this venture smacked of failure, impending doom. To race the winter storms was foolish at best. Had they left earlier, they still would have faced the uncertainty of the weather, unpredictable in the best of times. Now, they had little chance of outrunning it. Why had the trapper not urged Brigid to leave sooner, Henry wondered, though knowing Brigid, the stubborn woman, the trapper probably had informed her as much and she had balked. He slapped the reins of his buckboard. The wagon bucked and rolled amid the ever muddy ruts that caused his wheels to dip only to spring back up when they met a dry spot or a large stone. It would be slow going through the mountains. He slapped harder at the reins, determined to speak to Brigid before it was too late.

When he arrived at the farmstead, Henry discovered that Thomas had somehow commandeered a dozen or more prairie schooners, which some of the women were filling with bedding and supplies. Unlike the Conestoga wagon, the prairie schooners were smaller and more versatile, better suited for mountains like the Adirondacks. They also required fewer oxen to pull them. The only downside was that they slept a mere four adults, unless the women could rig up hammocks to accommodate more.

"Have you seen Brigid?" Henry called to Thomas.

Thomas lifted his chin and pointed to some vague spot over his shoulder. Sure enough, there stood Brigid, all five-feet seven of her, giving instructions to some of the women, who left at a run.

Before she could take off in a new direction, Henry whistled to get her attention. She paused, frowning, hands on hips. Then she lifted her skirts and made a beeline toward him.

"Excuse us," Henry said to Thomas, but his brother had already moved onto some other task. Henry ran to meet Brigid. Funny how a mere day had passed since he'd last laid eyes on her, yet viewing her anew he couldn't help but be struck by the icy cavern of her eyes that lit with a golden glow from within. In all his life, he'd never seen a woman with this unique characteristic. It lent her an intensity that was both disconcerting and magnetic, all at once. He couldn't help but be drawn to them . . . to her.

"Henry . . . Brigid." They spoke in unison.

"You first," Brigid said.

He chose to launch right in. "We can't go in fall. This is too dangerous. We are putting everyone at risk. No way will we be able to make it through the passes in time. Even if we did, we would have to face Alaric just before the beginning of the snowy season, with no place to stay, no food to hold us through the winter." To his surprise, Brigid's mouth drew up in a bow, and her eyes held a hint of mirth. "What?" he demanded.

"I spoke to Ingrid today."

"*Ingrid?* What on earth for?" He blinked at the superciliousness of his questions.

"I went to speak to Jax . . . about Heinrek. But he was helping Ingrid's husband with the milking. So I ended up speaking with Ingrid instead. And Henry . . ." Here she produced six Morgan coins from her pocket.

Henry shook his head in wonderment. What an odd turn of events. "Where did you get those?"

"From Ingrid . . . for the cause. And you know what else?"

Henry shrugged his shoulders, unable to hazard a guess.

"She has people in the countryside surrounding Alaric's fortress. They despise him as much as we do. They have offered us food and lodging when we get there."

Henry read the excitement ringing in her voice, a surge of hope lifting him of his earlier fears. And yet . . . He'd had no time to complete his thought when suddenly a commotion rang out and the very air around him seemed to hum with anger mixed with excitement as word spread around the camp. But word of what? Henry and Brigid turned as one at the sound of Thomas's frantic shout.

"Quick!" Henry said, grabbing her hand.

Before she could protest, he yanked her along, threading his way to where his brother stood in the center of a crowd of women. "Back up!" Thomas cried, making way for Henry and Brigid.

"What is it?" Henry asked. "What has happened?"

Thomas's face had paled to the color of an uncooked pie crust and his chest was heaving as he tried to speak.

"A message was sent by carrier pigeon," he said, breathing hard, his words dripping with sadness. "Our people have decided to wave the white flag, to allow Alaric to become the new ruler." With that, Thomas ran his hands through his hair and growled, followed by anguished cries that halted all other sound.

Henry felt as though he'd been pummeled. He rocked back on his heels and would have plopped down on the ground had there not been such a crush of people as to make that impossible.

"Henry," Brigid cried. "We can't give up. Not now. Not when we've worked so hard. I won't have it!" She stomped her foot. "*We* won't have it!" she cried to the women around her, her tone so flush with strength and assurance that a sliver of renewed hope rebounded through him.

Still . . . Henry turned to her and snatched up her hands in his. "We have no choice. It is done." He tilted his head in sorrow, but she refused to give in to despair.

She pushed him away and stood taller, if at all possible. "We will not cave!" she shouted, her voice rich with promise. "We will save our kingdom. I've promised the loom, and I will *not* go back on my word."

A cry erupted and fists shot up as one as a cry rang out. "For the cause!"

Excitement zinged through the air, a current all its own. "We will fight!" one woman shouted. "We will protect our people!" another agreed. "Liberty!"

The women repeated the word in a shout. "Liberty!"

To that, Brigid added, "And to freedom!"

"To freedom."

The ground fairly shifted from the weight of what they were

about to do. Henry wished he could be so optimistic. But he had seen what Alaric could do. He knew the danger they faced, but he didn't want to dampen the women's enthusiasm. "To freedom!" he shouted.

If only it were so.

21

I sent a notice to the Bookbinders and Sir Roger and Lady Penelope, signed by me, Henry, Thomas, and even Emma, who had been quaking in her boots ever since she'd learned of my intent. The message had gone by the same carrier pigeon. Together we stood in the clearing as the pigeon was lifted into the air. With trepidation, we watched him go. Once the pigeon disappeared over the forested area, each in turn sighed, as though releasing the tension we all felt.

"What will your parents do when they read it?" I asked, the question aimed as much at Thomas as it had been at Henry.

Both men peered at each other, followed by an uncomfortable silence, neither wanting to be the first to speak, it would appear. Finally, Henry gave into the interlude saying, "We have never disobeyed them about anything."

"Ever," Thomas added, as if to clarify Henry's meaning.

"Never?" I asked, Emma echoing me.

"Never," the men said in unison.

"Not even as teenagers?" I demanded, incredulous by their assertion that they had been angels their entire lives, nary a misdeed of any kind.

They paused for no more than a second when Thomas said, "Well, there was that one time you threw a dirt bomb at me right before we were scheduled to attend a dance at the Morrison's manor."

"Well, at least I didn't pour water off the turret over Aunt Seymore and Uncle Sedgewick. Father grounded you for a week over that one."

For the next fifteen minutes, the pair regaled me and Emma of their misdeeds, which were growing more legendary by the moment. So much for angelic children, I thought with a smirk.

"Okay, boys, time to pack. We have an army of women to move quickly if we're to make it to the other side before the pass freezes over."

That sobered everyone. One by one, we picked our way back toward camp, only to halt when a swath of humanity, as far as the eye could see, appeared over the horizon. I paused, frightened.

"Who are those people?" I whispered to Henry.

Lady Bookbinder heard rather than saw the pigeon as it fluttered through the window, then landed nearby as she helped the other women in the kitchen prepare the larder. They needed to be as stocked up as possible. After all, one never knew what the future would bring under Alaric's rule. When she caught sight of the pigeon, she shooed it into the other room, all the while muttering about sanitation and thoughtless pigeons. But when she saw what it was carrying around its neck, she called into Lord Bookbinder who was shuffling around in his study.

Though she knew she should wait for him, her worry mounted about what message the bird might have brought. Hands trembling, she reached over to the small metal container around its neck, surprised to discover that it was quite light in the palm of her hand. She unfastened it, and a tiny furled up paper fell into her palm just as Lord Bookbinder arrived in the doorway.

"What is it?" he demanded.

The writing was so tiny that Lady Bookbinder had to reach inside a drawer next to her knitting and hand-sewing basket to locate her magnifying glass that she used for those stitches too small for the naked eye, especially now that her eyes were aging. She studied the words, then peered up at Lord Bookbinder with a frown.

"What is it?" he asked yet again, his patience wearing thin.

Lady Bookbinder peered at him through round wire spectacles, her words escaping in a breathy sigh. "The women refuse to give up. They are on the march. In the meantime, they ask us to stay the course."

Lord Bookbinder flopped down into a chair, designed especially for him, one of two matching Karpen chairs complete with mahogany griffins framing either side of the cushions.

"You don't mean . . ."

"They plan to take the pass before winter."

Lord Bookbinder plowed hands through his hair, his brown

eyes wild with concern. "It would be suicide to march this late in the season. Even if the weather held and they met no obstacles, they could never arrive in time. They would have to move at a grueling pace." At that he stood. "I must go speak to them, talk them out of such foolishness."

"Sit down!" Lady Bookbinder urged. "You'll never make it in time to stop them. The only way is for us to send the blue falcon. He's fast . . . much faster than the carrier pigeon. I know Henry and Thomas will listen to you, but . . ."

"It's Brigid, isn't it? She has way too much grit for her own good."

Though he scowled, Lady Bookbinder detected a hint of respect for such determination in the young woman. Brigid took risks that few men or women were willing to take in these very strange times when everything they'd known had turned upside down, inside out. And yet they all stood to lose nearly everything if they didn't stand together. As her father's motto went, either they stood together or they fell apart. She peered at her husband, fearing what life would be like without him. He had been her rock, had carried her through many a storm. Now that Alaric had entered the equation, the storms seemed to come in multiples, amplified by his greed and hate. She bent down in front of the man she had loved all these years.

"We can't let Alaric rule the kingdom," she said, tears trembling on her lower eyelashes. "He will destroy it, destroy us. Don't you see?"

Lord Bookbinder sat unblinking, then finally bowed his head and nodded, a broken man.

"We have to try. To give it our all. For Henry. For Thomas.

For our unborn grandchildren."

His shoulders gave a shudder as he gave into the emotion that he'd held so tight since first announcing the cease fire. Relieved that he had finally released the festering emotion, she swept him up into her arms and together they made plans for the days ahead.

"Who are those people?" I repeated to Henry, who stood on the hillock next to Thomas and Emma, watching the growing contingent clamoring up the rise.

But before he would answer me, he lifted his spyglass from the leather strap at his side and held it to one eye, squinting with the other. He frowned, lowering it slightly, then lifting it to his eye once more. This time he ran the spyglass slowly over the entire entourage.

Worry claimed me as I tugged at his sleeve. "Henry, what is it?"

Henry gulped and exchanged a nervous glance with Thomas. "If I'm not mistaken, it's a band of many tribes. I recognize some Iroquois and Algonquins, by their dress, but I do believe it's a whole host of tribes from this area."

"Like who?" Emma asked, having grown up in the confines of Ma'am's manor.

"That's whom," Henry corrected.

"Who, whom, who cares? I just want to know who."

"Whom."

"Oh for goodness sakes," I said, ready to clobber the both of them. "We don't need a grammar lesson now. We need to know who is heading our way."

"It could be any number of tribes from the area: the Oneida, the Tonawanda, the Seneca, the Cayuga, even the Mohawk."

I shuddered at that last group, having grown up hearing harrowing accounts of violence, but when I told Henry that, he merely scoffed. "Those are old wive's tales."

But as they neared and he witnessed the red face painting of a Mohawk warrior, he gulped and paled, all in one measure. The brave wore a breechcloth with leggings and moccasins, his long black hair tied back and adorned with brightly dyed porcupine and deer hair as well as a splay of eagle feathers. I have to say, the warrior was more than a little impressive.

The tight phalanx of men, women and children entered the clearing and paused, the warrior at the center leaving the line while directing us to meet him in the middle of the clearing. He carried a staff bearing striped turkey feathers. He spoke in a mixture of what Henry explained was a form of the Iroquoian language with a smattering of English.

"What is he saying?" I whispered to Henry.

"How should I know?" he whispered in return, his pale face now forming two cherry-red circles at his cheeks.

"Hello," I ventured despite the fact that Henry assured me only the men should speak.

"Excuse me," said someone with a small voice.

I peered around, expecting someone my size. Instead, a tiny creature tugged on my sleeve, her wide brown eyes blinking up at me. "Who are you?" I asked, bending down to greet her.

"I am Kahwihta, daughter of Tier. He has asked me to tell you he has brought the Indian nations together to help you in your quest against their shared enemy, Al-oh-wick."

Though the girl struggled with the name, I knew who she meant. If we accepted this new group into our growing army, it would no longer be a women's army, and yet some men were already among us. As the community grew, so did the problems. The only way I could resolve them adequately would be to partner with the tribes who knew these woods, knew how to stay alive in winter.

Chief Tier must have recognized my dilemma because Kahwihta translated his next words. "We can guide you through the pass, keep you safe until we arrive at the fortress. Chief Tier says that the spirits are with you, that Mother Earth has granted you favor." She pointed toward the blue sky in explanation. "As a gift, we have made you moccasins." As if on cue, a woman from among the warriors stepped forward, moccasins in hand.

"What do you think, Henry?" I whispered, my eyes trained on the young woman and her gift.

"I think we need all the help we can get," he whispered back.

But since there were four of us, I asked the same of Emma and Thomas. Both readily agreed that we could use the help.

"Thank you," I said to the woman, "and please thank your chief."

Henry nudged me.

"What?" I hissed.

"We need a gift. It's impolite not to give them something in return."

All four of us peered down to see what we might give them that would be of any value. I had my feather, but only one. Surely we weren't expected to give away our only totem? As I questioned

235

each in turn, one by one they shook their heads. I could see by the set of the Chief's face that I would offend him should I turn up empty-handed.

Just then, I saw a flutter of wings in the distance. Blue wings. "Is that–?

Before I could finish, Henry blurted, "It's the Blue Falcon."

"Phinney?" I cried, seeing a way out.

Sure enough, it was Phinney in the flesh. I let loose a small whoop that stirred the tribes, a rustle rumbling through them like wind through maple leaves. As Phinney landed, she lost a feather. It floated down in a zigzag motion that seemed to take forever before it landed in my hand. I handed it to Kahwihta, explaining that it was a rare feather meant as a gift to the chief. She handed it to him with great care, recounting what I had said. The chief paused for no more than a minute, then nodded his head and spoke in his native tongue, thanking me as it turned out.

For the next hour, the chief sat with us, and together we mapped out a plan. We agreed to camp out for one more night before we began our journey.

That night, I couldn't sleep. I tossed and turned, the moon cascading shadows onto the tent wall. All around me, I heard the stirrings of others who could not sleep, Henry included. In the wee hours of the morning, I heard him huff, then struggle with the ties on his tent before coming to sit by the dying embers. I joined him there. His eyelids were heavy, too heavy for someone about to set out on a weeks long journey, but I doubted that mine were any different.

"You okay?" I asked, reaching for his hand. He nodded even

as he remained silent. "Want to talk about it?"

He shook his head, but then changing his mind, apparently, he turned to me. "What did you think of the message my parents sent along with Phinney?" he asked.

I read the question in his eyes. "They were giving you their blessing, Henry. I think even they know we cannot sustain this type of rule for long. And I also think they realize that we cannot go back to bludgeoning each other to maintain order. There has to be a better way, Henry. These people don't deserve this. They've placed their trust in us. They could possibly die for us, so why hurt them? The best rulers are the benevolent rulers who see the good in their people and foster that. Shame and pain can never win out over kindness and cooperation. We have to retrain people to begin caring about each other again, Henry. I *know* we can do this."

It was clear he wanted to believe, wanted the shame and pain to end, but he had been raised as a coddling infant in the ways of it. He knew nothing else.

"What will replace it? When people do things they aren't supposed to? What then?"

I squeezed his hands between mine. "We work together as one to help teach them the proper ways." My thoughts turned to a teacher I'd known as a child. She had been able to tame even the wildest of children. "I once had a teacher who knew instinctively how to get children to cooperate."

"Yes, but children are different," Henry protested. "They're not mature yet."

"Really, Henry?" I squinched my eyes. "You don't see similarities between children and adults?"

He had to laugh. "Well, I suppose so."

I pressed him further. "The teacher who most helped the students didn't yell, didn't shame or ridicule. Didn't punish. She simply stopped what she was doing to focus on the child, all other students focusing their attention as well, until the student soon stopped. Then she would speak to them in a quiet way. Only total miscreants didn't respond positively, and those types are mostly in Alaric's camp anyway. Don't you see, Henry? We should at least try something different. This isn't working. It's only causing frustration, anger, and retaliation. Worse, it's creating a system of fear and mistrust. A system like that can't stand forever. It gives people like Alaric an opening, a way in. People will choose any evil in hope of a lesser one."

Henry lay his head on my shoulder. "I suppose you're right. I'm just afraid."

"Afraid of what?" I asked, leaning my head against his.

"Of everything. Of change. Of no change. Of Alaric and this entire quixotic quest."

I placed an arm around his shoulder and held him to me. Henry was a flawed creature, but then weren't we all? I listened to the spit and the crackle of the dying embers, basking in the warmth it provided, all the while scanning the night sky. There, I reveled in the myriad stars that twinkled in the vast universe, a rare falling star emblazoning the inky void. A peace settled over me. Tomorrow? Well, I would face that when it came.

22

We set out at dawn, the first hint of the fall chill settling into our very bones. Overnight, it seemed, the common wood sorrel and Canadian mayflower had given way to red maple and orange sugar maple along with the yellow birch and big-toothed aspen, all adding to an array of magnificent color.

Most of the women chose to either walk or ride horseback. As we left the village, the townsfolk gave us a sendoff, many women directing their children to offer us stores of food, blankets, leather gloves with wool lining, anything they thought of use to a struggling army. Whereas the men had prepared weapons that they reluctantly gave us—for the cause. We thanked them profusely.

The Native contingent had gone ahead to scout the way, leaving a grouping of women and children behind to guide our less experienced contingent. Henry had been pensive since our talk from the previous night. I rode up beside him on an appaloosa that the stable master had offered up as yet another gift for our ragtag army. Though Henry's eyelids still drooped, the excitement of setting out on an adventure had given him a second wind and he seemed almost dashing on his mount, his eyes now alive with the unknown.

We were so caught up in the thrall of our forward march that I had all but forgotten Alaric and the damage he might wreck, if he knew we were in route to his lair. For now, we drank in the breathtaking beauty of the landscape as we exited town, the blue skies, the tall firs and fall foliage. The area north of us was known for its many lakes and waterfalls, an area clearly not meant for wagons, as we were soon to discover. As we marched along, single file, I wondered why the trapper had failed to forewarn us, or the chief, for that matter. But perhaps he didn't want to overstep his bounds until he got to know us well enough to explain how simple an idea our caravan had been. Perhaps this is why they went ahead, on foot and by horse.

Fortunately, as we soon discovered, the Indians had formed centuries old hunting trails, that although not wide, were wide enough for the wagons to trundle their way through. Any narrow passages were soon cleared of vegetation and dug out to allow transit for the wagons.

We wound our way through forests and maples, through hills and valleys, remaining close to the river, wherever possible. Our first stop was a lake that from a distance was drawn in the shape of a heart. As I stood on a precipice, viewing it from above, I could see a vast swath of color surrounding the heart-shaped lake, breathtaking in its grandeur. For it's as if the gods had seen this place and granted it favor, pulling out all the stops, draping it in its finest glory. As such, we determined it a good place to rest our weary legs and to give the horses a chance to forage, Phinney too.

"It's lovely, is it not?" Henry said, taking a seat beside me and allowing his legs to dangle over the granite towers.

"It is," I had to agree. Since I'd set out into the wilderness, my thoughts kept returning to my family. Where were they? Were they alive? So much had happened in the interim since I'd last laid eyes on them. I longed to know how they were doing, to know if they were happy, content. Did they miss me? Think about me as I did them? I flopped down next to Henry. Not a day went by that my mind hadn't turned over every stone from the past, wondering how things might have been different. Wondering if I had somehow played an unwitting part in the way things had turned out. Each of us thrown to the four winds, mere wisps of dandelion seeds scattered in every direction.

"Henry?" I asked.

"Hmm?" he said, sucking on a piece of grass that he had found sprouted in among a small mound clinging to the basalt rocks overlooking the heart-shaped lake.

"Did you ever wonder where you went wrong?"

He frowned, as though unsure of my meaning.

"It's just that I never thought we'd end up here, chasing down a man who means us harm." I shrugged my shoulders, realizing that I wasn't making much sense. "See, I had this vision of what my life would be like when I grew up and I'm the *last* person I would have ever imagined fighting such a battle. And, well, I'm a pacifist at heart, Henry."

To my surprise, he said, "Me too, Brigid. I always thought I would one day grow up to be the next Master Gardener–"

"*You?*" I said, cocking my head.

"Either that or a Master Birder. Thomas was meant to take over the manor, being the oldest. *He* should have been the one leading the battle, not me. But it turns out that he doesn't have a head for that sort of thing . . . and Emma–"

I sat up straighter at the mention of my friend. "What about Emma?"

"Well, she adores Thomas. She's terrified something will happen to him, so she has made him promise that you and I will be the ones leading the charge."

I lifted a brow and giggled until I realized he was serious. "You and I?"

Henry shrugged. "It makes sense, really. Neither one of us ever wanted this. I imagined building my own manor, inviting all sorts of tradesmen in to help me. Mother and Father offered me a parcel of land on which to build."

"What sort of house would you have wanted?"

He leaned forward and tugged at a leather satchel at his side. He pulled out a small piece of canvas. On it was painted a castle of sorts, modeled after one "from the old country," according to Henry.

"See the turrets?" he said excitedly.

They were drawn in a slate blue, a golden hue lighting the front, giving it a soft glow. Hovering in the night sky just to the side of the castle was the largest moon I had ever seen, its peaks and valleys carved in relief.

"This is the Mont St. Michel from France. Do you like it?

Of course my castle would be small by comparison," he said, appearing shy suddenly, his cheeks a dusty rose.

"It's beautiful," I murmured, and I meant it.

"But Brigid," he said, frowning now.

"Hmm?"

He turned to lay on his back, looking up at me, allowing me to see his vulnerability for the first time since I'd met him.

"What if we never make it home, never get the chance to see our dreams come to life? What if this is it, forever?"

I knew what he meant. What if we died on the battlefield, our dreams dying with us, never having had the chance to grow old, to follow our hearts, to see to our dreams?

"I don't know, Henry," I said, taking his hand. "Most people never do get the chance to see their dreams fulfilled."

The loss hung large between us—the loss of our families, our hopes, our dreams. "I just know that I'm glad I found you," I said, giving his hand a squeeze.

He paused, as though thinking through what I had said. Then his expression turned more serious. "And I'm glad I found you."

Alaric drove the arrow home, hitting its intended target with a "th-wop"--the heart of a stag he had stuffed and mounted from one of his previous expeditions. All across the stone walls of his fortress, he'd had the village taxidermists working overtime to make sure that his walls were well filled with his hunting trophies. He stuffed every manner of animal from moose to owls, bears to beavers. Even a particularly spectacular specimen of a loon with its wings outspread as if prepared for flight. He growled with laughter at his latest conquest, which his craftsmen were even now preparing—an especially large wolf that he had been hunting for well near seven years. It had been allusive, head of its pack. Never go for second, when you could go for the top dog. He laughed at his own pun.

"Sir?' his squire said. "Is something funny?"

Alaric shoved him aside, as was his wont. Let it be known that *he* was top dog now. He had received the word by carrier pigeon before target practice. The good news had added an especially well-formed arc to his aim.

"We surrender," his squire had read. "Please inform us of the next move."

Now that he was through practicing his aim, it was time to return to the fort. Alaric had commanded the cooks to prepare a feast for this evening's celebration. He could already taste the plump mutton chops, the roasted beef smothered in succulent gravy. He licked his lips recalling last year's mincemeat pudding and the custardy pawpaw pecan pie imported from the south. Rubbing his hands together in anticipation, he prepared his mount and rode into the fort, a veritable entourage lighting his way.

The victor to his spoils, he thought with a churlish laugh.

But he had no sooner dismounted and removed his leather gloves, than he discovered Seigfried waiting for him, and as always, he seemed to be fairly swooning with what was undoubtedly bad news.

What now?

Alaric ground his teeth together as he waited for the man to spit it out. "Well?" he shouted, tired of the charade. "Get on with it! Why are you in such a lather?"

"Your grace," the man said, wringing his hands together in anticipation of Alaric's reaction. "We've received a new missive."

"Oh?" Alaric demanded, the hackles on his neck standing at attention.

"The message you received earlier?"

Alaric closed his eyes, the man trying his patience. As nothing seemed forthcoming, he snapped them open and lifted his glove to strike the man.

"It's just that the manor has sent word."

"Oh?"

"They have withdrawn their surrender, and our spies have it on good account that the women's army is on the move."

"They are, are they?" Alaric growled, his eyes narrowing. "And?"

"And they have grown. A few men and many women have joined the group. Also, an entire band of natives from numerous tribes. They are headed this way, through the narrow passage of the Adirondacks."

Blood pulsed in Alaric's veins at this new announcement. So, this sophomoric group of women thought they could best him and his men, seasoned warriors who understood the use of brutality as a means to an end. He chortled at the very idea, even as his blood seethed with fury.

"Wait here. I shall have the last laugh," he said.

"Yes, sire," the man said, clearly relieved to see Alaric go.

Alaric mounted his steed once again and turned its head

toward the main gate. He rode for a good half hour until he found just the spot from which to train his magic on the bands of women and natives headed his way–a granite mountain top that was his and his alone. From there, he could overlook the canyon below. He spoke an incantation, then lifted his hand in claw-like fashion, spinning it. As he did, sparks flamed from his fingertips and the winds began to grow. It was a foul wind, an evil wind that sent fingerling projections cascading into the valley below in a howl of discontent, curling tendrils cascading like water across an arid plain. It picked up speed, whispering as it went, hissing like a timber rattlesnake that was ready to strike. Alaric howled with it so that the sound became one large cacophony of noise. No one would be able to withstand the wind's power. And with that, he whipped his horse until it reared onto its back legs, only to come crashing down as he drove it ever onward toward victory.

23

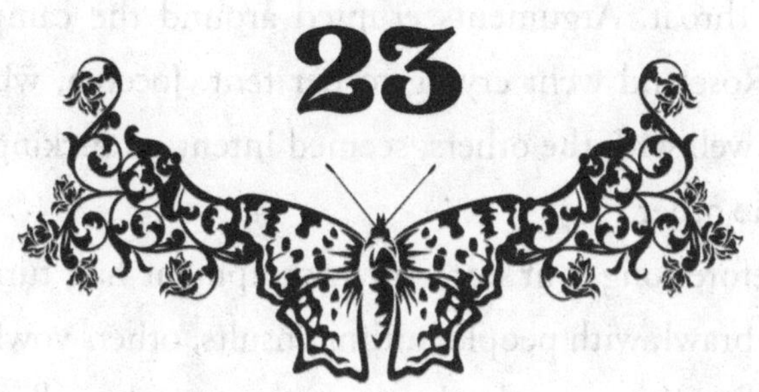

That evening, just before retiring to our tents, I sensed a shift. The wind grew balmy, but rather than settle us as it had on other occasions, it left each and every one of us with a feeling of unease. Conversation grew sparse. I heard the occasional grumble. Even Emma, who so often appeared cheery, was sullen and quiet. Unable to stand it further, I stood.

"I, for one, am going to bed," I announced.

As if the thought had been on everyone else's mind as well, the campfires were extinguished, except for a few, for those standing guard, or in case one of us couldn't sleep and needed a fire to warm us.

Within the hour, we were all tucked safely inside our tents, the sound of snoring lulling me into a fitful slumber. But as we lay sleeping, tendrils of wind tugged at our scalp like long scraggly fingers, teasing away the hair around our ears, whispering into the dark recesses of our brain. "She said . . ." "Did you know what so and so said about you?" "Why haven't you heard what she did?" "He thinks you're . . ."

Like a disease that floats upon the air, the whispered gossip woke us one by one, leaving us agitated, unable to sleep, the words a toxic brew of discontent. By morning, everyone was at each other's throat. Arguments erupted around the campfire. Kind, sweet Roseland went crying to her tent. Jocelyn, who normally got on well with the others, seemed intent on picking fights, one after the other.

Before long, our peaceful encampment had turned into an all-out brawl, with people hurling insults, others vowing revenge, and still others completely clueless as to what all the fuss was about and who had started it. The women began accusing one another of their motives. Words that earlier had seemed entirely innocuous were now dissected until they scarcely resembled the intended message. Soon, coffee pots clanked as they were thrust down onto the metal grates, plates slammed down so hard that if they were porcelain, they would have shattered into a thousand pieces. Even the oxen suffered as women shouted their misery at the poor beasts to do as told. But what chilled me to the very core was that most of the anger had been turned on me.

"You brought us here!" Winnifred cried, stamping her foot in a petulant manner unbefitting a female warrior. "If it weren't for you, I would be back home inside my barn with my inventions."

"And you never let me use the skills you promised," Yesimeh scowled.

Though we'd had scant use for fish intestines at the current moment, I groused, but fortunately kept my thoughts to myself.

Even Ma'am, who'd been my wise advisor in all this, gave an unfortunate grunt, as though she too had issues with me.

Soon, the women were all speaking at once, the accusations so scurrilous and unfounded that I withered beneath the onslaught and sought to escape to my tent.

For the next several days, matters only grew worse. Each and every word I spoke was parsed and dissected until I scarcely recognized them as my own. Every move, every sound I uttered was placed under a microscope only to be hurled back at me with such force that I fairly cowered beneath the weight of it all. Sabotage seemed to be the order of the day. Articles of clothing suddenly went missing, food either disappeared or was mixed with something highly unpleasant tasting to the palate. A misplaced pot. It was all too much. And because of the constant infighting, the party of hunters and gatherers had refused to go on daily forays, fresh food a thing of the past. As such, we soon grew thin, frail, every day fraught with some unknown peril, pitfall. Even the chief and his people, who had the good fortune not to understand the whispered insults, seemed to sense that we had all gone mad. We were no longer fighting the unseen enemy. We were fighting each other. My nerves were so nearly shattered that I kept dropping things and alternately grousing and crying for no reason. Something had to give.

Fortunately, Henry took me aside one evening after an exceptionally long day. He could see that I was shriveling right before his very eyes, my skin sallow, chest bones protruding. And we had made such slim forward progress that we were doomed to spend the winter deep in the Adirondacks. I knew we could not last a winter. Tears pooled in the corner of my eyes as I packed ahead for yet another day on the trail.

"Brigid, you have to get a hold of yourself," he said, taking me by the shoulders and shaking me gently.

"I know," I agreed, unable to look him in the eye. As each day passed, I heard so many angry whispers directed at me, some so perverse that I hardly recognized this person I had become in their eyes. As a result, I had become skittish of anyone looking my way. I had nothing but good intentions toward my friends and family. Yet in their mouths, I was evil incarnate. How? How had it come to this? Over the past week I had completely lost confidence in myself.

"Look at me, Brigid."

Henry refused to continue until I made eye contact.

"I know you, Brigid. You're a good person, a kind person. This is not them speaking. This is all Alaric's doing." He released me, anger flashing in his steely brown eyes. "He wants us at each other's throats. Divide and conquer, isn't that right? So long as he has us fighting each other, we'll be distracted. Lose sight of the goal. Then he has us." He flung his hands into the air, running his fingers through his hair before reaching out to implore me to see reason. "He is *lying*. Lying about you, about me, about everyone. Before he's done with us, he will have turned us all into murderers and thieves. That's what liars do. He's out to destroy us."

His words seeped into me like spring rain against the parched earth. How I needed to hear those words. For days I had gone over every word, every intention, wondering if there was any truth to the women's words, any truth at all–wondering if perhaps somewhere deep inside of me I had meant something perverse or unkind. I was so mixed up that I began to ponder my own existence. Had my family ever loved me? Perhaps they had sent me away on purpose, for not being the perfect child, for not being obsequious enough—the proverbial child who was to be seen but not heard. My ego had taken a bruising over the past week, so much so that I wondered if it was worth continuing. Perhaps I had been foolish to set about on such a journey as this. Me, a woman. *Nothing.* That is what I had come to believe about myself. That I had no value. Not here, not in society, perhaps not even in my family.

But dear, sweet Henry captured me in his arms and, as though understanding how deeply wounded I was becoming, said, "You have to believe in yourself, Brigid. You aren't those things they are saying about you. I have seen inside you. I *know* you. You're a good person and you *are* doing the right thing."

"Do you think so?" I said, fighting back a catch in my throat. I felt small, suddenly, as though indeed I had shrunk, not only in weight but in size.

"I know so." He gazed deep into my eyes, and for the first time I realized he didn't see my extraordinary eyes as different anymore. He saw only me. "But Brigid," he said, cupping my shoulders and giving me a gentle kiss on the forehead. "You have to make *them* believe as well." He pointed toward the opening of my tent, where even now women were bickering over who should stand guard, who should keep the fires burning. I decided then and there that I would have a talk with them in the morning. Set the record straight. But life has a way of destroying the best laid plans because by morning, the snow began to fall. The earliest snowfall in the history of the Adirondacks. I couldn't help but wonder if Alaric had a hand in this too. By afternoon, my boots developed holes and water and snow seeped in, filling my boots. Worse yet, the trapper had disappeared and it was feared he'd escaped into the night never to return, seeing an army of women as a poor bet. Thankfully, we had the tribes or we would have been lost indeed.

"What do we do now?" I mewled to Emma and Thomas, Ma'am and Henry, as we wedged around the fire, snow falling in swathes and covering my parka.

"First, we get you out of those boots," Ma'am stated firmly. "Emma, do you have a spare?"

Emma merely shook her head. Kahwihta, the daughter of Chief Tier, who for the first time joined us at the fires, took one look at me and pointed to her knee-length moccasins, fur-lined and covered in bear's grease to keep out the rain, snow, and cold. Though she had offered up a few as a gift prior to this, I had handed them off to the most needy of women, knowing that it would be the height of selfishness to keep them for myself. Seeing this, she stood and made a beeline for her encampment. She returned ten minutes later with a set similar to hers. Their clothing was clearly much more functional for winters spent outside in Upstate New York than ours. She must have realized it too.

"We have ex-tra cloth-ing," she said in the affectation of her language. "Not enough for everyone, but for some."

Some would be better than none. But we must find a way for all the women to receive proper clothing or we would have another mutiny on our hands. "Is there any way we could get more . . . from the tribes?"

She paused, her silky black hair mostly hidden behind her. "We could send for some deerskin tunics and furs, but it would take days."

Everything I had hoped for in this journey seemed to be unraveling. We didn't have time to linger, and yet we couldn't move without the proper equipment. I thanked her. After a quick head count, she left, returning an hour later with any spare clothing she was able to muster. Now for the unenviable task ahead. I called the entire group together. Chief Tier allowed us to use his large central teepee so that I could speak with the leaders of each group first before speaking to the rest, who were gathering outside. We sat cross-legged, filling the teepee to the brim. I quickly explained the situation. After some back and forth, we'd formed a consensus.

For his part, Henry had managed to roll a small boulder to a place just east of the Council fire. Once we had decided on our next course of action, the leaders and I exited the tent, whereupon I stood on the boulder, waiting for the murmurs of the women and few men to subside.

"Chief Tier and his daughter have been kind enough to offer us any spare clothing available. Emma, Henry, and Thomas will come around with a bucket filled with scraps of paper. Then we will pick numbers from the bucket. Anyone who would like a chance at the clothing can draw."

That said, the trio hurried through the encampment. Some turned down a chance to win, but most drew a number. When anyone who wanted one had chosen, I began drawing numbers. Yesimeh won the first draw. Gertrude won the second. The drawing continued until all the deer and elk-skinned dresses and moccasins were gone, Emma receiving a beautiful leather tunic given to her by Kahwihta herself as thanks for foregoing the drawing to give to others. Hers was unique, the top row of the tinkling bells looking for all the world like miniature drums. I admired them, but soon turned back to the task at hand.

To the rest of the assembly, I said, "The Mohawks and other tribes will bring us more leather tunics but it may take a few days."

When the next wave of murmurs had subsided, I called everyone to silence. "I have another matter to address," I said, steeling my courage with Henry's help. "I've noticed a lot of . . . infighting."

The women's eyes grew large as they turned to each other in sheepish acknowledgment of what I'd said. A smattering of nervous giggles ensued.

"Don't you see?" I implored them, gazing at each of them in turn. "This is Alaric's doing. The wind, the whispers . . . the lies. They are meant to keep us apart, to spend so much time attacking each other that we no longer fight the enemy. Is that what you want?"

I could see that the women weren't fully onboard yet, old grudges dying hard. "If we turn on each other, what do we have left? We stand to lose *everything*. Is that what you want? To be subjugated by a man like him who wants nothing more than to take every last freedom we possess? To starve, beat and pillage us to death?"

The tide had shifted slightly, and I heard a smattering of agreement among those in the crowd. *He stole our home. They came in the night, beat my mother, my sister, my brother. They absconded with every drop of grain in the silo. Not enough left for a mouse. They forced my father to become one of them or they would kill every member of our family.* That last voice was filled with tears. Soon, everyone had a tale of woe, each more hideous than the previous one. Relief flooded me followed by a wave of gratitude. They remembered. Remembered why they were here. Remembered what was at stake. Once again, we were back on track. I heaved a sigh of relief and mouthed a *thank-you* to Henry.

Now, to keep Alaric's black magic from reaching our ears in the future. Fortunately, I had come up with the idea of moss shortly after the whispering wind had first started. The tribes had agreed to hang it over a fire on drying racks while they waited out the storm. Then they had rolled the moss into small balls, small enough to stuff into the ear canal so that the winds could no longer confer damage on the women of our newly formed tribe. Emma, Henry, and Thomas once again passed the hat, so to speak, encouraging everyone to "close their ears" to the foul wind that had come our way. And just like that, I could see relief reflected in their expressions, which had appeared strained for days. Now, to find a way to communicate between ourselves. But that was for another day. Today, it was enough that we had found peace.

Already news of the early snow had traveled within the fortress walls, their dark, foreboding towers lending an almost Medieval quality to the surrounding area. Moments later, Siegfried brought Alaric the news. "The winds have subsided, sir, replaced by snow."

Alaric knew that already, but who had ordered it?

Standing beside his Friesian, Alaric stomped his boots of the white flakes, while encased in a warm ermine mid-length coat, the soft reddish fur lining the interior. Beside him, seated upon his pony, the equine ancestor of the one he'd brought with him from Mongolia, was the Kazakh his father had employed many moons ago. He was dressed in falconry gear that consisted of a warm wool-lined jacket with a hat bearing a rectangle brim made of red fox fur that draped the man's shoulders, the red crown of his hat done in felt. For an elderly man, the Kazakh was still quite spry, as attested to by the fact that he could lift a fifteen pound male golden eagle into the air with a single launch.

Alaric and the Kazakh had been hunting for nearly two hours. Already, they had bagged a snow-shoe hare, a marmot, and a gray fox. Alaric should have felt vindicated. Instead, he'd clamped his jaw together so many times his teeth hurt. All morning, he had felt unsettled, so much so that he had asked the alchemist to draw him up an herbal remedy. Something with valerian in it to calm his nerves. Yet still he champed at the bit.

"Sir?" Siegfried said, waiting.

"I heard you," Alaric growled. "I assume you have more news."

"Sir. The women have taken to stuffing moss in their ears."

"Moss?" Alaric countered.

"So that they will not be troubled by the whispering wind."

Fury rose from the very bottom of Alaric's toes to the tip of his tongue so quickly that he had no time to circumvent it, instead letting loose such a loud venomous rant that it unsettled the eagle and sent him scrambling before the Kazakh had time to quell its unease. The eagle flapped with such desperate need to escape that it nearly upended the Kazakh from his horse, while the talons of the bird nicked his chin, drawing a bead of blood that stained the black and white whiskers of his paltry beard. Fire danced in the Mongol's eyes, or perhaps it was a trick of the light flowing off the eagle's wings, for it seemed real enough. Alaric forgot his fury, apologizing quickly and obsequiously, the Kazakh having a reputation for ruthlessness when offended. The man said nothing, but his jaw clenched and unclenched. After some moments, the man bowed his head ever so slightly to let Alaric know that he had forgiven him. But he would not forget.

A chill traveled through Alaric's cold limbs as he thought of some way to ameliorate the man's wrath. *A gift.* He would search for a falcon . . . a rare *blue* falcon that the Kazakh so coveted, having only heard of but not seen such a beast. The idea calmed his racing heart. Now he just needed to find one before the man ordered Alaric's eyes pecked out the way he had the other man who had crossed him. But where? Where could he find a blue falcon?

24

With all that had happened over the past several days, I had neglected poor Phinney. I held her to me now and cooed, glad to have reunited with the aristocratic blue bird. In return, she pecked at my ear as though she would find a card there and perform a magic trick. Probably just preening as she would in the wild, seeking insects in among the other poor bird's feathers, but I had none to give her. Instead, I held out a sunflower seed, to mollify her. She took it in her beak, the greedy girl, quickly shedding the shell before downing it, then moved on to sit upon the tent, which was packed up and ready to move along with those in the rest of the camp. Emma strode over, her things long packed and ready with Thomas's help.

"It seems rather unfair that you have no real winter clothes," Emma said, dressed in the clothing given to us by the Indians. "Here you are leading us."

I shrugged my shoulders. No use complaining about what I could not change without further damaging my relationship with the other women who had struggled under similar hardships.

"I saw you shoveling the snow off your tent. Most women in your position would have asked for help." Her cheeks turned a light shade of crimson, and she bowed her head because she had asked Thomas to help her with her tent.

"Don't feel bad, Emma. You're lucky to have one such as Thomas to help you. He really is smitten, is he not?"

A shy smile lit up her face whenever anyone spoke of Thomas, and now was no exception.

"Has he asked you to marry him?" I asked, ducking down to meet her eyes.

Emma lurched backwards as though I had spoken of some hitherto agreed upon secret. "Of course not," she said, her green eyes widening, her auburn hair falling in ringlets around her doe-skinned tunic. "Well, not yet, at least."

"Maybe when all of this is over," I assured her.

She bit at her lip, frowning.

"What?" I asked. "What is it?"

She fidgeted a moment longer before blurting out the question that must have been near to her heart. "What if it never ends? What then? What if this war . . . or whatever it is, goes on forever?"

I reached up and cupped her chin which quivered slightly. "Well, then. You just go on with it. You marry. You have children. You—"

"But what kind of life could that possibly be?" she demanded, pulling away, anger furrowing her brow and pinching her lips more tightly closed. "How could I have a husband, raise a child? What if something happened to either of them?" she said, a catch in her throat. "What then? I couldn't bear it."

Her words ended in a whisper, but not before I had heard the tears lingering there. "Oh, Emma. I do understand." More than she would ever know, as I too was falling for Henry, my beloved Henry who had seen me through hard times, who had bolstered me up when my spirits flagged, who stood beside me in good times and in bad. Over the past few days I had longed to confess my feelings, my love for him, for the kindness he had shown me. Despite having been raised in a time when women were mere chattel, over the course of the journey, Henry had come to see me as his equal. Though it hadn't always been so, he now invited me in as his confidante. And I cherished him for it.

There were no words to make things better for Emma . . . or for me, so we simply hugged and prepared for the day ahead. While we finished loading our supplies, Phinney made little squawking noises as she flew from tent to tent as though inspecting them to see that the packing had been done properly. We laughed at her antics, the silly bird. Soon enough, she was back on my shoulder. Fortunately, Conestra had made a leather perch by which to land so that Phinney's talons wouldn't sink into my shoulder and leave their marks.

Today, the women seemed lighter, as though they'd been weighed down by all the gossip and innuendo that the wind had spread and could suddenly float. For the first time in days, I heard laughter and teasing. And the women were working together again, helping each other instead of at each other's throats. It pleased me to witness it. Henry must have noted my lightened spirits because he put a finger to his lips to keep Phinney silent, then tapped me on the shoulder opposite the bird and cried, "Boo!"

"You, too?" I laughed, shaking my head just as Phinney flew up into the sky and began to chatter to the women dancing below her.

It felt good to laugh again after this past week. Even the heavens seemed to have conferred goodwill upon our gathering, for the sun shone through the clouds and the snow began to melt, my toes not as frozen as before. Still, we had a long way to go and many challenges ahead, but for now, I refused to worry, instead lifting my head to the sun and raking in the warmth.

I had removed the moss from my ears, and I noticed that Henry had as well. Say what they may, the winds could not harm me today. As if they knew it, they shrank from the sun, their fingerlings of filth receding with them. And it was odd, this wind, because unlike an ordinary wind it was visible yet translucent, like water on a sandbank flowing in rivulets, only now it was flowing the opposite direction. Almost as one, the other women saw it too and pulled the wads of moss from their ears. Soon, a shout arose, filled with relief and delight, followed by dancing and hugging, for we had been freed of the foul wind that had settled over our little colony. It was as if we could all breathe again, the strain of the past few days gone. But I knew the forces of evil could just as easily return. We needed to be vigilant. So far, Alaric had yet to attack us twice in the same way.

As if the sun had cued to my change in temperament, it hid behind a cloud, but not for long as the women's happiness outshined my fears, thank the heavens. Henry swept me up in his arms and twirled me around. Before I could grasp what had happened, he kissed me. A celebratory kiss at first, but it soon turned into a long lingering kiss that took my breath away. When he finally released me, we peered at each other shyly, unsure how to proceed. But the forces that had held us at bay for so long were unleashed, and soon we were kissing passionately, our mouths seeking sustenance from the other, our lips greedy for the feel of each other. If not for the excitement of the women to see the wind gone, we might not have gone so unnoticed, but for a brief window of time, our emotions lay unfettered, and for that I was truly grateful. But they say all good things must come to an end, and so it was with us.

I felt another tap on my shoulder and turned, still breathing heavily, my cheeks no doubt rosy with the lustiness of the moment. "Emma!" Then I saw the tears in her eyes. "What? What has happened?"

"Come quick, Brigid, Henry!" she shouted, grasping my hand and fairly pulling me to a spot higher up, to a granite boulder, Henry close on my heels. "There!" She pointed into the distance.

All I could see was a bird. It appeared to be attacking another bird. The second bird kept attempting to circle back, closer to where I stood. I squinted, trying to see what Emma was seeing. Then it came to me in a wave of nausea that bent me in two. Phinney. The bird was kidnapping Phinney, and they were headed north. Poor Phinney made a final attempt to elude capture. She managed to fall from the sky as though she'd been shot, her body fluttering closer and closer to the earth.

"Pull up, Phinney!" I pleaded, waiting with dread for the

inevitable plop as my bird hit the earth. But at the last moment, she drove upwards and barrelled my way in one last ditch effort to reach me. "C'mon, Phinney!" I begged, my hands balled in fists, both Emma and Henry at my side. The two soon joined in.

"You can do it, Phinney," they shouted, Emma jumping up and down, lips pursed, Henry holding an arm out for the bird to land despite the damage the talons might do to his arm.

But it wasn't to be. Mere moments before the blue falcon could reach our trio, the second bird, a falcon too, I soon discovered–a peregrine if memory served–reached out with its talons and clipped Phinney. Precious feathers flew like eider from a down pillow and Phinney squawked, a sound that conveyed both fury and fear.

"No!" I screamed.

By this time the women had stopped their dancing and were now peering up at the aerial display overhead, gasping and silent in turn. Thomas, seeing the problem, rushed to get a gun and handed it to Henry, but the birds were so intertwined that there was no way to separate one without hitting the other. We could do nothing but watch.

Before Phinney could escape again, the peregrine falcon herded her up to a higher current and dipped and folded into the stream, forcing the blue falcon ever further north. I could see that Phinney was growing tired. At last, she struggled no more. The last I saw her, she dipped her head in a final goodbye, then she disappeared behind a mountain, gone.

"Here he is, M'lord," Siegfried said, marching Alaric to the front of the enclosure where the bird was being kept in quarantine in the rear of the aviary until she could be released with the other birds. "Her name is Phinney, according to the Kazakh."

From inside the leather-covered cage, the blue falcon eyed him warily, unblinking. Alaric felt as though a snake had slithered up his spine, such was his abhorrence of the very birds by which he hunted. They were more suited to the likes of the Kazakh. Both had a predatory quality that unnerved Alaric.

"Ah, good, so the Kazakh has seen the bird."

"He has," Siegfried assured him.

That meant there would be no more worry that one of the raptors might peck Alaric's eyes out . . . or his heart. He'd overheard one of the Kazakh's handlers telling another that falconers were known to have a secret pact. If any harm should come to either the falconer or their birds, the remaining birds would hunt the evil doer down and tear them to shreds. He'd shivered at the words, even as he assured himself that this was just superstition. Still, to be on the safe side he always treated the Kazakh well. No use tempting fate, after all.

Alaric bent down and eyed the bird, who steadfastly ignored him as though he were a mere speck of a human. Too bad the bird looked so bedraggled, feathers missing on the right side of its body. She had a bloody spot near her neck where the peregrine had attacked her. Jinchuang ointment, a mixture of lard, frankincense, dragon's blood and a whole host of other ingredients, had been used to help the healing. Still, the bird shivered lightly as though struggling with shock.

"Don't let anything happen to that bird," Alaric warned,

pulling himself upright.

Siegfried paled slightly. "Yes, sir."

Alaric was about to leave when he turned back to Siegfried who stood vigil over the animal as though willing it well by the very power of his presence.

"Seigfried?"

"Yes, M'lord."

"How did the Kazakh know the name was Phinney?" he asked, his voice low, like the echo from a cavern deep within the bowels of the earth.

Siegfried's color turned from white to crimson in a matter of seconds, his cheeks aglow with splashes of color. "Well, because he was raised with them. Says he speaks their language."

"Hmm." Alaric scowled, something just on the edge of his consciousness calling to him, warning him. "But why Phinney? Do all birds come with names?"

Siegfried shrugged. "According to the Kazakh wild birds do not, only birds who belong to people have names."

A warning shot rang inside Alaric's brain as he realized the implications of what Seigfried had said. "So *who*, exactly, owned this Phinney?" Alaric demanded.

Siegfried peered around him, as if caught in a trap with no way out. "Well, sir . . ." He fidgeted, ringing his hands together. "It belonged to a girl named Brigid."

A slash of light flashed before Alaric's eyes followed by a darkness so deep and so profound that he feared he might topple like an old tree following an ice storm. Fortunately, he'd thought to bring his riding crop with him, his horse stabled nearby. He reached for it now, where he'd laid it on a rock, and used it to steady himself.

"Brigid, you say. And where is this *Bri-gid* now?" he said, drawing out the name with distaste.

"Why heading through the pass, sir. Along with a contingent of natives." Siegfried stared at Alaric as though he'd grown three heads.

How have I not known this about the bird?

A low growl formed at the back of his throat. Once again, he had been outsmarted by a *girl*. He would not let it happen again.

25

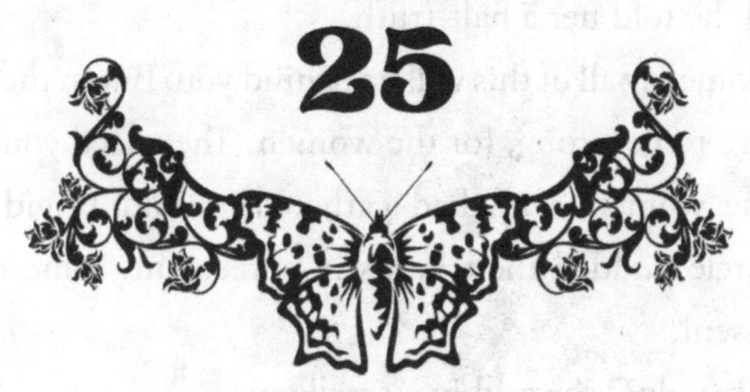

Brigid sat on the granite outcropping, her head on her knees and her hands covering her head. Henry could hear her weeping and longed to do something about it, but what? It's not as though he could grow wings and magically fly to find Phinney, rescue her and bring her back. Besides, he wouldn't know where to begin, what to do. He peered helplessly at Emma, who motioned for him to go to Brigid. He'd never had sisters and his brother never cried. He wrangled in a breath of fresh air before launching in. With unexpected resolve, he marched over to her and took a seat on the granite next to her. And still she buried her face in her hands, her shoulders heaving.

Henry leaned in and slowly drew her hands to him. Dark splotches surrounded her eyes. "Brigid, I know you're upset. I know it seems like nothing will ever get better, but it will, in time."

She shook her head then sniffed, peering up at him. "You think so?"

He wanted to tell her the truth, that this was the way of the world, only she was just now discovering it for herself. He longed to add that he wished it could be different, that life could be easy, that people could be kind, but that was not the way of things. Instead, he told her a half-truth.

"Someday all of this will be behind you. But in the meantime, you have to be strong, for the women. They need you."

The women, who had gathered around Brigid in a wide semi-circle nodded their heads in agreement, some murmuring their assent.

"They do?" she said in a small voice.

"Yes, Brigid, they do." And this was a whole truth, at least for most women. Some traded jealousy like candy, always stepping over other women to climb the ladder of success, only one brass ring available to women, and each woman competing for it, well at least those women who wanted it.

The women around him echoed his words. For the first time since Phinney's disappearance, Brigid lifted her head fully, and the women cheered.

"We'll find Phinney," Brigid said, her voice returning.

"Yes we will, won't we ladies?" Henry said.

The women assured them they would, all except for Gertrude. She had remained unusually silent during the entire ordeal. Even her sister Jocelyn seemed quieter today. Henry couldn't shake the idea that something was up, in that regard. He would make sure to keep an eye on them. In the meantime, he turned his attention back to Brigid whose color had returned and whose red, puffy eyes had begun to dry.

"Okay, ladies!" he called. "It's time to finish packing and head north. Who's ready?" Hands shot up everywhere. "Then let's go!" He helped Brigid up. Once all the women were gone to their separate quarters for last-minute preparation, Henry turned to Brigid. "I'll send a message to the Master Birder back home and ask her to send out a scout to find Phinney. In the meantime, we follow through with your plan."

Brigid ran an arm across her eyes one last time. "Thank you, Henry."

"What for?" he said, tipping his head slightly.

"For being you," she said, then giggled through tears.

It felt good to be back on my feet again, a little worse for wear, but definitely better. But poor Phinney. The odd thing is, when we set out on our journey that day, the women winding their way slowly up the mountainside, the weight inside the wagons shifting back and forth as if the contents might topple down the mountainside at any moment, I began to hear clacking. The sound was light at first, gaining speed as we walked. Finally, after hour upon hour of listening to it clack, I just had to see what the miniature loom was up to. I stepped out of the line and watched as a great sea of women and a few men marched 'round me like currents in a river rounding a fallen log. I knew better than to go against the flow, so instead I waited until the wagon with my loom caught up to me.

I whistled to gain Emma and the other driver's attention.

They slowed to give me time to reach them, then helped me up onto the buckboard, all the while, the impatient women behind swarmed on either side of the wagon, forcing us to move slowly so as not to crush them. Once I had caught my breath and was safely in tow, I climbed over the seat and into the back where my tiny loom lay anchored to the wheel well. I clung to one of the ropes that held the canvas bonnet in place as the wagon sashayed back and forth in an arrhythmic motion. With the other arm I reached for the loom. And there, in a tower was my precious bird . . . caged and forlorn.

"Phinney," I whispered, running my fingers across the strands of fiber as though I might make him magically reappear here, where he would be safe.

Despite the size of the tapestry, I could see that some of Phinney's feathers were missing, the others ruffled. Anger bubbled up inside me. Of course this was Alaric's doing. Why was I not surprised, but why Phinney? How had he even known about the blue falcon? I squinted, moving closer despite the jostling movement beneath my feet. That's when I noticed it . . . in the corner. A map! Of the fortress. For seconds, my heart stilled. I closed my eyes and spoke a prayer of gratitude. With a map, I could begin planning, begin searching for any chink in the armor of the fortified walls. For any advantage that I might find to throw the contest my way. And it was a contest of sorts. A contest for our very survival. A contest over who would lead, good or evil, darkness or light. I planned to be the light even to my last breath.

I let out a whoop of joy, realizing only too late that I had let go of the rope. For one brief second, I feared I might crash down onto the loom, but fortunately I was able to twist my body at the last moment and roll onto the floor, walloping my ribs against a barrel filled with eggs and cornmeal—the cornmeal placed around the eggs to keep them safe through the harsh travel. Without even feeling my ribs, I knew they were bruised as breathing proved difficult.

"Are you alright back there?" Emma called, concern in her voice.

Try as I might, I couldn't speak more than a squeak, and even that sent shards of pain riveting through me in waves so that I feared I might pass out. Of all the things that had happened to me, this was of my own doing. I ground my teeth together, angry at myself for being so foolish—better yet, careless.

"Emma!" I groaned, the best I could manage under the circumstances.

I felt, rather than heard, her rush toward me, falling onto her knees before the wagon had a chance to knock her off her feet as it had me. "Oh, for heaven's sake, Brigid. What have you done now?"

I had never seen her so exasperated with me. If it wouldn't hurt so much, I might have laughed, but one attempt was one too many for I scarcely opened my mouth for a mere giggle when the pain laid me out cold. I struggled to breathe, wishing that it were not a necessity at this exact point in my life, as the pain was almost too great to bear. But I would get past this as I had everything else in my life, I felt certain.

"Oh, Brigid," Emma said, as though I were the foolish child who once again had failed to listen to her mother's sage advice. "Why can't you be like the rest of us?"

"And . . . how is that . . . ex-act-ly?" I managed to say through gasps, small beads of sweat forming on my brow from the exertion.

"Normal," she said, then placed a hand over her mouth as though she might stuff the word back in her throat before it gained traction.

"Ah," I whispered.

So what was normal, precisely? Was normal causing other people pain if they didn't think and act as a single unit? Was normal stifling all emotion, bottling it up with a cork and shaking it until one exploded from the unspent feeling? What was normal? And if eschewing cruelty meant I was abnormal, then so be it.

For some reason, her words had brought me peace, as though it reminded me of my true self, the one not bound by petty, narrow rules . . . by conformity. I thought of all of mankind's inventions. Had those people given in to conformity, accepted things as they were, we might never have advanced as a people. Why, less than a century ago Frenchman J.M. Jacquard had developed the jacquard loom, and Thomas Newcomen had invented the steam engine in the early 1700's. One had only to view the Sistine Chapel and Leonardo da Vinci's portfolio of inventions to know that he was a nonconformist. For several seconds, I lay still on the floor, every bump an agony, every hoofbeat of the oxen feeling as though it were me instead of the ground lying beneath those hooves. I spied a bolt of cotton.

"Unfold it," I murmured through gritted teeth.

Emma did as asked.

"Wrap . . . it . . . around me."

She saw what I meant for her to do and lifted me with one arm as she struggled to place the wrap beneath me. For what seemed like an agonizingly long time, she wound and wound it around me until at last she tied it off, snipping it with a pair of scissors she found cinched to the side of the wagon.

"There," she said, inspecting her handiwork.

"Now help me up," I said, offering her my arm.

She eyed it warily, but did as asked. I tried to groan as little as possible, but I'm afraid I failed miserably. I could see the growing fear in her eyes, but finally I was able to sit up on my elbow.

"Now . . . all the way up." I spoke matter-of-factly to leave no doubt that I meant to stand.

In the end, we compromised. She lifted me to the bunk and laid a blanket over me. Then she gave me a draught of laudanum and assured me she would wake me should she need me.

I soon fell into a fretful slumber, where fortress walls beckoned me with a silky smooth voice meant to ensnare. Where Phinney pleaded for me to turn away from this godforsaken place before it was too late. But I would not heed her pleas, for I knew the alternative. Next time it would not only be Phinney inside that cage. It would be me. It would be Emma and Thomas and Henry. It would be all the people I loved, and I could not stand for it. No, I could no more walk away from those walls with the forbidding towers than I could go back to the life I had once lived, for it was the past and the past never comes but once in a lifetime.

26

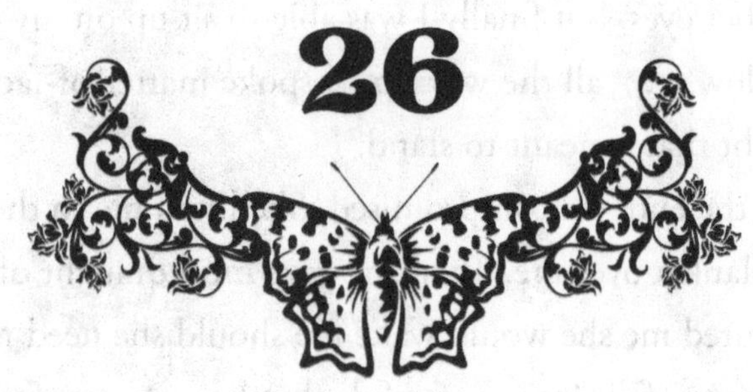

I had slept the sleep of the dead, but now that I was awake, I could feel every jarring bump of the road, every crevice, every nook and cranny as though I were lying directly on the road itself and being dragged across it. Tears hovered at the corners of my eyes, but I refused to give into them this time. Instead, I forced myself up onto my elbow and heaved a sigh. Then I sat all the way up, gauging my surroundings. I needed to pull myself upright, somehow walk to the head of the wagon and get off this wretched contraption. Easier said than done.

Outside, I could hear both Henry and Thomas alternately whistling to the oxen to keep them on course, and yelling directions to those among the wagon train. Did they know of my predicament? No doubt they were too preoccupied with keeping the train moving. After considerable wrangling, I managed to claw my way up front and to sit on the bench seat of the buckboard only long enough to plead for them to halt so that I could climb down.

"You shouldn't be out there walking in your condition," Emma said, wearing worry on her forehead like an old hat.

"No worse than being jostled to death," I said with a laugh, then immediately regretted it as I ground my teeth together in pain.

"Then I'm coming with you, to keep an eye on you." Emma called down to one of the women who was walking and had no trouble convincing her to trade places.

"Gladly," the other woman cried, helping me and Emma down, then leaping on despite her long dress.

Fortunately, like Emma, she was one of those who had received the allotment of fur-lined moccasins. We discovered that with so many of the women dressed like natives, we had begun to forget the differences between our groups and see the similarities instead. All doted on the children that the natives had brought along, including me. All helped in the chores, knowing that we each had a stake in our collective success.

Now that I was finally upright and on solid ground, I could breathe, if only marginally. However, I quickly found myself lagging behind, Emma having trouble matching her speed to mine. If she could have carried me, I knew she would. I just had to soldier on. We walked like that for mile after painful mile. Every joint in my body ached by the time we reached our dinner stop that night. A crescent moon hung in the sky bathed in a silvery-blue glow, twinkling stars dancing circles around the moon, whereas the mountains near Indian Pass were silhouetted against the sky giving it an ethereal quality that left me speechless.

How could so much beauty and so much pain be contained in one such space? One of the mysteries of the world, that. I sank down gratefully onto a log that Henry had maneuvered into position just for me.

"Stay!" he said, holding out a hand as though I were his pet spaniel and he, my master.

Yet it set me to giggling and moaning in turn, followed by a horrid case of the hiccups.

"See what you've started?" he said, tsking, as he set about work on both our tents.

When he'd finished setting up camp, he began preparing our evening meal, despite my many protests. As if a cracked rib weren't enough, the rain set in shortly after sunset. It started out slow at first, then gained speed until all of us dove for our tents. Yet even there, metered drips rained down on us in turn and I could hear the myriad groans amongst the women. Before long, I saw a shape emerge from the shadows and dip down to enter my tent, a small rolled bark torch in her hand for light. It was Kahwihta, dressed in fur-lined deerskin and oil-burnished moccasins. From all the discontented sounds we'd been making she'd figured out our dilemma and had come to help.

"Our teepees are large and dry," she offered. "If we divide the women up, they can hunker down with us tonight. Stay warm . . . dry. Then we grease your tents once they dry, yes?"

It took no more than a moment to make my decision, that and a large raindrop hitting me squarely on my left cheek and sliding down to my chin.

"I'll let the others know," I said.

I had only to tell Emma, who relayed my message to Thomas

and Henry. Soon the news had spread over the encampment and everyone, except Gertrude and Jocelyn and those who slept in the wagons, prepared for the trip to the nearby camp. Once there, Kahwihta divided us up into separate teepees, squeezing us in until we were all snugly ensconced around the warmth of a fire. Tier's daughter had placed me in her teepee along with Emma, Yesimeh, and Winnifred, who said "Righto" before dipping through the flaps of the tent. Scattered furs kept us warm.

For the next hour or more, we traded stories, laughing at the telling of many, especially the one about the grizzly bear raiding the Indian camp, only to discover that they'd been teased by one of the young men from a neighboring camp who had dressed up in bear skins.

After some time, we settled down, each with our own thoughts. As I lay between the folds of my fur blanket, I watched the fire dance, send off blue sparks that shot through the collar of the teepee then raced toward the heavens, the stars gathering 'round the flying sparks. I lay there for some time feeling both whole and lost, all at the same time. Whole because I had finally awoken to the world and it to me. Lost because I was no longer the innocent who believed that life would somehow work out as it was meant to, the way I had hoped it would. My childhood dreams of who I would someday become had slipped through my fingers like sand, nothing left but grit. Determination. And in the smallest corner of my brain, hope. But like the sparks that had escaped through the collar of the teepee, hope could be fleeting. I hung onto it as long as I dared. I lay like that for hours. Somewhere near dawn, I slept, but it was a restless sleep. One filled with dreams and nightmares that awoke me again and again. It set the stage for what was to happen on the following day.

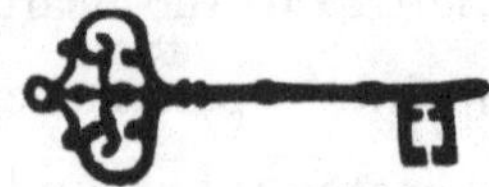

The Kazakh awoke to the sound of a bird high up in the tower. He knew it was a falcon because, although it spoke a slightly varied version of the peregrine falcon language, it was a language he understood. From infancy, he had been raised alongside falcons and hawks. Prey birds of all kinds. Eagles too. He'd grown up learning not only their language, but their habits, their emotions, and he could detect trouble brewing by the distressed cries of the falcon, its calls pitiful. The bird was searching for someone named Brigid. With a peregrine falcon on his shoulder, he peered up into the tower, the sound coming from high above.

"Who is crying?" he cooed in falconese.

"Phinney," the bird said, scarcely batting an eye.

"Ah, the new bird," the Kazakh murmured.

He had heard and seen so little out of Phinney since her arrival that he'd had trouble recognizing her voice, a different dialect from his falcons, to be sure. Alaric had kept her under lock and key after the Kazakh's brief introduction to her, but he had asked around among his birds. Learned her name. "Alaric said that one of his men found the bird, but I don't believe it. How did she really get here?" he asked in the bird's language.

"Alaric sent Old Grey out to find Phinney and bring her in." The bird stretched its talons before resettling on the Kazakh's shoulder.

The Kazakh frowned. Whenever something bothered him, he

became more focused not less, and he was focused now. "Why?" he asked simply.

"To give to you."

The Kazakh turned his head to get a better view of the falcon. "And why is that?"

The falcon lifted one leg, then another. "Because he's afraid of you."

"Afraid of me?" The Kazakh laughed, then immediately saw the error of his ways. Of course the bird was right. In most power dynamics, Alaric was strong, a bully, always getting his way. But in his relationship with the Kazakh, he had been more circumspect, never once stepping on the falconer's toes . . . until recently. He nodded, a certainty coming over him. The blue falcon was a peace offering. He blinked once. Well, so be it.

"Let's go see how Phinney is faring," he said in the deep melodious voice of his people, his words carrying a hint of menace.

But what he saw when he arrived at the top landing of the circular staircase had him fuming. For there, in a cage no bigger than that of a trapper's cage stood a very wounded, very forlorn falcon. Its neck feathers had been plucked and dried blood attached to its remaining feathers around the neck. But it was the stark feeling that he got of lost hope and sadness that made the Kazakh's blood swell and his pupils dilate. He loved the birds, respected them. How could anyone be so cold and uncaring as to do this to a bird? Well, he would bide his time. But he had a memory, some had said, like that of the ancients. And he would not forget. No, he would not forget. Ever.

It's said that time heals all wounds, and yet as I struggled to rise the next morning, my eyesight bleary, every breath causing me pain, I realized I hadn't yet spent enough time in purgatory, apparently, because my body reminded me with regularity that I had yet to serve my entire sentence. As if to punctuate that point, the rain had only ramped up its affliction by adding wind to the mix so that now it blew on blustery gales.

The previous night, I had dreamt that Alaric was watching me through a spyglass out on the ramparts of his fortress. Even though I knew it to be a dream and only a dream, I couldn't shake the feeling that he was indeed plotting and planning. As if to confirm my fears, when I returned to my own tent to find it soaked, all its contents sopping wet, I discovered too late that I had left the loom behind.

The loom.

I turned a full circle, panic setting in. I had placed it on a folding stool that I had brought along, in full view of anyone wanting to snatch it, as I now realized as I stood in the middle of the tent, unable to breathe. How? How could I be so foolish? Frightened beyond imagination, I raced toward the opening of the tent only to run smack dab into Henry.

"Oof!" he grunted, rubbing his chest. "Where were you headed to in such a hurry?"

"My loom, Henry. I've lost my loom. Someone has taken it."

His golden brown eyes widened at the enormity of what I had said, for it had been prophesied that whoever owned the loom, owned the kingdom. Did that include the smaller loom? I didn't know, but I didn't want to take any chances.

"Who could have taken it?" I cried, shaking.

"I don't know, but we've got to find out."

He grabbed my hand and together we bent down as we dashed through the raindrops, soaked almost instantly by the current downpour. All of us had been in the other camp, all except . . . I squeezed Henry's hand to bid him halt.

"Gertrude and Jocelyn were in the camp last night, as well as those inside their wagons."

I peered through the downpour in search of their tent. I spotted it on the outskirts of the encampment, near a stand of alder.

"There!" I cried.

And sure enough, they were packing their things. Somehow they'd managed to cover their tent with tree branches and a tarp so that their tent remained relatively dry. Ingenious, really. From now on, we would prepare our tents for the weather, once we were able to dry out our belongings, but at this moment, I wanted to speak to the pair, to find out what they knew, what they had heard.

But to my surprise, as the two of us bent down to enter their tent, they both stood with their backs to us inspecting something. I cleared my throat. They jumped slightly, as though caught red-handed. When they turned to face me, between them sat my loom.

"We were only protecting it!" Gertrude said, her expression dissolving into one of surprise.

"Yes, from the rain," Jocelyn added.

They were no longer the pie-eyed girls that I had met at the manor, dressed in their finest. They had matured considerably since we'd started out on our trip, from coquettish young girls into full-fledged women. As such, they stood to face me, unafraid.

"And what did you find?"

"Look for yourself," they chimed in unison.

They stood back. What I saw took my breath away, for the loom had indeed been working its magic through the night. At the bottom of a tall tower stood a giant of a man with a grizzled beard and bushy eyebrows. He wore a wide-brimmed felt hat covered in red fox fur, a long fur jacket and boots, and he wore one leather glove on his right hand. But what stood out most was the falcon on the glove attached to a leather lead. The bird wore a hood over its eyes, something I myself had used on Phinney when the need arose. I peered more closely to see if indeed it was my blue falcon, but no. This was a peregrine falcon, most likely. Hope swelled only to be dashed just as readily when I realized it wasn't the bird I had been hoping to see. But what did this Kazakh have to do with this bird or Phinney? It's then I saw what the Kazakh was peering up at—a window in the tower. And though I could not be sure, I spied something small, something blue.

I turned to Henry. "Do you think that's Phinney?" I asked excitedly.

Henry bent down and squinted at the object in the window. "Hard to say," he said, pulling himself upright. "But if the loom thought it important enough to show us, it must mean something."

"I think you are both missing the point," said Jocelyn, her shiny brown hair plaited over one shoulder, her green eyes piercing.

"And what's that?" I asked.

"Here!" She pointed to a spot on the tapestry, one I had

missed in light of the giant and his bird. She picked up a magnifying glass that she'd managed to procure somehow and held it to a spot on the tower closest to the forest.

Despite the use of the magnifying glass, I had to squint and turn the glass this way and that to see it clearly. But what I saw sent shivers skipping down my spine for it was none other than Alaric standing on the rampart wall facing us. To his eye, he held a spyglass. And for one brief moment I had the uncanny feeling that I was reliving my dream, for he was staring back with such an intense gaze that it felt as though he were looking directly into my soul and searching for any small chink from which to uproot me. To tear me from the very earth that I walked on and to send me soaring into the chasm of time, never to be seen again.

I must have paled because the two women gathered 'round me, while Henry grasped my hand and said, "Stay with us, Brigid. We promise not to let anything happen to you."

I gasped for air. How could he be certain? How could any of them be sure when evil lurked just over the mountain, an evil so terrifying that I thought I might be ill right then and there.

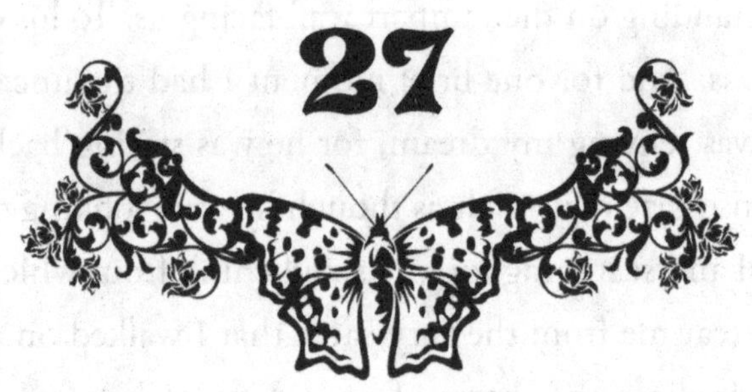

27

It was time. Alaric released the blue falcon to the Kazakh's care. He did it with great ceremony, calling in the Master Birder as well the others from the Council. Even the two generals were there in full regalia. They stood out on the military plains, Alaric in a garment more befitting a French gendarme than one from this region. He wore a badge at his neck to hold his wool cape in place. And on that badge was a coat of arms with a knight, only instead of the silver armor one might ordinarily expect, this one bore an ebony coating of armor that turned colors and glistened in the light, like the shimmery shell of a milkweed beetle. Alaric's boots came to his knees and his hat was not flat like a gendarme's, rather a black tricorn hat with a large ostrich plume he'd managed to procure from one of the returning ships bound from Auckland to New York on one of his many inland excursions.

All were on horseback, including the Kazakh who rode his

Mongolian pony as he and his forbears had for centuries prior. All in ceremonial garb. The Kazakh stood in the middle of the grounds looking bare with no raptor to garnish his gloved fist. But Alaric meant to change that. With anticipation bordering on glee, he announced the transfer of the priceless bird to the Kazakh. This should win the Kazakh's fealty.

Alaric bowed slightly, expecting the Kazakh to do the same, only lower. Yet when the Kazakh made no move, Alaric glanced to his right and to his left, at his generals and saw that they too had noticed the slight. His face flushed with undisguised fury, but he fought to quell the anger. No use upsetting the Kazakh more than he already had. After all, Alaric needed the birder to help him hunt for his real prey, Brigid and her many followers. No, he would bide his time. He finished the ceremony with words of accolades for the great huntsman, then when the ceremony was completed, he rode back to the fortress. His entomologist would be waiting for him. Together they would embark on a plan. A plan that would end Brigid and her followers once and for all. As he entered the fortress walls and reined his horse to a halt, he sat back on the horse's haunches before dismounting. Once he was on *terra firma*, he rubbed his hands together with glee. Now for the beginning of the end.

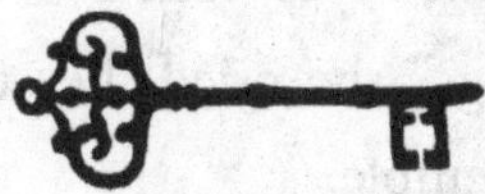

It was late afternoon by the time we had reached Tupper Lake and the autumn leaves rang victorious in their painted splendor. The rain had subsided by midmorn, replaced by a glorious sun that shimmered against the beads of water like bits of colored glass. Though my ribs still ached, I had pressed on beyond human endurance. Fortunately, Henry had agreed that we should take a brief respite, so he called a halt to our wagon train.

While we were there, a group arrived carrying a travois filled with clothing of all shapes and sizes: fringed leather tunics, skirts and leggings to wear beneath the skirts, as well as knee-length moccasins and fur coats. For the next half hour, women ducked beneath the canopy of trees to change into their new clothing, much better suited to fall in Upstate New York. Throughout the temporary encampment, I heard titters of excitement and laughter from the women. I donned a pale yellow hide tunic and skirt, admiring the care that had gone into the beadwork. I made certain that the tribes were well paid for this gift that would surely spare many of our lives over the days ahead.

Once we were all dressed and seated on downed logs, rocks, and buckboards, any place that would accommodate us, we began eating cold food–corn mush from the morning meal usually, with dried blueberries and a bit of jerky, if we could spare it. Despite the same rations nearly daily, we tucked in as though it was the first time, each of us hungry from the exertion of our trek.

We were nearly through and ready to press on when we heard a strange sound, a gnawing sound. From her position on one of the buckboards, Gertrude's eyes went wide.

"What's happening?" she cried, her teeth jolting together, causing her words to tremble.

And though the buckboard seemed to be vibrating only marginally, something about it sent a streak of fear racing through each and every one of us. Soon, the other buckboards were vibrating along with it. Suddenly a wheel fell off one, sending one of the women careening over the side. Fortunately, Thomas had been close enough to catch her.

"What the—" But I never had a chance to finish my sentence because all over camp we heard the same sound, saw the same sights. The wood from our caravan was literally crumbling right before our very eyes.

"Henry!" I cried, pointing. For a large termite ate through one of the side boards and plopped on the ground, its well-fed body writhing before us.

I leaped back with a scream only to see other termites gnawing their way through the wagons. So many, in fact, that the ground was soon littered with the mass of writhing insects.

Frantically, I searched for my loom, only to discover that it too had been eaten.

"What will we do?" I cried, all hope of learning anything new from the loom vanished along with the loom.

Henry, who had followed close behind me, looked on as I picked up the remaining remnants of the tapestry among the sawdust that remained. "I don't know, Brigid," he said, bending down next to me, "but we have to come up with a plan, and we have to do it quickly."

But as I attempted to formulate a plan of attack, I heard a great thundering and the ground shook beneath us until we were nearly knocked to our feet. Before we were able to react, to run to the forest or jump in the lake, we saw a mass of grizzlies like nothing I had ever seen before. They were galloping, if indeed grizzlies could gallop. And they were coming from every direction, making escape impossible.

Henry snatched me to him and hugged me, wrapping me in

his arms as if to protect me, but protection seemed unlikely given the circumstances. All I could do was to hold on and pray. I closed my eyes, expecting the inevitable, believing that Alaric had finally won. Here, today, beside this lake, he had truly and inevitably won. But to my surprise, I heard a slurping sound. Despite my constant quaking, I peeked out from beneath the shield of Henry's chest only to discover that the bears were lapping up the insects in a frenzy of delight, their mouths forming happy grins as they slurped down the wee beasts. I peered around, wondering what had happened when I caught sight of Winnifred who simply smiled.

"You?" I mouthed.

She nodded.

"Your gift?" I asked. "You can harness . . . *bears*?"

She shrugged, and once again nodded. "We helped an injured baby bear once, and he never forgot. Any time we need help, we just call on them."

Yesimeh had been right. I should have listened to her. All around me were women with gifts—gifts that might very well save us in the future. I saw this as the lesson it was. That we were all in this together, each and every one of us. From now on, I would trust the women more, and hopefully they would come to trust me as well. At least I hoped so.

Winnifred and I looked at each other and once again smiled. Now to figure out how to carry on without the wagons. But before I could formulate a way out of our predicament, the grizzlies sat while Tier's band fitted them with leather blankets and reins, as though they had imagined just such a predicament. How? How was this all happening? I spun around, searching for answers, but the women only shrugged.

Then, to my surprise Kahwihta explained that she, too, had gifts.

I shook my head to clear the cobwebs. "Gift, what gift?" I asked, deciding then and there that we needed to write down each of the gifts so that they could be used in the future.

"The gift of sight."

"You knew this was coming?"

"*Tkaie:ri*," she said in her native tongue. She added, "Yes. I have known for some time."

"And you said nothing?" I demanded, frowning.

"One can not change the future, only prepare for it," she said cryptically. "So, I brought you saddles and reins, and travoises. They are so much better than wagons, yes? How do you say it . . . ? Pr-ak-ti . . ."

"Practical?" I ventured.

"Yes, exactly." She smiled, clearly pleased with herself and her use of the English language.

I couldn't help but giggle. All around me were amazing women who could make our journey so much better, so long as we worked together, helped each other up instead of down. Women had positioned themselves so long for the meager crumbs thrown them that they had never been given the opportunity to work together to build something better—a better future for all women. I thought of my mother, how she and her friends had shared food, helped each other with their children, run errands for each other, but in the wider world, the world of men, they had been excluded almost entirely. That must change, but it could never change with the likes of Alaric.

For the next couple of hours we unloaded the crumbled wagons and reloaded the travoises. The women warily inspected the bears before gingerly climbing aboard. Most let out squeals of panic when the grizzlies rose with the women on their backs, but in the end, the grizzlies moved much faster than the cumbersome wagon trains. Though I missed the sound of the wheels, I was not unhappy to see the remaining shavings turn to dust beneath our feet. Not only could the grizzlies carry us through even the narrowest forest path, they hunkered in at night, providing warmth as the weather changed. Silently, I thanked both Winnifred and Kahwihta for their fast thinking.

When we arrived that evening at our next encampment on the north end of Tupper Lake and finished our meals, everyone tucked in early, including the bears. Some were a deep brown, almost black. Mine had a slightly copper color and appeared younger than some. As I burrowed into my furs, the ones that the tribes had allowed us to keep, I pulled my locket from beneath my tunic. I pushed the button and watched the orb open. Out popped my family. I gazed over to see what the grizzly would make of it but he merely looked at it and grunted, then closed his eyes. In the hologram, it was Easter this time and we were out on a picnic. We girls giggled and laughed as we went in search of Easter eggs, seeking the most elusive of eggs, the silver and gold. My sister Belinda came up with the silver but, try as we might, we couldn't find the gold. For hours, we searched, but in the end, we came up empty-handed. In exchange for the silver egg, my father reached behind Belinda's ear and pulled out a silver coin, which he handed to her with great ceremony. We girls all stood 'round, peering down at the coin in awe. The memory orb began to fade so I tucked it back inside my leather tunic for safekeeping. No one knew I had it, not even Ma'am or Emma. It was my own personal treasure, the one that tied me to the past if only by a slim piece of silver that hung 'round my neck.

I dove deeper under the covers so that the bear would not see my tears. Though I longed desperately for sleep, sleep was not to be had. Once again, I lay there 'til the wee hours of the morning, pondering all that had become of me since that fateful day when my family had been tossed to the four winds, never to return. Somewhere near dawn, I fell into a fitful slumber. This time a creature was stalking me. It was a great hairy beast with red eyes and fangs that dripped poison. I awoke with a start, only to discover that Henry had come looking for me when I hadn't awakened early as was expected on a sojourn such as ours.

"Are you all right?" he asked.

I squinted at my surroundings. The bear had long since risen, according to Henry and was now out foraging for food.

"You missed breakfast and the whole camp is packed and ready to go."

I patted my hair, strands headed every which way. I quickly tucked stray tendrils behind my ears and forced myself up on my knees, grasping onto the little makeshift table as I regained my bearings. Seeing my clumsiness, Henry offered me a hand.

He didn't even wait for an explanation for my tardiness. Instead he began packing for me. And as soon as he had me safely out of the tent, he set to work unpegging my tent and folding it up. When he was done, he whistled. That must have been the bear's cue, for it came lumbering out of the forest where it had found a nest of bees and honey, the goo dripping from his lips while several spare bees swirled 'round the bear's crown.

"What have we here?" I asked, amused.

The bear merely lumbered over and waited for me to place the saddle on his back. Henry helped me lift it up and cinch it around the bear's waist. Then he created a makeshift stirrup with his hands from which to lift me into the saddle. Once there, I yawned, determined to see my way through this day and whatever it had to offer despite the soreness that lingered from my earlier mishap. Already the entire camp was packed and leaving, Tier guiding the way. Henry and I were the last to leave. It felt good to bring up the rear, for a change, no one seeking me for guidance or asking me to resolve a problem. Yesterday's near disaster had proved a win for us, albeit a surprise win.

"You're awfully quiet," I said to Henry when the path had widened and he was able to pull up beside me on his grizzly, a decidedly older, slower grizzly. But the bear had personality. One dark eyebrow flared upward giving him an almost jaunty air, while one ear was misshapen where it had been chewed by another bear, most likely. But it was the large white patch on his stomach that gave the appearance of a bear at a ball in a tuxedo that caused me to grin most. The bear seemed almost dapper. I quite expected him to wear a spectacle and a watch fob.

"Just thinking," Henry responded glumly.

"About what?" I said, furrowing my brows.

"About a friend from my past."

"Oh," I said, unexpected jealousy rearing its ugly head so quickly that I had no time to tamp it down, to stuff it into the box it had come in.

"It's not like that," he added quickly, his eyes growing round.

"Just a kid I grew up with . . . Soren Langtree."

"That's quite a name."

"Hmm . . . yes, it was. A lot to live up to, actually. He was part of the Josiah Langtrees. A very prestigious family."

My world had spun around so fast that I knew what it was like to live on both sides of the equation . . . wealth, expectations—to poverty and subservience. As a result, part of me knew what it was like for a family to have those sorts of expectations, the other part quelled at the very notion of class and servitude.

"At any rate, he's long gone." I read the sadness in his eyes.

"What do you mean? Where did he go?"

For a moment, Henry merely licked his lips and swallowed down the lump in his throat, still used to forcing down emotion whenever it arose, no doubt. "He's dead," he finally managed. "Died quite a while back."

I gasped. "Was he ill?"

The emotion Henry had long since buried burbled up, and he turned his head away so that I wouldn't see the pain written there, but I had seen it. I could tell by the slump of his shoulders, the heaving of his chest.

"Was he sick?" I repeated, hoping that he would reengage.

"Yes," he said, rubbing his eyes with his sleeve before turning back to me, but I could see that his eyes were red. "He died of pneumonia."

I sat back on my haunches, which the bear took to mean that we were to halt. Henry's older bear did likewise. And despite the fact that those ahead of us were rounding a bend we remained stationary.

"Oh, Henry." I slid down the sloping back of the behemoth

and reached up to Henry, who pulled me to him. There we sat facing each other, our foreheads touching. "I'm so sorry," I said.

But Henry merely shrugged. "Nothing we can do about it now." Despite his stoicism, I could see that Soren's death had affected him greatly.

"What happened?"

The wind sighed in the tree canopy, an occasional bird chirping amidst the growing silence. Finally, Henry lifted his head to face me. "Soren was different," he began. "He wasn't athletic, but he was smart. He could have been an engineer. He could have created amazing things if he'd managed to make it to adulthood, but he never did."

"But why?" I probed, not allowing him to retreat behind the wall of silence he had maintained for so long.

Henry released a protracted sigh and peered up at the sky as though he might find inspiration in the fluffy white clouds. The cold had set in and each time he spoke, puffs of steam rose up with it.

"We were expected to defend our kingdom, don't you see? But Soren was not athletic. He was clumsy, tripped easily. His intelligence was his undoing."

He stared at me with those clear blue eyes as though I should understand what he was trying to say, but I didn't. I threw my hands up in frustration. "I don't get it, Henry. How would being smart cause a problem?"

Henry grasped the reins of his bear and shook it as though it might somehow shake the correct words from his brain. "How can I explain this so you can understand it," he said, squeezing his eyes shut and reopening them. "Those who lead our defense prize *physical* prowess. Anyone smart is thought to be 'too good' for the rest of us, so those in charge bring them down a peg. Make that a whole lot of pegs. They're made to feel–"

"--small," I said, finishing for Henry.

Henry nodded. "Jonathan had one such officer who wouldn't let up, always rode him. And he couldn't complain. It would have been like crying sour apples. It would have created even worse hazing, humiliation."

"So he stuffed his feelings."

"And it ate at him. Ate at him until he–"

"Until he what?" I demanded.

"They made him run in the cold, in the rain. They lowered his rations until finally he became sick." I could see him fighting down the lump in his throat.

"And died," I said, finishing for him.

Tears rimmed Henry's eyes as he nodded yet again. "It was a lesson to the rest of us. To endure. To keep our mouth's shut."

"Is that why you agreed to join me here?" I said, my hands splayed outward to encompass everything we had been through.

His voice came out a rasp. "It is."

"It happened back when the kingdom was united, before Alaric tried to overthrow our kingdom. But someone like the officer doesn't forgive or forget. I was Soren's friend. I attended his funeral. I wanted to tell his family the truth but–"

"--you were afraid."

Suddenly the sobs that Henry had held tight all those years burst from the dam of his contempt for himself, for his weakness, for his fear at having to face the officer should he be so bold or brave.

"Henry," I said, teeth gritted as I grasped his hands in mine. "His death was not your fault. Don't you for one second take the blame."

Henry balled his fists, his face contorted in anguish. "I should have said something to his family, while he was alive. Tried to make them see. Help."

"*Could* they have helped?" I said, lifting Henry's chin to peer directly into his eyes.

"Probably not. No one could."

I thought about what he'd said, my heart heavy. To have someone as kind and loving as Henry forced to bear such a loathsome weight on his shoulders. And indeed, the tragedy seemed to have weighed him down, for he sagged in his saddle, a broken man.

"I hate to say it, Henry, but this is what happens when you have a closed system with no outside checks and balances. One's happiness and survival are based on the benevolence, or lack of it, of their leaders."

A lump formed at the back of my throat as I leaned into Henry, feeling the warmth of his chest, smelling the sweet scent of his essence as though he had bathed in honey and cinnamon with just a hint of vanilla.

We stayed like that for some time, our lips coming together in a need so intense and so passionate that I could scarcely breathe for the want of him, and yet I pulled back, my breathing returning in great bursts. For several minutes, Henry ran his fingers through my hair, his eyes capturing mine, longing written into them. Finally, we came together in a final hug. We couldn't keep the troops waiting any longer. With reluctance, I slid off the tuxedoed bear and climbed back onto my much younger one. At the same time, we gave our reins a slap and yelled, "Hah!" to which the bears merely grunted and began moving.

But nearly forty minutes later, we still hadn't caught up to the rest of our group and the angle of the sun was beginning to lower in the sky. Nor could I hear movement that foretold our impending meeting. I flashed Henry a frightened glance and could see that he was as nervous as me, for we had no way of knowing which way they'd gone, and now there was a fork in the road. Right, left, or straight ahead? Fear gripped me in its silent talons. That's when I thought of Phinney. If only I could somehow conjure her to come find me. But Phinney had problems of her own.

28

The Kazakh had spotted them first. While on a hunting expedition in a glade surrounded by the pungent smell of firs, he'd located a pheasant, brought here from China, his neighbor to the south of where he'd once lived in Mongolia. He raised his hand and gave a short whistle. The blue falcon soared through the sky like the Kazakh knew she would. Though small, it was a mighty predator used to hunt prey. Grouse, quail, pheasant. Even small birds. But just as the falcon was about to snatch its prey it winged upward, flushed out by a thumping sound to the south. That's when the Kazakh saw them. A great phalanx of people 'rounding the bend just north of Saranac Lake. Some walked. Many rode atop bears of every kind, but mostly grizzly bears. He gripped the reins of his pony tightly, fear settling in his belly. Although the Kazakh had seen everything under the sun in his nearly eighty years, he had never seen this. It had to be magic of some sort. *Strong magic.*

He jerked his pony around, but it hadn't taken much coaching because the horse was just as unnerved by the phalanx of bears as he had been. The Kazakh gave another short whistle and saw for a moment the blue falcon pause, as though deciding which direction to go, north with the Kazakh or south with . . . *his people.* Fear gripped the Kazakh then, for he knew who was among them. The blue falcon's owner, this Brigid that Alaric spoke of. The leader of both people, birds, and as he now knew, bears. And as if to prove that point, the bird dipped down toward a woman riding alongside a man, but when the bear turned to face Phinney, the bird let out a desperate screech, snagging one of the woman's metal beads as she pulled upwards.

The Kazakh's pony bucked, nearly unseating him, but Mongols were great horsemen as everyone knew, and he caught hold of the pony's mane in order to right himself, even as the horse flew through the underbrush, knowing instinctively its way back to the fortress without the Kazakh needing to make a move, so well trained was the pony.

The air flew past him, the wind in his nostrils as he leaned in, gripping the sides of the pony with his knees. Though he despised Alaric, he knew he must tell him what he had witnessed. All these thoughts ran through his head as he raced up the final leg of his journey toward the hidden gate that veered behind a stand of trees so that one might assume that nothing was here except brush and trees. Before entering the hidden outcropping, he took one look back, searching for the blue falcon, but it was nowhere to be seen. So, the bird had chosen. Wisely, it seemed.

Alaric paced the ramparts, his spyglass trained to the expanse that lay between the fortress and the forest beyond. Loon Lake lay just to the east, so the women's army would have to come this way.

"Order the men in battle gear," he growled to his adjutant.

"Of course, sir," the adjutant said, then left, the generals already on their way to the tower.

Seconds later, the door flung open to Seigfried who announced the two generals' arrival.

"We came right away," said General Cedric as he strode across the room, General Weathermore not far behind.

General Cedric was a surprisingly small man with thinning white hair and a ruddy complexion. Perhaps not that surprising really. After all, Napoleon was a small man with an outsized personality, according to most, and look at what he had accomplished– sequestering most of Europe and beyond. General Weathermore, on the other hand, was a large man with an equally large neck and Roman nose that seemed to drip a good deal of the time. Though large, his movements were quite quick and a bit unnerving, if truth be told.

Alaric turned to greet them in his typically brusque manner. "We have a problem, Generals," he said, launching in without preamble. "None of what we've done has slowed Brigid's army of . . . *women*." He spoke that last word with disdain for the very thought that he might be bested by a woman caused him to seethe. He recalled the nuns at the orphanage. Smacking his hands until they were raw any time he'd made the least error. Forcing him to stand before the class, head bent, as penance for his many "crimes." Making him announce his bed wetting or his lack of hygiene in front of the entire class. He had smoldered with resentment then as he did toward Brigid now. When he had left that place, he had vowed he would never let a woman best him again. Treat him as though he were nothing, as little more than a worm. No. He ground his teeth together and forced air in through his nose. He would stop her, but how?

"I want her captured," Alaric announced, brooking no opposition.

The two generals gaped at each other in alarm. "But sir," Cedric, the more senior of the officers said, "we don't even know what she looks like."

"That should be an easy dilemma to resolve. The Kazakh said that she is in nearly constant contact with a Henry fellow and that she's wearing a tunic with metal beads. Since there are few men among them, simply find a woman and man together and collect them. I have a cell waiting in the dungeon. Do you understand?"

When they didn't respond quickly enough, he shouted, "DO YOU?"

"Yes, sire," they both said in unison.

But their eyes hid nothing. They didn't believe it possible. But they had better begin believing, because Alaric wanted the leader of this brigand placed behind bars. The sooner, the better. He sank down into his favorite chair, one with snarling jackals bordering either armrest.

"Now off with you," he said, waving his hand in the air,

Siegfried's cue to get rid of them.

Once they were gone, he stood and turned back to the rampart where he placed his spyglass up to one eye. His heart thrummed in his chest, for out of the forest, just as the Kazakh had foretold, came the first of the mighty beasts, a grizzly. And just as he'd said, a woman *and* a man were astride twin bears. He heard the jingle of metal beads.

"Brigid and Henry," he breathed in a sigh. "Now, you are mine."

He laughed until his lungs gave out and he could laugh no more.

Which way to go? I turned to Henry whose bear lumbered alongside mine. If I ambled down the wrong road, we might lose the entire group. And without my dear Phinney, we had no hope of finding them. I had lost the loom when the termites had arrived to eat anything wooden. All I had were the remnants of a tapestry. And from what I had seen of it, there was much to fear for it had revealed a dungeon, two people in it, but their backs were turned toward us, so that I was unable to decipher who had been captured. Though I fretted at the revelation, I could do nothing about it now. We must press on, no matter the outcome.

Just as we were prepared to take the middle trail, out of nowhere I saw a flash of blue, flapping wildly as though chased. It's then I realized it was Phinney—my dear, sweet blue falcon. A cry of delight escaped through my frozen lips as I reached out a hand, realizing too late that I wore no leather glove. Fortunately,

Phinney spotted the problem and came to rest on the tree branch closest to us.

"Phinney!" I screeched. "Look, Henry, she's back!"

"And what does she have in her talons?" Henry added, pointing to something torn.

The bird dropped whatever it held in its clutches. The swath of leather came drifting down, and with it something tiny that fell and rolled. I quickly slid off my bear and ran over to see what Phinney had brought us.

"It's a piece of leather, all right," I told Henry, "but it could belong to anyone."

He could see I spoke the truth for it was a shredded piece of leather tunic. When I peered up at Phinney, I could also see that she'd been in a brawl of some sort, for her left leg was slightly injured and she favored her right, something I hadn't noticed until now. And her beak was dripping with blood. I recalled the small item that had rolled.

"Quick!" I told Henry. "Help me find whatever rolled into the grass."

Henry slid off his bear and knelt down beside me as I cast the blades of grass aside with my fingers, inspecting every square inch of the meadow, it would seem. Just as the sun was about to set, I found it and lifted it to the remaining light. It was a bead—a beautiful Oneida trade bead. This one was unique in that it looked like a tiny . . . *drum*. Fear clawed up my back at the realization. Only one person had such a bead and that was Emma. All the rest had either rounded or flat beads.

"Emma!" I cried, rushing into Henry's waiting arms. "We've got to find her, Henry. To find Thomas."

"We can't take these trails in the dark," Henry protested, worry furrowing his brow.

I peered up at the waning light, a chill already settling in that had cooled me to my very marrow. Although I could see that he was right, the thought of anything happening to my dear, sweet friend left me bereft of feeling, willing to do anything, to go anywhere to help save them. Henry could see I had made up my mind.

He merely shook his head and sighed, then said, "I suppose the bears know their way around the forest in the dark. We will just have to trust them."

Relieved, I hugged Henry and thanked him profusely. Then I walked over to the bears. I had collected some treats the evening before in case we were unable to stop often to allow them to forage. I fished through my leather pouch and brought out dried jerky for us and worms I had managed to collect from a downed log that had decomposed nearly completely. The bears greedily downed the treats I had brought them. Then I sat, legs crossed, and explained what we needed to do to find the rest of our group. By Phinney's frantic hovering and diving above us, I felt certain she knew where they were located. But to my surprise, the bear lifted its nose and began sniffing like a dog, testing the wind. And as though it indeed had found something, it picked up its hind legs and the other one did likewise. Soon we were on the move again, only this time we were headed northeast to skirt Loon Lake to the west. Phinney seemed pleased with our choice of routes as she no longer flapped her wings in panic. Instead, she flew ahead and waited, finally succumbing to the effects of nighttime by landing on my pummel and nodding off, apparently having decided that the bears knew what they were doing.

Both Henry and I were also fatigued from a long night without sleep. Each of us tied ourselves to the pommel so that we wouldn't fall off. Before long, we were fast asleep, but only after we'd received reassuring nods that the bears would wake us if anything were amiss.

Apparently, I had slept long enough that I awoke to snuffling and two pairs of eyes staring back at us, that of a boy who could be no more than nine at best, and a little girl, six or seven, all told.

"And who might you be?" I asked.

The sound of my voice brought Henry around with a snort and a shake of his head to gain his bearings. "Wha–?" he said through rheumy eyes. "Who have we here . . . and where *are* we?"

The front door of a small hovel that edged the clearing opened to a woman carrying a basket. "For chicken eggs," she explained. "We've been expecting you."

"Expecting us?" both Henry and I exclaimed at precisely the same time.

"*Oui*, the others have arrived and are divided among houses. I was the only one left without guests because the other women assumed you would arrive last. And *voila*! Here you are."

"Here we are indeed," Henry said with a stretch and a yawn.

"We're the Martins," she said in a decidedly French accent. "My husband is Pierre, my son Jean, and my daughter Celestine. And I am Eleanor. We're friends of Ingrid."

"Ingrid!" Henry and I parrotted each other, both of us relieved to have been guided to the right place.

Eleanor wore a simple cotton frock, no doubt made from gunny sack when they'd purchased grain, cinched at the waist and with poofy sleeves. Celestine, on the other hand, wore simple white linen and boots, while the boy wore black pants and a tunic with boots up to his knees.

"Have the others given word of the whereabouts of a woman named Emma and a young man named Thomas?" I asked, fear making a home in my chest.

The woman closed up like a prayer plant at dusk. Her eyes darted to the left and the right as though searching for someone to offer her guidance. Finally, she handed the basket to her son and said, "You and Celestine go collect the eggs for this morning's breakfast. And hurry with you now. There are wolves and bears–" She halted before she could finish the sentence, her eyes straying to our two bears. Then she cleared her voice. "Just hurry," she amended. Next she turned to Henry and me. "Please, come inside. I have a fresh pot of coffee on the hearth. Your bears will be alright out here?"

I nodded. "They can forage . . . and watch out for the children, yes?" I said to the two grizzlies.

The pair grunted. I could only hope they would keep their word. We followed the woman inside. Her husband was already out hunting, she explained. "He tries to go just before daylight, when the leaves are moist. Less noise to distract the deer and elk."

Once she was busy pouring the coffee into tins, I tried again to ask about Emma and Thomas, and again she closed up like a night-blooming flower at dawn. She placed two biscuits on two plates and handed us each one. When she finally took a seat at the rough-hewn table, she said, "I'm *tres* sorry to have to tell you this, but they've been taken prisoner by Alaric and his men."

I leapt to my feet. "Why?"

Henry reached for my hand and tried to calm me. "Please, Brigid. Sit. Let her explain."

Slowly, I fell back into the chair. "How? What happened?"

"Alaric thought the pair were you and Henry, according to a woman named Ma'am. At least that's what she thinks since they called them by name."

I gasped and turned to Henry who sheltered me in the hollow of his shoulder. My hands shook at the news.

"Before you panic," she said, holding her hands up, palms facing me, "I've spoken to a neighbor who has an idea. When the children return, I will send Jean to fetch him."

Unfortunately, there was nothing I could do but wait. Henry, knowing how close I was to Emma, cradled me as though he'd been doing it for a lifetime, though I knew he was just as concerned about his brother, Thomas. Still, I melted into his arms, grateful for any comfort he could spare.

Ten minutes later, the children returned carrying a basket filled with eggs of nearly every color: blue, green, brown, white, and mottled eggs, some small, some as large as a goose egg. Eleanor grasped the basket from her son and set it on the table. Then she turned to her son, Jean, a small boy with pointed features and a wisp of brown hair that cascaded over his forehead.

"While I prepare these folks' breakfast, you go 'round and collect Master Clyde. He is the head of our clan. He will be expecting you, *oui*? And be quick about it!" she added for good measure.

Apparently, the boy could tell by the urgent tone of his mother's voice that she meant business, as he nearly flew out of the one-room cabin on winged feet. He returned twenty minutes later with a man I could only presume was Master Clyde, a rather smallish man with not a spare ounce of fat around his midsection. He wore a blue shirt and brown woolen vest with boots that fell just below the patched knees of his pants.

Anxious to hear word of my friend, I rushed to my feet, Henry doing likewise. "Have you heard? Where are Emma and Thomas? Are they safe?" I demanded, peppering him with questions.

Master Clyde held up his hands pleading for patience. As Eleanor tended to eggs cooked in bacon grease mixed with wild vegetables they had collected from the meadow out front—fresh sorrel, wild onions, and a hearty mess of dandelion greens—Master Clyde told us all he knew.

"They're in the dungeon, according to one of our lookouts."

"Henry," I cried. "It's just as the loom predicted. What will we do?"

Henry seemed just as stimied as I over what to do next. This was not in the least as I'd envisioned our triumphant entrance into the citadel.

Master Clyde took a seat at the table as Eleanor dished us each a plate. Despite my panicked state, the lack of food and the amazing smell of eggs upon our plates, with a hunk of brown bread and butter besides, sent my insides churning, my stomach growling.

"Eat up," Eleanor encouraged. "Master Clyde has a plan." She winked, then set a fresh pot of buttermilk onto the table.

I am ashamed to say that I tucked into the food greedily even as I listened to Master Clyde's plan, the eggs tempting my tastebuds, the bread sealing the deal.

"As a child, I accidentally found a hidden passageway into the dungeon. Actually, it's more like a warren of passageways that lead to all points in the fortress." Here Master Clyde pulled a map from his pocket that he had painstakingly drawn up, detailing the various parts of the fortress. "So long as you follow the directions I've given you, you will be safe. At least until you arrive at the dungeon. There are trap doors inside the dungeon itself. We have someone on the inside," he said, giving me a look that signified a promise owed on my part to never tell anyone what he was telling me today.

"Your secret is safe with me," I hurried to say.

"Good! He will be stationed there today. Make sure you are in as the light starts to fade and out before dawn so that you are less likely to be seen. Once you enter, there is a torch on the wall. Light it. But be sure to extinguish it before you leave. You must arrive in darkness and leave in darkness. Until then, rest up. You will need all your strength."

Henry and I readily complied.

"But Brigid and Henry," Clyde said, pausing, "whatever you do, if you miss the turn to the left here–" He pointed to a spot on the map. "--then you will end up here."

"What is up there?" I ventured to ask, for at the turn, one staircase stretched downward toward the dungeon, the other climbed upwards toward a tower.

"That is Alaric's private quarters. Wind up in the tower and there will be no saving you."

He didn't have to explain the dire consequences. Henry and I glanced at each other, the desire for food all but forgotten.

29

We spent the day inside an old barn, reconvening with the other women who were just as distraught as I about Thomas and Emma. One by one, each woman offered up their ideas. Roseland informed me that she had already sent out her carrier pigeon, which Lord and Lady Bookbinder had returned only recently, outlining our dilemma to the Lord and Lady. The pigeon should be arriving at the manor as we spoke. Peke had offered up her snake, despite the realization that she might never see it again, to help slow the enemy should we need it. And lastly Yesimeh had prepared a leather satchel filled with Isinglass made from sturgeon bladders along with a leather pouch filled with water to make the bladders sticky and concrete-like.

I saw that the parfleche made of an animal bladder with its colorful geometric designs had been donated by one of the Oneida. It's then I realized with a frown that I had yet to see any of the tribe members. Reaching up on my tiptoes, I searched for them but saw no one.

"Where are Tier, Kahwihta and the rest?" I whispered to Hannah and Yesimeh.

"They disappeared into the forest when Alaric's men commandeered Emma and Thomas. Without leadership, our plan to create a diversion and meet the enemy from both sides fell to the wayside." Hannah's complexion was much better since that day that the ogre wind had tried to snatch her in its maw and do away with her. Now, her blonde hair glistened in the dim light of the barn.

"Hmm," I murmured, my thoughts still on Emma and Thomas.

Knowing Tier and his daughter, Kahwihta, they were too wise to be caught in a snare. As such, they had done the only thing possible; they had hid until a plan could be formulated. I didn't want to give our plans away to the women just yet, but Tier needed to be ready once Henry and I returned from the fortress, *if* we returned. I must have paled at the thought because Yesimeh leaned in and patted my hand.

"Are you okay, Brigid?" she asked, her small, cherubic face drawn up with worry.

I nodded, forcing air into my lungs. The day was passing quickly and everything must be in place by nightfall if Henry and I were to have any chance at success. The leader of the clan, who had given us refuge, needed to know our plans. I hailed Master Clyde, who must have recognized my concern because he made haste to circumnavigate the throng of people filling the barn in order to come sit beside me. The courier pigeon was gone, unfortunately, so the only way I could get word to the tribe was to send Phinney, who was safely back at the house with Eleanor. But Alaric and his men, and more importantly, the Kazakh, who Master Clyde had told us earlier worked as a master birder on behalf of Alaric, would be on the lookout for Phinney. It was a fool's errand to send my bird, and yet what alternative did I have? I quickly explained all this to Master Clyde.

"It's too dangerous to send Phinney," he said, rotating his jaw back and forth as he contemplated the odds. "The Kazakh will make mincemeat out of him."

I shuddered at the image. Poor Phinney.

"What can we do?" I pleaded, recalling how the peregrine falcon had chased my dear sweet Phinney, plucking at her feathers. She had fought valiantly, but she still wasn't completely healed.

Master Clyde shrugged. "We have no choice. I will send word to Eleanor that Phinney is to fly immediately. Her best option will be to stay low. I will draw up the safest route for Phinney, but she will have to rise high enough on the currents to locate the tribes. That will place her in greater danger. My guess is that the tribes are holed up in one of the nearby caves. I will provide a map. Can Phinney read?"

I threw up my hands, for I had no idea. "I doubt it."

"Very well. Eleanor can explain it to Phinney then."

"Phinney is quite smart," I said, hopefulness in my voice. And yet smart enough to understand directions? But then again, she had found me. I held up something Tier had given me, a small pouch big enough to place my feather in. Although falcons weren't known for their sense of smell, perhaps Phinney had imprinted their smell enough to know what we were asking of her. It was worth a shot.

"When you enter the fortress, you'll want to be sure to take this," he added, handing me a vial of a somewhat clear liquid. "What is it?"

"Something to protect your skin."

"Why?" I asked, squinching up my nose as I smelled the liquid.

"You'll see," he said, mysteriously. "Just be sure to wear as much clothing as possible. Then cover the remaining skin with this liquid. You will be glad you did." Then with that, he was gone.

An hour later, Henry and I made our way back to Eleanor's house, the bears providing security along with one of Master Clyde's men, a reed-thin fellow who looked as though a wind could blow him over, but he did have a rifle. Though not particularly fond of guns, I was grateful for it now. After all, who knew what Alaric would do if he learned he had taken the wrong prisoners. By now, he surely knew that Emma and Thomas had been kidnapped by mistake. But he might also believe they would make good hostages. No, we simply had to free them before Alaric learned the truth. Nightfall couldn't come soon enough.

"Are you sure you're up for this?" Henry whispered as they knelt outside the thicket that would lead to the fortress dungeon. Nighttime hadn't yet settled in. But it wouldn't be long. Already dusk blanketed the forest, creating shadows that appeared dark and menacing.

He had thought that they would cross a moat, or that the door would somehow be in plain view, not hidden beneath poison ivy, of all things. "Supposedly, the door is just on the other side of this."

Brigid's eyes grew wide as she drew out the small vial from her satchel and together they slathered it onto their hands and face, which were already covered in ash to blend into the forest. Their clothing was dark as well, donated by the townsfolk who were just as eager to end Alaric's reign of terror as he and Brigid were. And in a satchel she kept at her side was the poisonous snake Peke had lent her and Yesimeh's Isinglass, a deterrent should they need it.

"Brigid," Henry said, feeling nostalgic suddenly. "Whatever happens tonight–" He paused to take her hand, his own hand trembling. "I want you to know that I love you."

Brigid gulped, her large eyes glistening. "I love you, too, Henry. I couldn't have done any of this without you. Couldn't have been so brave."

Henry kissed her mouth tenderly, tasting the sweet succulence of her. She was everything he had ever wanted in a woman, only he hadn't known it until this very minute, when their very lives were at stake. One of them might never return, or perhaps both. He sought to keep this memory forever, to hold it as tightly as Brigid did her family.

When he came up for air, he said, "Don't you know, Brigid? You have always been brave. It's who you are."

Tears hovered on her eyelashes. The two touched foreheads, staying like that until a twig snapped, reminding them of the urgency.

"Now," Brigid whispered.

"Now," he agreed.

They dove into the poison ivy where no one would think to find them. Inside was a curtain of darkness. Henry felt in front of him. Rough bark met his hands. And something else. A latch of some sort. He pulled it and heard a thin creak. Together they crawled inside. But to his surprise, they were not inside the fortress, as Master Clyde had predicted, but inside a massive tree complete with a door. On the wall of the hollowed out tree was a torch, just as Master Clyde had stated. Henry used flint, crushed up leaves and dry sticks to start a fire, then lit the torch. Beside him Brigid squealed with fright. And he could see why, for the very walls were draped in spiderwebs, most long abandoned and gathering dust. But some were active. Either way, it sent a chill through him that would take some time to quell.

"Hurry," he whispered. "We have no time. We must be back before dawn."

Brigid reached for his hand and clasped it tightly. "To freedom!" she cried.

"To freedom," he agreed. "To the cause."

"And to a better world, a kinder world," she added, her breath coming in short gasps.

"To all of that and more," he concurred, capturing her with his eyes and holding them there for what seemed a protracted time. He gave her one final kiss for good measure, then they set off to face their future. Together.

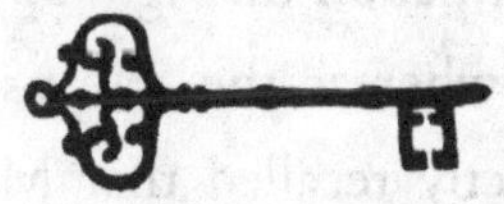

So many emotions were swirling through me as we ran the length of the tunnel with its twists and curves. My heart thudded in my chest and the very air clouded with each of our breaths as we ran dodging rats and creepy crawlies of every sort, most making me cringe in fright. Henry loved me. He had said so. Now, even as I ran terrified through the tunnel, that one thought warmed me, made me feel whole again, or at least partially so. I was so lost in the moment that I nearly stepped on a trip wire, Henry halting me at the last moment, just before my foot touched it. He snatched me back so quickly that the air squeezed out of my lungs.

"That could have killed us," he whispered. "Be more careful, Brigid. I don't want to lose you."

Unnerving as it was, I stepped over the tripwire, determined to watch for it on our return trip. If there was to *be* a return trip. But I couldn't think like that now. I had to believe in my heart of hearts that we would return with Emma and Thomas in tow. And in that moment, I saw it as if it were before me. Emma and Thomas, and the guard that Master Clyde had installed who would be given safe haven back at the manor once we had all escaped. But I also heard the jingling of keys just before my second sight failed me, returning in time to face the fork in the road that Master Clyde had warned us of. Left supposedly went down to the dungeon, right wound up toward Alaric's lair. I grabbed Henry's hand as he halted before the two tunnels.

"That's odd," I hissed, rubbing my eyes lest they deceive me further. But no, the tunnel on the right appeared to spiral down toward the dungeon, whereas the staircase on the left wound upwards, and I distinctly recalled that Master Clyde had said not to take the staircase toward the tower as that spelled doom. Perhaps age had dimmed his memory.

"What's wrong?" Henry whispered, his face alight with shadows against the flickering torch-light.

"Master Clyde must have got it backwards. The right staircase is the one to go down to the dungeon, not the left."

"That can't be," Henry said, pulling the map from his tunic pocket and unfolding it. "See? It shows right here that we are to go left."

"Yes, but left is up, and right is down. It's supposed to be the reverse." I cinched my hands into fists hoping for a miracle in deciding which way to go. Down as Master Clyde had urged, or left as he had indicated? "He must have made a mistake. I say we take the downward staircase."

"I don't know, Brigid," Henry moaned. "We should probably stick to the map."

"But he said *down* to the dungeon, never to go up or we might meet with Alaric and that would spell doom. Besides, he was just a child when he entered the fortress through the tunnel. Over forty years ago, by the look of him. He could have easily forgotten the directions in all those years."

I could see by the furrow of his brow that he was unconvinced, but with one last groan, he said, "Okay, we'll do it your way, Brigid. I just hope you're right."

"Me too," I said, then breathed one deep breath for courage and stepped onto the staircase.

Oddly, the moment I started downward, I could have sworn I was climbing upwards, as though my eyes and my body were deceiving me. After we had climbed, or rather descended—I couldn't say which—a couple of levels, I turned to Henry in the flickering light.

"Does this staircase seem . . . rather *strange* to you?" I whispered, the sound of my voice echoing off the tunnel walls. But before he could answer, I heard another voice, a deep man's voice from somewhere above me. "Do you suppose that could be Master Clyde's man?"

"I don't know," Henry hissed, the sound of his voice close to my ear. "But don't show our hand just yet. Walk softly to the platform and let's listen."

We tiptoed down (or up) the remainder of the stairs and crouched onto our haunches on the landing where I spied a door with a large keyhole from which to view any exchange.

Once there, I heard someone say, "What do you *mean* you captured the wrong people? Can you do nothing right?"

Heart pounding nearly out of my chest, I peered through the peephole and saw my nemesis, the man who would see me gone. Dead. Alaric. I pulled away, stunned.

"What is it, Brigid?" Henry mouthed, his face having turned ashen in a matter of moments.

I threw my head back against the sooty wall of the tunnel and closed my eyes in order to clear my head. When I'd gathered the energy to speak, I whispered, "We went the wrong way. This isn't the dungeon. This is the tower."

Alaric paced back and forth across the room, stabbing the air with his gloved fist. How had he managed to hire such incompetents? As if his anger had inspired the gloom, the candles shuttered sending shadows cascading so that he appeared like a shadow puppet across the wall, amplified to the size of a giant or troll, whereas his subordinate's shadow seemed to shrink as if to physically hide from him. He halted when he reached his writing table and used it as ballast before he turned and launched into the man.

"You . . . will . . . bring me . . . Brigid and Henry . . . or I will know the reason why!" he shouted, his fury shaking the very walls. "Now GO!" He pointed a finger toward the door. "And don't come back without them!"

With bulging eyes, he watched the man skulk out like a skittering mouse scarcely able to close the door behind him. When the man was gone, Alaric muttered, "Good riddance."

Though he needed men like Siegfried, he despised them almost as much for they were worms with little backbone. And yet he despised men like himself because they were competition. He'd learned early on that people were to be used. That was the key to success. Care for no one, just as no one had cared for him when he'd been dragged off to that god-forsaken orphanage.

Alaric walked over to gaze out of the tower window. "Where are you, Brigid and Henry? Where in blazes are you?"

30

I grabbed a hold of Henry's hand, my heart pattering in my chest like a wounded bird. "We've got to find the left fork in the tunnel, Henry," I said, starting off at a run. But before I'd got to the downward slope of the tunnel, or perhaps the upward slope–I didn't know anymore–I collided headlong into a giant spider's web that I had apparently ducked under on the way in. Before I could stop myself, I let loose a scream. Henry reached forward and grabbed my mouth to muffle the sound, but it was too late. My voice had awakened the dead, or at least Alaric, as I heard him shout, "Guard!"

Henry's eyes grew into two round saucers. Now it was he who grabbed hold of my hand and fairly yanked me as he flew down the corridor with me stumbling behind him. We ran until I could run no more and doubled up, panting. But he gave me no room to waver before grasping my hand yet again and forcibly tugging me to the fork in the tunnel.

By the time we reached the fork, I no longer cared that up appeared down, and down appeared up. This time we went left, and although it did look as though we were climbing skyward, I couldn't help but feel my feet trudging downward. We had just about made the x mark that Master Clyde had placed on the map when I began to let out another scream. This time Henry was prepared and covered my face with his chest, pressing me into him so tightly that there was no room in which to open my mouth, let alone scream.

Finally, when he released me, with trembling hand I pointed to the skeleton I'd seen seated against the wall of the tunnel, looking for all the world as if he'd sat down to eat lunch and had died before having a go at his meal.

But then I saw it. His dirty and decrepit clothing had a slice right where his vital organs should have been. Someone had caught up with the poor bugger and had done him in. I shuddered. Henry held me tight, placing a finger to his lips for silence. He peered down the hallway, and even now I could hear thumps somewhere far off as though running footsteps. No doubt headed for Alaric's lair. Then the guards would be set upon us. We had to collect Emma and Thomas, and we had to collect them quickly.

Henry must have had the same thought, for he carefully made his way 'round the skeleton, urging me to divert my eyes. I was only too happy to comply. Once we were on the other side of him, we ran no more than half the length of the hallway when we came upon a door, only our second door outside of Alaric's room.

Up until now, it had appeared we were running uphill,

but now that I was able to peer behind us, I could see that we'd actually been running downhill, the stairs nothing more than an optical illusion. I shook my head to clear the cobwebs. Then turned back to the door. Although dimly lit, it was easy to see that this was indeed the dungeon, for there was a tight metal grate, rusted from years of disuse, that faced into the chambers. At first, I saw nothing, but as my eyesight improved, I saw chains attached to a round hook in the wall. I stood on tiptoes, alongside Henry to see what lay below the chains. Sure enough, folded onto the floor and looking haggard were the pair that I had come to love as if they were my brother and sister. Emma and Thomas.

Before I could think to do otherwise, I hissed, "Psst! Emma! Thomas!"

Henry yanked me backward, dragging me into a kneeling position. "What do you think you're doing?" he whispered into my ear. "You could get us killed. What if there's a guard or other prisoners?"

Master Clyde had assured us that he had installed a guard of his own to watch after the pair tonight. A mole, as it were. Someone whose family had been close to Alaric, but who had tired of the ever increasing abuse of power and had vowed revenge. Yet I hadn't thought about other prisoners there to give us away. A tightness played at the back of my throat. To have Emma and Thomas so close, and yet unable to rush in and rescue them, set my heart racing and made my throat feel parched. But any comfort would have to wait. For now we had to come up with a plan to save my beloved friends.

"What should we do?" I whispered.

"Wait!" he said, lifting up just high enough that he could

peer through the grate. He moved side to side to get a better look, then he bent down, searching the ground for anything that could be used to roust Emma and Thomas without giving anything away.

I felt around until I discovered a tiny pebble that had come loose from the tunnel wall. "Here!" I whispered. "Try this."

Once again, Henry stood up just enough to peer through the grate. Then he gave a quick glance around and, satisfied that no one was within earshot, he tossed the pebble. I heard the tick as it found its mark, followed by a "What the—"

Too excited at the sound of Thomas's voice to remain seated, I got to my feet and peered through the grate beside Henry. Thomas, who had aged considerably since entering this god-forsaken place—his clothes soiled, and wrinkles lining the corner of his eyes—seemed to finally register that help was here at last. He nudged Emma who sat up, and like me forgot her silence as she struggled to sit upright, her hair a tangle and her face smudged with soot and grime.

"Help us!" Emma pleaded, tears gathering in her eyes.

"Shh!" both Thomas and Henry hissed in unison.

I heard the clank of keys and peered with trepidation over at the door opposite us that led into the room. *Please be Master Clyde's guard,* I prayed, hoping against hope that it was the man Clyde had promised.

We had only moments to learn our answer because the door flew open and within seconds the guard was on his knees, key in hand, unlocking the irons shackling Emma and Thomas.

"Hurry!" I pleaded, the sound of pounding footsteps nearing.

The guard freed Thomas first. But he fumbled with the

second lock, his nerves clearly getting the best of him. For one brief moment, I feared all was lost, when at last I heard a click and the shackles fell away.

Already, I heard the pounding of footsteps come closer, and even before Master Clyde's guard could unlock the rusty lock to the door that would set my friends and the guard free, the door to the prison chamber shuddered. Alaric's men tried to open it, to no avail, then heavy fists pummeled the door as the real jailer yelled for the key.

The door to the passageway finally opened, just as the sound of keys could be heard on the other side of the room. We quickly ushered the threesome through, then slammed the door shut and locked it. Then we tossed away the key, throwing the skeleton across the path in hopes that it would slow our pursuers down.

We had barely begun running down the corridor when we heard the door to the cell fly open with a loud thud that seemed to shake the ground we walked on. All I could do was to run and pray, in equal measure.

Fortunately, the ruse with the skeleton had worked, for we heard a crashing sound followed by curses and loud "oomphs" as man fell over man. But too soon, they were on their feet again and I could hear their shouts reverberate through the corridor as they gained on us.

I was so caught up in escape, that I had almost forgotten the satchel I carried with the poisonous snake. I said a quick prayer to the gods and goddesses, then released the snake behind me, never slowing to learn what had become of it.

Moments later a loud scream thundered through the tunnel as indeed the snake found its target. I knew it wouldn't stop them for long. We pressed on, our feet and our breathing the only sound, which seemed loud enough to wake the dead.

At last we were nearing the entrance to the tunnel, the poison ivy on the other side of the hollowed out tree. I had only moments to stop the remaining pursuers for good before we fled into the nighttime.

I halted long enough to pull out the isinglass and to wet it down with water from my flask.

"Don't get it on your fingers," Henry warned. "Now!" he hissed. "Toss it!"

I needed no further urging. I threw the sticky goo to the ground. Then we turned and quickly covered our extremities with the tea tree oil that would protect us from the poison ivy. With that, we raced out into the night on silent feet. But not before I'd heard a chorus of yells and groans as the men's feet were encased in the gooey substance that soon turned to cement, pinning them securely to the cobblestone floor.

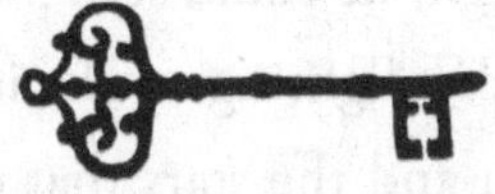

Alaric hadn't felt this furious since he'd first learned that the loom was out there, somewhere, just waiting to be found and giving him total access to power. He paced the ramparts, peering into the night with his spyglass but all he could see were the shadows below. Frustrated, he retired to his room to don his fur-lined cape before he went in search of the adjutant. But just as he was about to throw open the door, it burst in on him, barely missing him in the process while in popped the adjutant.

"Sir," the man said, tearing at his hair with his hands. "The prisoners have escaped through the tunnel. They had help. A woman and a man."

"A male and female, you say," Alaric murmured, stroking his graying goatee. "Hmm." He wondered if it could be the infamous Brigid and Henry whose loom he so coveted. He'd learned through the Kazakh's bird that Henry was brother to Thomas, the captive. The hostage, more like it. Now he had no bargaining chip. *Unless* he could locate Brigid and Henry.

"Where is General Cedrick?" Alaric demanded, pacing, then turning on his heel to pause before the beleaguered adjutant who appeared haggard against the candlelight.

"He has already sent a battalion of men into the forest in search of them."

"He has, has he?" Alaric growled, secretly relieved that the general was so inspired.

Alaric marched outdoors, once again facing the rampart, the chill of late fall instantly setting his cheeks afire, the adjutant close on his heels. Sure enough, he could see a flood of men streaming out into the night, torches lighting up the inky void below. Alaric peered up at the moon and the stars that danced around it, the cold calm a contrast to what was taking place beneath him. Through the forest, the sounds of dogs could be heard baying at the quarry that they had yet to locate. But locate them they would. Alaric let loose a hearty laugh. Soon, he would have not two but four prisoners, all bound in chains that would carry them to their final resting place.

But no sooner had he finished congratulating himself on a job well done than he heard something in the distance. A sound unlike any other that he'd heard. It was as though a trillion ants were chewing at wood, a grinding noise but small, as though created by a quadrillion wee little beasties. He thought of the termites he had sent down as a plague to halt their forward motion to the fortress. And yet, it wasn't that, for termites were his and his alone to do with as he pleased. No, this was something altogether different, but what?

Just then, a flood of insects descended in a rushing river of dark brown bodies, but as they neared, he could see them divide into phalanxes that moved like water. Screams soon followed and cries as far as the ear could hear, torches as far as the eye could see. As one, those with torches held them out and turned, racing back to the fortress.

"What the–?" the adjutant said, his eyes wide and his voice trembling.

"What are those pests?" Alaric hissed, rubbing his eyes.

"I believe they are mosquitoes, sir. Best come inside."

Alaric paused just long enough for one of the blood sucking beasts to have scaled the wall and landed on his neck. He slapped at it and pulled his hand back in time to see a tiny squashed insect marred by a healthy drop of his blood.

"Inside!" he yelled. "Everyone inside!"

But he had to say no more, for everyone on the outside who had been in pursuit of the foursome had flowed inside the fortress, mosquitoes and all, then raced indoors, boarding the windows and doors behind them.

31

Even before I had the chance to reacquaint myself with the outdoors, a hand reached out with a moistened towel, taking turns covering first my face and then the faces of those around me. I tried to scream but the sound was muffled. With all my strength, I fought to be free, but the hand held tight to my face, nearly taking my breath away.

"Be quiet," a voice hissed. "Do you want to get caught?"

Slowly, the man lifted the towel from my face. But no sooner had I breathed deeply of the cool night air than another hand reached out and scoured my face with a substance that smelled like peppermint.

"Hold still," a woman said as she plastered me with the oil.

I paused, recognizing the voice. It was Eleanor, the woman who had taken me into her home and cared for me and Henry as if we were family. Shaking my head so that I could get a better view of her, I saw that indeed it was Eleanor and Master Clyde.

"We knew you would need rescue," Master Clyde explained. "But we must hurry," he hissed, now that all of us were coated in peppermint oil.

"Why?" I tried to say. But I had scarcely said the word when I heard a loud hum, or chewing, I couldn't say which.

"Run!" Henry said, grabbing my hand.

Before I could determine what had happened, we were running, the forest alive with swarms of insects that wafted around me, occasionally hitting my face, filling my nose, my ears, any open orifice. I kept my mouth closed, eager to escape the onslaught. I kept my eyes open, a mere slit, hoping that my eyelashes would keep the gnats, or whatever they were, from entering my eyes. We couldn't speak, simply reacted. We plunged down the hillside at a high speed, twisting and turning to avoid trees that we could only see by way of a lantern that Master Clyde had thought to bring. The landscape sent an eerie shiver racing through me, for it consisted of shadows that leapt out to greet us, sending us careening in different directions. In the reptilian part of my brain, I feared I would lose the others, make a wrong turn, become separated from the rest. Yet every time I thought that might happen, one or the other reached out a hand to keep me going in the right direction.

My legs were trembling by the time I arrived at Eleanor's cabin. I knew we couldn't stay as we would be putting the entire group in jeopardy. As if Master Clyde had simultaneously come to the same notion, he showed me to four horses that had been coated in peppermint oil to prevent the mosquitoes, as I could see now, from biting at their haunches.

"Head southeast," the clans member suggested.

"But what about the other women? And the jailer who helped us. Surely, we can't leave them behind."

"Not to worry. We've taken care of everything. You will meet them at the folded rock."

"Folded rock?" I frowned, uncertain about what he meant.

"Folded rock," he assured me. "In the meantime, your blue falcon turned back, unwilling to leave you a second time. She will guide you."

In all the haste, I had almost forgotten my beloved falcon. She had opted to stay with me. *And* she was safe. But what of the mosquitoes?

"Your blue falcon can fly well above the mosquitoes," he assured me. "She'll see that you don't get lost."

I thanked the man profusely for his heroics in my hour of need as each of us mounted our steeds. Next I gave a teary farewell of gratitude to Eleanor, friend of Ingrid. Before I could fully comprehend all that had happened this evening, Master Clyde slapped at the haunches of our four horses and we were off, to destinations unknown.

It wasn't until a full day had passed with little rest and no sleep that we finally were able to lay our weary heads down on the bedrolls that Eleanor and Master Clyde had thought to provide. We no longer cared about the cold, and the mosquitoes had let up midway through the day. It was late for such things, and I wondered how they'd come to be so far north, this time of the year. Furthermore, why had they aided our cause? Heretofore, they had belonged in Alaric's camp, so why had they attacked not only Alaric, but his entire fortress of warriors? But I'd witnessed stranger things of late and no longer thought them as odd as I had in the past. As I lay huddled alongside Henry, his arm around me to keep me warm, I thought over all that had happened the past few days. The women warriors, the tunnel, the bears . . . The bears! What had become of them? But Henry assured me they would be safe with Master Clyde at the helm, then nodded off to sleep almost mid-sentence.

Thankfully, we now had Thomas and Emma safely at our sides. My relief was so overwhelming that tears laced my eyelashes. Just then I spied a shooting star fly overhead, then another and another in a display that filled me with wonder, so much so that I gasped and heard Henry stir. He sat up in his bedroll to see what had astonished me so. He let loose a sigh of contentment, waking the others. Soon, all four of us peered to the sky, eager to take in the fireworks display of showers.

As if that weren't enough, the northern lights shimmered down on us in an array of color: onyx blue, chartreuse, even burnt umber and sunflower yellow. We oohed and aahed, and giggled at the changes taking place in the night sky for we had been through hell and back and had survived. We were alive. As if Henry had just now recognized the seriousness of the past month, he hugged me tight and leaned in for a kiss. He tasted like cinnamon and honey, and all things right in the world. It was for these moments that I had pressed on, even in my lowest hours, and there had been many to claim that spot.

"Do you think we'll find the others?" I asked, once we'd come up for air.

Henry pressed his forehead to mine, a symbol of our shared

suffering. Our shared beliefs. "If Master Clyde said we would, then I have to believe him."

"But do you remember a folded rock?" I asked, peering up at him, his silhouette outlined in the glowing night sky.

"Can't say as I do."

I nodded, then leaned my head on his shoulder, grateful for his steady strength in the face of adversity. If only I could absorb some of it through osmosis. But then again, I'd done alright. After all, we'd saved Emma and Thomas, hadn't we?

Sometime during the night, as the moon rode the navy blue dome toward sunrise, I fell fast asleep, the others along with me. It wasn't until late morning that I heard the horses snuffling and stamping, ready to be off. Just like the large equines, determined to rule the roost over we mere mortals. I yawned and stretched, my breath a cloud of steam against the chill morning air. Now, more than ever, I felt grateful for what little sleep we had managed. For as long as I lived, I would remember last night, the shooting stars, the northern lights, the way Henry had looked at me as if I were all that mattered in the world. It would live on in my heart as long as I walked this earth.

We ate a quick breakfast over a roasting fire, then saddled up for destinations unknown. Phinney, who had taken up residence in a nearby tree, fluttered about impatiently for us to follow, as though she were a herding dog rather than a blue falcon. I laughed at her antics.

As we made the long winding trek through the forest, I wondered what had become of the tribes, who had disappeared shortly after our arrival at the fortress. Had they escaped as well? Returned to their camps? I wished I could have thanked them, told them how much their support had meant to me, to all of us, especially Kahwihta, who was like a sister to me.

We carried on through the moss and fern that stretched beneath the red spruce seedlings and common wood sorrel, the striped maple and the witch-hobble. I wondered where the name witch-hobble had come from, but knowing the history of the Salem witch trials, and the fact that the plants' pendulous branches snagged on anything coming into contact with it, I no doubt had my answer.

For mile upon endless mile, we rode. In the morning, before we had set out on our journey, we had been so happy to be free of the fortress and the evil that resided there that we had laughed and joked and sang rounds, Emma and I on one side, Henry and Thomas on the other.

But as the day wore on with none of the other women in sight, our laughter had waned and our spirits began to flag. Where could they possibly be? Furthermore, we had failed in our mission, for although the fortress was indeed besieged by mosquitoes, we hadn't won the day. All we'd managed to do was to escape with our precious cargo, Emma and Thomas, who both appeared sobered by the ordeal they'd endured, now that the laughter had worn off and reality had set in. Quite certainly, they were looking forward to a bath and a hot meal. For time to lick their wounds and to begin again toward their future as a couple. But I had a nagging feeling that what had happened to them had changed them in some way, made them more introspective. Quieter.

The sun was nearly setting by the time we reached the edge of Hart Lake, so named for its heart-like shape. We decided to camp as near the top of the mountain peak closest to it as possible, for two reasons. Just in case the mosquitoes returned, and secondly, so that should some of Alaric's men have followed our scent, we would see them. To our surprise, neither of these things occurred. Instead, from a distance, that we could only see through Henry's spyglass, was a white flag waving high atop the fortress wall. Over the course of the past two days, the mosquitoes must have so inundated the fortress, had taken their payment in blood, that all work around the kingdom must have halted, no one able to go outdoors. No doubt pandemonium had ensued until Alaric finally relented. We knew it was only a temporary truce, that he would bide his time until he could once again turn his attention to us. But at least this would give us time to regroup, to prepare and to come back stronger than before.

"Alaric's waving the white flag," Henry said, then let out a whoop, whereupon we all began dancing like children, Emma throwing her hat into the air while Thomas snatched her up in his arms and twirled her like a Whirling Dervish. "They've surrendered!"

"For now," I added, unwilling to let go of our temporary excitement.

When we all were done dancing, we fell to the ground, exhausted from the day's ride and the weeks of fear and uncertainty we'd all endured. For several moments, no one spoke. Then Emma, in her quiet way, said, "You don't suppose something has happened to the other women? Shouldn't we have spotted them by now?"

"We might have missed them," Thomas suggested, newly formed lines etching the corner of his mouth and eyes.

I peered up at Phinney, who was even now eying a meadow vole that hadn't yet taken shelter for the night. But seeing that we were watching her, she paused and let out a high cree, as if in protest of our judgment of her skills at location.

"Phinney wouldn't have missed them or steered us wrong," I said. Then, as if on cue, Phinney went back to hunting for her nightly dinner.

Too exhausted to set up camp, we merely ate dried food from our pouches and then pulled out our bedrolls and slept under the stars. Although the night air was frigid, we huddled together, Henry and I in one bedroll, Emma and Thomas in the other. Despite my fatigue, I found it hard to sleep.

"Henry," I whispered. "Are you awake?"

He rolled over to face me, his eyes like saucers in the bright moonlight. "Yes. What are you thinking?"

"I just wonder if things will have changed at the manor, when we return."

"You mean the punishments?"

I nodded, worry settling against my ribcage.

"Probably not," he said, though his eyes held an apology for what I must go through in the upcoming days.

"So what was the point . . . of all this? Why are we fighting Alaric only to return home and fight each other? I don't understand it."

"No one does," he whispered. "It's the way it has always been. It's so ingrained in the system that there's almost no way around it."

"But systems can be changed, can they not?"

Henry let out a long sigh and turned onto his back, one arm

draped across his forehead as if to ward off the inevitable. "That sounds easy enough, but it isn't because there's no one person able to fix it, so we are all bound by it. It's a great mechanism for control."

I could see that he was having trouble facing me, knowing how I felt about a system of abuse. And yet I could see no way forward.

We sat in silence for some time, when at last Henry spoke, his voice filled with anguish. "But I have to tell you, Brigid. This time with you, free from all that?"

"Yes," I said, cautiously.

"It was the best time of my life, and I will cherish it forever."

He needn't say more. We both knew what he meant. I reached out my hand to his and we threaded our fingers together in a tight embrace.

"I love you, Henry Bookbinder."

"I love you, too, Brigid Anne Dunsmore."

And with that, we said good night.

32

The following day dawned frigid, fall clearly having taken a turn toward winter. Though fog brushed my lips when I spoke, the colors of the leaves had turned the entire mountainside to a lush panoply of yellow and reds and oranges amid the rare remaining green of summer. We all seemed more energized as though certain we must be nearing not only the valley that began the Adirondacks, but the women as well. Surely, it couldn't be much farther now as Master Clyde had promised our success in finding the others. Yet as we decamped, the uncertainty once again tugged at each and every one of us, until finally, Henry spoke up.

"Look! We're never going to find them by sitting here, stewing," he said as he reached into his knapsack to pull out his spyglass. Once again, he surveyed the land before us. "There!" he offered at last. "I can see the trail is beginning to wind down. I recognize it from our trek up. We're on the right path."

As though incensed by our lack of faith in him, Phinney let loose a high cree and scowled down at us as he hovered above us in midair. Afterwards he took flight, causing us to hurry to keep up.

Soon we trekked down the mountainside. Over the next several hours, we glanced hopefully about, expecting to see our group of women at every turn. But as the hours droned on, and we grew tired and worn from the long trek, one by one we turned inward, each with our own thoughts. Mine centered on both what we had lost, and what lay ahead. The thought of going back to the way things were–the daily punishments, the constant jabs–left me feeling depressed. How could people live like that? Expect others to live like that. It was inhumane. As the sun rode high in the sky, yet filtered little warmth our way, I realized that I had been sheltered in many ways. Oh, I knew that evil existed. I wasn't a complete ninny. And I knew that it often hovered close by. But somehow, I thought it had escaped our small circle. That I could make life what I wanted by simply wishing it so. Now I knew, it was as if we were all caught in the web of a great evil machine that ate up people like spiders ate up insects.

"Penny for your thoughts," Henry said when I'd been quiet for some time.

"You don't want to know my thoughts," I replied churlishly.

Henry pulled back on his reins, causing not only my horse to halt, but Emma and Thomas' horses as well. My roan yanked at the reins, his head bobbing up and down in frustration to be moving again, knowing that until we reached another lake or stream, there would be no stopping for water and fresh grass.

"We might as well discuss your concerns," he said, "before we're back at the manor."

"Can't it wait until tonight, when we reach a resting stop?" Thomas demanded, sounding just as churlish as I had moments earlier.

Pragmatic Emma said, "But what if we meet up with the women? There will be no time to talk then."

Thomas merely shrugged a shoulder and rolled his eyes.

"Well?" Henry and Emma spoke in unison, all eyes on me.

"Well what?" I pouted like a child and I knew it, but I couldn't help the frustration I felt at the idea of once again being ensnared in a system that cared only for its own well-being, not that of the people that resided within it. When no one answered, I said, "Am I the only one who finds the entire system unbearable . . . cruel even?"

No one answered, too conditioned into silence to risk the wrath of a system that seemed to have ears in every village and eyes in every home. No wonder we were all so afraid. People, who once had seemed so friendly now seemed predisposed to maintain their silence, even to those closest to them. Once again, my thoughts turned to my family. Were they, even now, suffering the same fate as those at the manor and villages surrounding it?

"Everyone is afraid of everyone else. No one speaks, let alone laughs. Is this the life we all want?" I demanded. "*Is it?*"

Again, no one spoke, but this time in the silence I registered guilt and shame in their downturned expressions. We had all played a part in turning away from each other, from turning against each other. Divide and conquer, wasn't that the old adage?

Finally, Emma spoke up in a soft voice that carried on the

wind. "At least it was different, for a while . . . because of you."

Her words brought sudden tears to my eyes because I *had* tried, with every fiber of my being, to make things different for the women, to offer them hope of a better life, a life without constant pain and punishment. But had I succeeded in any real measure to make their lives better? Only time would tell, yet I feared the answer.

Slowly, we began our trek once more, picking up speed as we neared the village where we had first entered the Adirondacks. But just as we were so close I could almost taste the warm food, imagine the feel of the soft pillow at the inn, Phinney let out a high cree and began darting off to the east.

"What is that infernal creature doing?" Henry shouted, lifting up on the saddle to get a better view of the direction Phinney was taking us.

Sure enough, a path jutted off to the left, but where it went was anyone's guess. Henry peered back at me as if to say, get your blue falcon under control, but Master Clyde had said to trust Phinney's guidance, and trust him I would.

Though lodged in the fork of the road, I swerved my horse around Henry who appeared miffed, his face set into hard lines and his eyebrows curled in frustration. Emma and Thomas paused, as though unsure what to do next.

"I, for one, plan to follow Phinney," I said, then gave a flick of the reins and a cluck to get my horse going.

Behind me, Emma and Thomas followed, leaving Henry to make up his mind. Finally, he dug his heels into the side of his horse and soon he had caught up and was cantering beside me.

As the day waned and the sun rode low to the west, Henry

groused. "We would have been to the inn by now, eating mutton and potatoes with gravy sautèed in onions and mushrooms along with a mug of ale. We could have slept in a warm bed, taken a hot bath. Shaved."

And it was true, both Henry and Thomas had gone so long without shaving that they each had a short beard, making them appear older and more distinguished. I had to say, I liked the change. I brought my horse alongside Henry's and tweaked his beard, then laughed and raced off, to which he said, "I take that as a challenge, woman," and then set off after me at a trot. We were all laughing when we came around a corner and nearly crashed into each other at the sight, for there before us, in the distance, was a huge wall of folded rock.

Alaric surveyed the grand ballroom where the injured had come to nurse their wounds. Cots stretched out along the walls as well as two rows in the middle, filled with men, their arms and faces marked with small swollen dots of discomfort that led to an inordinate amount of itching and cursing. Nurses stood by to attend the wounded, but many of the men pulled their arms away as the nurse stood helplessly by. Fortunately, one enterprising nurse had thought to bring calamine lotion and was passing it out to those with swollen faces, ears puffed up to the size of a pufferfish. A murmur of grumbling and the angry glares tossed Alaric's way had him rethinking his strategy. Clearly the men blamed him for this.

"See to it that the men all get a week's rations while they

recuperate," he ordered. "We will meet with the generals later to determine how to proceed."

More grumbling. *So, this is how they plan to play it.* They would see reason. Later. For now, he attempted to win them with promises, both large and small, few he planned to actually keep once he got them through this bad stretch.

He bent down to a young boy who looked as though he'd barely reached puberty, a thin waif. Fortunately, he'd thought to bring a scribe with him to witness his magnanimity and to report it far and wide. A tingle of pleasure rippled up his arms as he spoke to the young man.

"None too worse for wear, eh?" he asked, clasping the young man's shoulder. "You'll be up and around soon."

The boy produced a painful smile, his lips swollen along with one ear and an eye. Even his hand appeared more like the custard-like southern paw-paw rather than an appendage meant for picking things up.

A man two cots down lifted himself up onto his elbow and shouted, "You did this to us! None of this would have happened if it weren't for you!"

Emboldened by this heretic, more men grumbled and took up the cry so that the room rang out like a discordant symphony of complaints. Alaric felt his temperature rise, his blood boil. How dare they create such a cacophony of noise with the scribe there to witness it.

"Take him!" Alaric ordered under his breath, speaking of the first man to show disloyalty.

"Sir?" the nurse asked with a twist of her head, her cherubic face revealing uncertainty.

To that he shouted at the top of his lungs. "Guards! Remove this man."

He pointed a finger at the man who peered down at him as though confused. But it didn't take long to get his point across as the guards rushed to take him away, the coverlet descending to the floor like a blossom from a magnolia flower fluttering to the ground following a gust of wind.

The scribe furiously dashed off words on his paper, never once realizing that Alaric had set him in his sights. Once he was done scribbling all that he could on the single sheet of paper and noticed the silence, it was too late. Alaric pounced. He ripped the paper out of its sheath and crumpled it into a ball, which he summarily pocketed for fear of it ever seeing the light of day.

Then, in a low voice so as not to be overheard, he growled, "You ever publish a word of this and you will never see sunlight again. Do I make myself clear?"

The scribe's Adam's apple bobbed up and down, his eyes wide behind round spectacles. For all the world, he appeared like a bug that had just been squashed. Then Alaric hurried off, eager to put this whole sordid mess behind him.

As he strode out of the room and made his way to the tower rampart, his favorite place from which to view his kingdom, he thought of what would come next. For although he had waved the white flag, he planned to bide his time. It might be weeks, it might be years, but he was a patient man. One day his kingdom would be more than the surrounding area. Far from it. If he was a betting man, his name would one day be known from sea to sea, across the entire continent. But first he must best this tiny pest of his, the woman who owned the loom. Yet make no mistake about it, he reflected as he lifted his head to take in the breeze. He would one day own the loom. Own her.

Brigid.

33

We raced toward the rocks at a gallop, our horses lathered by the time we reached the folded rocks where Master Clyde had prophesied we would find the women warriors. But as we approached the rocks that lifted out of the ground in waves, moving toward some unseen shoreline, we peered around and saw no one. Nor did we hear anything except the wind that had begun to howl through the leaves. I turned to the others. Surely this must be the place. One could find no clearer indication of folded rocks such as these, so where *was* everyone?

I didn't wait long for my answer, for atop the odd formation I heard a voice, and then another and another as the women came to peer down on our ragged procession. When they saw that it was us, a cry rang out among the women, and soon a lineup of faces peered down at us, one I was especially happy to see. Ma'am.

"You made it!" she shouted down. "There's a hidden trail to

the top. I've sent someone down to collect you."

Her words echoed off the canyon as if in Greek Mythology, the words of a nymph, it seemed. Henry and I clasped hands in relief, as did Thomas and Emma. We were found at last. Now we could be on our way . . . home. But where *was* home?

I thought back to the home of my childhood, gone now. To my time in the attic, that too gone. And lastly to the manor. It felt no more like home than the attic. But as the scout came down to collect us, little Yesimeh, who we soon learned had asked to be the one to take us to the top of the hill, I realized my home was here, with Henry and Emma and Thomas. With these women warriors. And yet, when we returned to the manor, nothing would change. We would still be expected to bury our thoughts and our words beneath a wall of silly smiles, proving us worthless in thought and deed. No one would know the amazing abilities of these smart, capable women. No one would hear the ideas these women had to offer to the world. We would be caregivers once again, nothing more. No stunning achievements. No station greater than the ones we were in before we left. These thoughts left me glum as we headed up the hillside, balsam fir and eastern redcedar brushing our cheeks.

But as we arrived into the daylight, all that changed. Our moods brightened with the robin blue skies dotted in cotton candy clouds. Furthermore, the closer we got to the women who were scattered in a semi-circle as far as the eye could see, I heard a rhythmic chant and saw Kahwihta stationed in the center of the mounded hill dressed in full regalia, dancing to the strikes of the drummers' powwow sticks and their rhythmic chants.

"She's doing the jingle dance," Ma'am said as she came to

stand beside us. She pointed to the metal cones that lined the white leather skirt and shawl, at the blue and yellow beaded front of Kahwihta's bodice. "It's a healing dance."

I watched as Kahwihta bent low, an eagle feather held out dipping in each of the four directions as she danced, her steps precise and unyielding, the sound of the metal like miniature bells, filling the hillside with song. When she ultimately raised her head, she lifted the feather to the sky as if seeking a blessing. All the while, she continued her guttural chant. Prickles of hope ran through me, up my arms and down my spine, for I needed this healing. How had she known? Maybe we all needed healing, I realized as I fought back tears for all that had passed and all that would be in the future. Here, now, I was where I needed to be. Perhaps one day things would change. We would become kinder, more caring, less punitive. Maybe that was the healing we needed–a healing of a nation unmoored.

As if she'd read my thoughts and the drummers too, the drumming stopped on a final collective beat and so too did Kahwihta. Next, she prayed in her language, the words drifting over each and every one of us, flooding me with too many emotions to name: grief, sorrow, intense joy. All wrapped up in need.

Henry clasped my hand and peered down at our joined fingers. Then slowly, his gaze met mine. I saw tears in his eyes, he too hoping for a different future, I felt sure, a better future. But it could only come if we willed it so. If we fought for it.

"I promise," he said, to a question I hadn't asked.

But before I could ascertain his cryptic meaning, Kahwihta lifted her hands to the winds. Phinney flew overhead, her wings fluttering as if in unison to the woman's movements. Then Kahwihta turned to me and spoke in a voice that seemed preternaturally loud on the silent hillock, the wind the only other sound.

"Brigid, leader of nations," she said, calling me forward to stand facing her. "The Great Spirit has asked that you be given a new name that represents your new life going forward. You are to be called Brigid, Dancer of Looms."

One of her tribe members brought Kahwihta lighted sage, which she then used to smudge me for purification. When she was done wafting the smoke over me, from head to toe, back to front, she turned me toward the people and said, "It is your turn to speak . . . from the heart."

I stood there, wondering what to say to these women who had endured so much with me over these past few months. I knew that they would return to the same life as before with no hope of change. For a few brief moments, I wallowed in self-pity for both myself and these women. But then it came to me in a flash of inspiration that although others might harm us, it didn't mean we had to harm each other.

I stiffened my spine and lifted my chin as Kahwihta had, to show that I would not be cowed. "I vow to you, from this day forward, that I will never harm a single one of you, and I hope that you will do the same." With that, I tapped my heart in pledge.

To my surprise, the women did the same. Then they did something that would touch me immensely, both now and in the days ahead. They clasped each other's shoulders and made a solemn vow to help each other only, never to hurt each other. So, this trek hadn't been for nothing after all.

Kahwihta stepped forward and once again turned me toward her. "Brigid, Dancer of Looms, I bestow upon you our most cherished possessions."

She lifted a blue and yellow beaded pouch strung in leather from around her neck and placed it around mine. In it were seeds of all the plants that provide nourishment for the tribe: corn, beans, squash, and the seeds of herbs for healing.

"We are sisters," she announced, turning to the crowd.

"We are sisters," I repeated, shouting for all to hear.

As if the wind were calling out to me, it swirled around me so that it was as if I were in the eye of the storm. No one else, just me and the wind. And I heard it like a song that echoed in on me. *Teach them joy and you change the world.* My eyes stung with emotion.

"Teach them joy and change the world," I whispered.

Was it really as simple as that? But I knew the goddess of the wind was right. If as much time and energy were spent in teaching happiness as it had been in creating war and misery, we would be a better species. We spent so much time creating punishments that we had forgotten to teach people the utter joy and happiness of creation.

Suddenly, the wind flew out in a swirl of movement that leapt up to the sky so that I could hear the single chant of the crowd: *We are sisters.* The words were swept away on a cloud to carry our vow to all the world. No longer would we be divided; no longer would we bow to the brutality of the world. In this, we were united as one.

Acknowledgements

My deepest gratitude goes to Darrin Brenner for the care and detail she gives to my book covers. And a huge thank you to Sara Rolat who not only edits my novels, but does my interior design as well.

Many thanks go to the people who have helped me with either my editing or writing over the years, people who helped mold me and made me a better editor than I would have been otherwise. You know who you are. Also, to the many people who allowed me the privilege of working with them on their "babies." To Valerie Brooks who has been a great support and who I appreciate immensely.

I can't thank the women in my writers' groups enough. First and foremost, starting with my earliest group and my partners at Colonyhouse: Valerie Brooks, Patsy Hand, Candy Davis and Chris Schofield. Next in line are Laine Stambaugh and Elaine Stek who always bring great insight to the table as well as fig newtons!

Thanks go to author Candy Calvert who graciously offered me a review on The Vast In Between and who is my soul sister in the garden, in baking, in writing, and even in interior design.

Thanks go to the many friends and family who have supported me through the years. Some who have passed, but many still very much present. And to my actual sisters, Anne, Barbara, Sue and Tanya, who have supported my writing through the years.

We can't forget new grandpa Scott, or those who are no longer with us, Howard and Dixie, my other writing partner, and Robert, all of whom had big shoulders.

Last, but most definitely not least, much love for all the support from my husband Les Craig, who helps keep me focused and on track, Sara Baker who makes me laugh on our many weekly walks, and to Kaylee Baker who was born with a zest for life. The three of you keep my world spinning. And after all, that's what Dancing the Loom is about. Love, pure and simple!

About the Author

Author Carol L. Craig has published three books in addition to *Dancing The Loom*:

The Vast In Between (Historical Women's Fiction)
A Thousand Bits of Wonderful (Romance)
The Great Unraveling (Historical Women's Fiction)

For over twenty years she has had the pleasure of editing a long list of traditionally published authors for Editing Gallery, LLC. She has been a guest speaker for Women Writing the West in Tucson, Arizona, has given one-on-one editing sessions at the Willamette Writers Conference. She has helped new writers get their start. And, she has spent many happy hours with friends at Colonyhouse, a writer's retreat in Oregon.

While at home in Oregon, she enjoys writing, reading, gardening and editing as well as coffee klatches with her husband and dog, Parker.

Be Sure To Sign Up For Her Newsletter At
www.editinggallery.com to read articles from writers, editors, artists, filmmakers, book cover designers, interior book cover designs, professional bloggers, as well as those in marketing.

You Can Find Carol At
www.editinggallery.com
facebook.com/EditingGallery1
Instagram: @clcraig7